M.R. Mackenzie was born an   d
at Glasgow University and h: n
Studies.

In addition to writing, he w~~~~~~~~~~~~~~~~~~~~~~~~~~~~~~~~as
overseen releases of films by a number of acclaimed directors, among
them Dario Argento, Joe Dante, Hideo Nakata and Jacques Tourneur.
Writing as Michael Mackenzie, he has contributed chapters to books on
cult cinema and regularly provides video essays and liner notes for new
releases of celebrated films. He used to work in a library, before leaving
to spend more time with books.

In 2019, his first novel, *In the Silence*, was shortlisted for the Bloody
Scotland Scottish Crime Debut of the Year and longlisted for the
McIlvanney Prize. His third novel, *The Library Murders*, was featured in
Crime Time's Best of the Year 2020 list.

Praise for M.R. Mackenzie

'Brings a fresh new voice to the field of Tartan Noir.'
JAMES OSWALD

'Writes with precision and passion.' CARO RAMSAY

'Splendidly written stuff.' BARRY FORSHAW, *CRIME TIME*

'An immersive slow burn of a tale, peppered with
disquieting fire-crackers of revelation.' MORGAN CRY

'Mackenzie has come up with something that defies easy
definition and is truly original.'
PAUL BURKE, *NB MAGAZINE*

'Up there with the best contemporary authors working today.'
DAVID B. LYONS

Also by M.R. Mackenzie

M.R. MACKENZIE

WOMEN WHO KILL

AN **ANNA SCAVOLINI** MYSTERY

MADHOUSE

Cover design by
Tim Barber / Dissect Designs

Typeset in 10pt Minion Pro

First published in 2023 by Mad House

ISBN: 978-1-9160948-6-4

Version 1.0a

www.mrmackenzieauthor.com
facebook.com/MRMackenzieAuthor
@landofwhimsy

They fuck you up, your mum and dad.

Prologue

'Guilty.'

The word rings out like a tolling funeral bell. For a moment, no one reacts, each individual crammed into the airless room privately digesting the verdict. Then, somewhere in the public gallery, a deep, full-bodied yell rings out. It sounds a bit like *yeeeeeaaAAHH!* – but it's less an actual, identifiable word than a raw, unfiltered expression of emotion. There's triumph in there, but also deep, agonising pain, harboured silently throughout the long months of the trial. Another sound, no less incongruous, follows from the other end of the gallery: a strangled laugh – less because the situation is genuinely funny, perhaps, than because it's the only means the person responsible possesses to release the tension bottled up inside them. As excitement spreads like an unstoppable wave, another voice rises above the wordless tumult.

'Rot in hell, you murdering bitch!'

At once, the mood seems to crystallise, as if these words have given voice to what everyone else has been thinking but, until now, has not been bold enough to articulate. A roar of agreement goes up at the back, someone lets out a whoop more suited to a rock concert than a place of solemn procedure, and a dozen more voices join the fray. As the noise grows to a crescendo, the judge – an old-school, donnish figure straight out of legal drama central casting – awakens from his torpor and calls for silence. This is not the way things are done. Not in his courtroom.

Silence resumes – gradually rather than all at once. Those that have risen to their feet retake their seats, chastened. All eyes are on the woman in the dock, flanked by a broad, white-shirted guard on either side, as the judge directs her to stand.

The public, seated behind her, don't see her face, though it's doubtful there's a single person in the country unable to recall its every detail with pinpoint accuracy. The strong, square jaw. The thick, perpetually unbrushed dark hair. The thin-lipped mouth, permanently set in a straight, unsmiling line. And, of course, the pale blue eyes that are her most distinctive feature and on which so many of the press photographs have focused, earning her the moniker that has become as well-known as her actual name.

Ice Queen.

The judge is speaking now, addressing her directly. His monologue will soon be a matter of record, reproduced in every newspaper and on every television and radio bulletin in the next twenty-four hours. He tells her that mere words are insufficient to convey the barbarity of her crime, but of course goes on to use a great many anyway to do just that. A shocking crime. An unbelievable crime. A crime committed not just against the three victims but against all who believe in kindness, decency and the rule of law.

And throughout it all, she doesn't move. Doesn't react in any way. Journalists stationed in the press section of the gallery will attest that her face remains expressionless throughout the address, even though none of them are in a position to actually *see* it, and no one who reads their words will seriously doubt the veracity of this claim. Everyone knows the Ice Queen is incapable of emotion.

And now the judge has finished speaking, and it's all over. Firm hands seize her upper arms and she is bundled down the steps leading from the dock, just like the condemned women and men taken straight to the gallows in days of old. Not that they hang people anymore in this country, despite how fervently several media pundits and members of the general populace might wish an exception could be made in this case.

The moment she disappears from view, pandemonium erupts in the gallery as press and punters alike scramble towards the exit. Edinburgh's High Court is located in the heart of the city – a stately edifice dating back to the seventeenth century, surrounded by the touristy trappings of the picturesque Old Town. Today, the cobblestoned road on the building's

2

north side has been cordoned off at either end, with a dozen uniformed officers deployed to police the sizeable crowd that's been gathering, in anticipation of a verdict, since before first light.

A prison van idles, facing away from the building, its tailgate slightly overlapping the kerb. The driver, leaning out of his window, flexes and unflexes his hands on the wheel. The mid-morning air prickles with nervous anticipation. Every face in the crowd is turned towards the building, each pair of eyes fixed on the plain wooden door, its 'FIRE EXIT – KEEP CLEAR' sign fooling no one. They're a diverse bunch, with no clearly defined profile. Young, old, female, male, rich, poor – every conceivable demographic has a witness present. Several of the women have brought their young children with them, as if hoping to prove a point. A fun day out for all the family.

Just then, a shout goes up. It's not clear what has prompted it, but a second later, the door opens and the first of the two guards steps out. Behind him walks the Ice Queen, wrists manacled in front of her, the hand of the second guard clamped firmly around her bicep as he brings up the rear.

The crowd presses forward, held back by officers armed only with batons where riot gear would have been more appropriate. Roars erupt. Jeers. Boos. A variety of colourful threats and epithets. The mothers with children present are among the loudest and most graphic in their descriptions of what they'd like to do to her. The machine-gun fire of camera shutters rattles unceasingly. Journalists bellow over one another, microphones and voice recorders thrust forward, as if they expect the prisoner to stop and take questions. She doesn't react, those brilliant blue eyes as blank and devoid of expression as a china doll's.

Something's wrong. The van door won't open. The first guard rattles the handle uselessly. Turns to his partner for assistance, or perhaps advice. One hand still on the prisoner, he moves forward and tries the handle himself with the other. No such luck.

The crowd is getting louder. Angrier. They've smelled blood, their prey almost within touching distance and barely protected. If just a few of them rushed forward en masse, they'd be unstoppable. The Ice Queen continues to stare straight ahead, seemingly unmoved by the precariousness of her plight.

Without warning, something strikes the first guard on the shoulder, hurled with considerable force from the rear of the crowd. He gives a grunt and looks down as a plastic water bottle rolls away from him over the cobblestones, a trickle of yellowish fluid spilling from its open end.

'It's *piss*,' he says in disgust, as more of the liquid drips from his shirtsleeve and the hair at the back of his head.

A moment later, another projectile is hurled, and then another. A rock, a half-eaten banana, a traffic cone – the floodgates open as people rush to pick up whatever is to hand. One particularly zealous individual even removes and throws a platform shoe, which glances off the side of the van, leaving a dent in the bodywork.

'Fuck*sake*,' the guard hisses as he continues to cling to the prisoner. 'They're gonnae lynch us.'

His partner redoubles his assault on the door, twisting the handle this way and that, hoping to find the sweet spot that will do the trick. The crowd surges forward on both sides, those at the front now actively grappling with the officers holding them at bay.

And then, as if by a miracle, the door swings open, and the two guards scramble inside, dragging the prisoner – who gives every impression of having been content to remain standing there to be torn limb from limb – behind them. The door slams shut, the engine revs, and the van takes off, the driver performing a ninety-degree turn in the narrow street that would put a professional stock car racer to shame. The police and the crowd part just in time as it roars up St Giles' Street towards Lawnmarket, serenaded on its way by a fresh barrage of missiles and a few well-placed thumps from nearby fists.

Inside, the two guards sit facing each other on opposite benches, sweating and catching their breath as the danger recedes in the rearview mirror. Their eyes meet. Both laugh nervously. As his breathing settles, the one responsible for the prisoner turns to his charge, sitting impassively next to him on the bench.

'Hope ye enjoyed that, darlin'.' His voice drips with undisguised glee. 'Wee taste of what the rest of yer life's gonnae look like.'

If the Ice Queen has heard him, she gives no indication. She continues to gaze straight ahead, those pale blue eyes unblinking, unseeing, unperturbed, as if all this is but a passing inconvenience to her.

PART ONE

JAILBIRD

1

It didn't look much like a prison from the outside – but then, Anna supposed, they never did these days. With its glass-fronted façade, reflecting the cloud-stippled mid-afternoon sky, it could just as easily have been the entrance to a shopping centre or an airport terminal. In front of the building – which the 'About' section on the Scottish Prison Service website disarmingly referred to as the Visitors' Centre – a large, rectangular granite slab occupied pride of place in the middle of the paved concourse, the words 'WELCOME TO HMP BROADWOOD' embossed on it in gold.

Broadwood, better known as the new women's super-prison – built, at considerable expense, on the banks of Broadwood Loch in Cumbernauld; now home to almost all of the three hundred or so women in Scotland currently serving custodial sentences.

Anna stepped through the revolving door – an architectural choice which seemed almost postmodern in its self-awareness – and into an eerily silent foyer sporting carpet-tiled flooring and pastel-hued walls stencilled with an array of positive affirmations. *'Sometimes the smallest step in the right direction ends up being the biggest step of your life.'* The waiting area was equipped with multicoloured polyester chairs and a children's soft play area which, with its safety netting walls, bore more than a passing resemblance to a miniature prison for tots. Which, given the often intergenerational nature of offending, seemed appropriate, in a perverse sort of way. Might as well get 'em used to it while they were young.

She approached the desk, manned by a girl in her twenties with blonde hair in a severe ponytail and lips so glossy they looked like they'd been lacquered. She fixed Anna with a gleaming, toothy smile.

'Welcome to HMP Broadwood. How may I help?'

Anna slid her Glasgow University ID across the surface. 'Professor Anna Scavolini, here to interview Martina Macdonald.'

It had started life as an idea for a journal article, or perhaps an extended essay: an account of women's experiences of the prison system, told in their own words. A chance to put the women themselves front and centre of the debate – a genuine collection of human stories as opposed to a dry academic treatise on policy which regarded them as objects on whom to 'do research'. But the project had grown legs, refusing to let itself be contained within the scope of a single article, and eventually one of Anna's colleagues – no doubt fed up hearing her lamenting this conundrum every day – had said to her, 'This sounds more like a book.' They'd put her in touch with an editor at a small, Glasgow-based academic press, who became duly excited by her pitch and commissioned her on the spot. Then, in short order, Anna was negotiating time off work to allow her to focus on researching and writing the book, freed from the obligations of teaching and running the university's Criminology undergraduate programme.

And now, here she was, three months into the project, stepping into the belly of the beast for the first time. She'd been inside prisons of various stripes before and had visited the now decommissioned women's facility at Cornton Vale half a dozen times over the years. But this felt different. All the women she'd spoken to so far for the book had been ex-prisoners – older women whose experiences of incarceration were rooted firmly in the past tense. Martina was the first woman currently serving a sentence who'd agreed to talk to her; the first who wasn't looking back on her experience in the rearview mirror. And, of course, there were Anna's own views on Broadwood and the circumstances surrounding its creation. Views which she'd already expressed forthrightly through a range of different forums – for what little good it had ultimately done.

But there was nothing she could do about any of that now. She just had to compartmentalise and focus on the task at hand. *Go in, get what you need and get out – and don't pick fights with the people that are just here to do their jobs.* And so she dutifully submitted to the biometric fingerprint reader and to being photographed and stepping through the body scanner. Satchel and phone in the plastic tray, jewellery and belt off, legs splayed and arms outstretched while a heavyset male officer patted her down … Really, it was no different to going on your holidays. Lanyard issued, bearing her mugshot and 'VISITOR' in bold red; belongings stowed in one of the thirty or so metal lockers, barring the stationery and voice recorder she'd received special dispensation to take in with her – not to mention the all-important participant information sheet and consent form, to be completed by the interviewee as confirmation that she agreed to her experiences and reflections being quoted in the published text.

And then she was through security and being led by the guard down a narrow corridor, at the end of which stood a tall, grey-suited woman of around forty-five, with a peroxide blonde perm and the sort of straight-backed, upright posture that suggested an equestrian lifestyle – or a stint in traction.

'Professor Scavolini.' She greeted Anna with an overripe smile and extended a perfectly manicured hand. 'So pleased to have you here with us today. I'm Ruth Laxton, governor of HMP Broadwood.'

She made it sound as if Anna was the one doing *her* a favour by being here rather than the other way round. It hadn't been easy getting the go-ahead for today's interview, her reputation as a critic of penal orthodoxy having doubtlessly preceded her. And then there were the safeguarding issues, which, Ruth had stressed, were her utmost concern. 'Many of our ladies are extremely vulnerable,' she'd said in her response to Anna's initial email, as if she anticipated this being news to her. 'I would require a cast iron guarantee that they will not be exploited or taken advantage of in any way.'

In the end, only one 'resident' – that was how Broadwood referred to those currently confined within its walls – had agreed to speak to Anna. Twenty-three-year-old Martina Macdonald was, from the little Anna already knew about her, an all too typical example of the trajectory of women within the prison system. In and out of a succession of care homes and young offenders' institutes from an early age, she was currently fourteen months into a three-year stretch for assault and robbery, committed to feed a heroin habit she'd picked up during one of her previous stints behind bars. There was a young child in the picture somewhere as well, which, odds were, was currently at the beginning of the same 'care to young offenders' institute to prison' trajectory as its mother.

'I thought,' said Ruth, as Anna fell into step with her, 'you'd prefer to conduct your business in one of our private legal visitation rooms rather than the general family room. It's slightly more of a trek, I'm afraid, but it'll give you a chance to see the facilities we offer.'

They headed down another corridor and through two sets of security doors, which Ruth unlocked using a key card, before emerging into an open-air courtyard. A wide, well-tended lawn spread out before them, bisected by a footpath which led to the centre of the courtyard before splitting off into three different directions, each leading to a three-storey, Y-shaped brick building. It was a scene that wouldn't have looked out of place on a modern university campus. Only the vertical bars in front of the windows hinted at the buildings' true function.

'As you can see, Broadwood has three houses,' Ruth said; 'Barbour, Inglis and Pankhurst. Each corresponds to one of three supervision levels – low, medium and high. At any given time, we can expect to have upwards of four hundred ladies staying with us – approximately seventy-five percent serving custodial sentences and the remaining twenty-five on remand. The number of women in custody in Scotland has almost doubled in the last decade, and the new facility has a fifty percent greater capacity than Cornton Vale.'

Anna, hurrying to keep up with the woman's brisk stride, said nothing, though she couldn't help noting Ruth's apparent pride in these statistics, and that, despite the warm words from politicians of every conceivable hue about seeking to reduce custodial sentences, the place had clearly been built in anticipation of a growth in demand.

Off to the left, a couple of young women in dungarees and T-shirts were working in a flowerbed, armed with rakes. As Anna and Ruth drew nearer, they stopped what they were doing and stood, watching.

'Haw, Mrs L!' the taller of the two shouted, cupping her hands to her mouth. 'Is that yer missus? Been holdin' out on us, so ye have.'

The pair hooted with laughter.

Ruth halted and stood facing them, hands on hips. 'If you've finished your chores for the day, girls, you are more than welcome to return to your rooms.'

The laughter died on the two women's lips. They quickly snatched up their rakes and began to till the soil with abandon, if not with any sense of purpose. Ruth watched them for a few seconds longer, then, seemingly satisfied, gave a curt nod and continued on her way.

'Several of our ladies come to us with behavioural problems,' she explained, as Anna once more hurried to keep up. 'They've not all had the best start in life. But we do our best to channel their energy into more productive pastimes. We're firmly of the opinion that few things are more conducive to a state of equilibrium than an honest day's work.'

They reached the entrance to the middle building – Pankhurst, according to the plaque above the door – and headed inside.

'Of course,' Ruth went on, as they made their way up a flight of stairs, 'it's not just endless grafting for no reward. Broadwood is equipped with multiple recreational facilities – separate football and netball pitches, a fully stocked library and lifelong learning suite, a state-of-the-art media centre … and all our guest-rooms are equipped with en suite facilities.'

'Lucky them,' said Anna, as they alighted on the first-floor landing.

'Needless to say, we also offer a round-the-clock counselling service and have a dedicated detoxification unit for those suffering from alcohol or drug dependencies. The mental wellbeing of our residents is our utmost priority.'

As they continued down yet another pastel-walled corridor, a girl in a T-shirt and jogging bottoms came hurrying towards them. Even from a distance, Anna could tell she was in a highly agitated state.

'Mrs Laxton, Mrs Laxton!' she practically bellowed, coming to a halt facing them. 'I need tae talk tae ye!'

'Indoor voice, please, Chantelle,' said Ruth. 'We've spoken about this, remember?'

'Sorry, Mrs Laxton.' Chantelle took a deep breath and stood, cheeks puffed out, one leg jiggling impatiently. She couldn't be much older than her late teens, though her manner struck Anna as that of someone considerably younger.

'That's better. Now, what's the problem?'

'It's Kellyanne, Miss.' Chantelle's voice was a petulant whine. 'She's took my cigarettes and she willnae give them back.'

Ruth sighed and folded her arms behind her back. 'And why did she take your cigarettes?'

Chantelle's gaze dropped to floor, unable to meet Ruth's eye. 'Cos I shoved her Snoopy hoodie down the bog.'

'I see. And you thought she'd just accept that lying down, did you?'

'But Miss, she's the one what started it, and—'

'I'm not interested in *who* started it. All I'm interested in is that you get it sorted pronto.' Ruth folded her arms and fixed Chantelle with an icy glare. 'Now, are the two of you going to sit down together and resolve this like grown-ups, or am I going to have to revoke both your recreation room privileges?'

'Yes, Miss.' Chantelle's voice was barely a mumble.

'Hop to it, then.'

With a final, hasty 'Yes, Miss', Chantelle turned tail and set off at a sprint, heading back the way she'd come.

'And no running in the corridor!' Ruth called after her. She turned to Anna and shook her head. 'A small taste of what we have to contend with. So many of these girls have no grasp of the ins and outs of civilised society – especially the ones who've grown up inside the system. They arrive here thinking they can resolve all their issues by engaging in tit-for-tat. It's our job to make honest women out of them.'

'Well, I wish you every success,' said Anna, her mind immediately turning to the levels of recidivism among former inmates.

Ruth gave a strained smile. 'And now, I'm sure you're eager to get on. I'll just find out if Martina's ready for you ... '

She retrieved her phone from the inner pocket of her jacket and, turning her back on Anna, dialled a number and put it to her ear. Taking the hint, Anna wandered in the opposite direction, admiring – if that was the right word for it – the tastelessly bland paintings of landscapes that adorned the walls. Behind her, she heard Ruth speaking in a low voice. Without meaning to, she found herself tuning into the words.

'When was this? ... I see. And is she ... ? ... No, no, you did the right thing. ... Yes, I'll tell her. ... What? ... No, I *don't* think that's a good—'

She stopped abruptly. Anna, facing the other way, felt the governor's eyes on her. A moment later, she heard Ruth's footsteps retreating further up the corridor. When the conversation resumed, she could no longer make out any of the words – just a low murmur, barely audible over the hum of the radiator.

At length, the conversation concluded and she heard Ruth's footsteps approaching. She turned, expression neutral but privately braced for bad news.

'I'm afraid we have a slight hitch,' said Ruth, folding and unfolding her hands as if she was trying to get grease off them. 'Unfortunately, Martina Macdonald is no longer available to be interviewed.'

Wrong-footed, it took Anna a moment to respond. 'Why? Has she withdrawn her consent?'

'Not in so many words.' Ruth had now taken to squeezing her hands together so tightly her fingertips were starting to go purple. 'She's become … indisposed.'

'Indisposed?'

'There's been … an incident. She's currently receiving treatment.'

Immediately, all manner of possible scenarios flashed through Anna's mind – everything from slipping on a wet patch of floor to serious assault at the hands of another prisoner to an overdose, accidental or otherwise. Given the wall-to-wall press coverage of the recent spike in drug-related incidents among the prison population, coupled with what she knew about Martina's own history, it was difficult not to regard the latter as the most likely.

'What's happened to her?'

Ruth winced. 'Unfortunately, I'm bound by our confidentiality policy, but I can assure you, she's being attended to and receiving excellent care.' She gave an apologetic shrug. 'Unfortunately, it looks very much like you've had a wasted journey.'

'So it seems,' Anna agreed.

In truth, she was less concerned about having come all this way for nothing than the wellbeing of a woman whose backstory positively screamed 'vulnerable inmate'. Though, given how much of an uphill struggle it had been to secure Martina's cooperation in the first place, she certainly didn't relish the prospect of starting the whole rigmarole again from scratch.

'I'd, ah, better show you out,' Ruth said.

As she spoke, Anna felt an unexpected pang of something approaching sympathy for her. This woman might be the living, breathing embodiment of a system Anna wanted nothing more than to dismantle, but she was also in an unenviable position and doing her best for the inmates under her care, however much she and Anna might disagree about the current settlement.

'Least I got a guided tour out of it,' she offered, with a slight smile.

Ruth managed a small, fleeting smile of her own. She took a step towards Anna, then halted abruptly. 'There is ... ' she began, then stopped herself.

'What?'

Ruth shook her head, dismissing Anna's question with a wave. 'No, no, forget it. It's nothing.'

But if there was one thing Anna wasn't going to stand for, it was having a carrot dangled in front of her and then immediately snatched away. She folded her arms, raising herself up on the balls of her feet to compensate for the height difference between them.

'No, come on – what were you going to say?'

For a moment, Ruth looked like she was on the verge of digging in her heels. Then she seemed to change her mind, her posture becoming marginally less rigid.

'I think, perhaps, this is a conversation that would be better suited to somewhere more private.' She extended an arm. 'My office?'

Ruth's office was on the second floor at the front of the building, the large slider window behind her desk affording an all-encompassing view of the courtyard and the rest of the prison complex. Her desk, a spotlessly clean mahogany affair, was bare apart from a ridiculously tiny laptop, a plaque bearing her name and a grotesquely oversized framed photograph of herself shaking hands with a former First Minister. It was a toss-up as to which of them looked more pleased with this state of affairs.

Ruth shut the door and stood behind her desk, presumably under the impression that it made her appear more in control of the situation.

'I debated whether to mention this,' she said, 'but I've concluded it would be dishonest of me not to say anything. Another prisoner has offered to talk to you in Martina's place.'

Anna could sense the unspoken caveat. 'Well, if she's happy to speak to me, I certainly have no objections.'

Ruth sucked air through her teeth. 'You might not think that once I tell you her identity.'

'Why? Who is she?'

Ruth hesitated for a moment before responding.

'The child-killer, Sandra Morton.'

2

Anna sucked in a heavy breath. 'The Ice Queen,' she murmured. As distasteful as the nickname had always seemed to her, it was so inextricably linked to the woman whose name Ruth had just invoked that it sprang to her lips almost unbidden.

From behind her desk, Ruth gave Anna a probing look. 'What do you know about her?'

Anna cast her mind back. To call the case 'infamous' was doing a disservice to the word.

'About the same as everyone else, I suppose,' she said. 'Convicted in 2002 of stabbing her husband and two infant sons to death while they slept. Pled not guilty, but eyewitnesses refuted her alibi. Multiple applications to the Appeal Court and to the Criminal Cases Review Commission, all unsuccessful. Received the longest sentence handed down to any woman in Scottish legal history.'

'Forty-six years. Even if she only serves the minimum tariff, she'll be eighty-one by the time she gets out.'

The overwhelming majority of women at Broadwood were serving terms of less than twelve months. Even among those convicted of the most severe crimes, minimum sentences were typically set at under twenty years. The length of the tariff had been controversial at the time, Anna remembered – though many had thought it too lenient.

'And why has she decided to talk to me?' This was, she belatedly realised, the most pertinent question.

Ruth hesitated – already, Anna could tell, regretting having said anything.

'She takes these fancies now and then. Hers is not the sort of mind that's suited to being locked up for twenty-three hours a day with no stimulation – which, as our highest security resident, is unfortunately her lot in life. For what I hope are obvious reasons, we keep her isolated from the rest of the population.'

She gestured to one of two cantilever chairs facing the desk, inviting Anna to take a seat. Anna did as she was bidden, waiting for Ruth to settle in the Chesterfield behind her desk.

'As you can imagine,' the governor went on, 'with someone of Sandra Morton's profile, all manner of journalists and psychiatrists are desperate to interview her, even after all the books and documentaries and podcasts. And, from time to time, Sandra obliges them with an audience. There's no shortage of experts who think they're the one who's going to crack her – to figure out what made her do what she did. Sometimes, she'll indulge them, feeding them a pack of lies about her childhood that can be disproved with even a cursory amount of research. Other times, she'll agree to speak to someone, only to change her mind at the eleventh hour – often after they've been waiting in the interview room for hours. A couple of years ago, she agreed to talk to a world-renowned FBI profiler from Quantico. He flew over specially, went through the whole rigmarole of getting the paperwork in order. Then, as soon as she was seated in front of him, she took one look at him, said "I don't like his tie", and asked to be taken back to her cell.'

Despite herself, Anna couldn't help but smile at the mental image of some self-important pseudoscientist having his balloon burst so spectacularly. Seeing Ruth's stony expression, she hastily rearranged her face and cleared her throat.

'And, in your opinion, is that what she has planned for me?'

Ruth considered the question. 'In your case, I'd say it's unlikely. You're already here, so there's a limit to how much of your time she can waste. If she does have an ulterior motive, it's likely to be something rather more elaborate than ensuring you're caught in the evening rush hour.'

'You don't think I should talk to her.' It was a statement of fact rather than a question.

Ruth looked pensive. 'I think,' she said, choosing her words carefully, 'that it would be better for the whole world if Sandra Morton simply faded into irrelevance instead of having her story dredged up again every six months in yet another lurid retrospective. I think engaging with her at *all* is giving her more attention than she deserves.'

Privately, Anna couldn't help but concur. How often had she herself lamented the media's grim focus on 'celebrity' killers, endlessly raking over the salacious details of their crimes, forcing their victims' relatives to relive their trauma again and again, all while feeding the public's prurient obsession with the worst excesses of human depravity? She was about to stress that that was the last thing she intended to do – that any interest she might have in Sandra Morton pertained purely to her experience of incarceration – when Ruth spoke again, her tone more conciliatory.

'Having said that, if you're looking for an up close and personal account of the prison experience, and assuming she *does* actually plan to cooperate, I doubt you'll find anyone with a more comprehensive knowledge of the system. I don't imagine there's anything she hasn't seen at least once.' She gave a small, fatalistic shrug. 'At the end of the day, it's your decision.'

Anna thought about it. If she left now, she'd probably make it back to Glasgow in time to pick her son up from playgroup herself and have nothing worse to show for it than a wasted afternoon. On the other hand, and despite her deeply held misgivings about the morbid fascination that invariably surrounded cases like Sandra Morton's, she had to acknowledge that at least a small part of her had more than a passing curiosity about this woman whose actions had generated so much public opprobrium; whose crime had become such a cornerstone of the zeitgeist that she felt she knew it inside out despite never having actively sought out information on it. She knew, if she passed up this opportunity, she'd be kicking herself for a long time to come. Plus, on a more straightforwardly human level, she recognised that Ruth, despite clearly having profound reservations, was trying to make amends for the wasted journey.

'I'll do it,' she said, getting to her feet.

Ruth rose from her chair too, disapproval still writ large on her features. 'In that case, I'll make the necessary arrangements. Just be forewarned: you can never be certain which version of Sandra you're going to get. She can be completely affable, or she can be so indifferent towards you that she won't even acknowledge your presence. It all depends what sort of mood she's in. Assuming she doesn't blank you completely or tell you to leave as soon as she lays eyes on you, I'd strongly advise against sharing any personal information about yourself.'

Anna couldn't help but give a wry smile. 'Yes, I saw that film as well.'

Ruth fixed Anna with a stony look. 'It's no laughing matter. Sandra Morton might not be capable of persuading you to peel off your face or swallow your own tongue, but don't for a minute underestimate how manipulative she is. If she senses a weakness in you that she can twist to her advantage, believe me, she'll use it – if only for the satisfaction of taking you down a peg or two.'

The décor of the visitation room was of a piece with the rest of the prison, but, for the first time, Anna observed cracks in the façade. The table was bolted to the floor, there was a brown stain on the pale blue wall where someone had hurled what she hoped was coffee, and several of the available surfaces had been augmented with graffiti – including the declaration, gouged into the tabletop, that 'Stacey B is gagging for muff'.

Seated facing the door, Anna busied herself with making sure her audio device was properly set up, laying out the consent form, information sheet and pen, then checking the audio device again. She clocked the slight tremble in her right hand and squeezed it with her left until it settled.

Stop it. She's just a prisoner like any other. Don't make her into something she's not.

She heard footsteps approaching in the corridor – several heavy pairs of boots, all moving at the same steady pace. She sat up a little straighter. Swallowed. Folded her hands on the tabletop, ready for business.

A moment later, the door swung open. A middle-aged male prison officer entered first, like a scout sent ahead to scope out the terrain. Others loomed in the doorway behind him – at least four, a mixture of male and female. Standing bang in the middle of the cluster – the odd one out with her grey sweater and bright red tabard amid a sea of white shirts and black ties – was the woman the press had dubbed the Ice Queen.

A part of Anna had expected Sandra Morton to be wearing an orange jumpsuit and clapped in leg irons, her movements restricted to the bare minimum. Even for someone as well versed in the particulars of Scotland's prison system as her, the influence of imagery from American maximum-security penitentiaries was hard to shake. Instead, the woman who now stepped into the room was completely unrestrained, though one of the officers forming the rear-guard – a young man with a bum-fluff goatee – followed closely behind her, one hand hovering in the general vicinity of her shoulder without touching her, as if he feared to make physical contact. The woman glanced briefly at the empty seat in front of her, as if checking it for cleanliness, before plonking herself down. She leaned back, folded her arms and looked Anna up and down.

'You're shorter than I expected,' she said.

As far as opening gambits went, it was certainly to the point.

'Has anyone offered you any refreshments?'

'Oh no.' Anna's response was instinctual, like a child conditioned never to accept sweets from strangers. 'I—'

'I'll have a black tea,' Sandra said, not addressing this demand to anyone in particular.

The officer who'd entered the room first, and who was clearly in charge, nodded to his colleague with the bum-fluff. 'See to that, Gary, will you?' He turned to the gaggle of officers milling in the corridor. 'The rest of you, clear off. This isn't a spectator sport. Plenty more work to be done.'

The officers dispersed, including Gary, shutting the door behind him on his way out. As the one who'd dished out the orders assumed an arms-folded position against the far wall, Sandra shot Anna a conspiratorial look.

'My entourage,' she explained. 'For my own safety. Curiously enough, plenty of folk in here would happily take a pop at me if the opportunity arose. Wouldn't be the first time.'

She pointed briefly to the side of her neck, where the skin looked puckered and papery – an old burn scar. It was known in the trade as a 'jugging': a form of so-called rough justice popular among the prison population involving a mixture of boiling water and sugar. Anna hastily averted her eyes.

'Ms Morton,' she began, fumbling with her paperwork to distract herself from the gruesome mental image, 'can I start by thanking you for agreeing to this—'

'Oh, Sandra – *please*,' said the other woman, her tone verging on camp.

'We keep things informal around here – first name terms only. One of the sainted Mrs Laxton's little initiatives – though you'll note she herself is exempted from this policy. First among equals, you see.'

She had a relatively neutral accent, not all that dissimilar to Anna's own: standard, educated Scottish, with few, if any, specific regional identifiers.

'Sandra, then. Before we start, I'd like to—'

'Your professorship's a recent appointment, isn't it?' Sandra cut in again, her tone measured but just loud enough to knock Anna off her stride.

Anna pressed her lips together and took a deep breath. She'd encountered this sort of thing before: the carefully timed interruptions, each one perfectly calibrated to throw her off her stride. In her experience, however, it was usually men of a certain age who indulged in this sort of behaviour. She couldn't remember the last time she'd been subjected to these disruption tactics by another woman.

She put down her paper and lifted her head, forcing herself to look Sandra square in those pale blue eyes. Like ice crystals, she thought – and just as impenetrable.

'What makes you say that?' She kept her tone measured and indifferent.

Sandra smiled enigmatically. 'You tell me.'

'I asked first.' Anna's expression didn't waver.

'Well,' – Sandra gave a slight eye-roll, as if she was spelling out something exceedingly obvious – 'given your relative youth, unless you happened to be a child prodigy, there can't be too many alternative explanations.'

Put like that, Anna couldn't help but feel more than a little foolish. She pressed on, speaking louder this time in an effort to forestall any further interruptions. 'Before we start, I'd like to ask whether you're comfortable with me recording our conversation.'

Sandra spread her palms, Jesus-style. 'By all means. When I received my sentence, I waved goodbye to all the rights we human beings normally take for granted, including the right to privacy.'

Anna pushed the information sheet towards her. 'If you could read this as well. It explains the purpose of the research, how your contributions will be used, your right to withdraw your consent and the steps that will be taken to anonymise the data.'

Sandra flashed an amused grin as she took the sheet. 'Anonymisation might be a tad tricky in this case. I doubt there are many others in the system with a comparable résumé.'

Anna pushed the consent form, and her pen, across the table. 'And I'll need you to sign this.'

Putting the information sheet to one side, Sandra picked up the form and began to read it. It soon became clear that, far from merely skimming it, she was intent on reading the whole thing from beginning to end, her eyes gliding slowly from left to right, pausing occasionally as she carefully considered – or pretended to consider – a particular clause before moving on.

The lull in conversation gave Anna an opportunity to properly observe her for the first time. She was a large woman – not in the sense that she was overweight or even particularly tall, but she seemed to fully *fill* the space she occupied. Anna had seen prisoners and ex-prisoners who, fearful of being attacked or having their food snatched from their plates, had become accustomed to sitting hunched over, shoulders tucked in, furtively guarding against wandering hands. Not so Sandra, who leant back in her seat, shoulders flung back, legs planted firmly apart, holding the page at arm's length in a way that suggested long-sightedness coupled with a reluctance to admit to needing glasses. For a woman in her early fifties, and one who wore no makeup, her face was remarkably free of any age-related blemishes. Her hair, scraped into an unfussy bun, bore a handful of grey flecks but was otherwise as thick and dark as it had been in the pictures of her that had appeared in every newspaper and on every television screen for months on end almost two decades ago.

Seemingly satisfied, Sandra put down the form, picked up the pen and signed her name – a languid, unfussy scrawl – before sliding it back across the table.

Anna folded and pocketed the form, then cast around for her pen, only to realise Sandra still had it. She watched as the older woman toyed with it, turning it this way and that as if trying to make sense of how it worked. Anna squirmed internally. People stealing her stationery was a personal bugbear at the best of times, and now her mind couldn't help but leap to all manner of extreme scenarios – everything from Sandra using it to pick the lock on her cell door to her leaping across this very table and stabbing

Anna with it before her seemingly catatonic minder even had a chance to register what was going on.

'Can I have that back, please?' Anna gestured to the pen. 'Um ... so I can take notes.'

Sandra frowned. 'Why would you need to take notes if you're recording the conversation?'

As Anna racked her brains for a believable excuse, a knowing smile crept over Sandra's lips. With a look that made it abundantly clear she knew only too well what Anna had been thinking, she reached across the table, holding out the pen.

'Thank you,' said Anna, taking it and laying it on top of her open notebook, positioning them both as far from Sandra as she could without making it obvious. 'Now, if you're happy to make a start—'

At that moment, there was a knock on the door.

'Ah, good.' Sandra glanced over her shoulder. 'Here are the caterers.'

'Come in,' the guard called gruffly.

The door opened and Gary entered, carrying a tray loaded with various items: a cup, with accompanying saucer and spoon, an urn, a pack of Tetley teabags and even a couple of digestive biscuits. As he set it down in front of Sandra, she nodded approvingly.

'Oh, Gary, you've outdone yourself this time.'

A brief smile flickered on Gary's lips, followed by a frown, as he tried to work out whether he was being mocked or genuinely complimented. At a nod from his older colleague, he withdrew from the room, shutting the door behind him.

Sandra poured water from the urn into her cup. As Anna watched, on the verge of incredulity, she selected a teabag, tied the string round her pinkie and proceeded to dip it in the water – an incongruously dainty gesture for such a brawny woman.

Anna shifted in her seat, anxious to get on but feeling somehow reluctant to interrupt this curious ritual. She was just on the verge of saying something when Sandra glanced up, gave her a quizzical look and nodded towards the voice recorder.

'Aren't you going to switch that on?'

Feeling decidedly foolish yet again, Anna reached for the device and switched it on, hands fumbling over the buttons. She placed it in the middle of the table, sat up straight and cleared her throat for what felt like the umpteenth time since she'd first set foot in this place.

'Anna Scavolini interviewing Sandra Morton at HMP Broadwood at 2.47 p.m. on Tuesday 5 March 2019.'

3

Anna glanced at her notepad, eyes skimming over the initial questions she normally asked interviewees – is this your first time in prison, what sentence are you serving, and so forth. They were intended primarily to put the subject at ease, but in Sandra's case, she didn't see much point in them. They certainly weren't going to yield any information she didn't already know, and Sandra didn't strike her as the sort of person on whom traditional ice-breaking techniques would have much effect.

'You've spent a considerable amount of time within the prison system,' she said, opting for a different tack, 'so I thought we might start by talking about some of the changes you've observed in how the service has been run over the last eighteen years.'

'Oh, it's been a veritable rollercoaster of twists and turns,' said Sandra, utterly deadpan as she gazed off into the middle distance. 'Real edge-of-your-seat stuff. Each new day brings fresh surprises.'

Anna acknowledged the sarcasm with a dry smile. 'I appreciate time probably moves incredibly slowly in the day-to-day sense. But when you take a broader view—'

'Still,' Sandra continued, as if Anna hadn't spoken, 'if one is being philosophical, it's hard to shake the sense that the more things change, the more they… well, you know how it goes.'

'Perhaps you could give some examples of—'

'So what d'you make of our all-singing, all-dancing new super-prison?' Sandra suddenly sat up straight, her brilliant blue eyes locking onto Anna as she stared at her intently. 'Quite impressive, no? A truly awe-inspiring monument to the principle of corrective justice.'

'It's ... clearly had a lot of resources put into it,' Anna said carefully.

'A hundred and forty million, to be precise – though I've heard estimates which put it at nearly double that. When politicians bang on about the societal cost of crime, do you imagine they include vanity projects like this one in their calculations ... or is that just me being cynical?'

Anna sucked in a deep breath, trying to keep a lid on her growing frustration. 'We're not here to talk about my views.'

'But your views are so much more *interesting* than some boring questionnaire!' Sandra protested, rolling her eyes at the ceiling. 'Here's an idea – let's do a trade. A question for a question. You answer one of mine, I answer one of yours.'

'I don't think so.'

'Why not?'

'Because, like I said, my views are irrelevant to why I'm here.'

'You were a lot more forthcoming with them when you were campaigning to have this place killed at conception.'

Anna's head jerked up sharply. She stared at Sandra, who merely smiled insipidly.

Right from the beginning, Anna had had a sense that the woman sitting across from her knew a whole lot more than she was letting on; that she possessed some advantage over her that she was keeping close to her chest until the perfect moment. And it wasn't as if Sandra didn't have her bang to rights. From the moment she'd become aware of them, she'd fought the plans for a women's super-prison tooth and nail, firing off reams of letters to her MP, her MSP, the local council, the Inspectorate of Prisons, the Justice Secretary, even the First Minister – all to no avail. Overnight, the same politicians who, with one face, had spoken passionately about the need for a more humane response to criminal behaviour had seemingly undergone a Damascene conversion and now extolled the virtues of retributive justice and a zero-tolerance approach to lawbreaking. A certain Groucho Marx quote summed it up quite well.

'My views are a matter of public record,' she said crisply. 'I don't see what's to be gained by rehashing them now – especially since you seem to know all about them already.'

'Touché. Though you must admit, there's a world of difference between reading an op ed in the *Tribune* and sitting down for a frank exchange of ideas.' As Sandra spoke, she untied the string from her finger and set the now thoroughly saturated teabag aside on the tray. 'Besides,' she went on airily, 'I find myself wondering how you'd fare in the hot seat. You know – when you're not hiding behind a keyboard or reading from a script. Perhaps I feel like making sure I'm not selling myself too cheaply.'

'That's up to you,' Anna retorted. 'But if you think I'm going to jump through hoops for you, we should knock this conversation on the head right now and stop wasting both our times.' She reached for the audio recorder.

'I wouldn't have thought you could afford to be so picky. It's not as if you're spoiled for choice when it comes to volunteers for your little project, is it?'

Anna stopped in her tracks. 'What makes you say that?'

'If they were queuing round the block to talk to you, you wouldn't be wasting your time with minnows like Martina Macdonald.' Sandra raised a knowing eyebrow. 'Am I right?'

Slowly, deliberately, Anna set the audio device back down. She leaned back in her seat, arms folded.

'OK,' she said, looking Sandra dead in the eyes. 'What do you want to hear? That I think places like this are an abomination and an affront to human dignity? That they represent a failed model which serves no purpose other than to give those calling the shots a chance to appear tough on crime, all while creating worse outcomes for those on the receiving end of their ideological posturing? That, if they just bothered to look, they'd realise there's a mountain of evidence out there showing that if you want to reduce crime, you start by funding social programmes and reducing the equality gap, not locking women and girls up in centralised facilities hundreds of miles from their families?'

Sandra almost whooped with delight. '*There's* the fire I was waiting for! Knew you had it in you.' She rubbed her hands together gleefully. 'See? Isn't life a whole lot more interesting when you turn off your internal filter and speak from the heart?'

Anna simmered silently. She was livid – both with Sandra for goading her and with herself for being so easily provoked. She was supposed to be a neutral observer, dispassionately documenting her subject's views and experiences, not some firebrand sermonising from her soapbox.

'So,' Sandra went on archly, 'you're one of *those*.'

'One of what?'

'Bleeding hearts. The ones who believe they can cure criminal minds with art therapy and airy-fairy lessons on the meaning of good citizenship.'

In for a penny, in for a pound. 'No – I just don't believe the solution is a single, high-security facility for the entire country. Nearly two-thirds of the female prison population are mothers. How is one from Lerwick supposed to maintain a relationship with her child if she's locked up in a jail in the Central Belt?'

'Some might say she should have thought of that before she chose a life of crime.'

'Then they'd be assuming all choices are made in a vacuum. That she had any choice in the matter at all.'

'In my experience,' said Sandra, 'most do.'

Anna swallowed a deep breath; counted to five in her head. She knew she was getting sucked into the very sort of debate she'd promised herself to avoid, but she couldn't help herself. Expecting a policy wonk like herself not to respond to an invitation to discuss policy was like expecting a duck not to quack – especially when the individual doing the inviting was making such incendiary assertions. And, regardless of the crimes the woman sitting across the table from her had committed, it was difficult to shake the sense that the two of them were, while coming at the matter from completely opposite viewpoints, at least versed in the same debates and discourses.

'Do you have a background in criminology?' Anna asked. 'Or are you speaking purely from a position of personal interest?'

'Open University, baby. You wouldn't believe the things you can learn without ever leaving the comfort of your own personal twelve-by-eight.' Sandra took a sip of tea, then carefully placed the cup back on its saucer. 'And yes, funnily enough, I do have a certain vested interest in prison policy – though, if you like, I can also regale you with my knowledge of the Russian Revolution, applied linguistics or the poetry of Emily Dickinson.'

Casually, she traced a finger round the rim of the cup. 'As it happens, when I first entered the prison estate eighteen years ago, I did so without a single qualification to my name. Now, I'm in receipt of six different degrees, including an MA in Law and Criminal Justice.' She smiled dryly. 'You could argue I'm proof the system works.'

'I think we'll have to agree to differ there.'

Sandra gave an amused snort. 'So, to sum up, you believe we're all just victims of circumstance with no free will of our own and if we could all just join hands and Kumbaya our way into the Garden of Eden, there'd be no need for places like this. Am I in the right ballpark?'

'I think,' Anna all but snapped, 'if you treat people the way you'd like to be treated yourself, they generally respond in kind.' She could feel her body temperature rising; hear her tone growing increasingly terse. 'And yes, I do happen to think treating custodial sentences as the default option is wrong – locking people up willy-nilly, whether their crime is something as trivial as shoplifting or…'

'Or stabbing your husband and children to death?' suggested Sandra, in a tone of bland indifference.

In the silence that followed, the very air seemed to evaporate from the room, and Anna was suddenly acutely aware of just how small and cramped it was, the squat, rectangular window near the ceiling offering only a distant glimpse of the sky outside.

'Oooh, elephant in the room,' Sandra smirked mischievously.

Anna said nothing. Until today, the women she'd spoken to for her research had all been convicted of minor offences like shoplifting, public solicitation or drug possession. And now here she was, debating policy with the most hated woman in the land.

'Come on, then.' Sandra rested her elbows on the table, chin thrust out impudently, like one child daring another. 'I know you wanna ask me.'

'What?'

Sandra shrugged. 'Same thing everyone asks, sooner or later. Did I do it?'

'I'm not going to ask you that.'

'Why not?'

'Because it's irrelevant to why I'm here.'

'Surely you're just a *wee* bit curious, though.' Sandra inclined her head, trying to catch Anna's eye.

'Not really, no.'

But even as she spoke, Anna wondered how true this really was. Was she really so aloof, so ideologically pure, as to be completely immune to the fascination surrounding the case that had gripped seemingly everyone else in the country? The fact she didn't think she could answer that question with any certainty unsettled her more than she cared to admit.

'Anyway,' she went on, attempting to banish these thoughts, 'it's no secret you maintained your innocence throughout the trial.'

'That's true,' Sandra conceded, absentmindedly twirling a loose strand of hair round her finger. 'But saying you didnae dae it in this place doesn't exactly make you special. *Everyone* says it. Isn't that right, Bob?' She inclined her head towards the guard.

Bob stirred from propping up the wall long enough to mutter a disinterested 'aye' before closing his eyes again.

'I know you've submitted multiple appeals against your conviction,' Anna said, taking care to avoid any inference from her tone of voice that she was expressing either sympathy or a view on the merits of this course of action.

'Four to date – all knocked back with increasing levels of glee. My theory is that the Court of Appeal spends vast amounts of time dreaming up ever more acerbic ways of saying "no" based on the degree to which it perceives its time as being wasted.'

'And you don't have one in progress right now.'

Sandra picked at something between her front teeth. 'Trouble is, each time you lodge an appeal, you need to come up with fresh grounds. You can't just say, "I didn't like the result I got last time. Kindly reconsider".' She paused to inspect whatever she'd retrieved. 'No, there hasn't been a fresh submission since 2014. Lately, my solicitor has been doing her best to let me down gently, suggesting it might be time to give up the ghost. In which case, that review into the conduct of my tormenter may well prove to be the last roll of the dice.'

Anna glanced up from her notepad. 'Sorry, what?'

Sandra grimaced. 'Yes, I know – I'm not a fan of mixed metaphors either, but it's late and I haven't had my forty winks. Best I can come up with in my current state.'

'What do you mean, your tormenter? What's this about a review?' The questions came pouring forth from Anna's mouth before her brain had a chance to catch up.

Sandra stretched her arms above her head, stifling a yawn. 'I'm sure you'll work it out. Like someone once said, it's all a matter of public record.'

Anna ignored the dig. 'Come on – what did you mean?'

Blanking her, Sandra turned to her minder. 'I think I'd like to be escorted back to my lodgings now, Bob. I'm feeling unaccountably wearied.'

Bob, who'd already peeled himself from the wall, offered Anna an apologetic shrug. 'You heard the lady. Time to go.'

Anna looked imploringly at Sandra, but her subject was busy picking imaginary crumbs from her tabard. As Anna, admitting defeat, switched off her audio device and began to gather up her equipment, Sandra exhaled a satisfied sigh.

'That was most invigorating,' she declared. 'It's not often I get the chance to trade philosophies with an intellectual heavyweight.'

Her lips curled into a facsimile of a smile which failed to reach her eyes. They gazed back at Anna, emotionless, unreadable, like two dazzling but empty voids, lacking any hint of emotion.

'I'm grateful for your time,' said Anna. She was in no doubt that she was being insulted, but she opted for detached civility instead of giving Sandra the satisfaction of seeing that she'd got to her.

'See?' Sandra nodded to the item Anna had just pocketed. 'You didn't need your pen after all.'

4

Anna returned to Pankhurst's foyer, escorted by the ever-obliging Gary, to find Ruth Laxton waiting for her.

'So?' Ruth said, as she and Anna set off across the courtyard towards the Visitors' Centre. 'A constructive time was had by all, I trust?'

'You could say that,' Anna replied evasively. 'How's Martina?'

'Oh, she's doing much better now – though I doubt she'll be up to receiving visitors for a while.'

This, Anna surmised, was Ruth's way of telling her that rescheduling the interview was off the cards for the foreseeable future.

'Well, tell her I'm sorry not to have had a chance to see her today, and that I hope she continues to feel better.'

They continued across the courtyard.

'So what did you make of our star prisoner?' asked Ruth. 'Quite a change from your usual interview subjects, I imagine. Was it a fruitful conversation?'

She was clearly fishing for juicy details, and Anna had no intention of indulging her. There was, after all, a little thing called confidentiality. Her responsibility to her interviewees might not be comparable to that of a doctor and a patient or a priest and a penitent, but principles still mattered.

'We covered a number of topics,' she replied carefully. 'She's certainly an interesting woman.'

'She is that,' Ruth agreed. 'I've had her in my care for a little over eighteen months, and I still don't feel I've fully got the measure of her.' She paused. 'And, er, did you feel you came away with any worthwhile material to use in your book?'

'It's early days. I'm still figuring out the overall structure.'

This was a lie. She had the shape of the thing mapped out more or less perfectly. But she was damned if she was going to be railroaded into giving this jumped-up schoolmistress a sneak peek – certainly not before it had been seen by the handful of people whose opinions she did value.

'Well,' said Ruth, 'I trust you'll send me a signed copy when it goes on sale.' She said it with a flighty little laugh, but Anna sensed that it was, in fact, a serious request.

'I'll see what I can do,' she said, non-committal to the very end.

'So what's next?' Ruth asked, after she'd buzzed them through the entrance to the Visitors' Centre. 'Back to the office?'

'Home, actually. I'm on a sabbatical while I write my first draft.'

'Lucky you! I sometimes think I could do with a sabbatical myself. Overseeing an establishment like this is no picnic, I can tell you.'

Anna chose not to respond. It would hardly have been the first time someone had assumed that being on sabbatical was synonymous with being on holiday, and it didn't get any less irritating with repetition. *Well, if you think it sounds so idyllic,* she felt like saying, *why don't* you *write the damn thing?*

They were almost back where they'd started. As the row of lockers where Anna had left her belongings came into view, Ruth halted.

'Well,' she said with a philosophical sigh, 'I'd better get back to it. No rest for the wicked! Unless there's anything else you need ... '

Anna was on the verge of dismissing her when she remembered something. 'Actually, there *was* one thing I wanted to ask. Towards the end of our conversation, Sandra said something about her "tormenter" – that there was to be some sort of review into their conduct. What did she mean by that? I take it she wasn't talking about you.'

Ruth laughed. 'I should be so lucky as to rate so highly in her esteem! No,' she went on, more seriously, 'the person Sandra refers to as her tormenter is the detective who led the investigation into her back in 2001. Dalton, I think, or Dawson. He passed on a while back, but a couple of years ago, her legal team received word that his name had come up in relation to a group of corrupt police officers called the Shadow Men. I assume you know about them?'

'I'm aware of the name,' said Anna, choosing to leave it at that.

'Well, as I understand it, his connection to them was enough to get his cases earmarked for re-examination by that new anti-corruption unit. Needless to say, Sandra isn't overly inclined towards sharing the particulars of her legal endeavours with *me*, but I like to think, if there'd been any meaningful progress on that front, that I'd have heard about it by now.'

'She told me it was all in the public domain,' said Anna, 'and then she refused to say anything else. It's like she *wanted* me to ask her about it.'

Ruth regarded Anna gravely. 'In my experience,' she said, choosing her words with care, 'Sandra's only ever interested in you to the extent that you're of use to *her*. If she was trying to pique your curiosity, she won't have done it on a whim.'

Safely aboard the train to Glasgow, Anna fished out her headphones and hooked them up to the voice recorder. Public transportation was always her preferred option when she conducted interviews, even on occasions like this, when it would have been quicker to take the car. It meant she could listen back to the recording and make some preliminary notes while the conversation was still fresh in her mind, before anything else had a chance to overshadow it. Not that she anticipated getting much of value out of this one. Her overriding sense was that the whole thing had been a complete bust – an excuse for Sandra to toy with her and waste her time, all while winding her up something rotten. Her worst fears were quickly confirmed. All listening back to the exchange achieved was to make her cringe afresh at her own increasingly shrill and indignant responses to Sandra's provocations.

She stopped the tape, disconnected her headphones and leant back with her eyes shut, trying to purge her mind of the whole affair. And yet, try as she might, she couldn't get the image of Sandra and her ice-blue eyes out of her mind. There was something undeniably compelling about the woman who'd taken so much delight in cutting her down to size. She'd been sharp-witted, unpredictable, even – at times – genuinely amusing; all qualities which Anna, despite having been on the receiving end of her caustic tongue, couldn't help but grudgingly admire. She could see why people were so drawn not just to the mythos of the Morton murders but to the woman responsible for them. It would be quite something to truly get inside her head.

Despite her best efforts, Sandra was still very much on her mind as she made her way down to the lower level of Queen Street Station and boarded the 16:51 on the westbound line. When the train pulled into Hyndland ten minutes later, she'd resorted to spelling out complex words backwards in an attempt to ensure that her head was clear of any inappropriate subject matter by the time she reached home.

Eyes alighting on the platform, she spotted two familiar figures: a woman, her red hair blowing in the breeze, and a small, dark-haired boy of three by her side. As the train juddered to a halt, the woman spotted Anna and bent down to the boy's level, whispering in his ear and pointing. As the boy grinned excitedly, she lifted him onto her shoulders and waved manically. Anna, struggling to simultaneously wave back and navigate her way through the crush of bodies, stepped onto the platform and made her way towards the grinning pair.

'Hey, Trouble!' She scooped Jack into her arms. 'What are *you* doing here?'

'Came tae make sure ye hadnae got lost, didn't we?' beamed Zoe.

'Make sure ye hadnae got lost,' Jack agreed solemnly.

'I was just about to send out the rescue dogs,' Zoe went on as they headed for the exit, Anna still carrying Jack. 'That's two trains we've watched come in without you on them.' She turned to Jack. 'Gonnae tell yer mum tae gie us a bell next time she's gonnae be late? Mibby she'll listen to you.'

Jack turned his head to face Anna, then solemnly proceeded to recite what initially sounded like gibberish but which, after a second or two, she recognised, from the cadence and general approximation of the various vowels and consonants, as his rendition of the pre-recorded station announcer's voice. *The next train at platform two is the 16:46 to Balloch, calling at Jordanhill, Scotstounhill, Garscadden, Yoker…*

'Some kid, in't he?' said Zoe, as Jack continued to prattle away contentedly. 'Who needs Traveline when we got our own walking, talking timetable right here?'

'…Rectum, Alexander and Bampot,' Jack finished solemnly. *Renton, Alexandria and Balloch.*

'Rectum's his favourite word at the moment,' Zoe grinned. 'Ever since he found out what it meant. Here – reckon we could rent him out for extra pocket money?'

Anna laughed. 'I reckon child labour laws might have something to say about that.'

'Rectum, rectum, rectum!' Jack chanted joyously.

'So,' said Zoe, as they continued on down to the underpass leading out onto Hayburn Lane, 'how was prison?'

'Eh ... ' Anna cast an apprehensive glance at Jack. 'Maybe better to leave that one till later.'

Zoe mimed zipping her mouth.

Jack looked at each of them in turn, eyes wide and inquisitive. 'What's prison?'

'Oh ... it's ... ' Anna gestured vaguely as she searched for the appropriate words. 'It's where people are sent if they're convicted of a serious crime.'

Jack squinted at her, completely lost. '*Whit?*' he exclaimed – an uncanny echo of the sort of incredulous retort Zoe was inclined to make when she found something absurd or incomprehensible.

'It's where ye go if ye're really, really naughty,' said Zoe, not missing a beat.

'Oh,' said Jack, Zoe's explanation evidently making complete sense to him in a way that Anna's had singularly failed to. He turned to his mother long enough to give her a *can't take you anywhere* sort of look. It was something he must have seen an adult do at one time or another, and his impression was so spot on that for a moment, it felt to Anna as if the normal parent/child dynamic had been completely reversed.

She decided to change the subject. 'I'm starving!' she announced. 'What's for dinner?'

'*Well,*' Zoe declared self-importantly, 'we went to the shops earlier and got pasta, fresh tomatoes, herbs and they wee bits of bacon that are just – *mmmh!*' She smacked her lips. '*So* good. How's that sound?'

Anna smiled to herself. In her experience, Zoe was a dab hand at picking out the tastiest ingredients but less so when it came to putting them to use.

'I'm sure we can rustle up something between us,' she said, as they continued up the hill towards the tall sandstone townhouse near the top of Clarence Drive that they called home.

It would be no overstatement to say that Anna's life had been completely upended in the last three years – first by her becoming a mother, followed in swift succession by Zoe moving in. At the time, it had been taken for granted that the latter was a temporary measure while Zoe found her feet again after the fallout from the Shadow Men affair – albeit one without an official expiry date. Over time, however, the routine into which they'd settled had put down roots, with neither of them feeling any need to fix something that clearly wasn't broken. At times, it almost felt like they were belatedly enjoying, in their mid-thirties, the early twenties student lifestyle they hadn't got to experience together when they actually *were* students: living in shared digs, leading their own separate lives by day before reconvening in the evening to set the world to rights over a shared bottle of cheap wine. Or, as the ever-eloquent Zoe had put it more than once, "like a pair of auld lezzas who never dae it anymair".

That evening, after the three of them had done justice to the pancetta pasta Anna had knocked up and the two adults had done the same to half a bottle of supermarket red, Anna retired to the living room while Zoe headed upstairs with Jack to give him his bath and bedtime story – the latter a duty from which she was more than happy to absent herself. She knew, from experience, that Zoe always made a far better fist of it, armed with her 'box of tricks' containing an array of props and costumes – a plastic hat, a feather boa, a stick-on 'tache – to be adopted and discarded as she switched from one character to another. And, of course, she did *all* the voices. Anna's more conventional attempts to read to Jack had always been met with disinterest at best, if not active resistance.

Tonight, though, it wasn't just her deficiencies as a storyteller that had motivated her to leave this particular task to Zoe. All throughout the evening meal and its aftermath, Sandra Morton had continued to prey on her mind. Despite repeatedly telling herself that she was a detached professional, that her duty was merely to record her interviewees' experiences of the prison system and not dwell on the details of the crimes for which they'd been incarcerated, she could no longer deny that she wanted to know more – no, *needed* to know more – about the particulars of the case that was widely regarded as one of the most horrific in the country's legal history.

So she kicked off her shoes, loosened her belt and settled back on the sofa with her iPad, loading up articles on the case from her usual go-to sources: JSTOR, The Free Library, the online editions of the *Tribune* and *Caledonian* newspapers, even good old Wikipedia. As she tapped away at the screen, Zoe's voice periodically filtered down from above, rising and falling with the ebb and flow of the story she was telling. From the brief snatches of dialogue Anna was able to make out, it appeared that Zoe, blessed as she was with a vivid imagination and a healthy disrespect for the rulebook, was refashioning the plot of *The Gruffalo* to her – and Jack's – own tastes.

Anna was still bookmarking articles when she heard footsteps on the stairs. A moment later, Zoe ambled in, greeting Anna with an easy-going wave as she headed over to the opposite end of the sofa. Anna shifted her legs, making room. Zoe sank down with a contented sigh.

Anna peered over the top of her iPad. 'Jack go off to sleep OK?'

'Aye, snoozing like a boss.' She slapped Anna's knee expectantly. 'So, c'mon – spill. How'd it go in the big hoose? What was it like?'

'It was …' Anna began, only to stop. Where to even start? She realised now that, until Zoe had raised the subject, she hadn't truly comprehended just how heavily her visit to Broadwood had affected her on an emotional level. In fact, she saw now that she'd spent the last several hours doing everything she could to distract herself with other matters.

'It was everything I expected, in all the worst ways,' she said. 'The whole thing – it's just so …' She grasped at the air, searching for the right word. ' … *broken*. Most of the women I saw there were like kids who'd never grown up – and let's be honest, who can blame them? So many of them've spent their lives in and out of institutions, prison's basically just an extension of the care system for them. It's like, when they decided to close down Cornton Vale, they had this golden opportunity to start over. To do things completely differently. But instead, they just shook their heads and said, "Actually, we'll have more of the same, but with lilac wallpaper and feng shui".'

Zoe gave a sympathetic grimace. 'All the same, it was never exactly gonnae be like summer camp, but. End of the day, they still made their choices. If ye cannae dae the time…'

'…don't do the crime?'

'Bit too harsh, ye reckon?'

Anna rubbed her eyes with the heels of her hands and groaned. 'I dunno. Maybe. Or perhaps I *am* just a pie in the sky idealist who doesn't live in the real world. I'm just sick of making the same points over and over and no one listening.'

Zoe rubbed Anna's leg reassuringly. '*I'm* listening, doll.'

Anna smiled wanly. 'I know, and don't think I don't appreciate it. But you know what I mean. I'm talking about the people with the power to actually change things. They know all about the overcrowding, the self-harm and substance abuse, the number of women who spend months on remand for crimes that ultimately don't result in a custodial sentence…' She let out a heavy sigh. 'And still they do nothing.'

Zoe's lip curled impishly. 'Tell ye what – if ye're still as riled up the morra, we'll go down there first thing, you and me, chain oursels to the railings and no go home till they agree tae knock it doon. Deal?'

Anna gave up trying to fight the smile, allowing it to extend across her face. 'I'll hold ya to it, pal.'

For a moment, they sat there in companionable silence. Then, determined to change the subject, Anna hauled herself into an upright position.

'Oh, listen – you'll never believe who I spoke to today.'

'Who?'

'Sandra Morton.'

Zoe stared at her, a mixture of shock and wonderment in her eyes. 'That nutter who knifed her hubby and weans to death? No kidding! What was she like? She a complete head-case?'

'She was tough to get a read on, that's for damn sure. I spent a good forty minutes with her and I still didn't come away with any feel for what was going on inside her head.'

'Well, at any rate,' Zoe tucked her arms behind her head and leant back contentedly, 'least there's *one* person everyone agrees deserves tae be banged up for life.'

'Seems so,' Anna agreed. It came out sounding a little more noncommittal than she'd intended. 'Actually,' she gestured to her iPad, 'I thought I might read up on her case a bit. Y'know – just to satisfy the old curiosity.'

'Aye?' Zoe raised a dubious eyebrow. 'Well, you do you. That's some freaky-deaky shite ye're dealing with, mind.'

Anna bared her teeth. 'I'm a big girl. I can cope.'

'Rather you than me, doll.' Zoe glanced uncertainly at the TV. 'Uh … gonnae mind if I've got the telly-box on?'

'Nah, you're grand. You know what I'm like once I've got my teeth into something juicy: takes an earthquake to distract me.'

She wasn't being entirely truthful, though it was fair to say that, in recent years, she'd become a whole lot better at ignoring the world around her. These days, life in the Scavolini household was considerably less ordered than it had once been, with Zoe's presence almost as significant a source of upheaval as Jack's. Magazines, toys and items of clothing were left lying around, areas were commandeered for functions other than those for which they'd been intended, and where once she could have heard a pin drop, it was now highly unusual for there not to be at least some form of auditory disturbance wrangling for her attention at any given time. By necessity, Anna, who'd always believed she needed absolute peace and quiet to work, had developed an impressive ability to tune out all external stimuli – be it the wheels of Jack's Tonka truck grinding the hardwood floor, Zoe popping into her office for an impromptu chat while she was busy chasing a deadline, or the rat-a-tat-tat dialogue from one of the several drama series and soap operas Zoe followed and somehow managed to keep track of.

'Awesomesauce. I reckon this ep's gonnae be a belter. Candice's been seeing Niall on the sly, but now Michelle's started getting wise tae the fact something's up and she's been asking questions.'

'Candice had better watch it,' said Anna gravely, as if she had the first clue who any of these people were.

Zoe grinned and reached for the remote as Anna once more picked up her iPad.

They settled in for the evening – Zoe curled up on one side of the sofa, eyes fixed on the TV screen, one foot folded under her, the other coiled companionably round Anna's leg; Anna stretched out with the iPad propped against her upturned thighs. As the theme music to the show began to play, Anna switched to the first tab in her browser and began to read.

At 23:09 on Sunday 6 May 2001, emergency services received a 999 call from a house in Hillend, a small village in Dumfries and Galloway, approximately six miles from the border with England. In the recording, a man's voice can be heard, garbled and incoherent, though at one point the word 'help' can be clearly discerned.

At 23:20, amid a torrential downpour that had begun some thirty minutes earlier, a patrol car reached the village from the neighbouring town of Annan – Hillend having no police presence of its own. Two officers, PCs Robert Strainger and Euan Higgins, approached the house – a detached bungalow at the top of the small hill from which the village received its name – and found it in darkness. Having found the front door locked and received no response to their knocking, they circled round to the back of the house to investigate, where they discovered the rear door lying open. After radioing back to base for instructions, they entered the building.

Inside, they discovered the homeowner, Guy Morton, aged 44 and subsequently determined to be the originator of the 999 call, lying face-down in the hallway next to the telephone stand, the receiver on the floor, a few inches from his outstretched hand. He had suffered multiple stab wounds to his back, arms and neck, and the officers were unable to palpate a pulse. While Higgins radioed for backup and an ambulance, Strainger ventured further into the house, where, in a bedroom at the far end of the corridor, he discovered Guy's twin four-year-old sons, Iain and Gabriel, in their beds – both, like their father, stabbed multiple times and showing no signs of life.

At 23:31, paramedics arrived and quickly determined that resuscitation of all three victims was impossible, pending official pronouncement by the divisional surgeon. Meanwhile, alerted by the emergency vehicle sirens, Graham Malone (72), sole occupant of the adjacent property, arrived at the house to investigate. He furnished the police with the names and ages of its occupants, allowing them to determine that the children's mother, Sandra (34), was unaccounted for. He also stated that, at around 23:10, he heard a door being thrown open followed by hurried footsteps slapping on the wet grass of the Mortons' back garden. Later, it would be widely agreed that, in all likelihood, what he had heard was the killer making his or her escape.

A third child – a teenage daughter, whose identity, as per the guidance on reporting on minors in relation to criminal proceedings in Section 49 of the Children's and Young Person Act, was not made public at the time – was later established to have been sleeping at the home of her paternal grandparents that night.

At 23:35, the duty officer on call for the area, Police Sergeant Tom Howie, arrived in Hillend, his journey having been disrupted by localised flooding resulting from the downpour. Once on site, he organised the attendance of CID and scene of crime officers from Dumfries, the nearest large town, some twenty-five miles away. He also requested additional manpower from neighbouring villages and dispatched officers to search Hillend and the surrounding countryside for Sandra – some on foot, some by car.

From around 23:45 onwards, the press began to converge on the house – alerted, it has long been alleged, by tip-offs from within the police force. As a result of poor management by inexperienced officers, some succeeding in gaining access to the house, including a freelance photographer, who photographed the blood-streaked walls and floor of the hallway corridor before being ejected. The pictures were rejected by every newspaper barring one, which published them – albeit in a heavily pixelated form – as a double-page spread. The original, unedited versions remain hot commodities among frequenters of true crime message boards, and negatives purporting to be the originals still surface periodically on the more unscrupulous auction websites.

*   *   *

At 23:49, two police officers – PCs Mark Bennie and Donald Coughlin – were driving south along the Shaw Road, approximately a mile and a half east of the Morton home, when they spotted a woman walking towards them on the grass verge. They later testified that the sight struck them as incongruous on two counts. First, the road – a narrow country lane with several sharp bends – had no footpath or streetlights, and was therefore extremely dangerous for pedestrians, especially after dark. Second, despite the continuing downpour, she was dressed only in shorts and a spaghetti strap tank top.

Though not officially part of the search for Sandra Morton, the two officers had been alerted, via an all-points radio bulletin, to be on the lookout for a woman matching the description provided by Graham Malone. Agreeing that the woman did indeed resemble that description, they pulled over and approached her on foot. Both later testified that, when asked whether she was Sandra Morton, the first words she spoke were, 'Are they all dead?'

After some cajoling, she was persuaded to join the officers in the car. They reported her demeanour as distant and absent-minded, to the extent that they wondered whether she was under the influence of a controlled substance. Nonetheless, she ultimately confirmed that she was indeed Sandra Morton. Following a brief debate as to what to do with her, they concluded that the best solution was to take her back to the Morton house.

At 00:03, they reached the house, where, by this time, a sizeable news presence had assembled. The same photographer who had earlier invaded the house snapped a picture of her emerging from the back of the police car. The image of her standing, blank-faced, in the doorway of the car, her nipples glaringly visible through the drenched fabric of her tank top, made the front page of the morning edition of a national tabloid better known for its spreads of topless models than for its news coverage. The more tasteful publications cropped the image above her shoulders.

At 00:08, CID officers, led by DS Malcolm Gunning (48), arrived from Dumfries, accompanied by the crime scene investigation team. A twenty-three-year veteran of the force with considerable experience as a homicide investigator, Gunning wasted no time in gaining control of the crime scene. The house and surrounding area were cordoned off and all unauthorised personnel ejected from the premises. While Gunning liaised with his superiors in Dumfries, both the divisional surgeon and the duty pathologist arrived on scene – the former to officially declare life extinct, the latter to view the bodies in situ and record his preliminary impressions as to the nature and cause of death. Sandra's clothes were also seized and forensic samples taken from her, including fingernail scrapings and hair specimens.

At 00:55, Sandra – who, for the last hour, had been held under guard in the living room – was taken to the police station in Annan. Under strict instruction from his superiors not to interview her until the senior investigating officer was present, Gunning instead placed her in the family suite, after first offering her the opportunity to contact a friend or relative, which she declined.

The man charged with heading up the inquiry arrived in Annan early the next morning. His name, contrary to Ruth Laxton's recollections, was neither Dalton nor Dawson but *Dalston* – Detective Superintendent Frank Dalston (52), an officer with thirty-two years' experience and a solve rate the envy of his peers. Following a short briefing from Gunning, a colleague of many years with whom he had worked on multiple investigations, he decided against interviewing Sandra straight away in favour of heading to the local hospital to attend, in person, the postmortem conducted by the duty pathologist, Professor Robin Arbuthnot.

The postmortem was, by all accounts, harrowing even by the usual standards of such affairs, and left the normally unflappable Dalston ashen-faced and uncommunicative for some time afterwards. Colleagues later noted that they observed a marked change in his overall demeanour following his trip to the hospital. He had always been tenacious in his pursuit of the law, but from that moment on, a fire seemed to have been lit in his belly, and he exuded a determination not to rest until he secured justice for the victims.

'He was like a man possessed,' one member of the investigation team stated off the record. 'I saw the look in his eyes and I thought, "God help whoever did this when he catches them".'

5

Looking up from her screen, Anna realised Zoe was staring at her, concern etched into her pursed brows.

'That bad, aye?' she said gently.

'Yeah,' said Anna, finding it unexpectedly difficult to speak. 'Yeah, it's pretty bad.'

She wasn't sure what involuntary sign she'd given to attract Zoe's attention, but whatever it was, she knew what had triggered it: an article on Guy and the twins' postmortems which referred to Gabriel, the younger of the two boys by seven minutes, as having been 'virtually decapitated'.

'You OK?' Zoe continued to eye her with concern.

'Yeah. Just … freaky-deaky, like you said.'

Seeming to accept this, Zoe turned to face the television once more. Anna could tell, though, from the way her eyes had lingered on her just long enough to make it awkward, that she still had reservations.

Anna slowly let out the breath she'd been keeping in. Since having Jack, she'd become considerably more emotionally sensitive than she used to be, to the point of finding it difficult to read about or watch depictions of violence, even in a fictional context. *But that's somebody's baby!* she'd think, if she saw someone getting punched or hit in a film, even though the rational part of her mind knew it was all make-believe. Her current reading matter was as far from make-believe as it was possible to get, and the thought of the violence that had been visited on these two young boys – only a year older than her own son, fast asleep and blissfully unaware just above her – was enough to turn her blood to ice.

Perhaps it would prove less harrowing in the fresh light of day. Perhaps it was time to call it a night, close the iPad and lose herself in the trials and tribulations of a bunch of improbably glamorous, larger-than-life characters with Zoe. But she couldn't. She had the bit between her teeth now and needed to know what came next.

She took a deep breath, tightened her grip on the iPad to still the slight tremor in her hands, and read on.

By now, Sandra had been at the police station for almost nine hours without being interviewed. With time very much of the essence, Dalston and Gunning held a brief strategy meeting, then summoned Sandra and the duty solicitor representing her to the interview room, where they cautioned her and proceeded to question her about the events of the previous night.

On the sliding scale of alibis, from entirely credible to hopelessly implausible, Sandra's ranked dangerously close to the latter end of the spectrum. Despite repeated entreaties to provide a more compelling explanation as to her absence at the time of the murders, the story she repeatedly stuck to was that she'd gone out to buy painkillers and had had to walk as far as the petrol station on the A75 road to Gretna, approximately two and a half miles north of the house as the crow flies. This, she claimed, was why she was gone for so long and picked up so far from home.

With no immediate grounds to arrest or charge Sandra, Dalston saw little option but to release her pending investigation, under strict instruction not to speak to the press or leave the area. Unable to return to the house in Hillend while it remained a crime scene or to provide the name of any friend or relative with whom she could stay, the police arranged accommodation for her in a B&B in Annan.

From the outset, Dalston made it clear to the more than forty officers seconded to what, by then, had been dubbed Operation Bluegrass that Sandra Morton was to be regarded as the main person of interest, and that their immediate priority was to establish a complete picture of her movements. While forensics continued their search of the Morton house and garden, officers began making door-to-door enquiries – a less time-consuming task than would normally have been the case, due to Hillend having fewer than twenty residential properties to its name. A team was also dispatched to the petrol station on the A75 to interview the staff and seize the CCTV footage from the previous night.

The sole employee who'd been on duty at the time, Paul Kempley, a nineteen-year-old from nearby Eastriggs, produced the first major hole in Sandra's version of events. His shift had run from 10 p.m. to 6 a.m., and during that time, he had no memory of having served a woman matching her description. It had been an atypically quiet night, and he insisted he hadn't been off the shop floor at any point, barring a brief visit to the bathroom at around 2.30 a.m. Kempley's testimony would end up being vital in disproving Sandra's alibi after it emerged that, owing to a recording failure, the CCTV tapes for the entire week leading up to the night of the murders were blank. The till roll, which provided only the value of each transaction rather than an itemised breakdown, proved to be of little use, while neither the paracetamol Sandra claimed to have bought nor a receipt for it was found on her person.

Sandra, when confronted about this discrepancy, would insist that both had been in the pocket of her shorts when the police had made her strip and turn her clothes over to them, and that if they could not be located, the only possible explanation was that they had lost them, either through carelessness or deliberate malfeasance. The officers responsible for bagging and cataloguing her clothing remained adamant that neither pills nor a receipt for them had ever been present.

An audit of the Mortons' phone records, meanwhile, established that a call had been placed to a local taxi firm at 22:47, just over twenty minutes prior to the 999 call Guy Morton made as he lay bleeding to death on the floor. The company confirmed that Mr Morton had rung to book a taxi for six o'clock the following morning – a regular occurrence on weekdays. It was therefore concluded that the attack must have occurred during the twenty-two-minute period between the two calls – and almost certainly towards its extreme tail end. On this point, Professor Arbuthnot was unequivocal: the violence would have been brief, frenzied and savage, with death having occurred within a couple of minutes at most. The children, killed in their beds as they slept, were almost certainly targeted first, while Guy – presumably roused from his own bed by sounds of disturbance – was attacked when he attempted to intervene. The image of the heroic father grappling with the killer as he tried to save his children was a powerful one, to which both the press and prosecution would repeatedly return.

In the days that followed, a shrine to the victims sprung up by the roadside on the approach to Hillend, complete with oversized photographs of Guy – a clean-cut, handsome man with a pronounced cleft chin – and the twins – every bit as photogenic and media-friendly as their father. Meanwhile, the investigation continued apace. The SOCO and forensics teams completed their examination of the house, finding no evidence of a break-in. Dalston ordered the net to be widened, with officers undertaking a fingertip search of the area surrounding the house in a one-mile radius, focusing on the field at the foot of the rear garden – believed to be the most logical direction of flight for a killer fleeing via the back door. The primary goal was to locate the murder weapon, believed to be a carving knife missing from the Sabatier block set on the kitchen counter. The choice of weapon and the isolated nature of the house were viewed as strong indicators that the murders were unlikely to have been committed by an outsider.

With the door-to-door enquiries having failed to bear fruit, Dalston took his message nationwide, fronting a televised appeal for information on the evening news on Tuesday 8 May. Few of the resulting responses – the usual mixture of well-intentioned fools and professional time-wasters – proved of any use. This was followed, on Sunday 13, by a second appeal by Dalston, this time accompanied by Guy's parents, Eunice (64) and George (65), who took turns reading an emotionally charged statement, pleading for any information that would lead to the murderer of their son and grandsons being brought to justice. Sandra herself was conspicuous by her absence – something Eunice and George were alleged to have made a condition of their participation. In what was portrayed by much of the press as a deliberate act of revenge, Sandra gave her one and only interview to the media that same day: an on-camera exchange with a reporter from Border Television, the content of which was widely believed to have done more to turn public attitudes against her than any other development in the case. The following morning, the *Scottish Daily Post* ran a front-page splash consisting of a zoomed-in freeze-frame of her face, alongside the headline 'ICE QUEEN' – the first documented use of that nickname.

The one solid breakthrough to emerge from the appeals was a call to the dedicated hotline from one Adjoa Asante, a forty-three-year-old Ghanaian national employed as a cleaner by a family in Browhouses, a few miles south of Hillend. At approximately twelve minutes past eleven, less than three minutes after Guy Morton made the 999 call with his dying breath, Ms Asante was aboard the last bus to Ecclefechan, where she rented a studio flat. As the bus wound its way north along the Haysend Road, which bordered the field at the foot of the Mortons' garden, she happened to glance out of the window to her left and saw a figure scrambling over the low stone wall at the bottom of the field, heading away from the house. Though she only saw the figure for a few seconds, she was unequivocal on two points. One: the figure in question was wearing a blue raincoat. Two: she was a woman with long, dark hair. The driver, the vehicle's sole other occupant, had been concentrating on the road at the time and saw nothing.

By interviewing various Hillend locals, the police established that Sandra owned a raincoat similar to the one seen by Ms Asante. However, no item of clothing matching its description was found, during either the search of the house or the wider search of the surrounding area. When confronted about this, Sandra claimed to have thrown the coat away two weeks earlier after she accidentally ripped one of the sleeves on some barbed wire. However, two separate eyewitnesses attested to having seen her wearing it more recently, with the most recent sighting occurring just three days prior to the murders.

From the beginning, a major stumbling block for Dalston and his team had been the fact that no forensic evidence was found on Sandra to support her guilt. Hairs matching hers were found on both Guy and the twins, but this was hardly surprising given their relationship. If, however, she had worn protective clothing – like, say, a raincoat – then it was plausible that she could have committed the murders without getting any blood splatter on the rest of her clothes. The torrential rain, meanwhile, could feasibly have washed away any blood that had ended up on her person. She could then have disposed of the coat as she fled – something which would also account for her being severely underdressed for the weather when she was apprehended.

With a lack of forensic evidence and a reliance on both eyewitness testimony and the holes in her own account, the case against Sandra remained circumstantial, but for Dalston, it was enough. On the evening of Monday 21 May, he brought Adjoa Asante back in for a further interview, at which she reiterated her account of her sighting and made a positive identification of Sandra from a photographic line-up. Immediately after concluding the interview, Dalston drafted and submitted a report to the Procurator Fiscal, naming Sandra Morton as the prime suspect. His report was supplemented by a profile of the killer drawn up by renowned forensic psychologist Professor Ronald Greenstreet. Though Greenstreet offered no opinion as to Sandra's guilt, he nonetheless stated that she was as close to a perfect fit for his profile as it was possible to get.

In the early hours of Thursday 24 May, police arrived at the B&B in Annan where Sandra was staying. She was arrested, charged with the murders of Guy, Iain and Gabriel Morton, and remanded in custody. The following day, she appeared at Dumfries Sheriff Court, where she was denied bail and committed for further examination. On Thursday 31 May, she was informed that she would stand trial for the murders. Following a second appearance at the Sheriff Court, she was fully committed and transferred to HMP Cornton Vale to await trial.

6

'Seen this?'

Anna looked up to find Zoe angling her phone towards her, a video open on the small, fingerprint-streaked display. As she sat up to get a better look, she recognised the interview subject framed in close-up as Sandra – younger and slighter of build than the woman she'd spoken to earlier today, but nonetheless immediately identifiable as the same person.

'What's this?'

'Interview with yer new bestie. I only seen the edited highlights before, but someone's uploaded the whole shebang.'

As Zoe spoke, Anna became aware of how quiet it now was in the living room. She soon realised why: the television was no longer on. She checked the time at the corner of her iPad's screen. 22:17. Zoe's programme would have finished over an hour ago. Had she really been reading for that long?

She gestured to the phone. 'Can I ... ?'

Zoe nodded. 'Aye, but scooch up. I wanna see the rest too.'

Anna shuffled along the sofa until she was next to Zoe. With the sides of their heads pressed together, they leaned into the glowing screen, Zoe holding it for them both.

The footage was clearly at least a couple of generations removed from the source, but the quality was still more than acceptable. The burned-in timecode at the bottom of the screen suggested that the footage had been sneaked out of the studio by some light-fingered employee committed to the principle of open access. Whoever had lit the set was clearly aiming for an ominous mood: Sandra was seated in a three-quarters view, her surroundings swathed in shadow. She wore a sleeveless lace top that was low cut enough to expose the deep cleft of her cleavage – which the cameraman had made sure was in frame – and, once again, very clearly no bra. All told, it was only marginally less revealing than the outfit she'd worn on the night of the murders.

'Guy's parents didn't want you to take part in today's appeal,' said the off-screen interviewer, his disembodied voice flat and tinny through the phone's speakers. 'Why is that, do you think?'

'Cos it's always gotta be all about them,' said Sandra immediately. 'Can't have anything taking the spotlight away from them and their *grief.*' She delivered the last word in a sneering tone, as if she regarded the very notion as contemptible.

It took a moment for Anna to realise what it was, besides her comparative youth, that seemed so different about this Sandra, but then it hit her. *The accent.* Whereas the Sandra who'd verbally sparred with her earlier today had spoken in a way that wouldn't have sounded out of place in the corridors of a university or reading the evening news, this one had a much harsher, more working-class inflection – all guttural vowels and glottal stops. She half-wondered if the numerous Open University classes Sandra had taken during her imprisonment had included elocution lessons.

'It has nothing to do with them believing you might be responsible?' said the interviewer.

'You'd have to ask them that.'

'But they're not here. You *are.* That's why I'm asking you.'

'Reckon she knows what she looks like, dressed like that?' said Zoe.

'Why?' Anna felt her shoulders drawing in defensively. 'What *does* she look like?'

Zoe gave her an incredulous grimace, as if she couldn't believe she was being so oblivious. 'Like, a big auld hoor?'

Anna almost laughed out loud. 'Oh, come on. That's hardly the most egregious aspect of this whole saga. 'Sides, ever heard the words "pot", "kettle" and "black"?'

'Aye, but it's hardly the time or the place, is it?'

Anna shrugged stiffly, reluctant to be drawn on the matter. She returned her attention to the screen, where the footage had now cut to the interviewer – a middle-aged man with a severely receding hairline.

'It's the question on everyone's minds,' he said, jabbing the pen he was holding towards Sandra, 'so I'm simply going to come out and ask it. Did you kill your husband and children?'

Sandra's lips parted in a silent laugh.

'Why is that funny?' The interviewer sounded genuinely wounded.

Sandra rolled her eyes. 'Well, I'm hardly gonnae say "yes", am I?'

'The point I'm making,' the interviewer continued, 'is that this is your opportunity to set the record straight. To convince our viewers that you're innocent.'

'What for?' Sandra shrugged belligerently. 'Everyone already thinks it was me. Nothing I say's gonnae change their minds. You lot've made sure of that. Only one person knows what really happened, and that's the person that did it. That could be me, or it could be you ... ' She lifted an eyebrow, as if daring him to argue. 'Or it could be someone else altogether.'

'Oh my God!' Zoe breathed. 'She's a cookie. An absolute, grade-A *cookie!*'

'Shh!' Anna hissed, her eyes not leaving the screen.

'The police—' began the interviewer.

'The police wouldnae know their arses from their elbows,' Sandra snapped, eyes momentarily flaring in what, to Anna, seemed like the first genuine emotion she'd shown so far. 'Too busy dragging me in for endless questions, never giving me a moment's peace.'

The view cut to the interviewer, arms folded, lips pinched. 'Some might put it to you that, if you really were innocent and wanted them to catch whoever did this to your family, you'd gladly submit to as many rounds of questioning as it takes to get to the bottom of what happened.'

'That's assuming you think they care about getting to the bottom of *anything.*'

'And that's your final word on the subject?'

The camera slowly zoomed in on Sandra's face as she sat, arms folded, chin jutting out defiantly.

'It is.'

In the silence that followed, the hum of the tape heads rolling could be heard on the recording.

'Sandra Morton, thank you for your time.'

The clip ended. Zoe lowered the phone and turned to Anna, exhaling dramatically. 'Yowza. S'nae wonder they thrown the book at her. 'Magine anyone thinking *she* was innocent after a performance like that?'

'There's still such a thing as due process, you know,' said Anna, though without much conviction. Given all she'd read so far, to say nothing of what she'd seen of Sandra herself, she wasn't overly minded to disagree with Zoe's assessment.

'Aye,' Zoe conceded, 'but ye've gotta admit, there's some folk, ye just *know*.'

'She doesn't go out of her way to do herself any favours, I'll give you that.'

'Got *that* right.' Zoe stretched and hauled herself to her feet. 'Right, I'm offski. Gonnae be long yerself?'

Anna shook her head. 'I'll be just behind you. Just got a bit more to read.'

'Well, don't come crying tae me if that stuff gives ye nightmares.'

Anna waited till Zoe's footsteps on the stairs receded into silence, then picked up her iPad and began to read once more.

Over the next six months, the prosecution and defence teams built their respective cases. The press, now constrained by the Contempt of Court Act in what they could say about the woman they'd dubbed the Ice Queen, contented themselves with reporting on tangential matters – like the growing public campaign, backed by two tabloids, a firebrand talk show host and a former Conservative MP, to reinstate the death penalty for cases of child murder, and the joint funeral for Guy and the twins. The service – held at St John the Evangelist Episcopal Church, Eunice and George Morton's regular place of worship, on Friday 6 July – was an intimate affair, closed to all but immediate family and a handful of friends, though press and public alike still crowded into the modest grounds. People came from all over the country to pay their respects, gripped by an apparent belief that this was a crime that had been visited on them all. 'TAKEN FROM US TOO SOON,' reads a banner held by one of the mourners in a photograph that featured prominently in the press coverage of that day.

On Monday 24 January 2002, the trial of Sandra Morton finally commenced at the High Court in Edinburgh. Over the next two months, a jury of fifteen relived the events of that fateful night blow by blow and pored over the competing testimonies of the various witnesses for the prosecution and defence. The former numbered considerably more than the latter, with Sandra's team fighting what amounted to a rear-guard action, seeking to undermine the prosecution's case through cross-examination rather than leading any earth-shattering evidence of their own – a state of affairs widely perceived as indicative of the paucity of their case.

Sandra herself did not take the stand – a decision from which the Judge, Lord Dornock, was duty-bound to remind the jury not to infer any guilt, though the public inevitably drew its own conclusions. The prosecution's two star witnesses – Paul Kempley and Adjoa Asante – were examined and cross-examined at length, both sticking resolutely to their accounts: Sandra was not present at the petrol station on the A75 on the night of the murders, but *was* seen fleeing the vicinity of the house minutes after her husband took his last breath. Each day, the public galleries were packed, with queues beginning while it was still dark. There were even reports of particularly dedicated individuals camping outside the courthouse overnight.

For sixty-six days, the trial of Sandra Morton gripped the country and its media like no other before or since. All other matters were relegated to the back pages, or to brief addenda on the evening news before the sports section. Then, on Thursday 21 March, the defence and prosecution presented their closing statements and the jury retired to consider the verdict. Their deliberation continued the following day and they were sequestered in a hotel for the weekend. Shortly after midday on Monday 25, the legal teams, press and members of the public gathered in Court Three to hear the jury's decision.

By majority, Sandra Morton was found guilty of all three murders. She showed no emotion as the verdict was read out or as she was led to the awaiting prison van. Two weeks later, she was sentenced to three terms of life imprisonment: a minimum punishment part of twenty-three years for each of the three victims, with the sentences for the murders of the twins running concurrently, for a total of forty-six years.

And so it was that the case of the person dubbed 'the evilest woman in Scotland' ended. But those who hoped the matter would end with her sentencing would be sorely disappointed. As one chapter drew to a close, so another began, in the form of the lucrative business of raking over and re-litigating her crimes ad nauseam on the printed page and on television screens, thus ensuring that Sandra Morton and the Hillend Murders would be remembered for a long time to come. The media, which had dined out on the case for almost a full year, continued to pick over its bones like scavengers sustaining themselves on scraps until the next scandal came along. Meanwhile, lauded by the press and public alike for having brought the Butcher of Hillend to justice, Frank Dalston became something of a minor celebrity, doing the rounds on the chat show circuit and finding himself much in demand as a consultant for television police dramas. When he died in 2015, the great and the good lined up to pay their respects to 'an exemplary police officer' and 'a towering figure in the field of law enforcement'.

Life in Hillend returned, as far as was possible, to normal. The Morton house was put on the market and was soon purchased by a married couple who were evidently unfazed by its grisly history – or, perhaps, viewed its notoriety as a selling point. Sandra and Guy's surviving daughter – spared the same fate as her younger brothers by, it seemed, the grace of God – returned with Guy's brother and sister-in-law to their home in Ontario, Canada, to be raised alongside their two similarly-aged children. And behind the walls of Cornton Vale, Sandra herself passed into legend, the subject of endless retellings and embellishments, until fact and myth rolled into one.

One final footnote deserves mention. Two years after the trial, the matter of Sandra Morton once again hit the headlines with the news that her surviving daughter had turned sixteen, thus allowing the ban on reporting on her to be lifted and for her to be named. Pictures of the pallid, blonde-haired Katie Morton were splashed across the front pages of every tabloid and broadsheet in the land, accompanied by the breathless recounting of various details on which the press had dutifully sat for almost three years. Chief among these was the revelation that, far from having merely been visiting her grandparents on the night of the murders, she had in fact been living with them on a permanent basis for a period of nearly seven months.

The reason behind this curious situation never came to light, as the grandparents refused all overtures from the media, and all efforts to trace Katie herself proved unsuccessful. In the absence of an explanation, most simply took it as proof that something had already been deeply wrong within the Morton household long before Sandra decided, apparently on a whim, to butcher her husband and infant sons to death one rainswept night in 2001.

7

Saturday 9 March

'Where *is* it?'

Anna frantically rifled through the contents of her shoulder bag, trying to locate the trilling phone she'd managed to bury beneath a mountain of detritus. As she continued to root around, Jack, installed in the child seat of the laden shopping trolley she'd been pushing when her phone had started to ring, tugged at her sleeve.

'Mummy. Mummy.'

'Hang on,' said Anna, through gritted teeth. 'Mummy's a *little* preoccupied right now.'

Finally succeeding in locating her phone, she fished it out and took the call.

'Hello?'

'Is that Professor Anna Scavolini?'

The voice at the other end of the line was female, soft and vaguely childlike, and Anna briefly wondered if the caller was a schoolgirl with an interest in criminology wanting to enquire about work experience opportunities – though, if that was the case, how she'd got hold of her personal number was anyone's guess.

'Speaking,' she said.

'Excuse me,' said a voice behind her.

She turned to see a middle-aged man facing her, his own trolley parked just behind hers. He glared at her expectantly, clearly wanting her to move, despite the fact that there was ample space for him to get by on the other side.

'I'm sorry to disturb you, Professor Scavolini,' the voice went on, as Anna signalled to the man to go around her. 'My name is—'

'MUMMY.'

'Just a moment.'

Anna covered the mouthpiece and turned to Jack, who glowered back at her mutinously.

'What?' she demanded.

'Want Thomas Tank.'

He was referring to the coin-operated Thomas the Tank Engine ride next to the photo booth beyond the checkouts. For Jack, it was the highlight of their weekly trips to the supermarket, and Anna knew from long experience that it was nigh on impossible to leave without first having been relieved of most of the change in her wallet.

'I told you,' she said, 'I'll take you for a ride on Thomas Tank once we've got all the shopping. Now, if you don't mind ...'

'Want Thomas Tank *now*.' Jack's expression was one of pure rage.

'Well, you can't *have* Thomas Tank now, so you're just going to have to be patient, aren't you?'

The middle-aged man, still waiting for Anna to move, cleared his throat noisily to attract her attention. She glanced briefly at him and once more mimed for him to go around her. Then, turning her back on both him and Jack to convey to them that she wasn't going to entertain any further interruptions, she raised the phone to her ear once more.

'Sorry, you were saying ...?'

'My name's Pamela Macklin,' the girl said. 'I'm a solicitor with Riddoch MacLetchie. I represent—'

'Mummy Mummy Mummy Mummy MUMMY.'

Jack banged his heels against the metal frame of the trolley in time with each shout. On the final one, he lashed out with his foot, delivering a ferocious kick to Anna's backside.

'*Ow!*' Anna yelped, more indignant than hurt. To pre-empt any further attempts to make mischief, she scooped him out of the trolley and held him against her body, one arm wrapped round his torso.

'Sorry,' she said into the phone, steadfastly ignoring Jack's efforts to squirm free, 'you represent who?'

On the periphery of her vision, she was aware of the man throwing up his hands in exasperation, before performing an awkward one-eighty-degree turn with his trolley and setting off in search of an alternative route.

'Sandra Morton,' said Pamela. 'I represent Sandra Morton.'

As Anna digested this information, Jack, who'd now ceased squirming, reached for a jar of mayonnaise from the nearest shelf and let it fall to the ground. There was an almighty crash, and shattered glass and creamy sauce went everywhere – including on Anna's shoes.

'Oh, *fuck!*'

She leapt backwards, still clutching Jack, who grinned up at her with savage glee.

'I'm sorry?' Pamela squeaked, her tone halfway between a question and a genuine apology for whatever transgression she assumed she'd committed.

'Oh, no, not you.' Anna attempted to keep hold of both Jack and the phone while rummaging in her bag in search of tissues. 'Just a minor condiment-related catastrophe. If you'd just give me one minute ... '

Placing the call on hold, she pocketed the phone and set Jack down on his feet.

'You,' she informed him, 'are a little terrorist. Stay there and don't move.'

'RECTUM!!!' Jack yelled, face puce with anger.

Crouching down at Jack's level, Anna was acutely aware of several of her fellow shoppers staring at her, their disapproving silence a damning indictment of her poor parenting. Cheeks burning, she ignored them and continued to rummage in her bag.

Just at that moment, Zoe came striding into view, holding a pack of ice lollies aloft.

'Here, Anna,' she exclaimed, clearly delighted by her find, 'have ye seen, they got these new banana flavour freezy pops, and—' She stopped short, taking in the mess on the floor before her. 'Jesus, Mary and the wee donkey, what happened here?'

'Take him for me for a few minutes, will you?' said Anna wearily. 'He wants a ride on Thomas Tank.'

Abandoning the fruitless search for tissues, she got to her feet and turned to face the two glum-looking store assistants who, having evidently drawn the short straw, had arrived, armed with a dizzying assortment of cleaning tools.

'I'm so sorry,' she winced. 'Just tell me what I owe and I'll pay for it.'

As the assistants began erecting a cordon around the detonation zone and Zoe departed with Jack in tow, Anna took a deep breath, composing herself, before putting the phone to her ear once more.

'Sorry about that. Let's start again, shall we? Why are you calling?'

'Oh. Right.' Pamela was probably wondering just what sort of dysfunctional domestic arrangement she'd interrupted. 'I gather you met with my client on Tuesday.'

'She was the one who initiated it,' Anna put in quickly, feeling strangely compelled to counter any impression that she'd done something wrong.

Pamela gave a tinkling, high-pitched laugh. 'To be honest, I wouldn't have expected anything else. Anyway, I wondered if I might be able to put a proposition to you.'

'If you can make it quick.' Anna shot one final apologetic wince at the two store assistants and moved to the adjacent, less busy aisle – partly so she could hear Pamela better, partly out of mortification. 'I'm kind of in the middle of something.'

'Actually, I was wondering if we could meet. I'm in Glasgow right now and … well, I think it'd be better if I explained in person.'

'I'm afraid I can't. I've got a ton of things to do, and I'm not in the habit of—'

'I'll make it worth your while,' Pamela blurted out. 'Um … what I mean is, it's something I think'll interest you. We can meet wherever's convenient for you. Just name the time and place.'

Anna opened her mouth to deliver another polite but firm rejection, then stopped. As reluctant as she was to admit it, she was more than just a little curious to hear what Pamela's mysterious proposition entailed.

'I can meet you in half an hour,' she said. 'Caffe Monza, at the corner of Vine Street and Dumbarton Road.'

'I'll see you there,' said Pamela. 'You won't regret it, I promise.'

We'll see, thought Anna, and hung up.

8

By the time Anna had made it through the check-out and reunited with Jack and Zoe, Jack had already had his fill of Thomas Tank and was sitting splay-legged on the floor, gnawing on an oversized cucumber. She helped load up the car, then dispatched Zoe to take the shopping and Jack home, before heading round the corner to the café where she'd arranged to meet Pamela. She arrived with ten minutes to spare; some habits were impossible to break, no matter how precious her time.

As she sat, perched at a table with a clear view of the entrance, her thoughts turned – as they often had over the last few days – to the state of play of her book. Since her visit to Broadwood, she'd gone back through all her old notes, hoping that somewhere within all the unordered sheets of paper lay the germ of an idea that she could use in place of the material that should have come out of her interview with Martina Macdonald. It was supposed to have been the last major chapter before her concluding remarks; a contemporary case study which shone a light on the plight of the average prisoner and gave everything she'd argued about the system and its impact on women's lives a sense of immediacy. Instead, all she had to show for her visit were a recording of a convicted child killer denigrating and belittling her and several hours sunk into reading up on the gruesome details of her crimes.

Just before midday, the door opened and a slightly built woman in her mid-twenties came striding purposefully in. She was wearing a double-breasted overcoat that looked like it had been bought with a much larger person in mind, her twig-like legs protruding below it like a sparrow's.

Her hair was scraped back into a severe bun that would have looked more at home on a pensioner, but by far the most incongruous aspect of her appearance was a pair of massive over-ear headphones that completely dwarfed her diminutive features. Anna took one look at her and instantly pegged her as the owner of the childlike voice she'd heard on the phone.

Her hunch was confirmed as the woman spotted her and made straight for her.

'Professor Scavolini?'

'Anna. You'd be Pamela?'

'That's *right*,' beamed Pamela, seeming genuinely tickled pink at having been correctly identified. She lowered her headphones and extended her hand. Her skin was cool and clammy to the touch.

'So good to meet you in person,' she said, laying it on a little too thickly for Anna's tastes. 'Thanks so much for agreeing to see me. Have you … ?' She gestured towards the counter, where the two baristas on duty were doing a roaring trade.

'Oh no,' Anna said quickly. She was half-hoping that, if she declined the offer of refreshments, they could get down to business and be on their respective ways before very much longer.

'What would you like?' said Pamela, then added hastily, 'It's on me.'

She looked so eager to please, Anna felt she could hardly refuse. Shortly thereafter, Pamela returned from the counter with their respective beverages: a coffee for Anna and a mineral water for herself.

'Now,' she said, after hanging her coat over the back of her seat and settling into it, 'you probably want to know what this is all about.'

'That would be good, yes.'

'*Well*,' she said, investing the word with rather more dramatic flair than the situation merited, 'first of all, I'd just like to say how refreshing it is that someone of your standing has taken an interest in Sandra's case. To be honest, I've always found it a bit puzzling, given its profile, that there's been so little academic material written on it.'

Anna had noticed this herself during her internet trawl the other night, and had wondered what lay behind it. A reluctance, perhaps, to give any more oxygen to the media circus surrounding the investigation. Or was it because of the way her actions disrupted pre-existing models of criminal behaviour?

'I need to stop you there,' she said, pushing these thoughts to the back of her mind. 'I'm not sure what you've heard, but I've not "taken an interest" in the case. I only spoke to your client because she volunteered herself as a last-minute replacement.'

'Yes,' said Pamela, in a tone that suggested she viewed this as a mere trifling detail, 'she told me your original interviewee was taken poorly. Anyway, the point is—'

'Yes, please do come to the point,' Anna interjected, her patience wearing thin. 'I was under the impression you had a proposition for me.'

'I'm getting to that. The point is, during my regular catch-up session with Sandra on Thursday, she told me she'd spoken to you and how impressed she was by you.'

Anna, who was in the process of raising her cup to her lips, did a double-take. 'She was?'

'Wouldn't stop singing your praises,' Pamela went on obliviously. 'She said you were a breath of fresh air. What an astute mind you had. What a pleasure it was to spend time with you.' She stopped, seeing Anna's expression. 'I'm guessing that wasn't the impression she gave at the time.'

'Not in so many words.'

Pamela gave an amused smile. 'In my experience, Sandra's rarely effusive in her praise. You must have made quite an impression on her. Did you know you're the first visitor she's agreed to see in five years?'

In spite of herself, Anna felt something stirring in her chest. She wasn't proud of it, but she knew she had a certain susceptibility to compliments of this sort – perhaps because she hadn't been paid enough of them as a child and now felt compelled to compensate by hoovering them up wherever she could get them.

'So, this proposition . . .' she prompted.

'Of course. Yes. Sorry. You know she's submitted multiple appeals . . .'

'All unsuccessful, yes.'

Pamela made a pained expression. 'The problem for Sandra is that her objection to her conviction is entirely predicated on her insistence that the jury got it wrong. But applications to the Appeal Court typically only succeed if you can demonstrate flaws in procedure during the trial itself. For Sandra, that's not on the cards. Both myself and her previous legal team have been through every aspect of that trial at a near-forensic level and found nothing suggesting procedure wasn't followed to the letter. You can't just decide you don't like the result and ask the court to reconsider its decision, and you can't typically lead new evidence unless it's so compelling it puts the appellant's innocence beyond doubt.'

None of this, strictly speaking, was news to Anna, though out of politeness – and a reluctance to prolong Pamela's extended preamble any further – she refrained from pointing this out.

'I understand. So where do I come in?'

Pamela fixed Anna with a solemn look. 'I wanted to ask if you'd be willing to conduct a review of the case.'

Anna almost spat out her coffee. '*Excuse* me?'

'I wanted to ask—' Pamela helpfully began again.

'Yeah, OK, OK,' Anna cut her off, 'I heard you. What I mean is … why me?'

Pamela shrugged, like it was no big deal. 'I've asked around. Spoken to various contacts. Everyone knows you played a significant role in solving the Kelvingrove Park murders …'

'Less significant than people think.'

' … and you were instrumental in bringing the Shadow Men affair to light a few years back.'

'Again, my role in that has been greatly exaggerated.'

Pamela smiled knowingly, as if to say, *Pull the other one*. 'The point is, you have *an astute mind*.'

'I also have a job,' Anna pointed out.

Pamela gave a small shrug, conceding this point. 'I'm not asking you to drop everything and devote months of your life to it. All I'm proposing is that you re-examine the evidence with an open mind. If you still think she did it, then no harm, no foul. But, on the other hand, if you were to find something to suggest a miscarriage of justice had taken place …'

'OK.' Anna mimed laying her cards on the table. 'First of all, I'm flattered. Genuinely. It's not every day I get headhunted in a field where I have no qualifications or expertise. But I'm sorry. I just can't. I'm not in a position to take on additional paid work—'

'Oh, I wasn't suggesting *paying* you.' Pamela gave a high-pitched, nervous titter. 'I haven't the resources for that. I'm practically working for peanuts myself.'

'Well, then – and at the risk of sounding utterly blunt – what could possibly be in it for me?'

'For a start, I'd have thought the interesting nature of the case—'

Anna laughed dryly. 'Thanks, but I'm afraid I've got more than enough intellectual stimulation to be getting on with.'

'Then there's the prestige that would come with overturning such a landmark conviction—'

'Unless I'm spectacularly hard to read, you must have worked out by now that fame is positively the *last* thing I'm interested in.'

'And then there's access to my clients.'

Anna opened her mouth, intending to deliver another rebuttal, then stopped short. 'Your … '

'I represent a number of prisoners currently housed at HMP Broadwood,' said Pamela, in a tone that suggested this was merely a matter of happenstance, rather than leverage she'd planned to use from the outset. 'I'm sure they'd be more than willing to talk to you about their experiences for your book.'

That certainly gave Anna pause for thought. She had to admit this wasn't something she'd been anticipating. Nonetheless, she found the resolve to remain resolute.

'I appreciate the offer,' she said firmly, 'but I don't need your help getting people to talk to me. I'm more than capable of doing that by myself.'

'From what I hear,' said Pamela, 'you've not been having much success so far.' She gave a sympathetic smile that, to Anna's mind, was far too artificial not to have been practised in the mirror beforehand. 'Ruth Laxton's been stonewalling your requests, hasn't she? Making sure you don't get access to any of the people likely to tell you the things she doesn't want you to hear about conditions inside her prison?'

Anna swallowed a mouthful of coffee to avoid having to admit that it was true. She gazed across the table at Pamela, who sat there, looking like butter wouldn't melt, and was forced to acknowledge that she'd misjudged her. From her childlike voice and youthful appearance, she'd assumed she was naïve and inexperienced, probably fresh out of law school. In fact, she was a far shrewder operator than Anna could ever have anticipated.

'Before you say anything,' said Pamela, with the cool patience of someone who knows they hold all the cards and just need to seal the deal, 'I do have something else that might be of interest.'

'What's that?' said Anna, with a weary resignation which stemmed from knowing she'd been comprehensively outmanoeuvred and that her acceptance was all but a foregone conclusion.

'A dossier.'

'What kind of dossier?'

'The kind that details the side of Broadwood Ruth Laxton and our political masters would rather remained their dirty little secret.'

'You mean…'

'I mean the self-harm, the wide availability of drugs, the excessive use of solitary confinement – the works. All based on firsthand testimony and verified by at least one independent witness.' Pamela arched a knowing eyebrow in response to whatever facial expression she'd caught Anna inadvertently making. 'What, you didn't think you were the only one with concerns about that place, did you?'

Anna said nothing. She wasn't often lost for words, but Pamela had succeeded in rendering her speechless.

'You can use it however you see fit,' Pamela went on. 'As fresh material for your book, or – you know, if you fancied making a splash with a well-timed leak to the *Tribune*…'

'You'd give me all that,' said Anna after a pause, 'just for looking over your client's case?'

Pamela smiled. 'Given that the ideal outcome is you uncovering some hitherto overlooked piece of evidence that results in my client being exonerated, I'd call it a bargain. Besides, you're able to reach people I can't, and vice versa. I've thought about going public for a while, but a double-pronged approach might be more effective.'

'Think you might be getting just a little bit ahead of yourself there,' said Anna. 'There's no guarantee I'll find anything.' As she spoke, she was aware, from her choice of words, that she'd already implicitly agreed to Pamela's proposition. 'In fact, I'd say the odds are overwhelmingly stacked against it.'

Pamela gave a rueful smile. 'I'm not a *complete* idiot. I know it's a long shot. But I have to try. I don't know how many more times I can tell Sandra we've no grounds for submitting yet another futile appeal without losing the will to live.'

Anna grimaced sympathetically. 'I don't imagine she's an easy person to say no to.'

Pamela gave a small nod of confirmation. 'Plus' – she sighed heavily – 'between you and me, I think her mental health is really suffering. When I first took her on three years ago, she still had real fire in her belly. But lately, it's like she's lost the will to keep going. Like she's just accepted this as her lot in life.'

A silence settled between them that made the air feel positively heavy. Around them, the cheer and bustle of the café continued unabated.

At length, Anna stirred. 'I'm going to need you to let me have whatever you've got on the investigation. Presumably that includes a copy of the original case file.'

'I do ...' Pamela acknowledged, 'but there's a catch.'

Anna waited for her to elaborate.

'If you remember, back in 2012, there was a major fire at the police archive in Giffnock. A whole bunch of files were destroyed, including parts of the one on Operation Bluegrass.'

Anna vaguely recalled it being in the news. At the time, it had been widely suspected to be arson, though the official inquiry had – as was so often the case with such things – come to no firm conclusions.

'That would have been convenient for a lot of people,' she said.

Pamela smiled grimly. 'But not so much for us. At a generous estimate, I'd say a little over half the Bluegrass file survived. Some of the documents are complete, others aren't ...'

' ... and others are missing altogether,' Anna concluded heavily. She contemplated the matter for a moment, before being struck by an idea. 'What about the courts? They'd hold copies of everything that was disclosed by the prosecution.'

'I thought that too,' said Pamela. 'Normally the Crown permanently preserves all files for cases that are especially serious, or that have attracted significant public interest or are of particular historical importance. But in this case, they were destroyed some time after Sandra's last appeal failed.'

'That was a pretty grave oversight,' said Anna, her heart leaden.

'And doubly so given the subsequent fire.'

'You don't think…'

'That someone was covering their tracks?' Pamela shook her head. 'I reckon it's a little too early to be discussing conspiracy theories.' She gave a weary smile. 'No, I don't think it's anything more sinister than an underfunded body with limited time on its hands having to prioritise how to best allocate its resources.'

Anna gave a small smile of acknowledgement. She knew all too well what *that* was like.

'What about her previous legal team?' she asked after a moment. 'Have you contacted them to see what they have?'

'They destroyed all their paperwork after the six-year minimum period elapsed,' said Pamela. 'The courts aren't the only ones who have to contend with tight overheads and limited space.' She treated Anna to an apologetic wince. 'So I'm afraid you're stuck with my copy of what survived the fire.'

Anna considered this. 'Then that's what I'll have to make do with.' She was already mentally plotting out her schedule for the next several days. 'How soon can I expect the file?'

'I'll book a courier as soon as I get back to Edinburgh. All being well, you should have it by Monday.'

'Monday it is, then,' said Anna, and drained her cup.

'There's one other thing.'

Pamela's words halted Anna in her tracks. She looked at the lawyer expectantly, satchel perched on her knee.

'It's really important Sandra doesn't know this is happening.'

Anna frowned.

'She doesn't know I'm speaking to you about this,' Pamela explained, 'and if she thought I was taking matters into my own hands…'

Anna looked at her, still not comprehending.

Pamela sighed. 'A year ago, I reached out to a private investigator about looking at the case file – you know, just to sound him out. I told Sandra and she hit the roof. Almost fired me on the spot.'

Anna raised her eyebrows, though she wasn't sure why she was surprised. From what she'd seen of Sandra, this reaction seemed perfectly in character.

'I know, right?' Pamela grimaced ruefully. 'Took a *lot* of grovelling for me to talk her down. The point is, she hates the idea of not being in control. Needs to feel she's the one dictating the terms of her defence at all times.

Plus, I reckon there's a part of her that just delights in making everyone's lives as difficult as possible – mine included.'

'Well, don't worry,' said Anna, in a half-hearted attempt to inject some levity. 'I wasn't planning on giving her hourly updates.'

Pamela smiled dutifully. 'Quite apart from anything, I just don't want her to get her hopes up only to have them dashed. You and I may know this endeavour has little chance of success, but she won't see it that way. And I'm not convinced she can take another setback.'

Anna nodded soberly. Sandra hadn't struck her as someone on the verge of breaking, but she knew how deceptive looks could be. More to the point, she knew all too well the toll prolonged incarceration took on people's mental health. There was no reason to suppose Sandra was any less susceptible to that awful, crushing despair than the countless others that had come before her.

Shouldering her satchel, she got up to go. She stood for a moment, gazing down at Pamela, who hadn't moved.

'You really think it's possible she didn't do it?'

Pamela was silent for several moments, her expression pensive. 'There's a Sherlock Holmes quote I've always quite liked,' she said at last. '*When you have eliminated the impossible, whatever remains, however improbable, must be the truth.*' She tilted her head upward, meeting Anna's eyes. 'That's what I'm asking you to try to find out. Nothing more, and nothing less.'

9

The case file arrived, as promised, just after 9.30 on Monday morning, in the form of three large, heavy cardboard boxes, which the deliveryman dumped on the doorstep, then took off the moment Anna had finished signing for them.

'Work-shy basturt,' Zoe grumbled as she helped Anna hoof them upstairs to the office. 'Does he not know we're just helpless wee lassies?'

They dumped the boxes in a row on the floor next to the bookshelf – the only place that wasn't already occupied by the assorted piles of books and paperwork that made up Anna's incomprehensible-to-everyone-but-herself filing system. Breathing heavily and massaging her overtaxed back, Zoe gazed down at their handiwork.

'Huh. So that's what a police file looks like.'

'Mm,' Anna agreed noncommittally. She was wondering where to start.

'S'no too late tae back out, y'know,' Zoe said. 'I mean, if ye want tae. Only we've been round the block a few times now, you 'n' me. We both know how this sorta thing usually ends.'

'This is different,' Anna insisted. 'I'm just going through some files relating to an old case. And the woman responsible is safely behind bars. I'm not in any danger.'

Zoe merely gazed back at her, one eyebrow slightly raised, which immediately left Anna wondering which of them, precisely, she'd been trying to convince.

73

'If you say so, doll,' she said, and headed out, shutting the door behind her.

As Anna gazed down at the three boxes, contemplating the task ahead of her, her phone rang. She checked the caller ID before answering it.

'Pamela. Hi.'

'*Hi!*' the solicitor exclaimed, as if she was greeting a long-lost friend. 'I just got the delivery notification. Just wanted to make sure everything had arrived.'

'Three boxes, all present and correct.' As Anna spoke, she bent down and lifted the lid of the nearest box, grimacing at the sight of the various loose, no doubt unsorted pages that had been crammed into it. 'Unless there's a secret fourth one you're holding back.'

'Nope, no fourth box,' said Pamela, evidently failing to pick up on the joke. 'Everything I have is in those three.'

'And you're absolutely certain this is all that survived the fire?' She knew it was a pointless question, but she felt she had to ask.

'Not really. But short of blagging our way into the police archives and trawling through a bajillion different files just in case there's a misplaced scrap of paper somewhere, I'm not sure what else we can do.'

Anna blew a strand of hair out of her eyes. 'It's funny.'

'What is?'

'Call me naïve, but I'd always assumed all the files relating to a twenty-year-old case would be digitised and sitting on a hard drive somewhere. 2001 wasn't exactly the Stone Age.'

Pamela chuckled dryly. 'Well, I mean, it kinda *was*. At any rate, it was that sort of in-between period where the police were using computers for reports and whatnot but still worshipped at the altar of the almighty hard copy. Like, you know those weirdos who, when they get an email, they feel they have to print it out instead of just reading it off the screen? It was that sort of thing, but turned up to eleven. I've heard stories about old geezers who'd spend hours typing out a report, one keystroke at a time, run off a single printout, then say "job done" and close Word without saving a copy.'

Anna grimaced. She always thought herself something of a luddite when it came to technology, but she wasn't *that* bad. She still had copies of her PhD thesis backed up onto multiple hard drives stored in different locations, just in case the house ever burned down.

'Actually,' Pamela continued, 'in a lot of respects it's a blessing these *haven't* been digitised. If they had, we could be looking at corrupted disk drives, obsolete file formats, original copies shredded... Believe me, in comparison to *some* of the case files I've seen, this one's in fairly good nick.'

'Hmm.' Anna lifted the lid on the second box. Its contents were, if anything, even more intimidating than the previous one.

'Listen,' she said, replacing the lid, 'it occurs to me we never discussed a timeframe for me getting access to your clients.'

'About that ... '

Anna stiffened reflexively. From the tone of Pamela's voice, some watering down of their original agreement was clearly on the cards.

'I'm going to need a bit of time to talk to them first. You know – warm them up to the idea. Most of them have been badly let down by every authority figure you can name. None too anxious to trust someone with a bunch of letters after their name, y'know?'

From direct experience, Anna understood this predicament all too well – not that it did anything to take the sting out of what was beginning to feel like a blatant bait-and-switch exercise.

'And the dossier?' she said. 'Same applies to that as well, I'm guessing?'

The slight pause before Pamela answered told Anna everything she needed to know.

'I think it's best if I hand that over once you've completed your investigation,' she said, before adding quickly, 'It'll mean I've more time to gather data – and we want this to be as airtight as possible, don't we?'

'Indeed we do,' Anna murmured dryly.

It was, of course, a fairly transparent ploy to dissuade her from reneging on her side of the bargain. A charitable interpretation of the situation would be that there had been no deliberate attempt on Pamela's part to mislead her; rather that, in her eagerness to convince Anna to take on the investigation, she'd overpromised on what she was in a position to deliver. She had half a mind to tell Pamela, then and there, that she was on her own. And yet, when push came to shove, she found she couldn't bring herself to do it – not least because she had to concede that the prospect of looking into the case had started to genuinely appeal to her. Her evening of reading after her visit to Broadwood had failed to satisfy whatever itch her encounter with Sandra had stirred.

'So how long do you reckon it'll take you?' Pamela's voice interrupted her thoughts.

'How long is a piece of string? I'm planning on getting started straight away, but I don't want to rush this. And I'm not going to let my other commitments fall by the wayside.'

'Your publication deadline. Of course. Wouldn't have it any other way.'

An awkward silence settled between them, each waiting for the other to make the first move to wrap up the call.

Pamela cracked first. 'Well, then,' she said, with forced cheerfulness, 'I'll let you get to it.'

'Just a minute,' Anna put in quickly, before Pamela had a chance to hang up. 'There was one more thing I wanted to ask you. Do you know anything about this investigation into Frank Dalston?'

'Hmm.' Anna heard a sound which she suspected was Pamela tapping the butt of a pen against her front teeth. 'If memory serves, he spent his early days in Glasgow as part of the old Strathkelvin force, back when Richard Monkhouse and his cronies were in the ascendancy, before transferring to Dumfries and Galloway when he made CID. Accusations were presumably made. Whether that amounts to guilt by association or something more concrete ... ' She trailed off, leaving the rest unsaid. 'But either way, it means the cases he oversaw will have been earmarked for potential re-examination.'

As Pamela spoke, Anna lifted the lid of the third and final box. To her eyes, this one looked a little more manageable than the others, though perhaps she was just becoming used to the sight of overwhelming chaos.

'As for what progress they've made,' Pamela continued, 'your guess is as good as mine. They've always been clear with me that they won't discuss ongoing investigations or comment on hypotheticals. But if you fancy giving it a shot ... '

Anna replaced the lid. 'I reckon I've got enough to be getting on with for the time being,' she said – though she nonetheless filed the idea away for future reference.

'All righty, then!' Pamela chirped. 'Good luck! Call me if you need anything.'

After they'd rung off, Anna remained standing, phone in hand, gazing down at the boxes as she contemplated the task that lay before her. Now that they were physically in the room with her, the scale of what she'd agreed to take on – for a deferred and not even guaranteed reward at that – hit home all the harder.

Her thoughts turned once more to what she'd referred to as her 'commitments'. Pamela had assumed she was talking about her book, and that was certainly part of it. Officially, she had until early September – when the new academic year began and she was due to return to work – to deliver a polished draft, and she was convinced this remained achievable provided she bulldozed her way through the case file now, then made up for lost time later. Even then, she suspected there was still room for manoeuvre, provided she could sell her editor on the idea that a delay would result in a better end product. That might well prove essential if Pamela remained steadfast in her decision to withhold 'payment' until Anna had done her bit. Regardless, it was a circle she'd square when the time came.

But it wasn't the whole story. Her duty to her publisher was one thing. Her responsibilities as a mother, on the other hand, were a red line she wasn't prepared to cross. Ever since returning to work when Jack was six months old, she'd made every effort to maintain a strict Monday to Friday, nine to five schedule, keeping her evenings and weekends clear for him. Being on sabbatical was no different: she might be home during the day, but she'd refused to treat that as an excuse to allow work and family time to bleed into one another. In part, it was because she knew only too well what it was like to grow up with parents who were absent – either figuratively or literally. Her late father had spent virtually every waking moment at the office, regularly leaving the house before she woke up and not returning till long after she'd gone to bed, and even on weekends, she'd barely seen anything of him or her mother, thanks to the hours of supplementary Jewish education they'd forced on her every Sunday – a charade that, to this day, she was convinced had had as much to do with a desire to get her out from under their feet as ensuring her indoctrination into a faith that, from an early age, she'd known she didn't share. She wasn't going to do that sort of thing with Jack. No way.

She looked at her watch. It was just gone ten o'clock. That meant she had just over two hours before he got back from morning playgroup. You could get a lot done in two hours if you put your mind to it.

Settling cross-legged on the floor, she removed the lid from the nearest box, took out the first sheet of paper that came to hand, and began to read.

PART TWO

YOU CAN'T KNOW EVERYTHING

10

Tuesday 12 March

All told, it would take Anna the better part of five days to make her way through the file in its entirety. She worked methodically, sorting the paperwork into piles based on their content – witness interviews, incident room logs, reports by police officers and so on. For a while, navigating her office became like a game of Twister due to the multiple piles occupying every available floor surface, each with its own coloured post-it note and a vague description – often partly based on guesswork – of its subject matter.

As she'd feared, there was precious little sense of organisation to the way the material had been stored. In several instances, documents had simply been shoved into whichever receptacle was most readily to hand, meaning that the contents of a particular folder often bore no relation to what was written on the label, or might encompass pages from multiple unrelated reports or witness statements. By the same token, different pages of the same report might be split across multiple folders or boxes. One interview transcript, for instance, jumped straight from page two to page seventeen and had several pages from an unrelated witness statement inserted at random in the middle. Worst of all were the multiple loose pages simply floating freely inside the boxes, with no indication as to the whereabouts of their parent files – or, in some cases, whether they even related to Operation Bluegrass at *all*.

The version of the file she'd received was, unsurprisingly, not the original.

All of the pages were photocopies, some several steps removed from the source, and to describe the quality as variable would be putting it mildly. Some were barely legible due to the generational loss of clarity. Others had been fed into the copier haphazardly, resulting in entire blocks of text being unceremoniously cropped off at the edges. All in all, the work she was undertaking felt more akin to archaeology than a case review.

Gradually, though, some semblance of a structure began to take shape. It was obviously far from complete, and there was no way of knowing the full extent of what was missing, but by Tuesday evening, Anna felt she'd succeeded in assembling the material in a way that made at least partial sense. From there, one of the first steps she undertook was to draw up her own timeline of the events of the night of 6 May, drawing on a mixture of witness statements, interview transcripts and police reports, augmented, where necessary, by the information available online. The latter proved remarkably consistent with the official records – owing, no doubt, to the extensive media coverage at the time of the trial.

One of the most illuminating outcomes of going through the file was the considerably more complete picture it afforded her of Sandra's version of events, gleaned primarily from the three interviews Dalston had conducted with her in the eighteen days between the murders and her being charged. Of these, the first two had survived in their entirety, while the third was missing a substantial number of pages from the beginning. The initial interrogation, conducted immediately after Dalston's attendance of the joint postmortem of Guy, Iain and Gabriel Morton, was the most coherent, with Sandra, for the most part, allowed to tell her story without interruption.

The Morton family, she said, had spent most of the preceding day in the garden, making the most of an unexpected spell of warm weather. After putting the twins to bed at around 7.30 p.m., Sandra and Guy retired to the living room, where Guy watched a documentary on the 1992 financial crisis and Sandra read a thriller by Lee Child. At around 10.30, Sandra, who had been suffering from severe toothache all day, concluded that she couldn't wait until morning and decided to walk to the local 8 Till Late – approximately one mile from the house, on the village's northern edge – to buy painkillers before it closed at eleven. Telling Guy – an early riser due to his lengthy morning commute – not to wait up, she set off. Though the sky was now severely overcast, it was still unusually warm, so she didn't bother either changing out of the shorts and vest top she'd worn during the day or putting on a coat.

She reached the 8 Till Late at around 10.45, only to find it locked up, with no sign of life inside. A note on the door informed would-be customers that the owner (and sole employee) had gone home early owing to a bout of food poisoning. Faced with the prospect of enduring a night of excruciating pain, she contemplated returning home, rousing Guy and persuading him to drive her to the nearest equivalent store, until she remembered the petrol station on the A75 to Gretna. By road, it was a long, circuitous journey, but only around a mile and a half in a straight line across the farmland north of Hillend.

As she set off over the fields, it began to rain steadily, but she opted to press on, on the grounds that, even if she turned back now, she would still be drenched. All told, the journey took close to half an hour, owing to the difficulty in traversing the rough, undulating terrain in the dark. She reached the motorway at around 11.15 and arrived at the petrol station a couple of minutes later. There, she bought a box of paracetamol, exchanged a few words with the teenage boy on duty and left.

With the immediate issue of her toothache resolved and not relishing the thought of a fresh scramble over the mud-clogged hillside in the dark, she decided to walk the long way home. Setting off in an easterly direction, she walked along the verge of the A75 until she came to the turnoff for Shaw Road, a lengthy stretch of country lane following the eastern contour of the large central reservoir that provided Hillend and several of the neighbouring villages with water. It was still raining hard, but she was soaked to the skin anyway, and the residual heat from the day was still sufficient that a walk of nearly four and a half miles was a not unpleasant prospect, despite being underdressed.

About twenty-five minutes later, while she was still making her way down Shaw Road, she heard a vehicle approaching behind her. Seeing that it was a police car, she moved onto the grass verge to let it pass. Instead of driving on, however, it pulled over just ahead of her. Two officers got out and approached her, asking her if she was Sandra Morton. They then proceeded to strong-arm her into getting into the car, before driving off with her in the back. At no point, she claimed, did either of them explain why they were detaining her or where they were taking her. Furthermore, she denied ever uttering the words 'Are they all dead?' or anything similar, on the grounds that, at that time, she was under the impression that her husband and children were asleep in their beds, safe and sound. When questioned by Dalston as to her dazed and apparently absent demeanour when she was picked up, she merely responded, 'That's my normal demeanour.' Contrary to the officers' statements, she also claimed to have been walking south, not north, and coldly insisted, during a later interview when confronted with the discrepancy, 'It's basic geography. Petrol station up there. House down there. I'd have thought even a complete halfwit would be able to work that out.'

The two officers, she recounted, drove her home, where a sizeable number of emergency services personnel and members of the press were present. They made her walk the media gauntlet into the house, where they handed her over to another officer, who appeared to be in charge. He, she claimed, showed her the body of her husband and took considerable delight in describing the nature of the injuries inflicted on her two sons – an assertion strenuously denied by the officers at the scene. This resulted in the following exchange:

> **FD (Frank Dalston):** Let's say, for talking's sake, I believe you. What possible reason would they have had to do this?

> **SM (Sandra Morton):** I don't know. Perhaps they're sadists.

> *(Silence for several seconds.)*

> **FD:** How did it make you feel? When you learned your husband and children were dead, how did you feel?

> *(Silence.)*

> **FD:** Are you upset that they're dead?

> **SM:** Of course.

FD: You don't seem very upset to me.

SM: No? How do I seem, then?

FD: You seem completely indifferent.

SM: And you seem like a cunt.

This altercation served as a model study of the dynamic between Sandra and Dalston. Whenever challenged, her demeanour would alternate between sullen silence, passive-aggressive cattiness and openly insulting her interrogator – none of which suggested a desire to do herself any favours. In the face of such naked displays of self-sabotage, Anna had to remind herself that, in theory, the onus was on the police and prosecution to prove the accused's guilt, not the accused to prove their innocence. *In theory.* In reality, Sandra had as good as signed her own arrest warrant from the moment the cassette wheels began to turn, seeming to revel in making enemies of the very people she needed to get on side.

More of the same was found in the two subsequent interviews, with a clearly discernible escalation in both Sandra's rudeness towards her interrogators and Dalston's exasperation with her. It was possible that this lack of decorum from both parties was driven, at least in part, by the absence of the duty solicitor, whose services Sandra declined from the second interview onwards – though, given his virtually non-existent contributions during her initial interrogation, this was debatable. The hostilities reached their apex in the incomplete transcript for the third interview, which began on page 64 with Dalston already at the end of his tether. Even in plain text form, with all the nuances of intonation and body language stripped out, the tension in what Anna imagined as a small, stuffy, windowless room in the basement of the police station was so tangible she could almost smell the stale sweat and cigarette smoke.

> **FD:** … around the block a few times, and I can tell you this for nothing: folk that are innocent don't sit and stare into space when the police ask them questions.

(Silence.)

FD: Let's go back to the eyewitnesses. The boy at the petrol station says he never saw you that night. How do you explain that?

SM: He's lying.

FD: And what possible reason would he have to do that?

SM: You'd have to—

FD: Ask him, yes. Believe me, we have. Repeatedly. He's sticking to his story.

SM: So am I. Looks like you've got a real problem on your hands, Mr Dalston.

FD: Oh, I've got a problem, have I? Rest assured, Mrs Morton, from where I'm standing, the problem's all yours.

(Silence.)

FD: All right, then. Let's turn to the eyewitness who saw you fleeing the house immediately after the murders. What's your explanation for that?

SM: Whoever your eyewitness saw, it wasn't me.

FD: She was very specific in her description. "A dark-haired woman of medium build, wearing a blue raincoat." Sounds a lot like you, doesn't it?

(Silence.)

FD: Well?

SM: It wasn't me.

FD: There just happened to be a second woman matching your description and wearing a blue raincoat like the one you own but claim to have thrown away fleeing your house immediately following the murders of your husband and children, while you were allegedly buying paracetamol from a boy who claims never to have seen you.

(Silence.)

FD: So one eyewitness is lying. The other … what? Just happened to imagine seeing someone bearing an uncanny resemblance to you? You expect anyone to believe that?

SM: You can believe whatever you want.

FD: Let me put an alternative scenario to you. Let's just try this on for size, hmm? You killed your husband and children in a fit of rage, insanity – whatever. Then, when you realised what you'd done, you panicked and fled the house with no thought in your head other than to get as far away from the scene of the crime as possible.

(Silence.)

FD: And when you were picked up and called upon to account for yourself, you told the first lie that came into you head – not realising, until it was too late to take it back, that we could easily disprove every word of it.

(Silence.)

FD: You think we don't already have ample grounds to the throw the book at you? All this – all this is only delaying the inevitable. Might as well save us the hassle so we can all go home. Come on – you help us, we help you, hmm? Otherwise, we'll do this all night if we have to.

(Silence.)

FD: You killed Guy and the twins.

SM: No.

FD: Admit it.

M: No.

FD: You'll feel better for getting it off your chest. Just say it. "I killed my husband and children."

SM: You killed your husband and children.

FD: Think you're something, don't you? Sitting there, playing the smart aleck, while the person you'd have us believe actually did it is out there, free as a bird. Does that make you happy, hmm? Knowing someone butchered your wee boys in their beds, stabbed their little bodies with a kitchen knife till they were dead, while you're sitting here wasting our bloody time?

(Silence.)

FD: Don't you want him caught? This mystery intruder you'd have us believe broke into your house and, for no reason whatsoever, hacked your weans to bits?

(FD shows SM photographs of crime scene.)

FD: Look at them. That's what was done to your kids. And if it wasn't you, and you're any sort of mother at all, you'll stop yanking my dick and help yourself, and help us catch the piece of shit who did it.

SM: I'm sure you don't need anyone to help you yank your dick, Frank.

(FD exits.)

MG (Malcolm Gunning): Detective Superintendent Dalston has left the room. Interview suspended at 21:06.

The transcript ended there. If the interview had been resumed beyond this point, the records were lost.

Reading these transcripts, Anna couldn't help noticing that Sandra's speech once again had a different quality about it – less florid than in her own dealings with the woman, but with considerably fewer colloquial inflections than in the interview with Border Television Zoe had found online. Obviously, the words on the page didn't convey Sandra's accent or tone of voice, but Anna had little doubt she was deliberately adopting a mode of speech that was designed to put Dalston in his place, conveying both her superior intellect and her ability to keep cool under pressure. If her intention had been to drive Dalston to apoplexy, she'd certainly succeeded – though at what cost to herself?

As well as the interviews with Sandra, there were several signed statements and transcripts of interviews conducted with members of the public, of which the interrogations of the two star eyewitnesses, Paul Kempley and Adjoa Asante, were the most significant. According to the information available online, both had been formally interviewed twice, though only a transcript of the second interview with Adjoa Asante was present in the case file. Though her exchanges with Dalston were somewhat stilted, thanks to her imperfect grasp of English – her sixteen-year-old son, Samuel, was present in the interview room and translated for her where necessary – she was nonetheless clear about what she'd seen that night, describing a figure matching Sandra's appearance scaling the wall bordering Haysend Road in a manner that closely mirrored the evidence she would later give on the witness stand. Paul Kempley was similarly definitive in both his – comparatively brief – interviews: no one matching Sandra Morton's description had come into the store while he was on shift, either at the time she claimed or at *any* point that night.

There were also umpteen statements from various members of the public to wade through – some preserved in their entirety, others incomplete. Few, if any, Hillenders had anything remotely positive to say about Sandra, who it seemed had done the square root of nothing to ingratiate herself to her neighbours in the four and a half years the Mortons had lived in the village. Still, beyond a general sense that there had always been something 'off' about her, none of the interviewees could point to any concrete evidence of her guilt.

A handful were less preoccupied with Sandra herself than with various 'strangers' they'd observed in and around the local area in the weeks leading up to the murders. Most of these Anna chalked up to typical small-town paranoia. With its minuscule population and lack of any main roads running through it, Hillend was clearly the sort of place people didn't make a habit of passing through on a whim and where every unfamiliar face was immediately noticed and treated with suspicion. Two recurring figures included a middle-aged, homeless woman – 'almost certainly of gypsyish origin', in the estimation of one particularly exercised pearl-clutcher – who'd appeared in the village out of nowhere and spent a couple of days knocking on doors and soliciting for money before abandoning the operation and moving on, and a younger man with long hair and something of a hippyish appearance, seen loitering in different locations within a square mile of the Morton residence. Anna knew from her online research that the latter had sparked a brief revival of the Satanic panic that had consumed much of America in the eighties, with a couple of the more fanciful newspapers even speculating that he was the leader of some sort of Charles Manson tribute act and that Sandra was a Satanist who'd sacrificed her family to appease the dark gods. Reference was also made to various unfamiliar cars, with a silver, G-reg Montego making a handful of appearances in various locations in the three days prior to the night of 6 May.

None of these accounts appeared to have been given much credence by the police – which, in Anna's view, was probably for the best. She'd always had a deep distaste for the sort of mentality that viewed anyone from out of town as a nefarious interloper and regarded trouble as something that could only ever come from without, never from within. That said, the lack of any record that these sightings had been followed up, if only to rule them out, seemed to Anna to point to a lack of diligence on the police's part and the first evidence she'd come across of anything resembling a significant gap in the investigation.

Anna eased herself out of her chair and arched her stiff back. She gazed down at the multiple stacks of pages on her desk and the floor, with their multicoloured post-its poking out from between the sheets. She'd been half-hoping the act of immersing herself in the case in such a concentrated fashion would satisfy whatever curiosity had compelled her to fire up her iPad and type 'Sandra Morton' into Google just over a week ago. Certainly, she'd done what Pamela had asked of her: she'd read the file to look for anything that would undermine her client's conviction. The fact she'd come up with nothing beyond a handful of reports of 'outsiders' that the police had, in all likelihood, correctly dismissed as the paranoid ramblings of a bunch of curtain-twitchers with a prejudice towards anyone who hailed from further afield than the next village was no fault of hers. She was well within her rights to deliver her report to Pamela and wash her hands of the whole affair.

And yet, perversely, all the act of reading the file had accomplished was to leave her hungry for more. After a lot of soul-searching, the only credible explanation she could come up with was that it had less to do with the particulars of the case than the enigma that was Sandra herself. She'd fascinated Anna from the off with all her myriad secrets and contradictions. Who was she, really? What was going on behind those cold, seemingly emotionless eyes?

Anna reached for her mouse and waggled it, rousing her computer from sleep, and once more typed 'Sandra Morton' into the search bar.

11

Over the following week, Anna worked her way steadily through the collection of reading materials on the Sandra Morton case she'd accrued through a variety of sources, from the local Waterstones to various online second-hand shops. Her reading was, by necessity, piecemeal, broken up by spells of either spending time with Jack or working on her book, which she had to admit she was increasingly having to force herself to get excited about. The enthusiasm that had propelled her to undertake the project in the first place had faded – partly because progress had, for the time being, been stymied by the lack of interview material, but also because something else had taken its place in her imagination.

She found herself experiencing the same familiar feelings she got whenever a project truly captured her mind. She'd lie awake at night, mulling over theories, or catch herself zoning out and thinking about it at the most inopportune moments, like when Zoe was trying, for the umpteenth time, to explain the plot of *Inception* to her, or the time she came to in the frozen foods section of Morrisons to find herself clutching a rapidly melting bag of peas, with no recollection of how she'd got there or how long she'd been staring into space. She even found herself experiencing what amounted to withdrawal symptoms whenever she was away from her office for an extended period, and took to sneaking back there in the evenings after Jack and Zoe were both in bed – a fact she kept from Zoe, whose disapproval over her continued involvement with the case, though never stated outright, was always implicit.

Broadly speaking, the books she'd acquired could be split into two categories, albeit with some overlap between them. In one column were what might crudely be described as the more highbrow publications, which sought to tell as dispassionate an account of the murders and their aftermath as possible, often with at least a fig leaf of intent to further the reader's understanding of the discourse on familicide. In the other were the more lurid offerings, often written by current or former tabloid journalists, which sought to convey the horrors of the case as graphically as possible, in the process elevating Sandra to an almost mythic status – a figure on par with Elizabeth Bathory who did everything short of bathe in her victims' blood. These books, reminiscent of what Zoe would have drolly referred to as 'misery memoirs' – the heavily discounted true-life paperbacks, with titles like *BETRAYED* and *INNOCENCE LOST*, that lined supermarket shelves and described, in leeringly voyeuristic detail, the horrors suffered by their protagonists – invariably left her feeling grubby all over, as if, by reading them, she was somehow legitimising their exploitative agenda. Nonetheless, she soldiered on in the hope that, like the proverbial needle in the haystack (or the solitary piece of corn in the steaming pile of effluent, to use a more apt metaphor), somewhere within their pages would be some crucial nugget of information that all the other accounts had missed.

And certainly, there were nuggets, buried among a whole lot of editorialising and conjecture. She learned, for instance, that the 8 Till Late in Hillend had indeed closed early on the night of the murders – a small but, to Anna's mind, compelling point in favour of Sandra's version of events. She was also able to establish that the Mortons were a quiet family who, for the most part, kept to themselves. Guy was characterised as a workaholic whose role as head of operations for a haulage firm headquartered in Glasgow meant he was rarely home apart from at weekends. He didn't appear to have forged close ties to any of the other inhabitants, other than their elderly neighbour, Graham Malone, who spoke of him in positively glowing terms, saying that he was forever offering to mow his grass or clear his guttering of leaves.

As for Sandra, Anna established that she'd had no form of gainful employment following the birth of her first child. Instead, she filled her days by going on long walks, and was frequently seen striding purposefully around Hillend or the surrounding countryside, her long, unkempt hair blowing behind her like a mane. Comments of dubious provenance painted a similar picture to that established via the statements her fellow Hillenders had given to the police: rude and dismissive when she deigned to speak to you at all, she was just as likely to blank you completely if you passed her in the street and hailed her with a how-d'you-do.

Concerns were also expressed about the welfare of Iain and Gabriel. A former employee at the nursery the twins attended in nearby Gretna, speaking on condition of anonymity, claimed that they routinely arrived unwashed and inappropriately dressed for the weather, while a fellow mother claimed to have witnessed Sandra dragging one of them along the pavement by the arm. Anna couldn't help noting that, despite such apparently deeply held concerns, no reports appeared to have been made to the appropriate authorities while they were still alive, with the relevant parties instead preferring to sell their stories retroactively, once the lucrative publishing deals came along.

As well as burnishing her newfound credentials as a consumer of true crime literature, Anna had spent an afternoon perusing old newspaper articles in the archive at the Mitchell Library. Based on the reading she'd done following her visit to Broadwood, she already had a fair measure of the overall tone of the press coverage of the murders and their aftermath. Now, though, as she truly immersed herself in the discourse surrounding the case, it became clear that it was even more problematic than she'd initially realised.

From the point of Sandra's arrest, the Contempt of Court (Scotland) Act 1981 had kicked in, restricting the media's ability to publish material that could prove prejudicial to the trial – a constraint that proved akin to shutting the stable door after the horse had bolted. In the eighteen days between the murders and Sandra being charged, the television media and printed press had been given free rein to report on the case, and on Sandra, however they saw fit, provided it fell within the confines of the law – or, perhaps more accurately, the interpretation of that law by their notoriously artful legal advisors.

The *Daily Post*'s initial front-page splash the morning after the murders, of Sandra, blank-faced, her erect nipples prominently on display, set the tone for what was to follow. From day one, she was front and centre in the coverage of the murders, her appearance and overall demeanour raked over as journalists devoted column inches to speculating as to whether it was appropriate for a grieving mother to wear a tank top, and what might be inferred about her character from the fact she'd never been seen to shed a tear for her husband and children. This vein of moralising ran through all the coverage, with the tabloids more blatant about it than the broadsheets, though even the latter invariably adopted a tone of stuffy indignation in their numerous *what-sort-of-a-woman*-themed thinkpieces.

While the police built their case against Sandra, the press did likewise, mining both her present and her past for as much dirt as possible. Hacks were dispatched to Fintry, the housing scheme in Dundee where she grew up, to secure anecdotes from former neighbours and 'family friends' about her troubled childhood as the youngest of three siblings, raised by an unemployed single mother with a history of alcohol abuse. They even succeeded in tracking down said mother – still living at the same address and now housebound due to severe COPD – and managed to secure a direct quote from her on her estranged daughter's current predicament.

'She was forever hanging out with the wrong crowd when she was a wean,' sixty-three-year-old Angela Carmichael told the *Chronicle* between deep drags on her oxygen mask. 'I'm no surprised she turned out the way she did. You know she's no been back to see me once since she upped and married?'

Following the marriage, Sandra and Guy – then the up-and-coming assistant regional manager at the Dundee office of TransAlbion, the haulage firm for whom she'd recently begun working as an admin assistant – had moved around a lot, from Broughty Ferry to Perth to Linlithgow to Newton Mearns, before finally settling in Hillend. This extreme case of itchy feet was said to have less to do with Guy's rapid ascent of the corporate ladder than Sandra's multiple affairs with local men – a tendency which (or so the anonymous sources claimed) continued following the move to Hillend. Several eyewitnesses attested to having seen her in the company of other men in bars and pubs in the neighbouring towns of Gretna and Annan, and at the trial, Jeff Morton – Guy's brother – testified that, not long before his death, Guy had confided in him that he believed Sandra was cheating on him and had begun actively investigating his chances of securing custody of the children in the event of divorce. The prosecution strongly pushed this as a motive for the murders – though, to Anna's mind, the notion that the woman who'd been pilloried as a negligent and disinterested mother would have been sufficiently exercised by the thought of losing access to her children to slaughter both them and the husband who sought to take them from her rang somewhat false.

These revelations unfolded against a backdrop of already heightened public interest in Sandra and Guy's marital relations and were, for many, merely confirmation of what they had long suspected. Almost from the start, rumours had abounded in the pages of the tabloids that all had not been well in the relationship, and, just twenty-four hours before Sandra was charged, the *Daily Post* went one step further and printed a series of photographs, taken and submitted by a member of the public, which showed her seated at a booth in the Black Swan pub in Eastriggs with a well-muscled man in his early thirties in a series of intimate poses: Sandra licking her lips suggestively, one hand resting on his knee … the pair of them leaning across the table towards each other, heads almost touching … and finally, in the *coup de grâce*, their lips connecting in a passionate kiss. 'THE ULTIMATE BETRAYAL!' screamed the accompanying headline.

It was difficult to escape the impression that, as far as the media was concerned, Sandra was on trial as much for her transgressions against the accepted model of femininity as for the crimes with which she would ultimately be charged. Anna knew she was far from the first person working in the field of criminology to make this observation, but it was an unavoidable truth that, while men who committed violent crimes were rarely, if ever, visible specifically as men, their female counterparts' womanhood was invariably placed front and centre and subjected to constant scrutiny. Everything, from the obsession with the way Sandra dressed to her apparent failings as a mother to her alleged infidelity, reinforced this – to say nothing of the language used in reference to her. *Ice Queen, Killer Mum, Femme Fatale, Angel of Death* … Each of these highly gendered labels, and more besides, had been ascribed to her at one point or another. Following her conviction, a particular favourite among the tabloids was "murderess" – a term Anna found so absurd and archaic she almost couldn't believe it had made its way past the copyeditors. If

Sandra had been a man, there was no way she'd have been described as a male killer or an *homme fatal.*

She said as much to Zoe when she dropped by the office with an unrequested but nonetheless much appreciated mug of coffee.

'Aye,' Zoe conceded, sequestering the spare chair in the corner, 'that's cos most killers are men, though, in't it?'

Anna gave a humourless laugh. 'Not that you'd know it from the number of *these* that get churned out.' She gestured to the stack of books on the floor by her desk. 'No one wants to talk about the fact that murder is overwhelmingly an issue of male violence. They just want to talk about the handful of women who break the mould.'

'I sorta get it, though,' said Zoe, her tone almost apologetic. 'I mean, if shit like this wasnae so unusual, it wouldnae be half as interesting tae read about. Let's face it, doll – if lassies like Sandra Morton were ten a penny, odds are you wouldnae have looked at the case twice … right?'

Anna said nothing. As much as she hated to admit it, Zoe's words had hit uncomfortably close to home. At various points over the last couple of weeks, she'd told herself that her agreeing to look into the Sandra Morton case was driven purely by the hope that she would get something in return – but that couldn't account for the fact that, in continuing her investigation beyond the case file, she'd well and truly exceeded the parameters of her original agreement with Pamela. Could she really claim that she was driven purely by dry, academic interest? Was it not more likely that, despite her repeated attempts to cast herself as somehow being above it all, she too had been sucked in by the same ghoulish, carnivalesque fascination with the case that had so gripped the press and public alike?

The primary reason why she'd always been so reluctant to engage with cases involving female killers, and female child killers in particular, wasn't so much the prurient nature of the discourse surrounding them – though, Christ knew, it was certainly a factor. No – it was the deep, bone-aching weariness that came from being accused by the usual suspects of making excuses for them whenever you dared to contextualise their actions by pointing out inconvenient truths like the motivating factors for their crimes and how they differed from those of their male counterparts. The mere existence of women like Sandra Morton meant they had a ready-made stick with which to beat any feminist who raised her head above the parapet to advocate for reducing female incarceration. It didn't matter that the overwhelming majority of women in prison were there for non-violent crimes. All of that could be dismissed out of hand because, eighteen years ago in a tiny village in Dumfriesshire, one woman had taken a kitchen knife to her husband and two young children as they slept, and hadn't even had the decency to wear a bra while she did it.

Anna might have continued in this vein indefinitely if things hadn't come to a head in the early afternoon of 21 March. From midday to 1 p.m. every Thursday, the bottom half of the pool at the local leisure centre was closed to everyone barring under-fives and their guardians. For the past year or so, Anna had been taking Jack there at least once a fortnight on the grounds that it was never too early to equip him with the swimming skills that might one day save his life. It helped break up her working day too, and provided her with an excuse to get out of the house that she might not otherwise have taken. Several of the other mums – and the handful of dads – who were regulars there had formed little social clusters, but Anna and Jack tended to keep themselves to themselves, Jack doggy-paddling around in determined circles while Anna kept a weather eye on him, ready to intervene if he ever got into difficulty.

That day, lulled by the sounds of splashing and the whooping and shrieking of the various infants surrounding her, Anna allowed her mind to wander, her thoughts straying – as they so often did of late – to the events of the night of 6 May 2001. She'd been through it so many times now, she knew the whole timeline more or less by heart, down to the very minute.

23:09. A dying Guy Morton manages to ring 999.

23:10. Graeme Malone hears a door slamming open and footsteps fleeing across the Mortons' back garden.

23:11. Adjoa Asante witnesses a woman matching Sandra Morton's description scaling the wall at the bottom of the field next to Haysend Road.

23:20. PCs Strainger and Higgins arrive at the property. They enter the building and find Guy lying dead on the hallway floor.

23:21. PC Higgins radios for help. PC Strainger finds Iain and Gabriel Morton dead in their beds, Gabriel virtually decap—

'Anna!'

At the sound of her name being called, Anna instantly snapped out of it and looked around wildly, momentarily disoriented. It took her a couple of seconds to locate Jack, who had managed to paddle away towards the deep end, putting a good six feet between himself and her. As she hurried over to him, she heard her name being called again. Turning, she saw Zoe standing at the edge of the top end of the pool, wearing a polka-dotted two-piece that, to Anna's mind, showed off an indecent amount of arse.

'Watch this!' she shouted, cupping her hands to her mouth. 'I'm gonnae jump!'

Wrapping her arms round Jack to prevent a fresh escape bid, Anna dutifully watched as Zoe backed up, then took a running jump and cannonballed into the water, much to the chagrin of the quartet of septuagenarian ladies whose sedate breaststroke was interrupted by the resulting mini tidal wave. A moment later, Zoe resurfaced, spitting out water and grinning delightedly.

'Did ye see?' she called. 'Was that no pure dead brilliant?'

Anna forced a smile and mimed applause as Zoe, still beaming, swam over to the edge and hauled herself out, pausing to yank her bikini bottoms up over her exposed arse-crack. As Zoe waved off the remonstrations of an approaching lifeguard, Anna relinquished her hold on Jack and watched as he resumed his paddling, her own elevated breathing slowly coming back down to earth.

This was getting beyond a joke, she told herself. It was time to knock this Sandra Morton business on the head before she ended up so far down the rabbit hole she wouldn't be able to dig herself back out.

12

Saturday 23 March

Pamela steamed into Caffe Monza, windblown and flustered. Before she'd even reached the table where Anna had been seated for the past twenty-five minutes, she was already in full flow.

'Oh my God, I am *so* sorry,' she babbled, collapsing into the empty seat facing Anna. 'I thought I was getting on the fast train that only has like six stops between Edinburgh and Glasgow but it turned out to be the slow one that takes the scenic route through Livingston and Airdrie. Classic rookie mistake. I was going to come in the car but it's such a faff and you can never get parked anywhere close to where you're wanting to go and—' She realised she was waffling and stopped abruptly, offering up a limp shrug of apology.

Anna forced a smile. 'Don't worry about it.'

She'd been in a foul mood all day – a mood that had darkened by the hour. It had begun first thing in the morning with an email from Ruth Laxton informing her that Martina Macdonald, though now fully recovered from her 'incident', no longer wished to be interviewed by her, now or at any point in the future. Though Anna couldn't be sure, she strongly suspected that Ruth had played a crucial role in Martina having reached this decision. She also hadn't been crazy about giving up part of Saturday to meet with Pamela, and her views on the subject hadn't exactly mellowed after having been kept waiting for nearly half an hour. But it was the only day Pamela was available, and Anna had to acknowledge that, right now, her own schedule was considerably more flexible than the solicitor's. She promised herself she'd make up for lost time with Jack later.

'So what's the skinny?' Pamela grinned. 'I've been on tenterhooks waiting for you to call. Did you find something? You must've found something, else you wouldn't have asked to meet.' She stared at Anna in eager anticipation.

'Pamela…' Anna began, her tone strained. There really was no gentle way of saying this. 'I asked to meet to do you the courtesy of telling you in person that I've got nothing.'

She watched as Pamela's face fell in real-time. The only thing missing was a sad trombone sound effect.

'I went through the police file with a fine tooth-comb,' she continued. 'I've also read just about every book that's been published on Operation Bluegrass. If there's evidence out there that shows your client is innocent, I've not been able to find it. I really think I've done everything I can. I'm sorry.'

For several uncomfortable seconds, Pamela said nothing. She looked utterly crestfallen, her shoulders drawn in as she gazed down at the tabletop. At length, she drew in a deep breath and lifted her head to meet Anna's eyes.

'You're right,' she said. 'It was always a long shot.'

She tried to sound matter-of-fact about it, but she wasn't fooling anyone. An awkward silence lingered between them, before Anna cleared her throat.

'Obviously, I'll return all the paperwork you sent me. In the meantime, can I ask what progress you've made on persuading your clients to talk to me?'

'About that…' Pamela seemed unable to meet Anna's eye.

'Yes, what about it?' said Anna, a tad tersely. She wasn't even surprised – not really.

'They'll come round, I promise.' Pamela sounded even more breathless than when she first came in. 'It's just… taking a bit more time than I was anticipating. I just need to find a way to convince them that it's in their interests to talk to you.' She winced apologetically. 'It's this world we live in. No one likes the thought of doing something for nothing.'

'Indeed,' said Anna, feeling very much like she'd allowed herself to be talked into doing just that. 'There was also supposed to be a dossier…'

Pamela clasped her hands between her thighs, practically squirming in her seat. '"Dossier" might have been putting it a little grandly. I've got notes,' she added hastily, as Anna made no attempt to hide her exasperated eye-roll, 'and you're welcome to have them as they stand, but they're a bit … sparse. I'm not sure how well they'd stand up to scrutiny.'

'You don't say.' Anna reached for her bag.

'I can only do so much without the cooperation of my clients,' Pamela wittered, flailing desperately to salvage the situation. 'Turns out they're almost as reluctant to talk to *me* about their problems as they are to talk to you.'

'D'you know what? Don't worry about it.' Anna got up to go, shouldering her bag. 'I'll make do without your clients *or* your vaunted dossier. I hope you have a safe journey back to Edinburgh.'

'But … but couldn't you keep going? I mean, just for a little while longer? Please.'

Something about the beseeching note in Pamela's voice caused Anna to stop in her tracks. She gazed down at the solicitor, noting, for the umpteenth time, just how small she looked. Small, and very much out of her depth. She genuinely looked like she might be on the verge of tears.

'Sandra ran out of road with the Appeal Court a long time ago,' Pamela went on, 'and we both know this investigation into Dalston is never going to amount to anything – even *if* it ends up happening at any point this century.'

Anna said nothing.

'Please.' Pamela gazed up at her plaintively. 'You're the only hope she's got.'

'What is it that makes you so convinced she's innocent?' Anna asked in exasperation. 'Why are you so determined to take her side?'

'Because no one else will!'

Anna blinked, genuinely taken aback by the note of utter desperation in Pamela's sudden outburst. Instinctively, she looked around, faintly embarrassed on both her own behalf and Pamela's, but the rest of the clientele seemed to be too wrapped up in their own conversations to have noticed anything.

'It's not about me thinking I've got it right and everyone else has got it wrong,' Pamela went on, her voice brittle but filled with utter conviction. 'It's about fairness. Maybe she did do it? I don't know. I wasn't there that night. I can't say for sure what happened. Neither can you, and neither can those so-called journalists who spewed their poison about her, then sat on their hands and refused to report the other side of the story. It might sound a quaint notion to you, but I believe everyone deserves a fair hearing, whatever they have or haven't done. Sandra never got that.'

For several seconds, Anna didn't move or speak. During the past week, one point which she'd found herself dwelling on repeatedly was the question of how fair a trial Sandra could, in fact, have received, given that the wall-to-wall saturation media coverage of the case meant the odds of finding fifteen jurors without any preconceived notions about the woman on whom they were being called to pass judgement must have been nigh on impossible. In her own way, Pamela had helped crystallise feelings that had long been gestating in her own mind. It wasn't about an innate belief in Sandra's guilt or innocence. It was about a belief in the principle of fairness as a virtue in and of itself. In the presumption of innocence until proven guilty. In the notion that justice wasn't justice unless it was truly blind.

Don't do this. You promised you were going to let it go. 'Before you end up so far down the rabbit hole', remember?

Ignoring the disapproving voice in her head, she lowered herself back onto her seat.

'All right. I suppose there's no harm in giving it another week or so. It's just possible there might be some avenues I haven't explored yet.'

Even with that simple utterance, Pamela's spirits lifted visibly. She gazed at Anna eagerly, eyes wide with expectation. Anna was briefly reminded of a Labrador anticipating a pat on the head.

'For instance,' she went on, keeping her tone level to temper Pamela's excitement, 'I could try to track down some of the original witnesses and see if they can shed any further light on what happened that night …'

'Of course!' said Pamela, nodding eagerly. 'What a marvellous idea! You never know, do you, what might not have occurred to them at the time?'

'… and I *am* going to try to get in touch with the police corruption unit and see if there's anything they can tell me about this supposed investigation into Frank Dalston. It might not be relevant to the Sandra Morton case, but it's a stone we can't afford to leave unturned.'

'Yes,' Pamela continued to nod like a bobblehead, 'they wouldn't tell me anything, but it's just possible they might to *you*. You *are* a Professor of Criminology, after all.'

'*But*,' said Anna firmly, studiously ignoring this transparent attempt to blow smoke up her tailpipe, 'if I'm going to keep going, I'm going to need *you* to do something for *me*.'

'Of course. Anything.'

'I need you to arrange a meeting for me with Sandra.'

Pamela's face fell.

'I know,' said Anna, not unkindly. 'I haven't forgotten what you said before about not telling her, but it's ridiculous for me to carry on chipping away at the edges while the woman at the centre of it all is sitting right there in a cell in Broadwood.'

'She won't cooperate.'

'We won't know unless you try. You said yourself, I seemed to impress her last time.'

Pamela's expression remained dubious, but at least she was no longer actively protesting the idea.

A thought occurred to Anna. 'What if we said it was research for my book? That I've decided to include a chapter on her case.'

Pamela's brows pursed as she considered this. 'It would certainly play to her ego.' She lifted her head, still unsure but slowly warming to the idea. 'Perhaps, if you said that, based on having met her, you'd decided to rethink the focus of your book ... '

At this rate, I might have *to*, Anna thought. The prospect of her ever securing an interview to replace the cancelled once with Martina Macdonald was looking more distant by the day.

'Of course,' Pamela continued, 'there's the question of how to explain *our* connection ... '

Anna shrugged. 'Tell her I approached you out of the blue, asking how to go about securing an interview with your client.'

'Yes.' Pamela's enthusiasm was becoming palpable. 'I actually think this could work. You'd have to be very careful of what you say to her, though,' she added, stopping just short of wagging a warning finger. 'The slightest hint we're trying to hoodwink her and we'll both be for the high jump.'

'Duly noted.'

'Of course,' Pamela continued to think aloud, 'we could be on a hiding to nothing. She could well say no.' She flashed her small, even teeth in a smile that was almost conspiratorial. 'But if I know Sandra at all, she's going to find the prospect of another one-on-one with you devilishly hard to resist.'

13

'This is Malcolm Gunning. Leave a message and I'll return your call at the next available opportunity.'

Beep.

'Hello, Mr Gunning, it's Anna Scavolini calling again. I'm not sure if you received the previous messages I left, but I thought I'd try again in case you were in. As I mentioned before, I'm Professor of Criminology at Glasgow University and I'm undertaking some research into the Sandra Morton investigation. If you're willing, I'd really appreciate the opportunity to ask you about your memories of the case at a time that's convenient to you. My contact details are ... '

She reamed off both her mobile and landline numbers, though without much hope of the act proving fruitful. She'd established, via the phone book, that a Malcolm Gunning *was* registered at the number she'd called and was as confident as she could be – from comparing the voice on the answering machine message to that of the former Detective Sergeant in his brief speaking appearance in a documentary on the Sandra Morton case she'd found online – that he was the one she was looking for. This was the third time in the last week she'd attempted to contact DSU Dalston's former second-in-command, and she was forced to conclude that he was either away on an extended trip or simply had no interest in talking to her. The latter was, she suspected, more likely.

Since her meeting with Pamela Macklin on Saturday, she'd thrown herself back into the Sandra Morton business feet first. A part of her, she had to admit, was more than a little glad that she'd allowed Pamela to talk her into keeping at it for a little longer. For now, her primary focus was on attempting to persuade as many people as possible who were connected to the case to speak to her, though so far it was proving to be a thankless task. After failing to reach Gunning – who, with Dalston long-dead, she felt represented her closest shot at getting inside the SIO's head – her next port of call had been Drew Barriscale, Sandra's solicitor at the time of the trial. She'd found his contact details easily enough via his professional website and had fired off an email asking if he'd be willing to answer some questions about his recollections of the case, either in writing or in person. His unexpectedly terse response had come through a couple of hours later, stating in no uncertain terms that he believed more than enough ink had been spilled on Sandra Morton, and that he had no desire whatsoever to relitigate the case now.

'My former client's conviction has been subject to multiple unsuccessful judicial appeals,' he wrote. 'What precisely is it you believe you can possibly find that everyone else has missed?' – a question she was glad was rhetorical, as it was one she'd been wondering about the answer to herself.

Graham Malone, the Mortons' next-door neighbour, had been the next name on her list, though reaching out to him was essentially a formality. Malone had been seventy-two at the time of the murders and, while it wasn't impossible that he was still alive at the ripe old age of ninety, the odds weren't exactly in his favour. Her suspicions were confirmed when, upon ringing the landline number corresponding to his address, the woman who picked up informed her that she and her husband had been living in the house for the past eight years, following the death of the previous occupant – whose name, after conferring with her other half, she confirmed as having been Graham Malone.

Another one bites the dust, Anna thought grimly, and scored his name off the list.

She was keen to build up a better picture of what had really happened on the night of the murders and establish whether it was remotely possible to reconcile Sandra's version of events with that of the two people whose testimony was reckoned to have been the deciding factor in the jury's decision to convict: Paul Kempley and Adjoa Asante. As such, from the very beginning, tracing them had been her number one priority.

She started with Adjoa, on the grounds that she would presumably be the easier of the two to track down, having the more uncommon name – in this part of the world, anyway. She began with a certain degree of optimism, only to spend the better part of a day, off and on, trying and failing to locate the woman whose sighting of a woman in a blue raincoat fleeing the crime scene had holed Sandra's defence below the waterline. She identified Adjoa's place of employment at the time of the murders easily enough: Browhouses, a tiny settlement on the coast of the River Esk, had an even smaller population than Hillend, and it only took her a couple of calls to the dozen or so houses in the area to find someone who remembered both her and her employer – who, as it turned out, was still alive and living in the same house.

The elderly, chipper Mrs Duffield was more than happy to receive Anna's call. (Anna assumed, from the level of her enthusiasm, that she didn't get many.) She spoke of Adjoa in positively glowing terms, but she regretted to inform Anna that her former cleaner had handed in her notice in early 2002 and left to take up a new posting elsewhere.

'I'm not sure where, dearie,' the clearly hard-of-hearing woman shouted down the line. 'Somewhere up north.'

However you sliced it, 'up north' was a pretty all-encompassing descriptor when you hailed from the southernmost part of the country. With only this vague indication as to Adjoa's post-Browhouses direction of travel to go on, Anna resorted to the usual tried and tested methods for tracing people in the modern age: the online phone directories, the electoral roll, the various social media platforms and, when none of these came up trumps, good old Google. The latter produced only a handful of results, none of which appeared to be the person she was looking for – not unless the Adjoa Asante who'd once cleaned houses for a living in Dumfriesshire had gone to medical school in the intervening years and ascended to the position of Director of Surgery at the Christiaan Barnard Memorial Hospital in Cape Town. She also spent some time searching for her son, Samuel, deeming him to be of an age more likely to be active on social media, but came up similarly empty-handed and was ultimately forced to abandon that line of enquiry.

Having decided, for the sake of her sanity, that she should take 'up north' to mean the North of Scotland, as opposed to anywhere north of the River Esk, Anna began to trawl the websites for local newspapers in the Highlands and Islands, in the vain hope that the woman she was looking for had done something noteworthy enough with her life to make it into one of their pages.

As is so often the case with breakthroughs, hers came at the point when she'd all but given up any hope of success. She'd found her way to the *Ullapool Courier* – a publication which purported to be a local community newspaper but was really just an amateur blog by another name, maintained by a single, dedicated volunteer. The search function was missing the graphic for the button – a fact which, in Anna's mind, didn't bode well. She was fully prepared for the site to return an error message – and yet, when she clicked what should have been the Search button, she was, after a longer than expected wait, taken to a fresh page displaying the following:

Your search for 'Adjoa Asante' returned **1** result(s).

Dated 15 September 2003, the article that loaded was the sort of puff piece typical of local newspapers, reporting on efforts by members of the community to raise funds to repair the leaking roof of a local church. After a thoroughly underwhelming start to their crowd-funder – during which it had begun to look very much like the church, declared unsafe by the council, would have to close permanently – a generous benefactor had stepped in and provided almost the entire amount single-handed. An image at the bottom of the article showed said benefactor, looking altogether too pleased with himself as he posed outside the afflicted building with four middle-aged women wearing floral dresses of the kind Anna had always associated with the sort of people who organised church fundraisers. Below it was a caption:

Generous local businessman Andrew Johnson celebrates with members of the fundraising committee. L to R: Mary Stapleton, Morag Cairns, Adjoa Asante and Dawn McKenna.

The woman second from the right – the only person of colour in the picture – was unquestionably the same Adjoa Asante who'd given evidence at the Sandra Morton trial. Anna recognised her from footage she'd seen on YouTube of her emerging from giving evidence at the High Court. Not only did she have the same stocky build and beehive hairdo, she also sported the same oversized cloth handbag with its distinctive floral pattern, hanging from her elbow.

A call to the church – still open fifteen years later as testament to the success of the repairs – established that Adjoa hadn't been a member of the congregation for some time. In fact, the woman at the other end of the line said, she left Ullapool just a few months after the fundraiser and therefore missed the grand reopening.

'But,' she went on, just as Anna silently mouthed a decidedly unholy curse, 'Cressida Bagshawe might know where she went.'

'Who?'

'Her employer. Kept her as a housekeeper for … oh, a good couple of years, anyway, before she moved on. If anyone knows what became of her, it'll be her.'

'Do you have her number?'

'As it happens, I do. She's on our tea rota. Half a tick – I've got it here somewhere.'

After a prolonged shuffling of papers, the woman reamed off the digits in question. Anna rang off and dialled the number, listening to the ringing tone with bated breath. A moment later, the call was answered.

'Oh-eight-four-nine, Bagshawe residence,' a plummy voice trilled.

As Anna gave her by now well-rehearsed explanation for her call, it briefly occurred to her that, by telling everyone she spoke to that she was looking for Adjoa in relation to her status as a witness in a murder trial, she might perhaps be giving more detail than was strictly necessary. Cressida, however, didn't seem remotely perturbed.

'Oh, how fascinating!' she exclaimed, her shrill voice like nails on a chalkboard. 'I do enjoy a good true crime story. Allows one to experience the thrill of the macabre from a safe distance, doesn't it?'

Anna agreed that it did. 'About Adj … uh, Ms Asante, I don't suppose—'

'She was a *marvel*, that woman. Simply a marvel, I tell you. So hard-working, and always with such a cheerful disposition. Grasp of English a bit shaky, but what she lacked in conversational ability she more than made up for with work ethic.'

'I'm very glad to hear it,' said Anna, hoping the sarcasm wasn't too readily apparent. 'So she worked for you from 2002 to—'

'Early 2004, yes. Initially, we employed her as a cleaner, but she ended up doing all sorts around the house for us. She and her son. You know about Samuel, do you?'

'Yes. I—'

'Such a well-mannered boy,' Cressida sighed, 'and utterly devoted to his mother! Thick as thieves, the pair of them were. Oh, not that I'm implying...'

'Of course not,' said Anna, who was getting a fairly good idea of how this woman's mind worked.

'No, I never once felt I was taking a risk by having them in the house. Not that we had much worth stealing – Alec's business had taken something of a downturn at the time – which was why, rather than paying them in cash, I provided them with free room and board. Which, when you stop to think about it, is all anyone needs, really.'

'Who could ask for more?'

'*Exactly,*' said Cressida, evidently pleased that she and Anna were on the same page. 'So many people these days seem to know the price of everything and the value of nothing. Adjoa wasn't like that. Very low maintenance; seemed entirely content with her lot in life. That's why I was so surprised when, one day, she and the boy simply upped and left.'

Anna experienced a sinking feeling in the pit of her stomach. 'What, just like that? No explanation or indication as to where they were going?'

'Not that I can recall. She just came to me one day and said, "Ma'am, I must leave tomorrow", or words to that effect – which, I can tell you, left me in a pretty pickle. Where was I going to find a replacement with a comparable work ethic at such short notice?' Cressida sighed heavily, recalling this highly inconvenient period in her life. 'But of course, I wished her well and said I'd gladly write her a reference should she need one. She never did take me up on that offer,' she concluded, sounding both puzzled and vaguely put out.

'And you've no idea where she went?'

'Ah, now hang on, I never said that. A few weeks later, I received a letter in the post, thanking me for all I'd done for her. I'm *fairly* certain it included a forwarding address...'

'And do you happen to have it to hand?' said Anna, her spirits lifting slightly.

'Not to *hand*.' Cressida gave a patronising little laugh. 'It was fifteen-odd years ago, you understand. And it's possible I may have thrown it away. But perhaps not,' she mused, seeming to lapse into talking to herself. 'It came inside a rather nice greetings card with a knitted cover. She was a dab hand at the arts and crafts, you see. No,' she concluded, with considerably more certainty, 'I doubt I'd have got rid of *that*.'

'Well, do you think you might be able to look it out for me?' said Anna, who was beginning to feel that this was like getting blood from a stone.

'I could certainly try,' said Cressida, after giving the matter some consideration. 'But I fear it won't be today. I have bridge at six, you see, and later—'

'Just whenever you have the time would be great,' said Anna, knowing it was the best offer she was likely to get. 'It would be a massive help to me. And if you do happen to find it...'

'I'll call you on this number, naturally.' Cressida gave an unexpectedly girly squeal of delight. 'Well, I must say, this *is* exciting. A bona fide missing person investigation!'

Accepting that, until Cressida got back to her, she'd advanced her search for Adjoa Asante as far as she could, Anna now turned her attention to Paul Kempley. Reluctant to embark on a lengthy trawl through the profiles of the multiple Paul or P Kempleys on Facebook and the even greater number on Google, she opted instead to start at the source: his hometown of Eastriggs. With its population of around 1,800, she surmised that anyone living there with the surname Kempley was either Paul himself or a close relative. Entering these details into the online phone book turned up a single result: a C Kempley of 12 Dunedin Place. Having forestalled Zoe's summons to the dinner table by shouting that she'd be down in a minute, Anna dialled the number and waited, phone to her ear.

'Hello?' a female voice asked sharply.

'Mrs Kempley?'

'That's me, yes.' There was a note of impatience in the woman's voice.

It occurred to Anna that she, too, was probably on the verge of sitting down to eat.

'I'm sorry to trouble you, but I was wondering… are you the mother of *Paul* Kempley?'

Silence for an uncomfortable moment, then:

'Who's asking?'

I'll take that as a 'yes'.

'My name's Anna Scavolini. I'm a criminology professor. As I'm sure you'll remember, Paul was a witness in a… in a criminal trial some years ago. I'm doing some research into the investigation and I'm keen to ask him about his memories from that time, if he's willing. I was wondering if you could tell me how I might go about getting in touch with him?'

Utter silence. She couldn't even make out the woman's breathing.

'Mrs Kempley? Are you still there?'

A pause, then, 'I'm here.'

'Did you—'

'I heard what you said.'

More silence. The woman's lack of respect for the normal ebb and flow of conversation was starting to make Anna feel genuinely uncomfortable.

'Mrs Kempley—'

'My son and I haven't been in touch for several years. I've no idea where he is or how to contact him.'

'Oh.' Anna was momentarily thrown. 'Then can I ask—'

'I really don't want to talk about it.' Mrs Kempley's tone allowed for no argument. 'I wish you luck with whatever it is you're doing, but I can't help you.'

And then, before Anna could formulate a response, there was a click and the line went dead.

She lowered her phone. The silence that now enveloped her office felt decidedly oppressive. She told herself it was nothing unheard of; that children fell out of touch with their parents for umpteen reasons, many of them perfectly legitimate. She knew that better than anyone. And yet the way the call had ended had left her feeling despondent in a way that went beyond mere disappointment at having hit another roadblock in her investigation. There had been such a sense of finality about it – such a lack of curiosity from Mrs Kempley about where her now adult son might be or what he might be doing with his life. It wasn't a natural way for a parent to behave – or at any rate, it oughtn't to be.

Anna took a moment to collect herself, then got to her feet, pasted on her happy mask and headed downstairs to join the others for dinner.

14

Friday 29 March

The following morning, Anna was at her desk bright and early, ready to knuckle down and tackle the task she'd balked at yesterday: scouring social media for possible leads as to the whereabouts of Paul Kempley. At least she knew, from the photographs snapped of him arriving at the court to give evidence, what he looked like – or rather, what he'd looked like two decades ago. Gangly and lank-haired, sporting an ill-fitting suit and a beard that made him look older than his twenty years, she hoped he still bore enough of a resemblance to his younger self for her to recognise him from his picture as she scrolled through the list of profiles on Facebook.

Though she began, if not exactly in a state of optimism then, at least, with a determination to see the assignment through, by midday she'd resigned herself to the fact that this was going to be a marathon rather than a sprint, and that, if she continued to focus on it to the detriment of everything else, she was liable to drive herself mad. She was also painfully aware that the weekend was almost upon her and was loath to allow her investigation to intrude on time she should be spending with Jack. As a result, she put Kempley to one side and forced herself to confront the task she'd been putting off for some time now but had known all along that, sooner or later, she would have to face: contacting the surviving members of the Morton family.

For obvious reasons, the prospect of dredging up traumatic memories for people who'd already endured more than enough suffering for several lifetimes was far from a pleasant one, but she didn't see how it could be avoided – not if she was serious about pursuing every available avenue of information. She'd already taken some half-hearted steps towards tracing both Guy Morton's brother, Jeff, and Guy and Sandra's surviving daughter, Katie, over the last couple of days, using the same methods that had failed to bear fruit for either Paul Kempley or Adjoa Asante. So far, she'd identified a handful of potential candidates, based in locations as disparate as Vermillion, Alberta and Raglan, Queensland, but she was reluctant to start messaging random people and asking them, 'Excuse me, but are you the Katie/Jeff Morton whose mother/sister-in-law brutally murdered your relatives?' It was therefore with considerable reluctance that she reached for her phone and dialled the number for the two members of the Morton clan whose whereabouts she *did* know.

At the time of the murders, Eunice and George Morton – then both in their mid-sixties – had been living in an old farmhouse on the outskirts of Eastriggs for around ten years. Sandra and Guy's move to neighbouring Hillend in 1997 had, according to multiple sources, been precipitated by a desire on Guy's part to be closer to his parents, so they'd be on hand to assist Sandra with the childcare. Following the murders, both grandparents had made little secret of their belief in Sandra's guilt. During the televised appeal from which Sandra had purportedly been barred, a recording of which Anna had tracked down on YouTube, Eunice had repeatedly used female pronouns when referring to the killer – something which, for a member of a generation that regarded 'he' and 'him' as gender-neutral terms, had immediately seemed noteworthy.

The press had quickly picked up that little love was lost between Sandra and her in-laws and dined out on this, drawing all sorts of conclusions about the fact that two such upstanding, salt-of-the-earth senior citizens had been unable to see any good in their daughter-in-law. Whilst, according to them, Sandra was a disinterested and negligent mother, Eunice and George were defined by their devotion to their grandchildren, selflessly rising to the occasion when their mother failed to measure up. Whereas Guy's parents were regular churchgoers – as if that, in and of itself, was somehow a virtue – Sandra's lack of Christian piety was treated with grave suspicion, and, at its most extreme, added further fuel to the already fevered speculation about Satanic cults. They got particularly good mileage out of placing Sandra and Eunice in direct opposition to one another, using the nurturing, self-sacrificing Eunice to remind people what a mother figure *should* look like. One tabloid even ran a piece entitled 'The Saint and the Sinner', listing Eunice's virtues in one column and Sandra's purported vices in another.

All this was to say that Anna recognised how important it was that she avoid giving any impression that she was investigating the case with a view to reconsidering the question of Sandra's guilt. The slightest suggestion that she was in any sense fighting Sandra's corner and she could kiss goodbye to any hope of them cooperating with her.

There was a click as the receiver was picked up at the other end. A moment later, it was followed by a breathy, quavering voice, evidently belonging to an older woman.

'Seven six double six?'

'Hello, am I speaking to Eunice Morton?'

'This is she,' said the voice, speaking in a raised tone and enunciating each word individually, as if she was used to not being understood.

'Good – I wonder if you can help me. My name's Anna Scav—'

'Pardon?' the voice interrupted. 'Speak up, dearie. It's a bad line.'

'Of course,' said Anna, suspecting that deafness was a more likely explanation than the perennial 'bad line'. She began again, matching Eunice's volume and diction.

'My name is Anna Scavolini. I'm Professor of Criminology at Glasgow University. I'm sorry to be calling you about this, but I wonder if you could spare a few minutes of your time to help me. You see, I'm researching the Sandra Morton case—'

She heard Eunice's sharp intake of breath at the other end of the line. 'Oh … I'm not sure … We don't …'

'I'm not a reporter,' Anna assured her. 'I imagine you've had more than your share of bother from them over the years. I'm looking into the case as part of a broader study of women's experiences of the justice system, and—'

'I … I'm not sure about that.' Eunice's voice seemed to grow even more tremulous. 'My husband … he deals with this sort of thing.'

Before Anna could interject, she was subjected to a shrill, drawn-out shout of 'GEOOOOORGE!' Silence followed, punctuated only by Eunice's somewhat laboured breathing.

'Mrs Morton … ?'

'He isn't answering.' Eunice sounded vaguely unsettled. 'He must … perhaps he's outside?'

'Don't worry about that for now,' Anna said, aware that her tone was the same one she adopted when Jack got upset and she was trying to reassure him. 'I'm sure you'll be able to help me just fine. As I say, I only have a few questions. Would you be willing to have a go at answering them?'

'Well … ' Eunice began uncertainly, 'I suppose … all right.'

'Thank you. Before we start, I appreciate how difficult it must be to have to revisit these events – so if, at any time, I ask you anything that makes you uncomfortable and you want to stop, we can absolutely do that. Does that sound OK?'

'Yes,' said Eunice, in a tone that failed to convince Anna she'd fully understood what she was agreeing to. She felt a pang of guilt at the thought that she could well be taking advantage of an elderly woman who she was beginning to suspect was in, at least, the early stages of cognitive decline. But, having got this far, she couldn't bring herself to abandon ship now.

'Thank you, I really appreciate your cooperation. Now, Guy and Sandra moved to Hillend in early 1997. Prior to that, they'd been living in Newton Mearns. Is that right?'

'Yes,' said Eunice, after a pause as she processed the question.

'That's quite a distance from Eastriggs. How much contact did you have with them back then? I mean, did you see them often?'

'Did we see them … Oh dear, I … I'm not … George would know.'

'That's all right, Mrs Morton,' said Anna, forestalling yet another ear-splitting bellow. 'After the move, you became heavily involved with the childcare arrangements, didn't you? Especially the twins. Can you remember, was that something Guy initiated?'

'Yes, Guy. He … well, he was a working man. And that woman, she wasn't … I mean, she couldn't be … She … He felt it was better.'

'Right,' said Anna slowly, trying to parse Eunice's scattered train of thought. 'And why did he feel it was better? Was Sandra … was she neglecting the children in some way?'

'She wasn't … she wasn't …' Whatever Eunice said next trailed off into an incomprehensible mumble.

'What, Mrs Morton? Wasn't what?'

'She wasn't *right*,' Eunice suddenly hissed, with such vehemence that Anna was genuinely taken aback. 'Not right. Not right.'

Before Anna could respond, there was a sound of footsteps at the other end of the line, followed by a man's voice.

'What's going on? Eunice?'

There was a fumbling sound, following by a thud as Eunice presumably dropped or set down the receiver. Anna listened to the muffled sounds of a two-way conversation. She couldn't make out the words, but could tell, from the gruff, terse nature of the man's contributions, that he was subjecting Eunice to an interrogation that seemed altogether more forceful than the situation warranted.

A moment later, the receiver was snatched up again and the man's voice came through loud and clear.

'Yes?'

'Oh!' Anna struggled to regain her composure. 'Um … I was speaking to your wife, I think? Are you George?'

'Why?' he snapped. 'Who are you?'

She began to tell him, reaming off the same script she'd used on Eunice, but more falteringly, any sense that she was in control of the situation now wholly jettisoned.

'Now you listen,' growled George, once she'd finally trailed off into an uncomfortable and vaguely penitent silence. 'I don't know what it is you hope to achieve, but we don't need this, you hear? We've suffered more than enough harassment from busybodies like you.'

'I'm sorry, Mr Morton. I'm just trying to—'

'You think it isn't hard enough for us, living with what that woman did to our family, day in, day out, without people like you dredging it up, forcing us to go through it all over again?'

'I can assure you, Mr Morton, it wasn't my intention to—'

'I don't want to hear it. I can't stop you writing this disgusting article of yours, but I'll be damned if I'm going to make it any easier for you. If you have a shred of decency in your body, you'll reconsider what you're doing.'

Anna said nothing. There was no point. He'd made up his mind about her and her motives, and nothing she said, even if she *did* get a word in edgeways, would make any difference.

'I'm hanging up now,' George Morton said, 'and if you call this number again, I shall be contacting the police to report you for harassment. Good day.'

There was a sharp click, and the line went dead.

Slowly, Anna lowered the phone to her lap, her ear still stinging from the rebuke. She'd been half-anticipating a response like this, but that didn't make it any more pleasant to be on the receiving end of one. She thought about what the family's experiences of the press must have been like – the constant phone calls and door knocks, entreating them day and night to publicly air their grief for the gratification of the public, coupled with an inability to tell them where to go due to the need to keep them on side … Ever since she'd begun the process, she'd told herself she was nothing like the tabloid hacks who hounded grieving relatives without scruple; that her motives were nobler and less prurient. And yet, at the end of the day, what comfort were motives to those on the receiving end? From the point of view of people like the Mortons, how was she any different from the amoral muckrakers who churned out copy for the *Chronicles* and *Daily Posts* of this world?

I deserved that, she thought, and scored Eunice and George's names off the list.

15

'... *cos it's always gotta be all about them. Can't have anything taking the spotlight away from them and their* grief.'

'*It has nothing to do with them believing you might be responsible?*'

'*You'd have to ask them that.*'

'Pause there!'

Instantly, the image of Sandra Morton in the Border Television studio froze, mouth open, eyes mid-blink, giving her a vaguely zombie-like appearance. In the bottom left corner, the badly green-screened video host gesticulated animatedly towards her face.

'Here you can see her chin is down,' he declared. 'She's in a pre-confession state. Now, let's talk about what that *means*...'

Anna hit the spacebar, pausing the video mid-flight and leaned back in her chair, the heavy puff of air she let out sounding almost deafeningly loud in the nocturnal stillness of her office. If her university colleagues could see her now...

At least she'd managed to confine herself to more respectable activities during daylight hours – or so she told herself. More respectable, though not necessarily any more fruitful. She'd spent a significant portion of the previous day being passed from pillar to post as she attempted to make contact with the reviews unit set up to investigate institutional police corruption in the aftermath of the Shadow Men affair. Eventually, she'd succeeded in tracking down the correct phone number on a freedom of information website and, after navigating a near-endless series of pre-recorded options, had been put through to an actual, sentient human – though, in the event, she suspected a machine might have proved more helpful.

'*If* any of Detective Superintendent Dalston's cases were under consideration for review,' the nasal-voiced Detective Inspector at the other end of the line had informed her, 'they would go through a process of thorough examination to determine whether there were grounds to escalate them further. As someone in your profession can doubtless appreciate, our workload is considerable, and our approach rigorously systematic. We don't simply bump cases to the top of the pile because they happen to be especially juicy.'

'I suppose there's no point in asking if there's any possibility of me being allowed access to any files you hold on the Sandra Morton investigation,' Anna had said, her expectations less than rosy.

'You suppose correctly,' the DI had replied, his tone dripping with undisguised glee. 'And now, if there's nothing else I can assist you with, madam ... '

Unable to come up with a suitably cutting retort on the spot, Anna had simply hung up. It was possible, she supposed, that her reputation had once again preceded her, her views on the police being almost as widely known as those on the prison system. Regardless of the reason, yet another avenue of her investigation had been stymied, and she once again found herself facing a brick wall. She dearly hoped she'd hear something soon regarding her request to re-interview Sandra. Even if the response was a flat refusal, at least she'd know where she stood.

In the meantime, she'd managed to fall down the rabbit hole that was the online discourse surrounding the Hillend murders. For the last couple of evenings, she'd sat up into the wee hours, watching YouTubers attempting to dissect the case and Sandra herself, offering up their opinions with the sort of self-confidence only the truly ignorant seemed to possess. She found these to be compulsive viewing, in part because of how much they riled her up. Case in point, the algorithm's latest offering: 'Body Language Expert REACTS to Ice Queen Sandra Morton's SHOCKING Interview!' screamed the title, accompanied by a thumbnail of the supposed 'expert' posing, hands to cheeks and mouth open in a parody of Munch's *The*

Scream, in front of a still of Sandra from her infamous interview. Her jaw was circled, the word 'RAGE' helpfully superimposed over an arrow pointing to it.

The insight provided by the 'expert' (because of course she clicked the video) was par for the course. Sandra was aggressive, defensive and evasive, he claimed, frequently pausing the footage to highlight minute changes in her facial expressions or make sweeping statements about what a particular gesture 'meant'. On more than one occasion, he made great stock of the fact that Sandra briefly glanced to the upper right before responding to a question – which, according to him, proved incontestably that she was lying. Identifying so-called 'micro-expressions' was another popular pastime. Detectable only by freeze-framing at the correct fraction of a second, these fleeting, involuntary facial expressions provided – or so he claimed – a window into Sandra's true emotions, and each one, from the micro-smile to the micro-scowl, invariably proved she was as guilty as sin.

She gazed at the screen, frozen with the host about to pontificate on some matter of great importance, index finger raised, mouth open in a wide 'O' as he inhaled a breath. Anna knew she should stop watching. She'd long since passed the point where any of the material she was consuming had genuine educational value. All she was doing was riling herself up and ensuring that she wouldn't be able to get to sleep when she finally *did* drag herself to her bed. But she couldn't help herself. It was like picking at a scab or rubbing a mouth ulcer with your tongue: the more you told yourself to stop, the stronger the compulsion to keep going. And the itch wasn't going to be satisfied until she'd dredged every last corner of the internet for material that related even tangentially to Sandra Morton.

She leaned forward and hit Play again.

It wasn't that she was being *completely* unproductive – or at least, so she kept telling herself. On and off, she continued her trawl of social media for Jeff and Katie Morton and Paul Kempley – half a dozen profiles checked off here, another half dozen there. And she still had one or two books on the Hillend Murders to finish reading, the most recent of which had only arrived late last week.

Published in 2008 and seemingly never re-released, *The Face of Evil:*

Sandra Morton and the Hillend Murders was the work of Niall McEnaney, a former reporter for the *Daily Post* who'd covered the investigation and trial extensively and had – or so he proudly claimed – been the one who'd come up with the 'Ice Queen' moniker. She'd ordered it back at the start of her dive into the case; dispatched from a second-hand seller in Arizona, it had taken so long to cross the Atlantic that, by the time it finally dropped through her letterbox, she'd more or less forgotten having bought it in the first place. One look at the revoltingly tacky cover – a head shot of Sandra with prison bars superimposed in front of her; the title in bold red, complete with blood dripping from it – was almost enough to make her wish it had got lost in transit.

The text was written in the same salacious style as McEnaney's newspaper articles, his primary goal clearly to shock and titillate rather than to inform. He went to great lengths to describe both Sandra (simultaneously eroticising her as 'busty' and 'fond of flaunting her body' and making disparaging references to her 'mannish jaw' and 'child-bearing hips') and the crime scene ('like an abattoir') as graphically as possible, and was fond of speculating as to how various people – the first officers at the scene, the victims while they were in the throes of death, the bereaved relatives – would have 'felt', with seemingly no basis in anything other than his own overdeveloped imagination. On several occasions, he wrote with what bordered on orgasmic glee about being asked to cover such a 'juicy' case.

And yet, perhaps it was merely in contrast to the intellectual black hole she'd allowed herself to be sucked into with her YouTube viewing, but as she continued to make her way through McEnaney's book, she found that, if you could get past the general grubbiness of the language, it did cover some genuinely interesting ground that had been ignored by the other publications on the case. For one thing, it was one of the few to touch on Sandra's life prior to the murders in any detail. The first few chapters devoted considerable space to exploring her early years in depth – including details which could only have come from talking to members of her immediate family, or sources close to them. He'd managed to interview one of her primary school teachers, who noted her propensity towards noncompliance and a seeming lack of interest in learning despite possessing 'a most perceptive mind'. She was a loner at school, deliberately antagonistic towards the other children and a frequent target of bullies due to being far sharper with her tongue than with her fists.

Most of these details were unsourced – a complete anathema to Anna's academic mind. There were, however, a handful of direct quotations attributed to Sandra's eldest brother, Fulton.

'She was always a bit of a black sheep,' he said. 'Obstinate, didn't make friends easily, went out of her way to make life hard for herself instead of just fitting in.'

Once Sandra moved to secondary school, or so McEnaney alleged, she began hanging out with an older crowd – mostly consisting of friends of her two brothers, from whom she was able to bum cigarettes and alcohol. She also became sexually active at a young age – certainly by the age of thirteen, if not earlier. McEnaney took great delight in painting her as a sexual deviant who routinely seduced boys much older than her, implicitly absolving them of any wrongdoing. That said, he laid most of the blame for the way Sandra had 'turned out' at the feet of her stay-at-home mother, Angela, whom he characterised as an ineffectual drunk with no interest in her daughter's development. Anna noted that he had comparatively little to say about her father, John, a welder, who was frequently absent for lengthy periods and eventually walked out for good shortly before Sandra's fifteenth birthday.

Sandra's teenage years were characterised by frequent truanting and periods of suspension. She ultimately left school at sixteen after flunking her O-levels, and proceeded to flit between periods of unemployment and a succession of menial jobs. The latter included a brief stint as an auxiliary at a local nursing home, from which she was apparently dismissed following repeated complaints about her manner towards both the residents and her colleagues. McEnaney further detailed an incident, when Sandra was around seventeen, in which a local boy a few years older than her and with whom she'd had a brief relationship served a prison sentence for severely assaulting another boy. Rumours abounded, or so McEnaney claimed, that Sandra had put him up to it after revealing to him that she'd slept with the future victim.

'Several sources who knew her well confirmed she had a manipulative streak,' McEnaney wrote. '"She was partial to setting the cat among the pigeons," a former classmate claimed. "She loved nothing better than whispering into someone's ear, then sitting back and watching the fireworks."'

The early years of her marriage to Guy followed, including the birth, in 1988, of their first child, Katie. McEnaney claimed Sandra had never wanted children and 'most likely got pregnant by making a mistake with her birth control' – a statement which, once again, neatly absolved the man in the equation of any responsibility. However, he contradicted himself a couple of chapters later, speculating that Sandra and Guy's marriage had been on the rocks at the time and that her getting pregnant was a deliberate ploy to prevent him from leaving her. Logical consistency was evidently not a requirement in McEnaney's world, provided women could be portrayed as devious manipulators and men their perennial victims, powerless to resist their wiles. (Anna strongly suspected this offered something of an insight into his own dealings with the opposite sex.) In 1997, the cycle began again with the arrival of the twins – a gap of nine years since the birth of their first child; long enough to suggest that they too had been unplanned.

The book then turned to the night of the murders. Until now, McEnaney's narration had adopted an omniscient point of view, recounting the events from the perspective of the all-seeing, all-knowing author-as-God. However, the moment Dalston entered the narrative, the tone changed. He immediately assumed the role of lead protagonist in a narrative that pitted the plucky, under-resourced police against a criminal mastermind, with the events of the two and a half weeks leading up to Sandra's arrest told almost exclusively through his eyes.

McEnaney seemed quite enamoured by the Detective Superintendent, describing his 'movie star good looks' and 'sheer single-mindedness in the pursuit of justice'. (From the pictures she'd seen of him, with his receding hairline and oily, blotchy skin, Anna was more inclined to liken him to the B-actor drafted in to replace the original star for the direct-to-video sequel.) These chapters constituted an almost blow-by-blow account of Dalston's thought process at each stage of the investigation, suggesting an intimate familiarity with the inner workings of his mind. At no point was he directly quoted, nor did his name appear in the acknowledgements section, but the implication was clear: assuming McEnaney hadn't simply made the whole thing up, he must have spoken, in some detail, to either Dalston or someone extremely familiar with him.

The book also covered the trial extensively, but there was little in these chapters that couldn't be found elsewhere, the ins and outs of the court proceedings having been covered by the press in exhaustive detail at the time. A handful of pages were devoted to its aftermath and the unsuccessful campaign to reintroduce the death penalty, before concluding with a timeline of significant events, including everything from Sandra's birth in 1966 to her conviction on 25 March 2002. A handful of additional events post-sentencing were listed at the bottom, including the prison attack that left her with the burn scar on her neck and shoulder, her first two unsuccessful appeals and the death of her mother, from COPD-related complications, in 2005.

Anna reached for the book and idly turned to the back cover. McEnaney's biography was printed at the bottom, alongside the barcode.

> Niall McEnaney first rose to prominence with his groundbreaking reporting on the Sandra Morton case for the *Scottish Daily Post*. A celebrated investigative journalist renowned for his straight-talking style, he has also covered the House of Blood murders and the 2007 Glasgow Airport terrorist attack. He lives and works in Glasgow.

The byline would have been written over ten years ago, at around the time of the book's original publication. Did he still live in Glasgow, she wondered, and was he still working for the *Post*? With Dalston dead and Gunning ignoring the answerphone messages she'd left for him, McEnaney was arguably the closest thing out there to a living link to the investigation. It was obvious, from reading the book, that covering the case had been the high point of his career. As such, and going by the self-aggrandising streak that so clearly ran through him, she figured there was a good chance he'd be willing to share his memories of a period in his life he evidently regarded with considerable fondness. And however much of an unprincipled mudslinger he might be, talking to him could hardly be any less intellectually stimulating than watching – she checked the next video in her YouTube queue – 'Chilling moment where Sandra Morton LAUGHS in TV interview'.

She reached across to her keyboard and typed 'Niall McEnaney contact details' into Google.

16

Thursday 4 April

From the outside, the Eagle on Govan Road looked like every old man pub she'd ever seen, and she doubted it would fare any better inside. But this was where McEnaney had insisted they meet. Under the circumstances, she could hardly insist on an alternative venue.

'Want me to come with?' Zoe had asked, when Anna had told her about her plan an hour or so earlier, deliberately leaving it to the last minute so Zoe had as little opportunity as possible to talk her out of it.

'Nah, it'll be fine,' Anna had replied. 'It's not as if I'll be drinking with a hardened criminal. 'Sides, someone needs to stay for Jack.'

Her thoughts turned, as they so often had of late, to her reliance on Zoe's unending willingness to drop everything to babysit Jack whenever the need arose. Not that Zoe ever seemed to have plans of her own these days. On the contrary, the one-time party girl seemed to have settled into a life of evenings in front of the telly with her feet up, or on her knees building Duplo on the floor with Jack. If she had any yearning for her old life, she was hiding it well. Still, Anna could hardly ignore the pang of guilt she'd felt as she headed out of the house. Perhaps it had something to do with the fact that Adjoa Asante and her clearly exploitative relationship with Cressida Bagshawe – who it occurred to her still hadn't got back to her with that forwarding address – were still fresh in her mind, but she couldn't help but be aware of the extreme imbalance in the power dynamic between herself and her best friend/lodger. She told herself the situation was completely different; that Zoe wasn't an indentured servant; that she was free to turn round and say, *Actually, naw, I'm heading out for a night on the lash.* But she never did.

Three years ago, when Anna had first taken her in, Zoe had been in a seriously bad place: still reeling from the fallout of her involvement in the Shadow Men business and racked by guilt and grief over the death of her brother six years earlier, with which she'd never truly come to terms. She'd spent much of that first year getting back on track – going to therapy, taking long, solitary walks with no destination, and basically learning how to live again. In the second year, she'd made some half-hearted steps towards finding some form of employment, but hadn't been able to stick at anything for more than a couple of months before getting itchy feet. At one point, Anna had used some of the discretionary fund to which she had access in order to employ her as a research and admin assistant at the university – basically tabulating data, scheduling student tutorials, typing up the odd handwritten letter. It really wasn't a role that was tailored to her skillset, and Anna had often had to redo the work herself – a fact she took care to hide from her. When Zoe's contract had come to an end, they'd both reached an unspoken decision not to renew it.

Instead, over the last year and a bit, she'd settled into an almost exclusively childcare-focused role. She'd been helping out with Jack already anyway – bathing him and reading him stories and whatnot – but gradually, Anna's involvement in that side of things had grown less and Zoe's had grown more. Like her unrenewed contract with the university, they'd never discussed it – it had just evolved organically, with the result that there'd never been any sort of reckoning about whether this was a desirable or even healthy dynamic for them to have. Not for the first time, Anna found herself wondering if, on some level, she was keeping Zoe in stasis because it suited her from a childcare standpoint and because she enjoyed having her around.

Now, as she pushed open the door and stepped into the low-ceilinged, underlit pub, she half-wished she *had* brought Zoe as backup. She'd have been only marginally more at home here than Anna was, but the thought of strength in numbers held considerable appeal. The place wasn't exactly packed, but she knew she stuck out like a sore thumb among the exclusively male clientele, who all had that faint whiff of loneliness and disappointment about them, perched on stools at the bar or hunched over the tables lining the opposite wall.

She'd arrived a good fifteen minutes ahead of their agreed 7.30 p.m. meeting time, and yet the door had barely swung shut behind her when a voice called out to her over the warbling vocals of the old-timey ballad playing on the speakers.

'Anna?'

She turned towards the far end of the bar, where a short, pot-bellied man with a rumpled trench coat and a monk's shiny bald head was seated. The sort of guy who wouldn't look too out of place in a virtually deserted movie theatre first thing on a weekday morning – and who you'd make a point of not sitting too close to.

She gave a nod of acknowledgement and crossed the sticky floor towards him. As she halted before him, he looked her up and down, eyes lingering slightly too long on her breasts before coming to rest on her face.

'Found it all right, then.'

His speech was a little slurred, and she had the distinct impression that the smell of beer fumes in the air had become decidedly more pungent since she'd entered his proximity.

'Been here long?' she asked.

It wasn't meant as a dig, but she saw, from the brief flicker of annoyance that crossed his features, that he'd taken it as one. It was painfully obvious from both his condition and the empty pint glasses lined up by his elbow that he'd spent the last several hours racking up a sizeable tab. A tab which she'd already agreed to settle as recompense for his time.

Licking his hand, he slicked back the long, lank strands of hair that hung beneath his bald crown and gave an oily smile.

'What can I get you, darlin'?'

She ordered a Diet Coke, despite McEnaney's protestations ('Sure you'll not have a *proper* drink?'), and settled on the stool next to him. She'd have preferred a table, but she didn't feel in a position to insist. And there was, after all, something to be said for being somewhere visible, even if she had her doubts that either the barman or any of the clientele would make much effort to intervene if he tried anything on with her.

'So where'd you get your hands on my book?' he asked, once Anna's Coke had arrived, along with a fresh pint for him.

'Arizona,' she said, sipping from her glass without taking her eyes off him.

He made a face, his bushy black brows pinching together. 'Bloody second-hand market. You know I don't see a penny from those?'

She made what she hoped was a sympathetic expression. Given the way he'd repackaged the murders of a man and two young children as glorified wank fodder, she wasn't inclined to lose much sleep over having deprived him of a sale.

'I'm hoping to republish it in a new and improved edition,' he went on, when she said nothing. 'Bring eleven years' worth of hindsight to the table. But the publishers aren't interested. Sandra Morton's yesterday's news, and as for me – well, I'm no longer the hot young thing, am I?'

He squinted at her expectantly, inviting her to disagree. She didn't.

'No one wants to read the recollections of an experienced journalist,' he continued. 'Now it's eighteen-year-old "influencers" getting handed six-figure deals left, right and centre whose life experience amounts to the square root of bugger all.'

Still, at least you're not bitter about it.

'So,' said McEnaney, attempting to fold one short, stubby leg over the other and failing, 'you're writing a book yourself.'

'I am,' Anna confirmed, sticking to the same story she'd authorised Pamela to spin to Sandra. Given McEnaney's dogmatic attitude towards her guilt, she suspected his cooperation would be unlikely if he perceived her as trying to poke holes in the conviction. 'It mainly deals with women's experiences of the prison system, but I'm planning to include a section on the Morton investigation and its portrayal by the media. A sort of case study, if you like.'

'Well, hate to burst your bubble, missy,' said McEnaney, with no small amount of satisfaction, 'but between you and me, I reckon you'll have a job finding any fresh ground to cover. It's a crowded field already, and, not to toot my own horn, but it's been said that I wrote the final word on Sandra Morton.'

Play to his ego, play to his ego.

'Which is why I was so keen to arrange this meeting. I want to speak to someone who was actually there, and' – this nearly stuck in her craw as she said it – 'you're widely recognised as the foremost authority on the subject.'

'So you came looking for a crib sheet?' McEnaney gave an amused chuckle. 'All right, all right. I'm not averse to giving a newbie a leg up in the game – 'specially not when she's buying.'

As he spoke, his eyes strayed down to her knees, visible beneath the skirt she now fervently wished she hadn't worn.

'So what is it you want to know, darlin'?'

17

She got him to start at the beginning, setting him at his ease by inviting him to discuss his memories of how he first came to be involved in covering the case. As he launched into a blow-by-blow account of his escapades, she did her best to convey the impression of hanging on his every word, making sympathetic noises when he described being dispatched to Hillend while it was still dark and nodding sagely in agreement as he heaped opprobrium on the local press.

'Hadn't a clue what they were dealing with, those provincials,' he snorted. 'Bloody amateur hour, it was. All that lot were good for was writing about stolen tractors and runaway sheep. Never seen a case this big in their lives. Same with the local plods. When I got there, they were standing around gawping like a bunch of tourists. It's no wonder they called in the big guns.'

'Meaning Detective Superintendent Dalston.'

'Among others,' said McEnaney, preening.

'You had a close relationship with the police, I understand.'

'A *mutually beneficial* relationship, it might be fairer to say.'

Anna eyed him expectantly, inviting him to elaborate.

McEnaney smiled indulgently. Then, as if speaking to a wide-eyed child, he continued, 'That's how it works with the major investigations. You get to know the men working the case and they get to know you – 'specially when you're a bunch of out-of-towners, all kipping in the same hotels, propping up the same local bars after hours. Tongues become lubricated; things are said that weren't signed off by the press liaison officer.

'Of course,' he went on grandly, 'none of us were under any illusions as to what was for public consumption and what was strictly bar room talk. But if, say, they wanted to make it known they weren't entertaining the notion of break-in gone wrong ... ' He made a "greasing the wheels" gesture with his hand.

'So the police used you to influence the public mood,' said Anna.

'They didn't *use* me,' said McEnaney, affronted. 'I told you, it was a mutually beneficial relationship. Certainly, it was in their interests to get their side of the story across, and part of that was through the media. But don't be thinking I was some glorified stenographer, just regurgitating whatever I was told. I'll have you know I've got more than thirty years' experience as an investigative journalist under my belt. I'm more than capable of sorting the wheat from the chaff.'

'The reason I'm asking is that, from the word go, the coverage of Sandra was ... well, it was all quite one-sided, wasn't it? I don't just mean your own reporting. I'm talking across the board. Tabloid and broadsheet alike.'

'And what does that tell you?' McEnaney had the defensiveness of a man who'd been challenged on this subject before. 'If every paper in the land's saying the same thing, it's not because they've all been handed a script and told to parrot it unquestioningly. It means there's a consensus of opinion.'

He adjusted his position into one that he evidently believed would allow him to expound more readily. 'Take 9/11 as an example. Or the London tube bombings, or any other atrocity you can name. Open any paper the day after and they might have used slightly different words, but I guarantee they all said basically the same thing. Awful, catastrophic loss of life. Cowardly, subhuman perpetrators. Spare no effort in pursuit of justice. No one, not even the looniest lefty tract, was saying, "Well, actually we think those innocent people deserved it." He leant back with a self-satisfied shrug. 'I'd say the coverage was more than fair under the circumstances.'

'I really don't think that's a reasonable comparison,' said Anna. 'No one's saying Guy and the twins *deserved* to be murdered. But we're talking about every news outlet in the country lining up to condemn an individual before a shred of hard evidence emerged to put her in the frame.'

It hadn't taken much, she thought ruefully, for her to give in to her compulsion to relitigate the crimes of the press.

'Oh, come on,' McEnaney scoffed. 'It was obvious from the word go she was guilty as sin. There was never anyone else in contention.'

'Why? Why was it obvious?'

He shrugged. 'Because.' Then, as if repeating it somehow made his case more compelling, *'Because.'*

Anna continued to gaze at him expectantly.

McEnaney sighed, clearly regarding having to explain himself as an unreasonable imposition. 'When you've been in the game as long as I have, you develop a nose for that sort of thing. You get to be able to sniff out a wrong 'un a mile off, and Sandra Morton stank from the very start.'

'Just so we're clear,' said Anna, 'this is about intuition? It's not that the police tipped their hand to you that they had something on her – say, something that wouldn't stand up in court…'

'Like what?' said McEnaney, not hiding his amusement. 'A secret tape of her confessing that couldn't be used because someone didn't read her her rights first?' He cackled uproariously. 'That would've been a scoop and a half in and of itself. No,' he went on, once he'd regained his composure, 'there was no secret nod of the head or dodgy dossier passed under the table.'

'Oh,' said Anna quietly. For some time now, the thought had been percolating in her mind that the media's extreme antipathy towards Sandra might have been fuelled by some knowledge about her that, for whatever reason, they'd been unable to reveal. But no – it appeared it really *was* all just a matter of them collectively deciding, based on a gut feeling, that she was guilty.

'But we all knew it was her,' McEnaney went on grandly, as if to prove her very point, 'right from day one. And I think I speak for all my colleagues in the press when I say we knew we had a job to do, equal to or perhaps even greater than that of the police. We couldn't convict the cow ourselves, but we could give a voice to the ordinary man and woman on the street who wanted something *done.'*

'Uh-huh,' said Anna, unable to help herself. 'And where do the comments about her appearance, her promiscuity, her choice of clothing fit into that?'

McEnaney held up both hands. 'Hey, it's a free country. She was a public figure. She was fair game.' Seeing Anna's look, he sighed and rolled his eyes in what she supposed was meant as a gesture of admission. 'All right, some of it was pretty close to the knuckle, I'll grant you. The stuff about her whoring herself around and what have you. That sort of thing wouldn't fly in today's politically correct climate, where it's a woman's prerogative to spread her legs for as many blokes as'll have her. But, on balance, I reckon we captured the public mood.'

'Let me guess – you just hold up a mirror to society.'

'Hey.' McEnaney slammed his hand down on the bar-top, causing the contents of both their glasses to ripple and dance. 'If I wanted to pat myself on the back for making an upstanding contribution to society, I'd have become a charity worker. It's a business, nothing more. If I'd taken the moral high ground, someone else would have been more than happy to fill my place.'

Anna said nothing, but her contempt must have been writ large on her face, for McEnaney took one look at her and scoffed, shaking his head, as if unable to believe her naïveté.

'You weren't there. You have no idea how … ' – he waved a hand in the air vaguely, gesturing for the right word – ' … *febrile* the mood was then. How intense the pressure. Folk were angry. They wanted justice.'

'And you were more than happy to throw them some raw meat.'

But McEnaney didn't seem to have heard her. 'It was the height of the bad old days,' he continued. 'The police's reputation was in the sewer. They desperately needed a story where they were the good guys. And they were under tremendous pressure from above. The top brass was breathing down their necks. They wanted the case wrapped up in a neat little package with a ribbon on top. It's what the public wanted too. Last thing they needed was the thought of some madman on the loose who went round breaking into random people's homes and stabbing them to death in their beds. And, if the plods happened to have someone in the frame for it, and it suited them for that to be common knowledge, even if they couldn't come out and say it … ' He folded his arms and leaned back with a self-satisfied smirk. 'Besides, they got her bang to rights with the dodgy alibi. A jury of her peers found her guilty in a court of law. Case closed.'

'And you honestly don't think the way the press covered the case had any bearing on that verdict? You've no regrets about anything you wrote?'

'The only thing I regret,' McEnaney snapped, 'is not playing devil's advocate a tiny bit more. Not because I think that woman deserved better than she got, but because it would've put paid to all the accusations from do-gooders like you who want to turn her into some sort of Joan of Arc figure. Oh yes,' he smiled thinly as Anna's face once again betrayed her thoughts, 'I looked you up before I came here. I've got your number all right. You're one of those rad fem types who turn women killers into martyrs and make out they're all victims of "the patriarchy".' He made air quotes with his fingers. 'Folk like you are no better than those women who mail their knickers to men on death row. Well, I'm telling you, Sandra Morton's no victim. She's a vicious, murdering bitch who did what she did because she's pure, unrequited evil – not because—' He suddenly stopped midstream.

Anna looked up sharply. 'Not because what?'

'Nothing,' said McEnaney, altogether too quickly.

'No, you were going to say something. What was it?'

'It wasn't anything. Just local tittle-tattle.'

'I'd like to hear it all the same.'

McEnaney eyed Anna dubiously, a part of him perhaps wondering if what he said next would result in her treating him to another tongue-lashing. At length, his posture slackened as he relented.

'All right.'

He leaned in towards her, lowering his voice conspiratorially. Anna found herself battling the competing urges to recoil and to lean in herself in order to hear him.

'When I was digging into Sandra's past, doing research for the book, I picked up murmurings about something that happened when she was fourteen. Early on in 1981, she was off school for several weeks. Glandular fever, *allegedly*.' He did the air quotes thing again. 'But I heard from more than a couple of sources that, right around the time she took off, she was starting to show.'

'Show as in ... '

'As in up the duff.' McEnaney waggled his eyebrows suggestively. 'Seven or eight weeks later, she rematerialises – from a spell of recuperation staying with an aunt in Kyle of Lochalsh, supposedly – and she's her usual svelte self once more. Now, far be it for me to put two and two together and come up with five, but: teen pregnancy, family of Catholics, ergo "mortal sin", goes away suffering from some mystery ailment, comes back right as rain … Supposedly, the aunt was even bonking an obstetrician at the time.'

'You think she had an abortion.'

'Either that or she gave birth to something that would've stood no chance of surviving in the wild.'

'No, I suppose not,' said Anna quietly. She was thinking back to her own pregnancy and at what stage *she'd* first begun to show.

'And that's not all.' McEnaney raised an index finger. 'Once more, local tittle-tattle, usual caveats apply, yadda yadda yadda. But I heard the *real* scandal wasn't a fourteen-year-old girl getting knocked up. It was who did the knocking up.'

Anna began to feel slightly sick as she sensed where this was going.

'Apparently,' said McEnaney, 'it was an open secret in the neighbourhood that Daddy liked 'em young. Keep your daughters at arm's length from Old Man Morton, that sort of thing.' He gave a dirty chuckle. 'Now, I'm not saying this proves anything, but around the time of his darling daughter's "illness", he scarpered with the family chequebook and never showed his face in Fintry again.'

He looked at Anna expectantly, as if waiting for her to propose an alternative theory. Anna was far too busy trying to ignore her roiling stomach to formulate a response. She wasn't sure she was ready to believe this, though whether because she didn't think it credible or because it simply didn't bear thinking about, she couldn't say.

'You spoke to her older brother Fulton, didn't you?' she said, finally finding her voice. 'Did he have anything to say on this?'

'Shut me down the second I broached the topic. Which, if you think about it, lends weight both to the pregnancy being more than just a rumour *and* to them keeping it in the family, so to speak.'

'Maybe.' Anna wasn't convinced. 'This aunt … '

'Aunt Jackie,' said McEnaney. 'Mum's younger sister. Died a few years back, 'case that was going to be your question.'

It was. 'And did you ever put any of this to her?'

McEnaney affected the air of an injured pheasant. 'What sort of journalist d'you think I *am*? 'Course I did my due diligence.'

'And … ?'

'Soon as the words "pregnancy" and "abortion" passed my lips, she told me in no uncertain terms that she'd sue me into next Tuesday if a word of what I'd just said ever landed up in print. By then, she'd dumped the OB and shacked up with a lawyer. Now you tell me, do those seem like the actions of someone with nothing to hide?'

'Possibly not,' said Anna, still not entirely on board.

McEnaney smiled, altogether too pleased with himself given the subject matter. 'I'm just saying – knocked up by Daddy Dearest, spirited away under cover of dark for a termination, whole family sworn to secrecy… An experience like that would've given anyone mental problems. But enough to turn 'em into a psycho child-killer?' He sucked air through his teeth. 'Who can say?'

Once again, Anna said nothing. For a while now, she'd been considering the 'diminished responsibility' argument and how it might apply in Sandra's case. Was it possible that the catalyst for her actions had been some past trauma that, for whatever reason, had been triggered that night in May 2001? It certainly fitted with established patterns of female offending, where so many of those convicted of violent crimes were themselves victims of male-originated violence.

'When you think about it,' McEnaney's droning voice intruded on her thoughts, 'there's a pleasing sort of symmetry to it all, isn't there?'

'In what sense?'

'Well,' said McEnaney, in a tone that suggested it was obvious, 'it all kicks off with one brat being aborted, and ends with her stabbing another two to death alongside Hubby – who, in this scenario, may or may not have served as a stand-in for her old man. Kinda delicious when you think about it, isn't it?' He saw Anna's stony expression. 'No? Oh well.'

Anna didn't dignify that with a response.

McEnaney emptied the dregs of his glass down his gullet. 'And then of course there's Katie – the one that got away.' He signalled to the bartender for a fresh glass. 'We knew all about her, of course – that business with her living with the grandparents. But we weren't allowed to write about any of it. Bloody Children's and Young Person's Act.'

Anna succeeded in swallowing her disgust at McEnaney's earlier comments sufficiently to find her voice again. 'And you've no idea what that was all about. You didn't pick up any rumours.'

'Not a squeak. 'Course, that didn't stop us coming up with all sorts of suppositions – 'specially when we realised we couldn't report on it. There were a bunch of theories: that Sandra was neglecting her or locking her in the basement or what have you; that Guy and the grandparents had intervened to keep her safe. But we never came up with anything concrete.' He shook his head. 'It's a weird one and no mistake.'

Anna was silent. For perhaps the first time since she'd sat down, she found herself in total agreement with him.

'It's funny,' McEnaney mused, 'village that toaty's not exactly the sort of place anything stays under wraps for long. But then, they were a secretive bunch, the Mortons. Who knows what was really going on behind closed doors?'

Who knows indeed, thought Anna. Who could guess what went on behind *any* family's doors?

McEnaney scratched his jowls thoughtfully. 'Wonder what's become of her. That wee girl.'

'You've not picked up any word about her whereabouts, then.'

'If I had, you can bet your bottom dollar I'd have been on the first flight to Canada to pump her for all she's worth.' He sighed wistfully. 'Can you imagine the fortune to be made from *that* exclusive?'

Anna, who didn't really want to think about McEnaney pumping *anything*, declined to respond.

'They still around, out of interest?' McEnaney enquired. 'The old coffin-dodgers. The grandparents,' he clarified, seeming to read Anna's look as incomprehension rather than distaste. 'Eunice and George. Still in the land of the living, are they?'

'They are,' Anna replied stiffly. 'I tried to talk to them, but I got a chilly reception.'

McEnaney laughed mirthlessly. '*They* haven't changed, then. Got a similar response myself when I approached them about an interview for the book.' He cleared his throat noisily and, mercifully, washed the phlegm down with a mouthful of beer rather than spitting it out. 'You'd think they'd show a bit more gratitude towards a member of the press after the easy ride we gave them. We could've dragged them through the bloody mud – rescuing wee Katie but leaving the twins under the same roof as that monster. But we didn't,' he concluded, with great magnanimity. 'Let them keep their saintly reputation intact.'

Anna nodded distractedly, only half-processing what he was saying. She was, to put it mildly, less than fully convinced that this was a case of the grandparents having saved Katie but decided the other two children were expendable. All the same, though, she had to agree that the whole situation was beyond strange. For the umpteenth time, she cursed the fact that everyone who was in a position to enlighten her as to what had gone on inside the walls of that house was either untraceable or unwilling to talk to her.

'And Gunning?' said McEnaney. 'You've spoken to him?'

'I've tried. He won't take my calls.'

'Pity. Thick as thieves, him and Dalston. Old Malcolm practically worshipped the ground he walked on.' McEnaney gave a fatalistic sigh. 'But if he won't pick up the phone, there's not a whole lot you can do.'

'Did you have any direct dealings with Dalston at all?' Anna asked, pretending not to have noticed the gloating note in his voice. 'During the investigation, or …'

'I didn't have a direct line to him, if that's what you were asking. But his people kept me abreast of what was going on – made sure I was never left looking like a mug while some rival paper got a scoop.' He hacked up another mouthful of phlegm. 'I did do a couple of sit-down interviews with him for the book, though. There was even talk of him writing the foreword at one point. That would really have meant something – back then, his star was in the ascendancy. But when he saw the finished draft, he hit the roof. Said I'd made him look obsessive, blinkered, like he had tunnel vision.'

McEnaney shrugged philosophically. 'I thought I'd been more than fair to him. But he didn't see it that way. Threatened to sue if I didn't take out all the direct quotations from him and pull his name from the acknow-ledgements.' He gave a disgusted snort. 'Then I found out he was in talks to write an autobiography of his own, and suddenly it all made sense. 'Course, it never did see the light of day.' He folded his arms, clearly delighted at having had what he perceived as the last laugh.

An awkward silence settled. Anna sipped her Diet Coke gingerly, wondering how soon she could extricate herself from this encounter.

'Who else have you tried to track down?' said McEnaney, breaking the silence. 'You never know – I might be able to point you in the right direction.'

As much as she wished to be in as little debt to this odious man as she could possibly manage, Anna knew she couldn't afford to pass up this opportunity.

'Well, the two eyewitnesses, obviously,' she said. 'Adjoa Asante and Paul Kempley. They both seem to have dropped off the face of the earth.'

McEnaney smirked knowingly. 'That's the trouble with an open-door immigration policy. They come into the country, no one keeps track of them, they disappear below the radar ... '

'And Paul Kempley?'

'Tried to track him down myself back when I was writing the book. No dice.'

By the sound of it, he hadn't even *attempted* to track Adjoa down. It wasn't entirely surprising: in McEnaney's world, immigrants presumably had nothing of value to contribute beyond being an easy source of scaremongering headlines.

'And then there's Jeff Morton,' Anna said. 'After he went back to Canada—'

'Oh, he's back in Scotland now,' McEnaney said, quite offhandedly.

'He's *what*?'

'Returned to the motherland a few years back with his tail between his legs after his marriage and business venture both went tits up. He's staying in Troon now, in a natty little one-bedroom flat above a chippy. Just goes to show, we're none of us safe from the effects of Newton's law of gravity.'

His relish was tangible. Evidently Niall McEnaney was one of those people who came to terms with their own misfortune by taking comfort from the thought that there were others who had it just as bad or worse.

'How ... ' Anna began. Why the hell had it never occurred to her to look for Jeff in his country of birth? 'Never mind. Troon, you said?' She fumbled with her phone to make a note of it.

'That's right. Hey.'

Anna looked up.

'If you manage to persuade him to talk to you, maybe you'll put in a word for me? Might help to have one of the original cast on board if I'm to get this new edition off the ground.'

'I'll see what I can do,' she said, without really meaning it. She reached for her bag. 'And now I really do feel like I've taken up too much of your time.' Before McEnaney could get a word in, she turned to the bartender. 'Can we settle up, please?'

'You're not going already, are you?' McEnaney sounded surprised and disappointed in equal measure. 'I thought we only just got started.'

'I'm afraid I have to.' She'd already shouldered her bag.

'But ... but is there not anything else you want to know?'

Anna, now on her feet, gazed down at him and saw a lonely, desperate man whose former glory, such as it was, was long behind him. Despite everything he'd said and done that utterly nauseated her, she couldn't help but feel just a tiny bit sorry for him.

'If I think of anything else,' she said, 'I know how to get in touch.'

'Right.' McEnaney's disappointment, though momentary, was palpable. 'Well, one more for the road, then.'

He signalled to the bartender, who, fresh from presenting Anna with the bill, began to pull another pint. Anna looked at the tally – it was considerable, though not quite as considerable as she'd feared – and settled up. She extricated herself as smoothly as possible and left McEnaney nursing his latest pint. As she turned to glance back at him from the doorway, she suspected he'd probably be there till they turfed him out.

As Anna headed along the pavement towards Govan subway station, she checked her mobile for messages. The red dot next to the green phone icon told her she had a voicemail waiting for her. She tapped the icon and put her phone to her ear.

It was from Pamela Macklin. The solicitor was already mid-stream as the recording began, gabbling away in her usual breathless, borderline manic style. As Anna listened, she came to a standstill at the station entrance, incurring a stream of invective from a youth whose passage she'd inadvertently blocked. Ignoring him, she remained stationary as she listened to the message to its end. When Pamela's rambling, detour-strewn message finally ended, she lowered the phone slowly, still digesting what she'd just heard.

Sandra Morton had agreed to see her again. Their next meeting was scheduled for Monday afternoon.

18

Monday 8 April

Anna's escort for her second visit to Broadwood proved to be far less loquacious than Ruth Laxton. The redoubtable governor was nowhere to be seen today as the stone-faced, monosyllabic guard who'd met her in the Visitors' Centre led her to the same interview room as before, the set of keys clipped to his belt jangling with each step. He ushered her into the cramped, airless room with its tiny window, table and two chairs, then left her to it, the door closing behind him with an ominous clang.

As before, Anna took the seat facing the door and, to give her restless hands something to do, busied herself setting out her voice recorder and stationery. A part of her still wasn't prepared to believe that this meeting was actually going to happen until she saw Sandra in the flesh: she hadn't forgotten Ruth's stories of her keeping visiting dignitaries waiting for ages, only to renege at the eleventh hour.

Since her encounter with McEnaney, his revelations about Sandra's childhood, true or false, had seldom been far from Anna's mind. Even now, four days later, she still wasn't sure what to make of the information, or what to do with it. She'd gone back and forth umpteen times on whether to raise any of it with Sandra herself. She supposed she was just going to have to play it by ear; do what seemed right in the moment.

In one respect, she *had* made some progress in the last couple of days, even if it felt like a case of 'one step forward, another step back': thanks to McEnaney, she'd succeeded in locating Jeff Morton. It had required little effort on her part once she'd known where to look – namely, the telephone directory for Troon, where, as it turned out, he'd been hiding in plain sight all along. He'd been less than enthused about the prospect of talking to her about his memories of Sandra and the investigation when she'd rung him on Saturday morning, claiming he had a lot on and would need time to think about it. She nonetheless took heart from the fact that she'd got what amounted to a 'maybe' out of him rather than an outright refusal and had resolved not to push it, giving him time to come around to the idea rather than demand an immediate 'yes' or 'no' and risk getting the latter.

She heard approaching footsteps and straightened her back in readiness. When the door opened, the first person to enter was Bob, the middle-aged prison officer who'd served as chaperone last time round. Sandra came in behind him, once again wearing her grey sweater and red tabard combo, a book tucked under one arm. Her eyes lit up as they alighted on Anna.

'Professor Scavolini! We meet again. So we didn't scare you off for good last time.'

'Evidently not,' said Anna, as Sandra settled in the seat facing her.

Sandra's smile broadened. 'I'm so pleased. It's not often I have the pleasure of a repeat visitor. I tend to have something of a repelling effect on people,' she added in a theatrical whisper.

'I appreciate you agreeing to see me again,' said Anna, keen not to waste any time. 'I have some—'

'Just a moment,' Sandra interrupted. 'Before we get underway, I wondered if you might perhaps indulge me a little. Since we last spoke, I took the opportunity of procuring this.'

She slid the book across the tabletop. At the sight of the cover, Anna felt a bolt of electricity shooting up her spine.

RETHINKING JUSTICE: NEW APPROACHES TO FEMALE OFFENDING

ANNA SCAVOLINI

She picked it up, tracing its contours with her fingers. She'd had umpteen journal articles published over the years, and perhaps a dozen chapters in edited collections, but this was, to date, her only venture as the sole author of a self-contained published work. It hadn't been circulated widely, which made it all the more impressive that Sandra had managed to get her hands on a copy.

She looked up at Sandra, who affected a simpering, fangirlish smile.

'Would you be so kind as to do me the honour of adorning it with your autograph?'

Anna hesitated. She was deeply uncomfortable with the very idea, feeling that it somehow signalled their relationship as something more than merely that of interviewer and interviewee. And yet she couldn't deny that another part of her felt ever so slightly flattered ...

'Ah, go on.' Sandra clasped her hands under her chin like a child at prayer. 'It's not every day one gets to bask in the presence of a famous author.'

For a moment, Anna didn't respond. Then, unable to see any obvious harm in indulging the request and calculating that it might even encourage Sandra's cooperation, she picked up her pen and opened the book to the half-title. On the facing page, a black and white photograph of herself in a freshly ironed trouser suit stared back at her. Even now, it still made her cringe inwardly, the tight, pinch-lipped smile making her look unbearably smug, though in reality it had been the product of nerves rather than pride. She held her own gaze for a moment longer, then hastily scribbled her signature under the title, shut the book and slid it back across the table.

Sandra opened the book and inspected Anna's handiwork. Seemingly satisfied, she closed it and proffered it to her minder.

'Look after that for me, will you, Bob?'

Evidently used to such requests, Bob exhibited no surprise. He separated himself from the wall for long enough to take the book and tuck it under his arm before resuming his earlier pose.

'Feel free to have a browse while we're chatting,' Sandra told him. 'It's really rather thought-provoking.'

Bob grunted an acknowledgement but showed no inclination towards taking up her offer.

Sandra turned to face Anna, a knowing smile playing on her lips. 'So, you and wee Pamela have been trading notes on me, have you?'

Anna experienced a momentary surge of panic. 'Sorry?'

'Nice little sleight of hand using her as a go-between. Mrs Laxton would no doubt have conveniently mislaid your application if you'd gone through her.'

Anna felt her muscles unclenching.

'Exhausting, isn't she?' Sandra rolled her eyes. 'Like an eager little puppy trying to hump your leg.'

'She's just doing her best,' said Anna. As much as she agreed with Sandra's assessment, she nonetheless felt compelled to defend Pamela given that she wasn't there to account for herself.

'Oh, well, if she's doing her *best* …' Good intentions, in Sandra's world, seemingly didn't count for much. 'Still, I'm sure you didn't come all the way out here to discuss the merits – or lack thereof – of my legal representation.' She folded her hands on the table. 'So then, what shall we talk about?'

'Did Pamela tell you I've been rethinking the scope of my book? That I'm planning to include a chapter on your case?'

'Just one?' Sandra shook her head and tutted. 'How disappointing. I thought I'd have merited at *least* two. Yes, she told me, and I'll say to you what I said to her at the time: sounds like weapons-grade bollocks to me. I didn't have you pegged for one of those sickos who get their kicks drooling over true crime stories.'

'In fairness, I could hardly ignore the case,' said Anna carefully. 'Given its significance, I couldn't let it pass without *some* mention.'

'But it's been done to *death* – if you'll forgive the obvious pun.' Sandra leaned back into a full body stretch, arms above her head. 'It just seems like such a waste of your talents. Besides, I'd far rather continue our debate on the merits of the prison system.'

'If you've read the book, you'll already know my thoughts on—'

'But I want to hear them from *you*! An open exchange of ideas is so much more mentally stimulating. What makes you so reluctant to defend your ideological positions?'

'What makes *you* so reluctant to talk about the crime you're adamant you didn't commit?'

For a moment, Sandra didn't respond. She leaned forward, elbows on the table, chin resting on her folded hands as she regarded Anna with a look of amused understanding.

'You're trying to solve the case yourself, aren't you?' she said.

'I'm not,' said Anna automatically. 'I'm just—'

'You *are*. You're trying to figure out whether I really *did* do what they say I did. You've got it into your head that you're going to uncover some hole in the prosecution's case an entire army of lawyers managed to miss.'

Anna said nothing. There seemed no point in trying to deny it.

Sandra gave a delighted little chuckle. 'All right, Miss Marple. I'll play your little game. But I'm going to want something in return.'

'What's that?'

'A trade. We'll do swapsies. You answer my questions about your views on the prison system, I answer yours about the case.'

Again, Anna didn't respond. Not for the first time, Sandra seemed to have read her with disarming ease. She supposed she just had to thank her lucky stars that, as yet, she didn't appear to have divined Pamela's part in all of this.

'Of course,' Sandra mused, 'we can sit here playing "you show me yours, I'll show you mine" till the cows come home. One of us has time on her side. The other, I'd say, has . . . ' She looked up at the clock on the wall. 'Oh, about thirty-eight minutes.'

Anna stifled a sigh of exasperation. In so many respects, this reminded her of the sort of battles she'd had with Jack when he'd dig his heels in and refuse to do as he was told – only she somehow doubted she'd be able to threaten Sandra with no trip to the swing park if she didn't fall into line.

'Tell you what.' Sandra unfolded her arms and spread her palms. 'I'll give you a freebie to get us started. Go on – what's your most burning question?'

Anna didn't respond immediately. She was busy considering the upsides and downsides to going along with this ludicrous trade. The obvious downside was that she'd be acquiescing to spending a significant chunk of the forty-five minutes she'd been allocated going over a whole lot of well-trodden ground – no doubt purely so Sandra could belittle her views for her own amusement. But then, it wasn't as if refusing to play ball would be any more productive – other than in the sense that Sandra was likely to call a halt to the meeting there and then, allowing her to go home early but empty-handed.

She sighed inwardly. There was really no choice at all.

'All right,' she said, choosing her question carefully in case it was the only one she got to ask. 'Two separate witnesses, Adjoa Asante and Paul Kempley, both gave evidence which contradicted your alibi for the murders. If your account was true, then both of them must have been either mistaken or lying. Why would two completely unrelated witnesses both be wrong about your whereabouts?'

'You'd have to ask them,' said Sandra. Her sly smile left little doubt that she'd correctly surmised Anna had failed to trace them.

'I'm interested to hear your thoughts,' Anna said. 'I'll concede it's possible Adjoa Asante could have been mistaken, but Paul Kempley seems a bit of a stretch. With all the hue and cry, I don't imagine he'd have simply forgotten having served the woman whose face was plastered across the front page of every newspaper the following morning.'

'No,' Sandra agreed, 'I don't imagine he would have. Stared at my tits the entire time, the grubby little pervert. Mind you,' she added, with a philosophical shrug, 'can't say I entirely blame him. I wasn't exactly dressed for the occasion – and, if I say so myself, I didn't cut too shabby a figure in those days, 'specially for someone who'd squeezed out three ankle biters. Of course, that was before eighteen years of sedentary living, along with the sort of diet it should be illegal to feed to a pig. Hey!' Her eyes lit up. 'You should include that in your book – the adverse effects of prison food on inmates' physical wellbeing.'

'Well, then,' said Anna, ignoring this crack, 'why do you think he came down with such a severe case of amnesia?'

'Simple. Someone had a word in his ear.'

'That someone being—'

'My tormenter.'

'That doesn't make sense. Why would he perjure himself just because Dalston told him to?'

Sandra shrugged. 'Who can say? I can think of a dozen and one reasons why a slack-jawed youth would do what the big bad policeman told him. Maybe he'd been nabbed for smoking blow or buggering sheep and was told the charge could be made to disappear if he did as he was told? Or maybe he just had a general fear of authority figures. Plenty of people do. But like I said, that's a question for him. See also the receipt and painkillers that vanished when they took my clothes from me, and the CCTV that mysteriously failed to record that night. How truly convenient that there was no impartial record to prove, beyond a shred of doubt, whose account was accurate!

'And now,' she rubbed her hands with anticipation, 'it's my turn. *Now*' – she leaned forward towards Anna, hands steepled together in an imitation of an eager interview host – 'it's no secret that you're no fan of this country's approach to criminal justice. But I'm curious, is there a different model which *does* meet with your approval?'

'All this is covered in the book,' Anna protested, her skin prickling in irritation. 'I don't see what's to be gained by—' She managed to stop herself before she could say anything more. *Just play her game.* She sighed. 'All right. I think the Scandinavian model has a lot going for it.'

Sandra chuckled. 'Why am I not surprised? And why, pray tell, is that? What are our Nordic cousins getting so right that we get so wrong?'

'They don't routinely put women in places like this, for a start. They prioritise rehabilitation over punishment. Custodial sentences are viewed as a last resort, and when they *are* deemed necessary, every effort is made to maintain mothers' contact with their children and to ensure they serve their time in smaller, local prisons close to their own communities.'

'And what about the fact that Nordic society looks radically different from our own? These countries have a far stronger sense of collectivism baked into them. A greater willingness to comply with social norms. You think your average repeat offender fae Carnoustie is going to turn over a new leaf if you pat her on the head and tell her she has a responsibility to make a meaningful contribution to society?'

'And just why *is* this hypothetical woman from Carnoustie a repeat offender? Does the fact she keeps coming back for more not prove that the system isn't working?'

'Or that the punishment isn't harsh enough to act as an effective deterrent. But yes, a point well made. Score one to the Prof!' Sandra grinned. 'See? Isn't this fun? Your go.'

This time, Anna was ready right out the gate. 'I'd like to look at the various claims and counterclaims made by you and the police officers who dealt with you on the night of the murders. In several instances, one side disputed the other's version of events.'

'You're not going to waste another turn on "he said, she said", are you?' said Sandra, incredulous. 'All right, all right, it's your decision. Fire away.'

'For instance,' Anna continued, pretending Sandra hadn't spoken, 'the two officers who picked you up on Shaw Road claimed you asked them, "Are they all dead?" You've no memory of saying that?'

'I'd have to have been pretty fucking stupid if I had,' Sandra snapped. 'Talk about hanging a whopping great "guilty" sign round your own neck.'

Was it Anna's imagination or had Sandra's old, guttural accent from her Border Television interview just slipped through momentarily?

'One theory,' said Anna, choosing her words carefully, 'is that you suffered some sort of dissociative episode and killed Guy and the twins without knowing what you were doing. Then, when the police found you, you were disoriented, confused, with no memory of the incident—'

'Then it makes even less sense for me to have said it, doesn't it? If I offed them in a fit of blind delirium, I wouldn't have known I'd done it, so it wouldn't have occurred to me to ask.'

Anna, who had no ready-made response to this seemingly incontrovertible logic, bit the inside of her cheek and said nothing.

'My turn,' said Sandra, her tone now unmistakably chilly. 'Why do you hold women to a lower standard than men?'

Anna's jaw almost hit the floor. '*Excuse* me?'

'You infantilise them. You claim they're not responsible for their actions. It's been a recurring pattern in both your writing and your exchanges with me. But you'd never excuse a man for beating his wife to a pulp because of "systemic factors".'

'I'm not trying to excuse—'

'Yes you are. You're saying it's not really their fault if they turn to a life of crime because the mean, nasty man made them do it. They're victims of circumstance, society, the patriarchy – whatever. But in your eyes, a man who snaps because he's having a hard time at work and his wife is constantly nagging him at home isn't a victim of anything. He's just a bad man.'

Anna sighed inwardly and said nothing. However she responded, she knew Sandra would simply ignore or twist it to her own ends.

'Some women *are* just irredeemably bad, you know,' Sandra went on, 'and not because Daddy didn't show them enough love, or too much, but because that's the way they were born. Take Megan Dodds, my next-door neighbour on Barbour. Charming woman. Impeccable manners. Eight years ago, she killed her baby by putting it in the tumble dryer to stop it crying. And in those eight years, she's shown no remorse whatsoever. Tells her psychiatrist, first chance she gets, she's going to have another kid. Does *she* sound like the sort of woman who'd benefit from a nice, short stay in an open prison followed by a swift return to the bosom of society?'

'That's—'

'Or take me, if you prefer an example that's closer to home. Let's say, for talking's sake, that I really did what they say I did. What would you consider an appropriate punishment for me? A community order? A few rounds of talking therapy?' Her smile faded. 'Or perhaps, just perhaps, the judge got it absolutely right when he decreed that I would spend the rest of my natural life caged as far away from civilised society as possible.'

She fell silent. Outside, the sun moved behind a cloud, causing the room to suddenly darken. Anna watched Sandra out of the corner of her eye, trying not to make it obvious that she was studying her. She couldn't help noting that one of the first examples of a traumatic experience Sandra had gone to had been that of a father abusing his daughter. Had she merely plucked that out of the air at random, or was there more to it than that? She thought again of McEnaney's 'tittle-tattle' and swallowed heavily, the saliva sticking in her throat like glue.

She became aware that Sandra, in turn, was studying *her*, her head tilted to once side. She straightened up, suddenly self-conscious.

'What?'

'I make you uncomfortable, don't I? I disrupt your nice, ordered little view of the world, where men are bad and dangerous, and women are virtuous and vulnerable.'

'I—'

Don't worry – you're not alone. Feminists the world over are split down the middle on me. To some, I'm a gender traitor who's set the cause back decades. To others, I'm a *cause célèbre* – either because they're convinced I'm innocent and yet another victim of the male establishment crushing women under its jackboot or because they think I *did* do it and that makes me a hero for breaking the shackles of the patriarchal family unit. Of course, that view hasn't gained much traction outside of the lunatic fringe, but it's amazing what folk are willing to excuse in pursuit of an ideology.' Sandra glanced sidelong at the guard. 'Don't you think, Bob?'

Bob merely grunted. He, it seemed, held no strong views on the matter either way.

'Is there a question at the end of this,' said Anna, 'or is this just a treatise on how people like me are all idealistic tub-thumpers with no understanding of the real world?'

Sandra appeared not to have heard her. She sat in silence, gazing up towards the corner where the two walls and the ceiling met, seemingly lost in her own thoughts.

'D'you know what I'd do if they let me out?' she mused, after a moment.

Anna's curiosity got the better of her. 'What?'

'Binge on TV for a solid month.' Sandra turned to Anna with a dry smile. 'I haven't watched it since they put me away. Did you know, if I want a set in my cell, I need to pay for a rental?'

Anna shook her head.

'From time to time, I wonder if I should just pony up for one, but then I think, *No, don't give those petty bureaucrats the satisfaction.*' She paused for a moment. 'Is *ER* still on?'

'I think that finished about a decade ago.'

Sandra let out a low exhalation of disbelief. 'Unbelievable. You forget the world outside continues to turn because, in here, time doesn't move. Of course, I read newspapers and all that – I know, in a broad sense, what's going on out there. But somehow, in my mind it's still the spring of 2001. What were you doing in 2001?'

Anna considered the question. 'In Spring 2001, let's see … I'd just turned twenty. I was finishing up my second year of university.'

'Which means you're now thirty-eight.'

'Almost.'

Sandra shook her head. 'Jesus. Last time I breathed free air, I was younger than you are now.'

Anna watched as she once more gazed up towards the ceiling, a far-off look in her glacier-like eyes. Despite all her repeated mantras about objectivity and maintaining a healthy sense of detachment, despite the horrific nature of the crimes for which Sandra had been convicted, Anna felt a sudden, powerful paroxysm of sympathy for this woman who'd spent close to two decades in what amounted to solitary confinement, shut away from the rest of the world. Guilty or innocent, the state of limbo in which Sandra existed was so far removed from anything Anna had experienced herself, she could barely comprehend it.

They resumed their conversation, the earlier *quid pro quo* format having given way to a more free-flowing exchange of ideas. Sandra spoke about her experiences of prison – the dreadful food, the round-the-clock banging and shouting, the sclerotic pace at which each day unfolded. When you had nothing to look forward to except more of the same, she said, the passage of time ceased to have any meaningful significance. Especially if you were a lifer, the only way to avoid complete, soul-crushing despair was to take things one minute at a time, focusing entirely on reaching the next milestone – be it the next mealtime, your allotted hour in the exercise yard, or lights out.

All this was, of course, precisely the sort of detail Anna needed for her book, and it occurred to her as she listened that she'd forgotten to switch on her audio device, so wrong-footed had she been by being presented with a copy of her own book. And yet, when it came down to it, she saw no point in asking for permission to turn it on now – partly because she didn't want to derail the conversation, but partly too because it just didn't seem to matter to her anymore. The book was now so far down her list of priorities that she couldn't remember why it had ever gripped her imagination in the first place.

Along the way, she got the chance to slip in some questions pertaining to the case – questions which Sandra now seemed perfectly willing to answer, the demand that each of her responses be paid for in kind discarded by the wayside. In the process, Anna was able to clarify a handful of details about Sandra's purported movements on the night of the murders. Mostly, however, they merely served to establish that, close to two decades after the fact, Sandra continued to stick rigidly to the account she'd given to the police on 7 May 2001, down to the smallest detail. Anna would have dearly loved to ask more, of course, particularly about Katie and the particulars surrounding her moving out of the family home, but she knew better than to push her luck. She and Sandra seemed, against all the odds, to have established something approaching a genuine rapport. If they ever got as far as a third interview, perhaps she could afford to be more adventurous. For now, she resolved to play it safe.

They were comparing the differences between Broadwood and the old site at Cornton Vale when Anna glanced at her watch and saw that it was nearly quarter past three. They'd been talking for over an hour.

'Shit!' She scrambled to her feet.

'What?' Sandra's eyes flicked up sharply.

'The time. I need to pick up my son from playgroup in less than an hour.' She gave Sandra an apologetic grimace. 'We're going to have to call a halt, I'm afraid.'

'Pity. I felt we were well on our way to putting the world to rights.'

'I felt so too,' said Anna – wondering, as she spoke, whether she was merely being polite or if a part of her genuinely felt this to be the case.

'Well, any time you fancy picking up where we left off … ' Sandra's lip curled playfully. 'It's not often I have guests to entertain, and I do enjoy our little chats.'

Anna shouldered her satchel and stood before Sandra, gazing down at her with what she was now forced to acknowledge was genuine regret.

'I'd like that,' she said sincerely.

Sandra smiled enigmatically. 'Until next time, then.'

19

Anna hared along the road towards Hayburn Park playgroup, glancing at her watch as she ran. It was well after four. Until the point when the train from Broadwood had ground to an unceremonious halt just outside Queen Street Station, she'd still been labouring under the belief that she was going to make it in time. When it had become clear she wasn't, she'd rung Zoe to ask her to pick Jack up, but it had gone to voicemail. She'd then tried calling the playgroup itself, only for her phone to conk out while she was still keying in the number – the result of yet another late-night YouTubing session that had left her so shattered that, when she'd finally dragged herself to bed just shy of 2 a.m., it had completely slipped her mind to put it on to charge.

She hurried into the main hall, out of breath and perspiring freely, to find it deserted. Her eyes immediately racked to the coat stand by the far wall, where Jack's familiar red duffle coat looked devastatingly forlorn on its lonesome.

She felt her chest tightening, the pinpricks of pins and needles in her extremities and a growing lightheadedness that threatened to overwhelm her. Ever since Jack had come into her life, all the anxieties she'd once felt for herself had ended up being channelled into him. Where once she might have worried about missing an important appointment or, at the more severe end of the spectrum, running into the wrong man in a dark alleyway, her fears now ran the gamut from Jack missing one of his immunisations to this, the ultimate nightmare scenario for any parent.

Someone's taken him someone's taken him someone's taken him someone's taken—

'Excuse me. I think this one's yours.'

She swung around as a short-haired woman in a long-sleeve smock dress emerged from the doorway to the adjoining kitchen area, shepherding a small figure in front of her.

'Jack!' Anna almost sobbed with relief.

If she was expecting any sympathy from her offspring, she was fresh out of luck. Jack's mutinous expression told her just how he felt about having been kept waiting. Nonetheless, she hurried over to him and scooped him up into a hug. Jack, his body rigid in her arms, merely gurned and turned his head away.

Still clutching Jack, Anna turned her attention to the woman. 'God, I am *so* sorry. I thought I'd left in plenty of time, but the train from Croy got held up for absolutely ages at Queen Street, so of course I missed my connection to Hyndland, and then my phone ran out of—' She realised she was babbling and stopped, dipping her head in contrition. 'Sorry,' she muttered again.

'Well, you're here now,' said the woman cheerfully, 'so no harm done. I'm Simone, by the way – one of the play leaders. Everyone else has gone home, but I volunteered to stay behind with Jack till you got here. We figured you wouldn't be long. I was just fixing him a snack to keep him going. I hope that's OK.'

Anna nodded, slightly dazed. She was trying to remember whether she'd met Simone before. Most of the staff there were volunteers, fitting their sessions at the playgroup around day jobs or taking care of their own children, and the line-up of faces was constantly changing. It was hard to keep track of them all, especially when she only dropped Jack off or picked him up herself once in a blue moon.

'Well,' she said brightly, 'we'll be out of your hair now. Thanks for waiting with him.' She lowered Jack to the floor. 'Let's go find your coat, kiddo.'

'Just a sec.' Simone's voice stopped her in her tracks. 'I was wondering if I might have a word.'

Here it comes, Anna thought. *The inevitable and richly deserved you're-not-fit-to-be-a-parent speech.*

She nodded tightly, then turned to Jack. 'Go get your things.'

Jack headed off without a word, stomping across the hall towards the coat rack, clearly determined to make as much noise as possible.

Anna turned to face Simone. 'I'm *sorry* I was so late,' she began. 'I know there's no excuse, but you know it's not something I normally—'

'Oh, it's nothing to do with that,' said Simone. 'These things happen to the best of us. What I actually wanted to ask was … how should I put this? Does Jack have any friends his own age outside playgroup?'

Anna simply stared at her, not knowing what to say. Of all the possible turns she'd anticipated this conversation taking, this was positively the last.

'The only reason I ask is that … well, Jack's very good with puzzles and problem-solving, and for a child his age, his vocabulary is frankly intimidating. But when it comes to his interaction with the other children … well, he does seem to prefer his own company, doesn't he?'

Anna's instinctual response was one of defensiveness. *There's nothing wrong with preferring your own company,* she wanted to say. *It's often a hell of a lot more enjoyable than the alternatives.* But then, she wasn't sure why she was getting so prickly about this. Was it because Simone was being an interfering busybody – or was it because she recognised she had a point?

'I've got a little boy myself, you know,' Simone went on, oblivious to Anna's thoughts.

'Oh?'

'Oscar. He's Jack's age, only he goes to Partickhill.' Simone made a rueful face. 'I didn't think it would be fair, making him attend the same playgroup where his mummy works. He's a lot like Jack, in fact – very focused, very driven, but not too hot at the whole social interaction side of things. Anyway, I was thinking – how would you feel about perhaps setting up a playdate for the two of them? Of course, you don't have to,' she added hastily, 'not if you don't want to. The last thing I want to do is muscle in where I'm not wanted. But I reckon it'd do them both a world of good and … well, the offer's there.'

For a moment, Anna didn't respond. She remembered only too well the various playdates her parents had engineered for her when she was younger, usually involving some child with whom she had nothing whatsoever in common. Given the choice, she would far rather Jack develop friendships in his own way and at his own pace rather than being forced into ones concocted by well-meaning but meddlesome grown-ups. But then, she sometimes wondered whether, if she'd made more of an effort to get along, or if her parents had persisted just a little harder in their efforts to get her to socialise, she wouldn't have grown up to be such an awkward, cantankerous so-and-so who could count her close friends on one hand. At the very least, she supposed it wouldn't hurt to try it just the once.

She managed a warm smile. 'That sounds like a lovely idea.'

'Really?' Simone's whole face lit up with delight – or was it relief? 'Oh, that's marvellous. We really must arrange something soon.'

'Yes,' Anna agreed, getting out her phone. 'We should …'

She trailed off, remembering the battery was dead, and smiled ruefully. As she and Simone exchanged some awkward laughter, Jack materialised by her side, trailing his coat behind him. He glowered up at her.

'Go now?' he said.

They made their way up the road, Jack trudging alongside Anna, squeezing her hand with a ferocity that belied his diminutive stature. His interaction with the other children might leave something to be desired, but if there was one thing he *was* good at, it was making her feel like a world-class heel.

At length, she broke the silence.

'Are you mad at me, Jack?'

Jack considered the question, then nodded vehemently.

'Bad Mummy,' said Anna ruefully.

Jack nodded emphatically. 'Bad Mummy.'

'Rectum?'

'Rectum.'

She almost laughed but managed to stop herself, fearful of putting his nose even further out of joint. One of the unanticipated challenges of being the mother to a young child was that you never quite knew which iteration of them you were going to get. Right now, it was the sullen, uncommunicative version, but he might just as easily turn, in the blink of an eye, into the hyperactive, carefree Jack who wanted to ride on her back or run through the house with no pants on while she chased after him. Almost every day, something about him changed, hitting her in the solar plexus with the realisation that he was no longer the newborn who'd suckled at her breast and nestled against her in his sling. His personality, his appearance, his voice were all in constant flux, and the lack of a steady anchor onto which she could latch was something which she found profoundly disorientating.

As they reached the front steps to the house, the door swung open and Zoe came bounding out, a massive grin plastered on her face.

'You are *not* gonnae believe it,' she said, as Anna alighted on the top step. 'I have got *the* most amazing surprise for yous.'

'What is it?' said Anna, a little apprehensively. 'And how come you weren't picking up your phone?'

Zoe rolled her eyes. 'It's a *surprise*, fannybaws. 'Mon through to the living room.'

Mystified, Anna followed her. Jack, who had a far more favourable view of surprises than she did, trotted eagerly ahead of her. They stepped into the room to find a woman standing with her back to them, gazing out of the large bay window.

'Surprise!' boomed Zoe.

The woman turned to face them. She was in her mid-sixties, perhaps a little over five feet tall, with frizzy, shoulder-length hair, narrow shoulders and thin, pinched lips that made it look like she was permanently sucking on a sour lemon. She wore a navy-blue blazer, matching trousers and a cream-coloured blouse with a frill collar. As Anna's stomach lurched into her throat, the woman looked from her to Jack and back to her again.

'Well, Anna,' she said coolly, 'you *have* been busy, haven't you?'

Anna swallowed heavily.

'Hello, Mother,' she said.

PART THREE

TALK TO ME, TALK TO ME

20

The group that sat down to dinner at the kitchen table that evening might best have been described as eclectic. Of the four of them, only Zoe seemed fully at ease. Anna sat with her shoulders drawn in defensively, every muscle in her body tensed for battle, while Jack, his food largely untouched, gazed wide-eyed at the strange woman seated opposite him who, an hour earlier, had bent down to give him a formal peck on the cheek and said, 'Well, young man, aren't *you* a handsome specimen?'

The meal Anna had thrown together reflected her present mental state: a mismatched jumble of cold cuts; a hastily arranged salad; a couple of hunks of cheese; half a baguette, slightly stale – basically, whatever she'd been able to find in the fridge. She watched her mother, who'd always had decidedly bird-like eating habits, adding items to her plate as if they were charged by the milligram. A lettuce leaf here, a couple of cherry tomatoes there … As she poked and prodded the meat platter with her fork, searching for a cut that met with her approval, Anna noted that her attitude towards religious observance remained as selective as ever: not so intractable that she'd go hungry rather than eat non-kosher chicken, but drawing the line at anything that came from a pig.

Over the clatter of cutlery and chewing of food, the conversation ebbed and flowed, with her mother and Zoe doing all the heavy lifting. To give Leah Scavolini her due, she appeared remarkably unfazed by her newly discovered status as a grandmother. Zoe, who'd been like a pig in the proverbial all evening, hung on her every word, responding to each fresh utterance as if it was the most fascinating thing ever, her periodic *no way*s and *aw, I know*s setting Anna's teeth on edge. She sat in sullen silence at the head of the table, picking disinterestedly at her plate and stoking the grievance that burned inside her. There were any number of questions with which she'd dearly have loved to confront her mother, but there was one in particular that she kept circling back to:

What the hell are you doing *here?*

'How was your flight?' Zoe asked Leah, through a mouthful of bread piled high with ham and cheese.

'*Dreadful.*' Leah's verdict was unequivocal. 'For my sins, I was seated directly behind an entire family of noisy Middle Easterners. Jibber-jabbered the whole way to each other about goodness knows what.'

'How inconsiderate of them,' said Anna, 'speaking a language *you* can't eavesdrop on.'

'I'm just *saying,*' Leah said, addressing her response to Zoe, 'not everyone appreciates a running commentary while they're trying to catch forty winks. I'd have said the same if they were speaking English, French or Esperanto.'

'So why mention them being Middle Eastern?'

Leah sighed. 'Oh, for goodness sake.'

'What brings you to town, then?' Zoe asked, giving voice to the very question that was at the forefront of Anna's mind.

'Oh, you know.' Leah waved a hand airily. 'Felt it was high time I paid the old Dear Green Place a visit. After all these years, I'm a Glasgow girl at heart.'

Anna let out an involuntary 'Ha!' of contempt. As Leah looked sharply in her direction, Zoe once again dived in to salvage the situation.

'Well, it's totally amazeballs tae see you. So is this a flying visit, or … ?'

'I've yet to decide,' said Leah, with a certain amount of relish which Anna felt sure was directed at her. 'There are a few things I want to do while I'm here. People I'd like to look up.' She glanced pointedly in Jack's direction. 'I appear to have a lot of catching up to do.'

'And how's bonny Saint-Tropez?' Zoe went on, either failing to pick up on the tension in the air or putting in an Oscar-worthy performance pretending not to notice. 'Bet ye're still terrorising the local hunks, aren't ye?'

'Now, Zoe,' Leah brushed imaginary crumbs from her blazer, 'I did very little terrorising, even in my younger years – as you well know.' But she caught Zoe's eye as she spoke, and a conspiratorial look passed between them which, for reasons Anna couldn't explain, only served to enrage her even more.

At length, she became aware that Leah had stopped eating altogether and was watching her, frowning slightly as if trying to make sense of something.

Anna put down her fork and shrugged belligerently. 'What?'

'You've put on weight,' said Leah. She stated it as if she'd only just noticed, but Anna could tell, from the calculated nature of her delivery, that she'd been working up to it for some time. 'You can see it around your cheeks and your bust. You were always a top-heavy girl, but you need to watch you don't put on any more. Carrying too much excess weight never looks good on short women.'

Anna glowered and said nothing. This was a sore point for her. She knew she was heavier now than in her pre-pregnancy glory days. Not by much, but the dreaded baby weight had stubbornly refused to shift – exacerbated, in no small part, by the far more sedentary lifestyle she'd adopted since going on sabbatical.

'Sure I think she looks grand the way she is,' said Zoe cheerily. 'Better tae have a bit of meat on yer bones than be a complete skinnymalink.'

Leah turned to Zoe with a beatific smile. 'I think you look lovely as well, Zoe. I like what you've done with your hair. It makes you appear very grown-up.'

Zoe beamed. 'Aw, cheers, Mrs S. I like what *you've* done wi yer face. Ye'd hardly know it'd had any work.'

If Anna had said anything even remotely close to this, it would have triggered a Fukushima-level meltdown. But because it was Zoe, Leah merely threw back her head and laughed uproariously.

'Oh Zoe, you're a caution! Promise me you'll never change.'

In the vacuum that followed, Jack – who, so far, hadn't spoken to Leah other than to give monosyllabic responses to her occasional questions, but had been studying her with quiet interest for some time – suddenly piped up:

'Are you the Child Catcher?'

Leah turned to look at Jack, blinking in surprise and confusion. 'Excuse me?'

'Mummy says if I'm bad, Child Catcher'll come to take me away.'

Leah stared first at Jack, then at Anna, who suddenly found herself both extremely flustered and incredibly tongue-tied.

'I ... I ... I never said that,' she stammered. 'That was ... a reference ... to the film ... and ... ' She turned to Jack, giving him as reassuring a smile as she could muster. 'No one's coming to take you away, Jack.'

As Jack continued to look nonplussed, Leah, evidently concerned for his state of mind, reached across the table and patted his hand. 'I'm not the Child Catcher,' she assured him. 'Would you like to know who I *am*?'

Jack nodded, wide-eyed.

'Well,' said Leah, with a slight wince, as if she was apologising for the thoroughly unorthodox circumstances surrounding this introduction, 'it just so happens I'm your grandmother.'

For a moment, Jack merely gazed back at her, his expression not changing. 'Oh,' he said eventually, then stuck a piece of bread and butter in his mouth, the matter clearly of no further interest to him.

Leah shot Anna a dark look, the meaning behind which Anna understood all too well. She shrugged, pretending to be none the wiser, and busied herself nudging a cherry tomato around her plate with her fork.

'Mind like a steel trap, this one,' said Zoe, with considerable pride. 'He can ream off every train station fae here to Balloch.' She turned to Jack with an encouraging smile. 'Go on, munchkin. Say yer party piece.'

But Jack merely shook his head and looked down at his plate.

'Aww, he's just shy around new people,' Zoe told Leah. 'He'll come round tae ye.'

Leah pursed her lips in consternation, gave Anna another disapproving look, as if she viewed Jack's shyness as a black mark against his mother's character, and reached for the water jug to refill her glass.

'Aye,' Zoe continued to gaze at Jack approvingly, 'right wee brain-box, so he is. Takes after his mammy in that respect. Ye know Anna's a professor now?'

'A professor?' Leah set the jug down and turned to Anna with a frown. 'I thought you were one of those already.'

'No, Mother.' Anna spoke through gritted teeth. 'I was a Senior Lecturer in Criminology. Now I'm a *Professor* of Criminology. It's not the same thing.'

Leah pursed her lips and gave one of her trademark 'what a silly thing to get worked up over' laughs. 'I'm confused. I'm sure you told me, nigh on a decade ago, that you'd been made a professor.'

'That was—' Anna began, before stopping herself. She wasn't sure whether her mother was intentionally winding her up, but either way, it was certainly having that effect. She took a deep breath, then began again, trying to speak calmly and levelly.

'In Italian universities, all faculty positions above researcher level include the title *professore*, but over here it's a considerably more prestigious appointment. Only those at the very top of their field ever make it.'

'I see,' said Leah, who clearly didn't. 'So you've had to jump through two separate sets of hoops just to get the same job title. If you ask me, it hardly seems worth the effort.'

Well, I didn't *ask you,* Anna thought.

'And what does it get you, this new, old title?'

Anna was thrown by this question. 'Well . . . status? The respect of my peers?'

'But not a pay rise.'

'Well, a nominal one.'

Leah gave a self-satisfied little tut.

'If money was my sole concern, I'd be in the wrong career, wouldn't I?' Anna snapped.

Leah sighed, as if Anna was being deliberately obtuse. 'Lecturer, professor – it's all just so terribly abstract. I've always said, if you can't define a job in three words or less, it's—'

'—not a real job,' Anna finished. 'And *I've* always said, if you're incapable of understanding a concept unless it's boiled down to words of one syllable, that's a *you* problem.'

'Take your father, for instance,' Leah went on, ignoring her. '*He* had a real job.'

'Stop.' There was a warning note in Anna's voice.

'He worked hard every day in his life, providing for his family. And to this day, you and I continue to reap the benefits.' Leah gave Anna a withering look. 'What – you're not going to pretend you could have afforded this house on your *college* salary? I know about the nice little nest-egg he left for you, even if you never—'

'Well, I think it's important tae have a healthy balance.' Zoe's voice sounded unnaturally loud and breathless as she cut Leah off. 'A well-paying job's grand an' aw, but if it's no bringing ye any joy ... well, living tae work's no really living at all, is it?'

'And what is it *you* do, Zoe?' Leah enquired, any interest in Anna's career immediately forgotten. 'I bet *you've* got a job you can define in three words.'

'Do we really want to spend the entire meal talking about people's jobs?' Anna interjected, before Zoe could respond.

As Leah looked at her curiously, she shut her mouth with a snap, immediately wishing she could take her words back. She'd intervened in an attempt to avert any potential embarrassment, but she now wondered precisely whose blushes she was trying to spare – Zoe's or her own.

''S OK, Anna,' said Zoe evenly, before turning to Leah once more. 'Actually, I'm no in work at the moment, Mrs S. The right job hasnae come along, plus I went through some bad shit ... sorry, some bad stuff a while back, so I'm sorta taking a wee bit of time out. But I'm happy helping out with Jack and that.'

Leah took all this in, her expression unchanging, then smiled approvingly. 'Well, I must say, I'm glad to hear you're taking your own self-care seriously. I wish more people would take a leaf out of your book.' She shot a meaningful glance in Anna's direction. 'It really doesn't do to get so wound up all the time.'

Not trusting herself to say anything, Anna shoved a crust of bread in her mouth and chewed in sullen silence.

The meal continued with no sign of the tension abating. By seven-thirty, Jack was yawning every thirty seconds and clearly struggling to keep his eyes open – a fact which Anna swiftly seized on as an excuse to make good her escape.

'Right, you.' She scooped him out of his seat and into her arms. 'Time for bed.'

'D'ye no want me tae do it?' said Zoe. 'Give ye more time tae catch up wi yer mum?'

Abso-bloody-lutely not, Anna thought. 'It's fine,' she said breezily, already heading for the door. 'I'll be fifteen minutes, tops.'

Fifteen minutes proved to be an overly generous estimate. She got Jack changed into his pyjamas and into bed, then settled next to him with his well-thumbed copy of *The Very Hungry Caterpillar.*

'Where Zoe?' demanded Jack, features pursed into a bewildered frown.

'Zoe's keeping your grandmother entertained,' said Anna. 'I'm afraid you've got me tonight.'

'No!' Jack picked up his pillow and hurled it in her direction. 'Want Zoe.'

Deep breaths, Anna. 'Well, you can't *have* Zoe. She's busy. Now settle down and listen. "In the light of the moon, a little egg—"'

But by now, Jack had kicked off the covers and was on his feet, bouncing up and down. 'Want Zoe! Want Zoe!'

In the end, Anna was forced to admit defeat. Head low, she sloped back downstairs to the kitchen, where Zoe and Leah were deep in conversation about Leah's views on French cuisine (uncharitable).

'He wants you,' she muttered to Zoe.

An uneasy silence lingered as Zoe got to her feet and headed for the stairs. Anna reluctantly resumed her seat, unable to look her mother in the eye. Leah waited till Zoe's footsteps receded before drawing an intake of breath.

'Don't say it,' said Anna.

'Say what?'

'Whatever you were going to say.'

'Well, that's rather limiting. As it happens, I was going to ask if Jack's often difficult when you're putting him to bed.'

'He's not "difficult",' Anna snapped. 'He just wants Zoe to read to him tonight.' *And every other night.*

Leah sipped her water, all the while regarding Anna appraisingly. 'You know, if you simply roll over every time he gives you trouble, he's going to grow up expecting to always get his way.'

'I see. *Spare the rod and spoil the child.* Well, forgive me if I don't think tough love is conducive to raising a happy, well-adjusted child.'

Leah sighed. 'There's no need to be so melodramatic. Was I ever cruel to you?'

Anna didn't dignify that with a response.

'Of course not,' Leah went on. 'But we laid down boundaries, your father and I. We provided you with *structure*. And I like to think it paid off, even if you *do* delight in rubbing my nose in all the ways—'

'Hey.' Anna's eyes flared. 'When I want advice from you on how to raise my son—'

'My *grandson*!' Leah shot back, with a vehemence Anna wasn't expecting. 'My three-year-old grandson of whose existence I only learned this afternoon.'

Her words seemed to reverberate in the silence that filled the room. She looked at Anna with a mixture of hurt and incredulity.

'Were you *ever* planning to tell me?'

'I was going to,' said Anna, automatically defensive. 'It just wasn't something that came up.'

'In all our phone calls, it never once occurred to you to mention it?'

'*All* our phone calls? We have a couple a year at best.'

'That's still at least six!'

Anna had no response to this. She simply stared across the table at her mother, her expression incredulous.

'Why are you even *here*?'

Leah sniffed. 'I came to visit *you*, didn't I?'

'But *why*? Why now, after all these years? You – what, just decided on a whim to rock up out of the blue?'

Leah shrugged irritably and said nothing. In the silence that followed, Anna's eyes widened as realisation dawned.

'You've broken up with whatsisname, haven't you?'

Leah merely folded her arms and pursed her lips, avoiding Anna's eyes.

'Oh my God, you *have*!' There was a note of glee in Anna's voice that she didn't even *attempt* to curb. '*That's* why you're here. Trade you in for a younger model, did he?'

'We haven't broken up,' Leah replied stiffly. 'We're just…on a bit of a break, that's all.'

'Well, if you *will* insist on chasing after blokes half your age…'

Her mother snorted. 'You're one to talk – burning through men like tissue paper, none of them ever living up to your lofty ideals. How often *does* Jack see his father, out of interest?'

Anna said nothing.

'Does he even *know* he has a father?'

Silence.

'Well, there's the problem right there,' said Leah, with some satisfaction. 'Is it any wonder he acts out, without a proper role model to teach him right from wrong?'

'He has me,' said Anna, through clenched teeth.

Leah gave a strained, thoroughly patronising smile. 'I know you feel the need to flout your feminist credentials at every turn, but it really oughtn't to come at the expense of your own son's wellbeing. All the experts agree – a child should have both a mother and a father.'

This had always been one of her favourite debating tactics: claiming that there was universal expert agreement to support whatever spurious point she'd just made, then refusing to listen to any evidence to the contrary. Under any normal circumstances, Anna would have had all the facts ready to throw at her. Right now, though, she was too angry to think straight. She scraped back her chair and got to her feet, glowering at her mother with unbridled fury.

'Yeah, well,' she snapped, 'I didn't find having either to be anything to write home about.'

With that, she stormed out of the kitchen, grabbed her coat and marched out into the gloaming, slamming the front door behind her.

21

'It's pure braw having yer mum here,' declared Zoe, perching on the end of her bed as she tugged off her leggings. 'Who'da thunk it?'

Anna, already changed into her night things and sitting propped up against the headboard on the other side of the bed, made a non-committal noise at the back of her throat and said nothing. With Leah having arranged no accommodation for herself and all three bedrooms in use, there'd been no choice but for two of the four people under the roof to double up. Faced with the unappetising prospect of sharing a bed with her own mother, Anna had grudgingly surrendered her room to her and retreated down the corridor to Zoe's with the armful of clothes she'd hastily grabbed.

'Tell ye,' Zoe went on as she continued to get undressed, 'I got the shock of my life when I opened the door tae find her parked on the doorstep. Mind you, she hasnae changed one iota – and I'm no just talking about the Botox. Still the same old battle-axe through and through.'

'You're not wrong there.'

'And nice for Jacko tae finally meet his granny.'

Anna opened her mouth to respond, then changed her mind. Zoe wasn't stupid. There was no way she'd failed to pick up on the tension between mother and daughter, even if she wasn't fully clued into the specifics. Her pretence that everything was hunky-dory was beginning to wear seriously thin, and yet Anna hadn't the heart to tell her to cut it out. She knew that Zoe, in her own slightly guileless way, was doing her best to keep the peace, even if that meant putting on an act which no one, herself included, was seriously buying.

Zoe slipped under the covers and turned to face Anna, chin propped up on her elbow.

'Y'all right, love?'

Anna nodded tightly. 'I'm fine. Just … busy day.'

'Aye, nae kidding. So how'd it go earlier? Yer trip tae the jail?'

Anna felt her shoulders tensing. Her mother's return had obliterated Sandra Morton from her mind, but now Zoe had broached the subject, all her unprocessed thoughts from today's interview came flooding back.

'It was productive … ' she said, 'I think.'

Zoe was silent for a moment, her eyes not leaving Anna's face. 'You were seeing *her* again, weren't ye?'

Anna, knowing all too well Zoe's thoughts on the matter, was on the verge of denying it, but she stopped herself. She and Zoe didn't have secrets – at least, not that she knew of.

'I was, yeah.'

'Proper got under yer skin, hasn't she?'

'I suppose.'

'Ye think she didnae do it?'

'I … ' Anna began, then stopped, not sure how to answer that question. She was silent for several heartbeats, chewing on her bottom lip.

'I think,' she said eventually, 'I think there are definitely questions that haven't been adequately answered. And until I get those answers, I'm not going to let this go.'

For a moment, Zoe continued to eyeball Anna without saying anything, her expression giving nothing away. Then she sighed, her features crinkling into a forbearing smile.

'Well, that's you tae a T, in't it? Ye're an obstinate auld boot, but I wouldnae have ye any other way.'

She squeezed Anna's shoulder, then leaned over and turned out the light.

'By the by,' she added, as they lay side by side in darkness, 'if I start snoring in the night, just roll me over like a beached whale.'

Anna smiled. 'Will do, bestie.'

Long after Zoe succumbed to sleep, her snoring, for now, at a tolerable level, Anna lay awake, gazing up at the ceiling, her mind refusing to power down for the night. Like the bursting of a dam, Leah's return had unleashed a flood of old memories which now swirled around inside her head, dislodged from time and place. They were scattershot, a tumult of semi-coherent images and snatches of conversation. Gradually, though, the babel coalesced into a single, isolated event which she remembered as clearly as if it had been yesterday.

It was a warm evening in the summer of 1999, she'd recently turned eighteen, and the envelope had arrived earlier that day containing her all-important sixth year exam results. Four straight As – Maths, English, Sociology, Biology. A testament to all the long hours she'd put in studying, and one that left her with the luxury of her choice of the various courses she'd applied for at a variety of different universities. Each one of them would have fallen over themselves to have her. But there was only one she wanted. Only one she'd *ever* truly wanted, despite the umpteen other applications she'd fired off to appease her parents. And now the inevitable moment of confrontation had arrived.

Silence hung thick in the living room of the house on Cleveden Road, the late evening birdsong muffled to a distant chirp by the double glazing. Anna stood resolute, feet planted apart, fists bunched by her sides. Her mother sat on the sofa, arms folded, chin tucked into her neck. Her father occupied the straight-backed wicker chair that sat perpendicular to the sofa, resting his hand on his cheek, fist bunched but for the index finger that extended upwards, rhythmically stroking the skin in front of his ear as he contemplated a spot on the otherwise pristine carpet.

'No,' he said finally.

'What d'you mean, no?' Anna's voice sounded shrill and intransigent in her own ears.

'I mean forget it.'

'I'm going to Rome.'

From the sofa, she heard her mother sigh and tut under her breath.

Tall, thin and long-limbed, Francesco Scavolini unfolded himself from his chair. It had always been a source of some amusement to Anna that, while both she and her mother barely surpassed five feet on a good day, her father towered over them both at six foot four. His neck, normally hunched due to a lifetime of adapting to a world not designed to accommodate tall people, was, for once, perfectly straight as he regarded his daughter with cold, barely suppressed fury.

'Say it, then,' he ordered her. 'Lay out for us just what it is you're proposing to do.'

Anna met his eyes, her gaze unwavering. 'I'm going to study sociology and psychology at the Sapienza,' she recited in a monotone, 'then, once I've completed my doctorate, apply to be a lecturer in criminology.'

Her father shook his head.

'You can't stop me. I'm an adult. You haven't got any power over me.'

'It's not about "stopping" you.' Francesco pinched the bridge of his nose, as if the very act of saying this physically pained him. 'It's about being practical. How many positions are there out there for criminology lecturers?' He left a brief silence, which she instinctively recognised was intended not so she could respond but for her to consider his point. 'Not a lot, I imagine. You've invented this … this dream scenario for yourself, putting all your eggs in one basket, just assuming it's all going to work out. Well, what if it doesn't? What if it all goes belly-up? What then? What's your fallback?'

'I don't *need* a fallback,' Anna retorted. 'It's going to happen. I know because I'm going to *make* it happen.'

Her father sighed. 'I know you think that now, but you're making the mistake of confusing the world as it *is* with the world as you'd like it to *be*. And in all likelihood, you're going to end up with a qualification that's of extremely limited value outside a highly overcrowded field.'

Anna folded her arms. 'Can I ask a question?'

Her father gestured for her to go on. 'Please.'

'Why the sudden concern? You were happy enough to watch me apply for it – this degree you're so convinced is a one-way ticket to penury. Why wait till I've got the results I need to get in before bringing it up?'

'Because we didn't think you'd get them!'

His sudden, uncontrolled outburst reverberated in the light fixtures and the glass bowl on the coffee table. A stone cold silence descended on the room. Anna felt her shoulders drawing in, her jaw tightening, her breathing becoming low and shallow.

To give him some credit, her father clearly realised he'd gone too far. 'W-what I mean is,' he backtracked, running a flustered hand through his prematurely greying curls, 'we always knew it was a long shot. So did you. We assumed you'd be accepted onto one of the other courses you applied for and that would be the end of it.'

Anna bit back a humourless laugh. 'I suppose, if nothing else, I ought to appreciate your honesty. Always helpful to know when your father thinks you're a no-hoper.'

'Oh, come on, Anna. You know I don't think that. Today's results should put that beyond any shadow of doubt.' He began to pace the floor, attempting to channel his exasperation at her refusal to see things his way into some kind of physical action. 'Think of all the other offers you've had. Courses in finance, law, economics... All degrees with clear pathways to secure, well-paying jobs. You can have your pick of them. And if you're so set on it, I'm sure it'll be possible for you to do a sociology module alongside your main degree.'

'Yay,' Anna deadpanned. 'I can hardly wait.'

He stopped pacing and spun around to face her. 'Anna, be serious for a moment.'

Anna's eyes flared. 'I am being serious. I've never *been* more serious.' She looked at each parent in turn. 'Have the two of you been walking around with your eyes and ears shut for the last three years? You know this is my passion.'

'I see,' said Francesco quietly. 'And that's all that matters, is it? Your "passion".'

Anna said nothing. She turned to her mother, silently beseeching her to say something. Leah's continued silence made clear that she stood foursquare with her husband on this matter.

'Well, let me tell you a thing or two about passions,' Francesco continued. 'Passions don't put food on the table. Passions don't put a roof over your head. If everyone simply followed their passion with no thought to their responsibilities, the world would grind to a halt pretty bloody sharpish. So stop being so damned self-indulgent and think about your long-term future.'

Anna continued to say nothing. The blood was pounding in her ears as she struggled to keep a lid on the rage building inside her.

'Do you think,' her father said, 'if I'd followed my dreams and done whatever I felt like, that I could have afforded to raise you in a three-storey house in one of the most expensive parts of the city? To send you to one of the best schools in the country – a school that equipped you with the skills and knowledge to achieve those impressive grades? Hmm?' He jabbed a finger at her. 'Let me tell you, missy – I haven't sacrificed almost every waking moment of the past eighteen years just to watch you throw it all away chasing a dream.'

Anna glowered at him, her head low, her lips curled back in a snarl. 'Well, d'you know what?' she said quietly. 'I'd rather be broke than a miserable, joyless fuck like you.'

For several long, painful seconds, her father just stood there, gazing at her in silent rage. Then, without another word, he strode past her and stormed out of the room. Anna listened as his footsteps receded down the corridor and the door to his study slammed shut.

'Well,' said Leah, finally finding her voice, '*that* went well.'

Anna stared at her mother with unbridled fury. In that moment, her refusal to intervene seemed somehow worse than anything her father had said. Then Anna too turned on her heel and stormed out. She clattered up the stairs to her bedroom and, throwing the door shut behind her, collapsed face-down onto her bed, the duvet muffling her angry sobs.

Anna lay in bed, gazing up at the ceiling, the sense of injustice that burned inside her over an incident she hadn't thought about in years as raw now as it had been that night two decades ago. Her final few weeks in the house before her big move to Rome had been among the most tense and uncomfortable in her life, her relationship with her father having devolved to the point that they could barely stand to be in the same room. On a handful of occasions, he'd attempted to raise the subject again, still trying to make her see reason. There had been offers to pay for her accommodation, alongside a generous allowance, if she agreed to accept one of the various other offers. That had always been his approach: when in doubt, throw money at a problem until it went away. She'd refused every overture, and eventually he'd stopped trying.

In the end, she'd arranged everything herself – the apartment in Rome, the student loan to pay for it, even the plane ticket and, when the time came, the taxi to the airport. Her relationship with her parents – already thoroughly strained for a myriad of reasons, most of them ideological –

never recovered, and the rift between her and her father had remained until his death seven years later. Even when she graduated top of her year, when she completed her PhD, when she was appointed *professore aggregato di criminologia* at the age of twenty-seven, there was no acknowledgement from her mother that she and Francesco had been wrong; that Anna's ambitions *hadn't* just been a crazy pipe dream. In fact, if anything, it had only served to deepen the acrimony between them. And now Leah had come barging back into her life, and all the old wounds had been ripped open anew.

She turned her pillow cool side up, rolled onto her side and waited in vain for sleep to come.

22

Thursday 11 April

Over the next few days, the four of them settled into what it seemed, for the foreseeable future, was to be the new normal. In the time that they'd lived together, Anna and Zoe had become a well-oiled machine, their daily routine a perfectly choreographed ballet. Leah's arrival turned all that on its head. Suddenly, Anna found herself unable to rely on the bathroom being free when she normally had her morning shower or for there to be enough semi-skimmed left when she took a fancy for some coffee – this despite Leah having procured her own personal carton of almond milk, which Anna knew better than to touch lest she bring about the Apocalypse. To make matters worse, and despite a litany of complaints about everything from the lumpiness of Anna's bed to the flow and temperature of the water, Leah showed no inclination towards finding alternative accommodation, ignoring Anna's thinly veiled hints that she might find a hotel more to her liking – preferably one on the other side of the city.

It was, therefore, something of a mercy that Leah was often out and about, working through the laundry list of old friends she was determined to look up while she was in town. When she *was* around, Anna holed up in her office as much as possible and tried to make some genuine headway both on the Sandra Morton investigation and on her book, which by now was seriously behind schedule. Matters weren't helped by her mother's continuing inability – or, perhaps more accurately, refusal – to respect the concept of set work hours. She would barge in at the most inopportune moments, usually when Anna had just succeeded in building up some momentum with her current task and almost always for some trivial reason, such as to demand to be told where the teabags were kept or which colour of bin her apple peel should go in.

'I'm just not clear as to what it is you *do* in there all day,' she told Anna on one occasion when they collided in the hallway. 'Is it too much to ask for you to take a break and spend some time with your son every once in a while? The poor boy barely sees you.'

'He sees more of me than he would if I was going out to the office first thing every morning and not coming back till late at night,' retorted Anna – a pointed reference to her own father's work pattern which she was sure wouldn't be lost on Leah.

Leah drew back her chin and regarded Anna coolly. 'You know, traditionally it was the husband's role to go out and earn a living while the wife stayed home to raise the children.'

Anna met her mother's gaze without flinching. 'They also used to burn witches at the stake. If we're resurrecting primitive traditions, perhaps we should start there.'

Despite the ongoing upheaval, during this time Anna did, nonetheless, achieve two major victories. First, she succeeded in arranging another meeting with Sandra at Broadwood. Scheduled for midday the following Thursday, she made the appointment without first running it by Pamela Macklin. Given Sandra's obviously low opinion of her solicitor, and said solicitor's proclivity for making mountains out of molehills, Anna surmised that involving her would only complicate matters unnecessarily. She was determined to build on the rapport she felt she'd established with Sandra at their last meeting and seek, this time, to engage her about her past, if only to put the rumours about her father and the supposed clandestine abortion to rest once and for all.

Secondly, she managed to persuade Jeff Morton to agree to speak to her about his memories of Sandra, Guy and the rest of the family. It had taken several phone calls to him, during which she gradually chipped away at his resolve, culminating in her offering to drive down to Troon to meet at a time and place of his choosing. Her willingness to meet him face to face seemed to be what sealed the deal – or perhaps forced the issue –

and he proposed that they rendezvous at the South Beach Kiosk at eleven o'clock on Friday morning. In truth, the prospect of a mini road trip appealed to Anna considerably. She knew she was going stir crazy holed up in the same house as two other adults and a toddler, and a drive down to the coast seemed the perfect excuse for her to get Leah out of her hair for a few hours.

As Anna added Jeff to the 'Agreed to Interview' column in her notebook, her eyes were drawn to another name – one that, for one reason or another, had been driven from her mind in recent days. It was now over a fortnight since she'd spoken to Cressida Bagshawe – plummy, jolly hockey sticks Cressida, who'd promised to unearth Adjoa Asante's forwarding address and ring her back. By even the most generous measure, Anna had left it more than long enough. If Cressida hadn't called by now, it was safe to say she was unlikely to ever do so of her own volition.

Time to take matters into her own hands.

'Oh-eight-four-nine, Bagshawe residence.'

Anna tried not to wince as the shrill voice boomed in her ear. 'Uh, yes, hello. This is Anna Scavolini. I'm not sure if you remember, but we spoke—'

'Why yes, the true crime author! Of *course* I remember you.'

'Well, I'm not … I mean, I was wondering if you'd had any success in locating that card.'

'Card?' Cressida repeated pleasantly.

'The greetings card with Adjoa Asante's forwarding address,' said Anna, through gritted teeth.

'The card! Well, why didn't you say so? As it happens, I'm afraid it *completely* slipped my mind. You know how it is – busy busy busy!' She gave a tinkling laugh that set Anna's teeth on edge anew. 'But I'm sure it won't take me long to locate it. I keep most of these things in the bureau.'

'Can you look now?' Anna was grateful that Cressida couldn't see her expression.

'Since you asked so nicely. Two ticks.'

There was a sound of papers being rummaged at the other end of the line, followed a moment later by an exclamation of triumph.

'Here it is. I told you about the hand-stitched cards, didn't I? Such exquisite craftsmanship. Now, let's see … *Dear Mrs Bagshawe, I wish to thank you and your husband for the great kindness you showed to myself and Samuel—* et cetera, et cetera … *Sadly, circumstances have dictated that—* bla bla bla … Ah, yes! Here we go. *If any post should arrive addressed to me, I would be most grateful if you would forward it to me at my current whereabouts.* Ready?'

'Fire away,' said Anna, pen at the ready.

'Dungavel House, Strathaven, South Lanarkshire ML10 6RF.'

For several heartbeats, Anna sat there in stony silence, phone pressed to her ear. 'Are you *serious*?' she said eventually, her voice like ice.

'That's what I have here,' Cressida replied cheerfully. 'Why? Is there something wrong?'

'I'll say there is,' said Anna. 'Dungavel is an immigration removal centre.' *You absolute fucking moron,* she very nearly added.

'Oh.' Cressida was evidently wrong-footed by this revelation, though she quickly recovered. 'You know, I always had my suspicions that there was something not quite right about that woman. Far too cagey about her past for her own good. Of course, if I'd had the *slightest* inclination she was an illegal, I'd *never—*'

'Thanks for your time,' snapped Anna, and stabbed the End Call button before she said something she *really* regretted.

She sat in livid silence, unable to believe such ignorance and casual indifference could be possible. Gradually, the blood pounding in her ears subsided, to be replaced by a sickening sensation in the pit of her stomach. Why had she never considered the possibility that Adjoa had been deported? If she'd been trying to evade the immigration authorities, it would certainly explain why she and her son had moved around so much, and why they'd seemingly disappeared off the face of the earth. She could imagine only too clearly what must have happened. Conscious that the Home Office was closing in, she'd quit her employment with Cressida and gone on the run with Samuel, only to be picked up some time later and then almost certainly repatriated to Ghana. Deferential to the last, she'd even taken the time to send a thank you letter to the woman who'd so shamelessly exploited her.

Anna thought back to her own visits to Dungavel. She'd been there twice, both times to document the experiences of the women incarcerated there while they awaited deportation, many for trifling crimes or for being in the country without leave to remain – which, as far as she was concerned, was no crime at all. She would never forget the barbed wire fences; the haunted, hollowed-out expressions in the inmates' eyes; the crushing sense of despair that seemed to knock the very breath from your lungs; the total absence of anything approaching basic human dignity. Academic rigour and her own family history made her wary of facile, knee-jerk comparisons, but the similarities between the centre's exterior and the photographs she'd seen of the camps in Germany and Poland were difficult to ignore. What fate had befallen Adjoa and her son? Had they been dragged, fighting tooth and nail, onto the plane that had been chartered to fly them out of the country and dump them nearly five thousand miles away in the place that, for whatever reason, they'd left all those years ago? Or had they gone compliantly, knowing it was useless to resist?

She knew there was no point contacting the Home Office to ask for information on the Asantes' current whereabouts. They'd be unlikely to divulge anything to a third party, and in any event, the odds that they even *possessed* any information on the current whereabouts of former detainees were slim to non-existent. Once they were forcibly ejected from the country, Adjoa and her son would, in the eyes of the authorities, have ceased to be their problem.

She told herself it wasn't hopeless – that there were still steps she could take to try to pick up the trail again. But deep down, she knew she'd reached the end of this line of enquiry. Adjoa Asante had, like so many other victims of the aptly named Hostile Environment policy before her, fallen through the cracks and vanished into the ether.

That evening, anger continued to fester inside Anna – anger towards Cressida Bagshawe for her casual bigotry and general cluelessness, anger towards the system for its indifference and cruelty, and most of all anger towards herself for her inability to do anything about any of it. She sat at the table, head bowed, tapping away on her phone while Zoe and Leah conversed amiably and picked at the leftovers from the evening meal, seemingly oblivious to her mood. She didn't normally bring her phone to the table, but she knew she needed to channel her pent-up rage into something productive to avoid saying or doing something she'd later regret, and she figured continuing her social media trawl was the best option available to her at present.

She'd recently succeeded in identifying a Facebook profile that looked like it could be a potential lead for Paul Kempley. PJ Kempley, with 197 friends, listed his current place of residence as Düsseldorf, Germany, where he worked as a mechanic at Express Autowerkstatt, but he also described himself as an 'exiled Doonhamer' – 'Doonhamer' being the local term for a native of Dumfries. Kempley had grown up in Eastriggs, not Dumfries, but he'd attended secondary school there, which Anna supposed just about qualified him for honorary status. Furthermore, his profile picture was the insignia of the town's football club, Queen of the South FC. PJ Kempley hadn't posted since 2009, when the platform had still been in its relative infancy, and the page featured little in the way of content besides a handful of photos of landscapes and urban locales, as well as a few of a pretty, gap-toothed blonde woman in a leather jacket. She looked to be around her mid-twenties – which, judging by the accompanying timestamps, would have made her more or less ages with Kempley.

It might just be worth a shot, Anna told herself. At any rate, she had nothing to lose.

As she finished tapping out a private message to the account holder, she found herself tuning into the ongoing exchange between Leah and Zoe. Her mother was grousing about the various inconveniences associated with life on the French Riviera, such as the difficulty in sourcing Jacob's cream crackers and the reluctance of local shopkeepers to speak English – which she was convinced was born out of obstinacy rather than a genuine unfamiliarity with the language.

'Yes, I'm sure they do it just to spite you,' muttered Anna, unable to help herself.

Leah set down her wine glass and gave Anna a frosty look. 'Do I detect a note of sarcasm?'

'From me?' Anna pretended to be surprised. 'Perish the thought! No – I'm just slightly concerned that, despite living there for nearly thirteen years, you've somehow failed to pick up enough of the native language to get by.'

'I get by just fine, thank you very much,' Leah replied primly. 'I just happen to believe it's not unreasonable for paying customers to expect a little courtesy from the local retailers. After all, they'd be nowhere without us expats keeping them in business.'

Anna rolled her eyes. 'Oh, *God*! You lot with your little monocultural enclaves and your refusal to even *countenance* rubbing shoulders with the locals unless they're bagging your groceries or serving you drinks on the veranda while the theme tune from *The Brittas Empire* plays in the background. You do realise expat's just rich white person speak for "immigrant", don't you?' She leaned across the table, openly goading Leah. 'Because that's what you are, Mother. Say it. *Immigrant.* It's not a dirty word.'

She wasn't sure whether it was the fact that the conversation specifically revolved around both immigration and a master/servant dynamic or just Leah's general snobbery and disregard for those she perceived as below her in the pecking order, but Anna found herself taken straight back to Cressida Bagshawe and all the unresolved anger that had arisen from their earlier conversation. That was why she'd lashed out, she supposed – not because of anything Leah had said herself but because she adhered to the same worldview as the woman who'd so casually cast Adjoa Asante aside the moment she learned her ex-housekeeper had been an 'illegal'.

But if Anna had been hoping her mother would allow herself to be goaded into a direct confrontation, she was sorely disappointed. Instead of responding, Leah merely turned to Zoe. 'She takes things very literally, your friend Anna,' she declared wearily. 'I've often wondered if she might have a touch of the autism about her.'

'For goodness' sake, Mother,' Anna snapped, as Zoe stifled a guffaw by turning it into an explosive cough, 'you can't just go around deciding people are autistic. Do you have any relevant qualifications in the field?' She held up a hand. 'No, don't answer that. Of course you don't.'

Leah shot Zoe a triumphant look. 'See what I mean? *Entirely* literally.'

Zoe glanced momentarily in Anna's direction, flashed her a surreptitious wink, then turned to Leah again. 'Well, I gotta say, anytime I've been in foreign parts, I've always been grateful tae find a local who can parlay a bit of ye olde Anglais. 'Course Anna puts us all tae shame. See me, I never had much of a heid for languages, but here's her, fluent in three like it's the most natural thing in the world. And ye know me, Mrs S – I'm aye full of appreciation for a cunning linguist.'

Anna – who, perhaps unwisely, had chosen that precise moment to take a sip of wine – choked into her glass, most of the mouthful coming out of her nose. It was an old game she and Zoe had played as teenagers:

slipping thinly veiled sexual innuendos into conversations in the presence of Anna's parents or Zoe's granny, seeing how far they could push the envelope before one of the adults cottoned on.

'What can I say?' she said, with an airy shrug. 'It helps to know your fromage from your frottage.'

As Zoe threw back her head, mouth open in a silent cackle, Leah regarded them both with withering opprobrium. 'You must think I was born yesterday. Don't think I can't see what the pair of you are up to.'

'We were just—' Anna began, trying desperately to keep a straight face.

'No.' Leah raised a sharp index finger. 'You weren't just *anything*. Much as it may surprise you, I happen to know precisely what frottage is, and I'm astounded you think it's a remotely appropriate topic to discuss in front of a three-year-old.'

With perfect timing, Zoe let out a loud snort through her nose. As she clapped both hands over her face, desperately trying to contain any future outbursts, Anna, struggling to keep from corpsing herself, forced herself to maintain a straight face.

'I'm sorry, Mother,' she said, in her most serious voice. 'You're right – it's not—'

She got as far as the first syllable of 'funny' before doubling up in hysterics, clutching her stomach as both she and Zoe descended into peals of laughter, while Leah sat in stone-faced silence and Jack looked on in bemusement.

'It's Zoe, Mum,' Anna explained, once she'd regained a sliver of self-control. 'She brings out the juvenile delinquent in me.'

'Hey, dinnae look at me,' said Zoe, mock affronted. 'I was just an innocent wee lassie till I got led astray by her wicked wiles.'

In the silence that followed, Jack, who'd listened to the whole conversation with rapt attention, chose that moment to speak up.

'What's frottage?' he asked, with cherub-like innocence.

'It's a type of cheese, darling,' said Anna, not missing a beat.

The only sound that followed was the gales of laughter erupting from Zoe as she gave up any pretence of trying to maintain her composure.

'Thanks for that,' Anna said to Zoe later that night, once they'd both retired to Zoe's room. 'Been a while since I had a proper inappropriate cackle.'

She was seated on the end of the bed, stripped down to her bra. Behind her, Zoe was getting changed into her night things.

'Ach, don't mention it. Atmosphere down there was getting just a wee bit on the suffocating side. Felt I'd better see if I couldnae dial it back doon tae something breathable.'

Anna laughed softly. 'Well, no one can say you don't know how to push my buttons.'

Having finished changing, Zoe shuffled across the bed and, kneeling behind Anna, began to massage her shoulders. 'Fuck me, ye're tense as buggery! Even yer knots've got knots in 'em.'

Anna winced as Zoe kneaded a particularly tender spot. 'Ow! You're not kidding. Bit lower? Yeah, that's the spot.'

'It's this Sandra Morton business, in't it?' Zoe continued to dig into Anna's shoulders. 'Told ye ye shouldnae be letting yersel get sucked in.'

'It *has* been getting to me,' Anna admitted, with some reluctance. 'But it's not just that. It's everything else – Mum being back, the memories it's sparked off …'

'I hear ya. But I think she *is* trying. I'm no saying it's easy, but gonnae mibby ease off a bit on the whole argy-bargy side of things, if ye can?'

'Me?' Anna's shoulders instinctively drew together. 'She's the one who barged in uninvited and made herself at home. She's turned all our lives upside down and she doesn't give a shit.'

Zoe sucked air through her teeth. 'See, that's sorta what I'm getting at. Sometimes it takes one o' yese tae take the first step – tae be the bigger person. Might no seem fair, but … mibby dae it for Jack's sake, if nothing else?'

Anna craned her head over her shoulder to look up at Zoe. The mention of Jack had got through to her, even if nothing else had.

'I've no had the full skinny on what's going on 'tween the pair of yese,' Zoe went on, 'and I'm no gonnae ask, but I *do* know it cannae be good for him seeing his mum and his granny at each other's throats the whole time. So just … gonnae take it back a notch?'

For a few seconds, Anna said nothing. She continued to meet Zoe's gaze, Zoe's gold-green eyes boring into hers. At length, she gave a slight smile and dipped her head in surrender.

'All right,' she said. 'I'll try.'

23

At 10.45 the following morning, Anna pulled into the town of Troon in her Skoda Estate. She followed the main road south along the coastline, pebbledash houses to her left, the choppy grey waters of the Firth of Clyde to her right. It was one of those overcast, blustery spring mornings, and as she pulled into the car park next to the South Beach Kiosk, she noted that the place was virtually deserted, with only those determined to get their salt air fix having ventured out to trudge along the windswept seafront.

She remained in the relative warmth of her car till just before eleven, then got out and approached the kiosk. She turned up the collar of her coat, jammed her hands into her pockets, set her back to the wind and settled in to wait, hoping she'd be able to recognise Jeff Morton. There had only been a handful of photos of him online, all of them two decades out of date.

Time passed. Eleven o'clock came and went. She was beginning to wonder if he'd stood her up when she noticed a heavyset figure in a cagoule making his way along the esplanade towards her, accompanied by a massive Bernese Mountain Dog, straining at its leash. He was in his late fifties now, and he'd gained considerable weight since the pictures had been taken, but she immediately recognised the Kirk Douglas-esque cleft in his chin – a feature he'd shared with his late brother.

'Anna?'

'Jeff?'

They shook hands rather awkwardly.

'And this is Ludovic,' said Jeff, gesturing to the dog, who grinned up at the pair of them, tongue lolling excitedly.

'Is he friendly?' Anna asked. She wasn't, as a rule, afraid of dogs, but she was never quite sure how to behave around them – especially the bigger ones that looked like they could knock her over with a single bound.

'Oh, you're quite safe with him,' said Jeff cheerfully. 'He's a big sook, really.'

For a moment, Anna toyed with the idea of patting Ludovic, then concluded it was unwise to do anything that might encourage the great beast to mount her.

'Thanks for agreeing to meet me,' she said. 'It's really good of you.'

'Don't mention it.' Jeff half-turned towards the beach. 'Mind if we walk while we talk? I promised Ludo his morning constitutional.'

The cold sea wind whipped at Anna's hair as she and Jeff strolled along the sand in a southerly direction, Ludovic capering before them like a mad creature. Jeff carried a severely chewed tennis ball which, from time to time, he tossed ahead of him – at which point the big mutt would go bounding after it, throwing up great clumps of sand as he dived on it, then come lolloping back towards them, carrying it proudly in his mouth.

'I flew out the morning after it happened,' he said, after pausing to throw the ball. 'Mainly so's I could be there to support Mum and Dad. I saw up close what the grief did to them – Mum especially. She doted on those two wee boys. To say nothing of what it was like to lose a son.'

Anna nodded sympathetically. 'It wasn't just them, though. You lost your brother. That must have been incredibly hard for you too.'

'It was, right enough. But I knew, whatever I was feeling, I had to bury it for their sakes. Someone needed to be strong for the rest of us, and – well, I was the one who'd had the least contact with Guy and the boys over the years, so it seemed obvious I was the one best equipped to do that.'

Ludovic returned with his ball. Jeff wrestled it from his mouth, pitched back and threw it long, then walked on, Anna keeping pace.

'I shielded Mum and Dad from the press as much as possible. They were a right bunch of jackals – treated the whole thing like it was a bloodsport. They didn't care about the emotional toll on us. Just wanted their juicy scoop.'

Anna gave an understanding grimace. 'Your parents were convinced from the outset that Sandra was guilty. Why *was* that, do you think?'

'You'd have to ask *them* that,' said Jeff, a little stiffly.

'I did. They wouldn't speak to me.'

'Then I'm afraid I'm not able to answer on their behalf.'

Anna wondered briefly whether that meant he genuinely didn't know the answer or was holding something back. She considered pressing the matter, then decided against it. There was nothing to be achieved by rocking the boat.

'Can I ask about your niece Katie? I gather she lived with your parents for several months before the ... the event.'

'That's right.'

'Can you say why?'

Jeff hesitated before responding. 'To be honest, I'm not altogether clear on that myself. It's not something that ever came up, and I didn't like to ask. I thought it best not to dwell on the past.'

'And after the trial, when she went to live with you in Canada—'

'That was Cheryl's idea,' said Jeff, his expression brightening momentarily. 'It made total sense from a practicality standpoint. Mum and Dad were starting to get on in years. Losing Guy and the twins had taken a lot out of them. And then there was the press to consider. They weren't allowed to report on Katie, her being underage – but you just knew, the moment she turned sixteen ... ' He left the rest unsaid. 'Plus she was roughly ages with Christopher and Isobel – that's our two – so I thought, *Why not? Take her as far away from all this as possible. Let her start again someplace fresh.*'

'Does she ever talk about her mother?'

Jeff shook his head. 'She doesn't talk about that period in her life at *all*. It's as if it never happened. As if her life didn't begin till she moved to Ontario. And she's *super* Canadian. Got the accent and everything.' He chuckled softly. 'You'd never know where she was from originally.'

Anna got the sense this was something he didn't entirely approve of – and yet she herself couldn't help but applaud the young woman for putting her past so firmly behind her; for refusing to be defined by her roots. There was no law which said you had to retain some sort of allegiance to your country of birth. Identity was a complex thing, and she was firmly in the camp that it had more to do with where you chose to make a life for yourself than where you happened, by accident of birth, to come from.

Ludovic returned with his ball. As Jeff stopped to prise it from his jaws once again, Anna's eye was drawn to a round, black pebble poking out of the sand directly beside her foot. On a whim, she bent down and picked it up. She turned it in her hand, stroking the smooth surface. Then, noticing that Jeff was now some way off, she slipped it into her pocket and quickened her pace to catch up with him again.

'Can I ask about your impressions of Sandra?' she asked, once she'd drawn level with him once more. 'What did you make of her?'

Jeff tossed the ball for the boundlessly energetic dog. 'To be honest, I was a bit surprised when Guy took up with her. Even more so when I heard he was going to marry her. At the time, I didn't think it could possibly last. He was busy making his way up the corporate ladder and she was this lowly office girl.' He winced apologetically. 'It sounds dreadful, I know – but honestly, they were like chalk and cheese. I figured for sure it was just a rebound fling and he'd soon come to his senses.'

'Oh? He'd just come out of a relationship?'

'Not just relationship. He'd just come out of a *marriage*.'

'A marriage?' Anna stared at him in surprise. In all her reading on the case, this wasn't something that had come up.

Jeff nodded. 'Miranda, her name was. She worked for TransAlbion too. They were together just over three years. They were both too young at the time, probably, and there were certain … irreconcilable differences. A situation I myself know only too well.' He chuckled grimly. 'Perhaps it runs in the family?'

Anna managed a dutiful smile. That none of this had ever been mentioned in the media coverage couldn't help but feel to her like a deliberate omission. It would have been the easiest thing in the world for some enterprising reporter to dig up details of a previous marriage, and she could only assume it had been felt that such a revelation would have undercut Guy's image as a devoted family man. She wondered just what those 'irreconcilable differences' had been, but once again decided not to push it. She mentally stuck a pin in the subject, resolving to return to it if an appropriate opportunity arose.

'But what about Sandra herself?' she asked, noting that Jeff had studiously avoided answering the question before. 'I assume you met her.'

'No more than a handful of times. After Cheryl and I married, I wasn't back in Scotland all that often. She wasn't much of a traveller, and she wasn't big on me leaving her on her own. I was there for the wedding, of course, and a handful of other times after that – just after Katie was born, for one.'

'And how did she seem to you?' Anna prompted, sensing once again that he'd gone out of his way not to answer the question.

'She was…' Jeff pursed his lips, his pace slowing as he mulled over the question. 'To be honest, she didn't seem like much of *anything*. Like a blank slate, almost. She certainly didn't strike me as much of a people person. Both at the wedding and at Katie's christening, I remember, while the rest of us were all milling about, talking and drinking and generally having a good time, she mostly just sat on her own in a corner, not speaking to anyone. I wasn't sure whether she was rude or just shy, but I got the impression she didn't want to be there – or perhaps didn't want *us* there.'

As he spoke, Anna couldn't help thinking that he could just as easily have been describing *her* at any large gathering. She disliked such events intensely and invariably ended up retreating into herself whenever she was forced to attend one – something she knew made her appear rude and standoffish in the eyes of the sort of people who were completely at ease in social situations and expected everyone else to be the same.

She realised Jeff was still speaking – recounting, she quickly realised, an incident that had occurred at the christening party.

'She was crying and crying,' he said, 'and I can still picture it as clearly as if it was yesterday – Guy standing there with a screaming baby in his arms, saying, "For God's sake, just *hold* her!" and Sandra just getting up and walking away. I mean, what sort of a mother *does* that?' He turned to Anna, clearly expecting her to agree wholeheartedly.

To Anna's mind, there were a million and one reasons why a new mother might not want to pick up her baby – everything from just needing a moment to herself to something more serious, like postpartum depression.

'Did you ever get the impression Guy pressured her into having children?' she asked. She wasn't sure how the question would be received, but a part of her was still smarting from Jeff's offhanded dismissal of behaviour for which he had no context.

Jeff scratched a jowly cheek, brows furrowed as he contemplated the question. 'I'm not sure,' he said eventually, 'but from what I saw of her, Sandra didn't have a maternal bone in her body. I'd be surprised if the idea came from her – let's put it that way. And I know having children was important to Guy. In fact, it was a key factor in the breakdown of his first marriage. Miranda wasn't able to get pregnant.'

Sounds like a relationship built on a solid foundation, thought Anna glibly.

They'd been walking now for about a kilometre and found themselves facing a rocky outcrop that barred their way. Turning, they began to head back the way they'd come.

'At the trial,' Anna said, 'you testified that Guy had confided in you that he thought Sandra was being unfaithful to him.'

Jeff nodded. 'That's right.' Then, realising that she was looking for him to elaborate, he went on:

'He spoke to me about it a couple of weeks before … before it happened. We didn't ring each other often, but once in a blue moon, one of us would get a notion to get on the blower to the other and we'd spend a couple of hours making up for lost time. I can't remember which of us it was that initiated that particular conversation, but I do remember, after we'd been shooting the breeze for a half-hour or so, out of the blue he said, "I think Sandra's cheating on me".'

He paused momentarily and whistled to Ludovic, who had fallen behind them and was nosing around a patch of seaweed. The dog stopped what it was doing and came cantering after them.

'It wasn't the first time he'd said something like that to me. There'd been various … incidents … over the years. In fact, it was the reason they originally left Broughty Ferry. The whole town knew what she was about. It wasn't just something the tabloids dreamt up. Anyway, he went on to say he'd picked up rumours about her being seen with various men, most of them quite a bit younger than her. He also said, two or three times over the last couple of months, the phone at the house had rung and there was no one there when he picked up – or rather, there *was* someone there, but they weren't saying anything. Just what sounded like a man breathing.

'I could tell he'd talked himself into the idea that something serious was going on. At the time, I thought perhaps he was reading too much into a couple of heavy breathing pranks calls. I mean, I'd known he wasn't happy in his marriage for a while, so I figured this was him trying to convince himself he had a concrete reason to end things. For the first time, he even spoke about suing for custody of the kids – cutting her out of the picture completely. But as we know, the courts always favour the mother, so he obviously needed to build a proper case against her first. That's why he hired a private investigator.'

Anna, who'd been too preoccupied by Jeff's obviously self-pitying comment about the courts, took a moment to process what he'd just said.

'I'm sorry … did you just say he hired a PI?'

'*I* thought it was a bit over the top myself, but he said he'd tasked someone to tail Sandra while he wasn't there – to gather evidence of infidelity or anything else that could be used against her. And before you ask, I've no idea who this investigator was, or whether they handed anything concrete over to Guy before he died – but I'd say it's kind of immaterial at this point.' He laughed grimly. 'I mean, they got her for something a lot worse than screwing around.'

Anna didn't join in. Evidently, indulging in a certain amount of gallows humour was how Jeff coped with his grief, but she saw nothing funny about the situation and didn't feel it was appropriate to pretend she *did*.

'How come you didn't say anything about this at the time?' she asked instead.

Jeff cast Anna a sidelong look before lowering his eyes to the sand. 'To be honest, I didn't think it reflected particularly well on Guy. Made him look underhanded and paranoid. The whole family had already been through enough – Mum and Dad especially – without doing anything to blacken his reputation.'

He fell silent, tramping stolidly across the sand with his eyes cast downwards. Watching him, Anna sensed that there was something more he wasn't telling her. With them already more than halfway to their starting location, she also concluded that now was the moment to ask the question she'd avoided earlier.

'You said there were other factors in the breakdown of Guy's first marriage besides the fertility issues,' she said. 'Would you mind elaborating on what those were?'

Jeff gave her an apprehensive look. 'You're not going to be putting all this in your book, are you?'

'I won't be going out of my way to tarnish his memory,' Anna assured him, then immediately wondered just how wise it had been to make that promise, and when it had become her role to do anything other than uncover and document the facts without fear or favour.

Jeff was silent for a long, contemplative moment. Ludovic stared at the tennis ball, dangling loosely from his hand, tail quivering with anticipation.

At length, he stirred. 'The thing about the media,' he said, in a tone which implied that this was a speech he'd been rehearsing in his head, 'is that they love their heroes and villains. Sandra was the villain, obviously, so of course it stood to reason Guy must have been an absolute saint. And I'm not saying he was all bad. But in putting him up on a pedestal, they glossed over a bunch of things about him that cast him in a less positive light … or perhaps they just didn't look too hard for them in the first place.'

'What things?'

Jeff turned to Anna with a look that she read as one of shame. 'Quite a few things came out about him during the divorce proceedings. Miranda claimed he had a controlling nature – that he was big on telling her how to dress, how to wear her hair, on policing her friendships outside their mutual circle. She also said he did a whole lot of … well, she called it gaslighting. I had to look that up. I hadn't heard it before. I'm guessing you're familiar with it?'

Anna nodded. 'Lying to make her question her own sanity.'

'Right. I don't know how much truth there was in it all; whether he really did all those things to her or if she was just looking to increase her share of the divorce settlement. In the end, they basically each got half of everything and agreed to go their separate ways, and the allegations never came to anything. Of course, *he'd* have said she was just being paranoid; that she was the one trying to create a false recollection of events. And maybe she was? Still, I've always wondered.'

Ahead of them, the South Beach Kiosk loomed into view. Anna was silent for the remainder of the journey, deep in thought. However, as they reached the foot of the ramp leading up to the esplanade, she halted and turned to face Jeff.

'One question. Miranda – what was her maiden name?'

Jeff frowned. 'Why?'

'Just curious.'

Jeff gave her an odd look, followed by a shrug of acquiescence. 'Hayes, I think. Yeah, that's it – Miranda Hayes.'

'Thanks. And listen – I really appreciate you talking to me today. Before we wrap things up, I just wanted to ask if you'd be willing to do me a favour.'

'Depends what it is,' said Jeff, a look of suspicion entering his eyes.

'I wondered if you could put me in touch with Katie.'

'No.' His tone was adamant. 'Absolutely not.'

She'd had a feeling this was how he'd respond. 'I completely understand why you'd want to protect her, but I'd *really* like to ask her about her memories of her mother – and especially why she was no longer living with her parents at the time of the murders.'

Jeff's stony expression didn't falter. 'She's been through *more* than enough. She's put that part of her life behind her. I'm not having you dredging it all up again and undoing two decades' worth of healing.'

Anna suppressed a sigh of frustration. On one level, she was entirely sympathetic to his stance. Indeed, she felt a certain amount of admiration towards him for his protective stance towards his niece. But on the other hand, Katie was no longer the helpless thirteen-year-old whose identity had been subject to an interdict to shield her from the malign attentions of the press. She'd be in her thirties now – a grown woman, fully capable of making her own decisions without her uncle acting as her self-appointed gatekeeper, however well-meaning his intentions.

'Well,' she said, 'in that case, perhaps I can persuade you to pass on *my* details to *her*. That way, she can get in touch with me if she chooses to do so, and if not ... '

For a moment, Jeff said nothing. He evidently wasn't happy with the proposal – possibly because he recognised it as eminently reasonable.

'All right,' he said, with considerable reluctance.

'You'll do it? You'll give her my contact details and explain why I want to speak to her?'

'I said I'd do it, didn't I?' he growled, and for a moment, his eyes flared in anger. 'Sorry,' he muttered. 'I'm not trying to be difficult. It's just ... well, you'd do anything to protect your kids, wouldn't you?'

'You would,' Anna agreed. She found it unexpectedly touching that he clearly thought of Katie as his, just as much as his biological children.

'She won't talk to you,' he added, leaning down to scratch Ludovic – now sitting next to him and panting restlessly – behind the ears.

'We'll see.'

'We're not in touch all that much these days,' Jeff went on. 'She's got her own life now over there, and since I moved back here ...' He shrugged.

'All I can ask is that you try. And thanks again for agreeing to talk to me. It's been very helpful.'

Jeff gave a nod of acknowledgement. 'Don't mention it.'

As Anna turned to go, she suddenly thought of something. 'Just one thing. Supposing it came to it, would you be willing to go on the record about this with the police at some point in the future? The stuff about your brother's first marriage and the private investigator and all that.'

From the look on Jeff's face, it was clear he wasn't overly enthused by this idea. 'I guess ... if you think it's important.'

'I think it might be.'

'This ... this isn't going to get her off, is it? It's just, you hear all the time about convictions being rendered unsafe for utterly spurious reasons, and I don't ...'

'It's way too early to be thinking along those lines,' said Anna firmly. Then, remembering Pamela Macklin's words, she added, 'Besides, you need to have truly compelling new evidence in order to trigger a retrial – and this isn't that.'

'Good,' said Jeff. 'I mean, I didn't know her well, but from what little I saw of her, something about her just seemed ... well, *off*. She gave me a bad feeling.'

You and half the known world, Anna thought.

24

'I'd forgotten this place existed,' Leah remarked as she and Zoe strolled along the path, Jack charging ahead of them at a determined, knock-kneed clip.

Dowanhill Park, located about a half-mile from the house, was a little oasis of greenery nestled in the middle of the concrete criss-cross of the West End's streets, its existence a jealously guarded secret among local residents. Its footpath formed a figure eight, in the centre of each half of which was a children's play area – one decked out with swings, a slide, a roundabout and so on, the other a bare grassy patch overlooked by park benches. It was towards the latter that Jack now made a beeline, clearly on some vital mission, the details of which were known only to him.

'Don't go too far now, y'hear?' Zoe called after him. 'Me 'n' yer granny are just gonnae stop here for a blether.'

Jack toddled off purposefully while Zoe and Leah claimed one of the benches, Leah sinking into a sedentary position with a satisfied groan. 'Aaah! I tell you, these old bones aren't what they used to be.'

'Aye, it's a sin,' said Zoe sagely, as if speaking from personal experience. 'Should be some sorta law against these rampant displays of exertion when us old-timers are around tae see.' She waved a hand towards the play area, where a gaggle of infants from the nearby nursery were tearing around, watched over by their minders in their colourful tabards.

They sat in silence for a while, watching as Jack ducked behind a pine tree and peeked out from behind it, grinning up at them, seemingly oblivious to the fact that its narrow trunk did nothing whatsoever to hide him.

'He seems a well-adjusted little boy,' said Leah.

'Aye, he's brand new,' Zoe agreed, eyes not leaving her charge.

Leah opened her mouth to say something, then stopped, having seemingly changed her mind. A moment later, she tried again.

'And Anna … how is she?'

Zoe glanced sidelong at her. 'How d'ye mean?'

'Is *she* well-adjusted?'

Zoe frowned, trying to decipher the meaning behind the question. 'Aye?' she nodded slowly, trying to buy herself some time. 'She's grand, so she is. Work keeps her busy.'

'Mm.' Leah pursed her lips. 'So I've noticed. But does she have anything else going on in her life besides work? No man on the scene I don't know about?'

Zoe hesitated, wondering whether what she was about to say counted as breaking Anna's confidence. 'There *was* this detective at one point. For a while, it looked like it mighta gone somewhere. She liked him. He liked her. But' – she shrugged – 'y'know. They come, they go.'

By her side, Leah gave another 'Mm' – which might have meant *Mm, I know that only too well* or *Mm, that's not good at all* or something else altogether. A moment later, she drew in a sharp breath, and when Zoe turned to look at her, she found to her surprise that the older woman was dabbing her eyes with a tissue.

'Ye all right, Mrs S?' Zoe laid a hand on her shoulder.

Leah batted her concern away with her free hand. 'Ignore me. I'm just a silly old woman, I suppose. But no mother likes to think of her daughter being all alone.'

'She's not all alone, but,' said Zoe gently. 'She's got Jack, and she's got me.'

From Leah's lack of a response, it was clear she was far from reassured by this statement.

They lapsed into silence again. Jack continued his elaborate game of solitary hide and seek. Zoe's eyes drifted aimlessly over to the other side of the park, now considerably less congested than it had been, with only a dozen or so children remaining. Her eyes were unavoidably drawn to one of the three adults supervising them – a woman of about thirty, wearing a faded denim jacket and baggy, oversized cargo pants, and sporting a short shock of neon-pink hair that caused her to stand out like a glowing beacon in comparison to both her surroundings and the other grown-ups. Zoe had seen her before, and had always assumed she must work in the nursery, though it now occurred to her that the lack of a coloured tabard ran contrary to this theory. She looked a bit too young to be a mum – though, Zoe supposed, thirty really wasn't all that young at all. Plenty of people had kids far younger than that. Still, on the balance of probabilities, she reckoned 'childminder' was more likely.

She stirred, aware that Leah had spoken again. 'Sorry?'

Leah smiled patiently. 'I was just asking if there was anyone in *your* life? A man, or ... '

'Me?' Zoe smiled and shook her head. 'Naw, no top-secret toyboys in *my* life. I'm happy on my lonesome ownsome.'

She cast another glance in the direction of the play area. The pink-haired girl had disappeared from view.

She stirred. 'Best get a shifty on. There's a right nip in the air. Last thing we want is Jacko catching a chill.'

Anna got back in the early afternoon to find the house empty. A note in Zoe's handwriting informed her that she and Leah had taken Jack to the park. For a moment, anger flared inside her at the thought of them having gone ahead and done this without first running it by her. Then it occurred to her that if it had just been Zoe taking Jack out by herself, it would have been a non-issue. The fact that Leah had also tagged along should have been neither here nor there ... and yet, when it came down to it, it *did* make a difference. Anna reminded herself she was supposed to be trying to get on better with her mother. Finding pointless things to get mad about really wasn't the best way to go about doing that.

Concluding that the empty house afforded her an opportunity to follow up on the revelations from her conversation with Jeff while they were still fresh in her mind, Anna headed up to her office with a hastily thrown together sandwich and began searching for contact details for Guy Morton's first wife. She found her without too much difficulty. As she'd suspected, the one-time Miranda Morton had reverted to using her original surname of Hayes, and a LinkedIn profile in that name listed a two-year stint as a junior marketing executive at TransAlbion Ltd between 1982 and 1984. According to her profile, she was still working, having been employed as head of global corporate communications at Luminar, a PR agency in Dublin, since 2006. The 'About the Team' section of the company's website, however, contained no mention of a Miranda Hayes. It wasn't until Anna did a Google search for the name that she discovered the reason: according to multiple articles on a variety of news websites, Miranda Hayes had passed away in 2012 while still employed at Luminar. The cause of death was never explicitly stated, but several articles referred to a history of unspecified 'mental health issues', inviting readers to draw their own conclusions.

Anna sat back in her seat, the silence of her office feeling somehow cloying and oppressive. She was obviously disappointed as, for what seemed like the umpteenth time with this case, a potential lead had been shut down almost as soon as she'd become aware of its existence. Mostly, however, she just felt desperately sad for a woman who, from what Jeff had told her, had been treated abominably by his brother. As to whether there was any link between the aforementioned 'mental health issues' and her marriage to Guy Morton, Anna was in no position to draw any conclusions. But at the very least, it showed an urgent need to seriously consider the possibility that Guy's alleged treatment of his first wife had also extended to his second, and what impact this might have had on *her* state of mind.

Though she'd generally avoided engaging with the discourse surrounding female family annihilators, Anna hadn't spent the last twenty years immersed in feminist criminology without acquiring at least a working knowledge of the field. While the data was limited by virtue of just how rare such cases actually were, two factors she knew recurred time and again among women who murdered their families were the presence of an overbearing, often abusive male partner and a fear – real or imagined – of losing their children, with the act of pre-emptively killing them serving as a means to reassert some measure of control over a situation in which they felt powerless. Limited evidence also suggested social isolation to be a major factor.

On paper, Sandra Morton seemed to tick all the boxes: the wife of a controlling, coercive husband who had – seemingly intentionally – isolated her as much as possible and, shortly before his death, had told at least one person he was planning to sue for sole custody of their children. Of course, Sandra's lack of any apparent affection towards those children would seem to discredit the notion of her having had an existential fear of them being taken from her ... And yet, in making that assumption, wasn't Anna falling prey to the same reductive thinking as the voices who'd monstered her for her failure to conform to an arbitrary set of standards as to what constituted the 'correct' response to being told her husband and infant children had been murdered? Who was to say how she'd really felt about them, or how she would have responded to the threat of losing them?

People, she knew, liked to view the world through the reassuring lens of good versus bad. Heroes and villains. Offenders and victims. Lock up the guilty and protect the innocent. Move along, nothing to see. The reality, of course, was somewhat different. If you charted the lives of the three hundred women currently serving custodial sentences at HMP Broadwood, from birth to the present day, chances were that the vast majority would turn out to have, at some point, been subjected to one form of male abuse or another, be it physical, sexual, psychological or some other variety. She recognised now that the idea of Sandra as a victim in her own right had been taking shape in her mind for some time. It had begun with the media's coverage of the case – a highly personalised campaign of vilification conducted within the pages of the nation's newspapers and on its television screens – and had continued with McEnaney's gleeful recounting of the rumours surrounding her father. But, in the last few hours, Guy Morton had emerged as a deeply suspect figure in his own right, creating the unsettling possibility that Sandra had been a serial victim of abusive men.

The prosecution, Anna noted, had gone to considerable lengths during the trial to sell the idea that Sandra was mentally unstable and had snapped on the night of 6 May, killing Guy and the twins in a fit of psychotic rage. What they'd never done, as far as she could tell, was make any effort to explore *what* had made her snap – a glaring lack of curiosity that was echoed in the newspaper columns and TV bulletins. When a man murdered his family, considerable emphasis was invariably placed on the "tragedy" angle and speculation as to what pressures could have driven him to such desperate measures. But, when a woman did the same, there was rarely any consideration of any extenuating circumstances. It seemed to be taken as a given that whatever was wrong with Sandra was something innate within her rather than the result of any external factors. She'd simply been born that way and there was nothing anyone could have done to change it. No need for child services to intervene. No need to teach boys that women weren't objects or property. No need for any introspection or uncomfortable questions about the role of society in the monster's creation. Lock her up and throw away the key. The evil is vanquished. Job done.

None of this, of course, diminished the horror of what Sandra had done – assuming, of course, that she *did* do it. Indeed, if anything, the presence of these factors somehow made it more plausible to Anna's mind that Sandra *was* guilty – because it provided an explanation for her actions beyond the simplistic bromides of madness or badness. One of Anna's primary motivations in becoming a criminologist had been a desire not to merely document crime and explore its effects but to understand the reasons for it – both the broader, overarching, societal ones and the more intimate, personal ones. It wasn't enough simply to record the data dispassionately – she needed to understand *how* and *why*. The Sandra Morton case was no different in that regard. It had been naïve of her to believe she could ever be content to merely review the existing evidence and leave it at that. She didn't just *want* to follow the trail all the way back to the source – she *needed* to, and she was now more determined than ever to confront Sandra about her past at their next meeting.

As she sat there, watching the dust motes dancing in the light from the window facing her desk, she heard the front door opening and closing below her, followed by footsteps in the hallway and, a moment later, Zoe calling up the stairs in her best fifties housewife voice:

'Honey, we're *ho*-ome!'

25

Thursday 18 April

'Well, well! The prodigal one returns! This is getting to be quite a habit.'

This time, Sandra was already in situ at the desk in the interview room. She'd laid claim to Anna's usual chair – the one facing the door – and sat dipping a teabag in a mug of hot water, using the same 'string on pinkie' manoeuvre as before. Bob, the prison officer, occupied his regular position against the wall.

'How goes progress on the new book?' Sandra asked as Anna set out her voice recorder and other paraphernalia. 'Or is it rude to ask? Forgive me – I'm not *au fait* with publishing etiquette.'

'It's going fine,' said Anna noncommittally. 'Slow but steady.' She didn't overly feel like telling Sandra that progress had stalled almost completely.

'Well,' said Sandra, 'it may interest you to hear that, since we last spoke, I've finished reading your previous tome.'

The way she said it make it clear that she had Thoughts with a capital 'T'. Anna didn't invite her to elaborate – partly because she saw no point in encouraging Sandra to take a steaming dump on her work and partly because she knew Sandra was going to tell her her views regardless. Sure enough, after pausing to extricate the teabag from her finger and deposit it on the tray, Sandra folded her hands in front of her and launched into her critique.

'You write well – I'll give you that. You avoid the trap into which most academics fall of showing off their vocabulary at the expense of the point they're trying to make, and moment to moment, your arguments aren't entirely unpersuasive.'

'But … ?'

'But it has the same problem as all scholarly treatises on the subject – namely that you're too fixated on theory to see the practicalities. You propose a range of solutions that, yes, sound all well and good on paper but would fall apart the second they collide with the immovable force of a con who decides she doesn't want to play ball.' Keeping her palms together, Sandra spread her fingers into a V-shaped shrug. 'Sorry to be blunt.'

'No you're not,' said Anna, but without rancour. 'All I'll say is that lived experience matters, but so does the big picture. And I think you might be just a little too close to the ground to be able to see the wood for the trees.'

Sandra bared her teeth in something that looked too close to a snarl to properly qualify as a smile. 'Perhaps. Tell me, then – how have you been keeping yourself amused since our last chinwag? Any luck tracing our two elusive eyewitnesses?'

On her way to the prison, Anna had decided she was going to be full and frank with regard to the progress of her investigation, in the hope that such a spirit of openness would encourage Sandra to be more forthcoming herself. As such, despite a historic dislike of dwelling on her own failures, she now filled Sandra in on her efforts to find Paul Kempley and Adjoa Asante, including the likelihood that the latter had been deported some years ago.

'Well,' said Sandra, when she'd finished, 'it's not as if they were what you'd call reliable witnesses to begin with. One a horny teenager prone to memory lapses and the other an undocumented migrant who barely spoke the language.'

'The jury seemed to think they were plausible.'

'Ah, yes.' Sandra gave a knowing smirk. 'A representative cross-section of society. A certain George Carlin quote about the intelligence of the average person springs to mind.'

'Think of how stupid the average person is, then remember that half the world's population is even stupider?'

'Exactly.'

Anna didn't exactly disagree with the sentiment, though she wouldn't have phrased it quite so bluntly. She'd long held grave misgivings about the concept of trial by jury – the idea that the accused had no recourse but to put their trust in a randomly selected group of people who brought any number of in-built prejudices with them to the table. Such qualms had been far from allayed by the succession of sensationalised scoops and exclusives that had occupied the front pages in the days and weeks following the murders, each insinuating Sandra's guilt with varying degrees of unsubtlety.

'So' – Sandra's voice cut into Anna's thoughts – 'I trust adequate childcare arrangements are in place today? I'd hate for you to go scurrying off again to collect your son just when we're getting into the good stuff.'

'No,' Anna replied offhandedly, 'he's being well looked after today. Got both my housemate *and* my dearly beloved mother looking after him today. I'm sure they're all having a whale of a time.'

As soon as she'd spoken, she knew, from the look of glee that had entered Sandra's eyes, that the carrot she'd deliberately dangled had had the intended effect.

'*Oooh!* Do I detect a touch of familial strife between you and Mummy dearest?'

Anna pulled a rueful face. 'You could say that. She showed up unannounced a week ago. Since then, she's been sticking her nose into everything. I thought I was past having my mother trying to run my life, but evidently I was mistaken.'

Sandra's lip curled. 'Well, you know what Philip Larkin said about mums and dads.'

Anna laughed dryly. 'I'm not sure how typical my upbringing was, but mine certainly did their level best to prove him right.'

Sandra dipped a finger in her mug of tea, spinning a lazy whirlpool. 'In my experience, parents come in one of two flavours. They're either overbearing tyrants who try to control every aspect of your life or they're the polar opposite – feeble, weak-willed non-entities who don't give a toss about their offspring. Either way, they invariably let you down when you need them most.'

'Do you feel let down by yours?'

'And what about this son of yours?' said Sandra, as if she hadn't heard Anna's question. 'Making her presence felt where he's concerned, I'll bet.

Let me guess – she's muscled in with her own ideas about what constitutes good childrearing?'

'You could say that. Just the other day, Jack asked me if God can see you when you go to the toilet. I've never mentioned God to him in his life. Turns out his grandmother's been putting daft ideas in his head – telling him he's always watching you or some such rubbish.'

'Have it out with her, did you?' Sandra asked, with undisguised relish. 'What did she say when you put her on the spot?'

'At first, she pretended not to know what I was talking about. Then she tried to downplay it, saying why did it matter so much. Then, finally, she treated me to a lecture about how all children need some form of moral and spiritual grounding if they're to grow into well-adjusted adults – the inference being that he's not getting any of that from me. I told her to keep her proselytising to herself while she was in my house.'

Even as Anna finished speaking, she knew she'd gone further than she'd intended – and yet, she couldn't deny that there was something undeniably cathartic about the act of sharing her frustrations with someone who at least gave the *impression* of understanding them.

'They're all the same, really,' said Sandra. 'People of *faith*.' She uttered the phrase with undisguised contempt. 'It's the lack of introspection that really gets to me – the absolute certainty that their belief in a higher power automatically makes them more righteous than those who don't share it. But it doesn't – it just makes them more credulous.'

'You sound like you speak from experience.'

Sandra gave Anna a withering look. 'You already know I do, or else you *really* haven't done your research.' She tutted and shook her head. 'Poor effort, I'm afraid – this transparent attempt to segue into rooting around in my past, trying to locate the inciting incident that made me the way I am. I've already had plenty of that from the litany of shrinks and psychoanalysts who've spent the last eighteen years lining up to ascribe this condition or that mental imbalance to me. Don't tell me I'm going to have to endure it from you too.'

'I wasn't,' Anna insisted, unnerved by how easily Sandra had seen through her. 'I asked because I'm genuinely interested. In the last few weeks, I've probably read every book and article ever written about you, and not one of them has come even close to conveying a sense of your perspective in all of this. Most of them were too busy going out of the way to vilify you as the devil incarnate.'

Sandra smirked. 'Whereas you see me not as a monster but as an actual *person*. How very touching.'

'For *instance*,' Anna went on, ignoring her, 'I gather it was your husband who asked his parents to take a more active role in caring for the twins. I'm curious – was that a decision you were on board with?'

Sandra's only response was stony-faced silence.

'It's just that I can't help but notice a pattern of people overriding and undermining your wishes. Were children something you wanted, or was it more down to Guy pressuring you to fulfil what he regarded as your obligations as a wife?'

She knew she was playing a dangerous game, trying to provoke an unguarded response, but with Sandra having seen through her original plan, the softly-softly approach wasn't going to cut it.

'The thing is,' she continued, as Sandra continued to sit in silence, 'women are expected to just take to motherhood like ducks to water – to have all the answers to everything; to never lose their rag, even when their kids are winding them up to high doh; to never let on that sometimes, just sometimes, a tiny part of them wishes they'd never them had in the first place. But mothers aren't supposed to admit that they struggle, are they?'

Sandra gave an amused smile. 'Is there a question in there somewhere, or is this purely a personal confession?'

'Whose idea was it for Katie to go and live with her grandparents? Not yours, I'm guessing. Did Guy and your in-laws make the decision, or was it something Katie requested herself?'

Silence.

'Either way, it must have been painful.'

Sandra snorted. 'That's what you think, is it? That I was an uncontrollable, burbling wreck? That they had to wrest her from my arms and drag her away while I cried big, salty tears? Please! You've read every word ever written about me. What do they say about me?'

Anna gave a small shrug, inviting Sandra to tell her herself.

'I'll tell you what they say. That I'm cold. Emotionally distant. An unfit mother.' Sandra's voice was rising now. She was displaying a genuine anger that Anna hadn't encountered in her before. 'And they're right. Every word they say about me is true. The day they took that brat off my hands was the best day of my life.'

'I don't believe that, and I don't believe you do either,' said Anna, firmly but levelly. 'The people who wrote those words might have fooled themselves into believing they had you all figured out, but they had no way of knowing what was really going on inside your head.'

'And I suppose you *do*?'

'I know what it is to carry a child to term. To nurse them. To raise them. You don't do that without developing a bond with them, even if it wasn't the life you originally envisioned for yourself.'

Sandra folded her arms and leaned back in her seat. 'Is there a point to this, or are you just trying to impose your own embarrassing life experiences on me? Whatever happened to the big picture, Professor Scavolini?'

'There's something of a pattern, isn't there,' Anna went on, refusing to take the bait, 'of children being taken from you.'

No response.

'Because it wasn't just Katie, was it? I spoke to your brother-in-law. He told me your husband had told him he was planning to leave you and take the kids. That he'd even hired a private detective to build a case against you.'

Nothing.

'And according to at least one source, you got pregnant at fourteen and were sent away to have an abortion.'

Still nothing.

'What's more,' Anna decided to go for broke, 'according to that source, there were even suggestions that the man who impregnated you was your own father.'

Sandra continued to sit in silence, but Anna thought she detected a slight movement at the corner of her mouth. It was little more than a flicker, but it was enough to convince her that she was on the right track. Then, she became aware that Sandra was making a strange noise at the back of her throat – something between coughing and gagging. It took her a moment to realise what it was. Sandra was laughing – a deep, contemptuous, ugly cackle that barely sounded human.

'Oh, that's good,' she purred, once her laughter subsided, 'that really is.

Pray tell – what fourth-rate "source" told you that? No, no,' she added, before Anna could respond, 'don't tell me. Let me guess. It'll be one of those peddlers of smut and innuendo who cashed in and wrote their grotty little tell-alls about the case once the commissions from the gutter press dried up. Cochrane, maybe, or McEnaney.'

Anna's expression must have given her away, for Sandra's eyes lit up, her sardonic smile widening. 'It *was?* Well I never! So you let yourself be taken in by *that* bottom-feeder? I have to admit, I'm genuinely surprised. I'd credited you as a better judge of character.' She shook her head and sighed mirthfully. 'Let's see if I'm up to speed here. We've gone from the theory that I snapped and killed darling Guy and the twins while I was in the grip of a dissociative episode to me being a poor, messed-up girly who got knocked up at fourteen by her daddy, was made to get rid of the baby to save the family's honour and – what, years later, the discovery that my husband was planning to relieve me of my offspring triggered some delayed response in me and, convinced that history was about to repeat itself, I decided to off them pre-emptively, on the grounds that, if I couldn't have them, no one could?'

Put like that, it sounded hopelessly far-fetched, and Anna felt a wave of embarrassment washing over her. What had seemed so seductively plausible in the cloistered safety of her office had been ripped to shreds before her very eyes, the bloodied remains dumped unceremoniously in her lap.

'The criminology journals are full of mothers who murdered their own children for that very reason,' she said weakly.

Sandra rolled her eyes. 'Criminology journals are written by dullards who think they know far more than they actually do. In the hierarchy of intellectual blowhards, they rank just above psychologists in terms of idiocy. One lot's obsessed with drawing dodgy conclusions from inadequate statistics, the other with finding a Freudian explanation for every minor character defect.'

'That's a rather reductionist view. Some of the most significant advancements in our understanding of crime have come from—'

'I suppose I shouldn't judge too harshly,' Sandra went on, once again acting as if Anna hadn't spoken. 'After all, indulging in navel-gazing is what you lot do best. But you're wasting your time on all these esoteric theories when you should be concentrating on the umpteen holes in the original investigation. Take the multiple strangers seen hanging around Hillend in the run-up to the murders, for example – why were those never properly followed up? That one with the Charles Manson hair – he seems like a prime candidate. Why aren't you pulling out all the stops to trace *him*?'

Anna looked at Sandra curiously. Was it her imagination, or did this sudden interest in eyewitness sightings have more than a whiff of deflection about it? Deflection from *what*, though? If she was right, if Sandra *was* attempting to steer her down a blind alley, then it could only mean that she'd touched on the truth – or at least something close enough to it to give Sandra cause for concern – without realising it.

'Well,' said Sandra, lazily running a hand through her unbrushed hair, 'that's us put the "loony psycho mum" hypothesis to bed. Any others you care to float?'

For a moment, Anna didn't respond. She knew it was a mistake to indulge Sandra; that she'd only be opening herself up to further ridicule. However, it was beginning to dawn on her that, given the way things were going, this could well be the last opportunity she got to put any questions to the woman facing her. If this was to be the last hurrah, she might as well make the most of it.

'One other possibility,' she said, more or less thinking aloud, 'is that we've been looking at this all wrong – that the killer wasn't you but *was* known to you. Someone you're covering for. A lover, perhaps – someone who was jealous of your relationship with your family and wanted to clear the decks, so to speak.'

Sandra laughed and clapped her hands in delight. 'Ooh, I *like* it! Straight out of the pages of the penny dreadfuls! Just one problem with your little theory: I didn't have a lover. And even if I did, I certainly wouldn't have chosen to spend the rest of my life behind bars to protect him.'

'So there's no truth in the rumour that you were seeing multiple men?'

'That's different.' Sandra raised a corrective finger. 'They weren't lovers. They were men that I fucked.'

As Anna gazed back at the woman facing her, the thought idly occurred to her that Sandra was not a conventionally attractive woman, and that perhaps this was partly why the fact she'd flaunted her sexuality so overtly

– by dressing provocatively, by conducting affairs with multiple male partners – had been deemed so scandalous.

'And you felt nothing for any of them,' she said.

Sandra shrugged. 'I'm the Ice Queen. I don't *have* feelings.'

'You keep doing that.'

'What?'

'Hiding behind the persona the media created for you whenever we touch on territory you find uncomfortable.'

Sandra stifled a yawn. 'This is becoming tedious. Any other ideas in your bag of clichés? Come on, Professor – think back to your under-graduate lectures. Why do women kill their husbands and children?' She clapped her hands like she was keeping time. 'Quick, quick – this is textbook stuff.'

'Some women—' Anna began, before stopping herself. She knew they'd long passed the point where there was anything to be gained by playing Sandra's game.

'Yes? Some women what?' Sandra's pale blue eyes bored into her intently.

'Well,' she muttered, sounding far more defensive than she would have liked, 'there have been cases documented of women who've experienced prolonged spousal abuse snapping and killing both the abuser and their children.'

'So dear, sweet Guy was roughing me up behind closed doors and I'd had my fill – is that it?' Sandra threw back her head and cackled. 'Oh, *my*. I know you feminists love your stories of battered wives, but the idea of that mummy's boy ever lifting so much as a finger against me is quite possibly the most inane thing you've come out with all afternoon – and that's saying something. The Morton men might like to think they're the ones in control, but, to a man, they're nothing but weak-willed, spineless milksops.'

'Abuse doesn't have to be physical. There are other, equally insidious forms. Isolation, for one. Or gaslighting, or neglect, or—'

Sandra feigned a loud and overly theatrical yawn. Like the breaking of a dam, this proved to be the final straw for Anna. Abandoning any last vestige of decorum, she leaned across the table towards her, as if the increased physical proximity would make her case more persuasive.

'Come on – if you really are innocent, let me help you. I'm here to be convinced. I've not written you off as the spawn of Satan like everyone else. I'm willing to give you the fair hearing no one else has ever afforded you.'

'Oh, very good.' Sandra rolled her eyes and rocked back in her seat, arms folded. 'My own personal saviour! You think, if you just look deep enough into my eyes, you'll see the truth that lies behind them?' She barked out another ugly laugh. 'Well, no one can accuse you of having an insufficiently high opinion of yourself. And what then, once I've convinced you? You'll use your superior skills of persuasion to compel the courts to strike down my conviction and let me go? *That's* the grand scheme you and little Pamela have cooked up together?

'Oh yes,' she went on, as Anna's eyes involuntarily widened in surprise, 'I know it was her who put you up to this. Sussed it out the moment that visitation request came through. You think you're both *so* clever, scuttling around behind my back, thinking I wouldn't work it out. You're like a couple of silly little girls playing detective, flattering yourselves into thinking you'll succeed where two separate legal teams and four appeals failed. Well, I've got news for you: you'll crash and burn like the rest of them, and I'll be watching from the sidelines, enjoying every minute of it.'

Anna gazed back at Sandra in disbelief. There was cutting off your nose to spite your face, and then there was actively sabotaging the best shot at having your own conviction overturned purely for the satisfaction of seeing the person attempting to orchestrate it fail. She opened and closed her mouth multiple times, trying to formulate a response, but before she could get a word out, Sandra turned to her guard and addressed him in a tone of bored indifference.

'I'd like to go back to my room now, Bob. The company here isn't what it once was.'

Anna continued to stare at Sandra imploringly. 'Work with me,' she said helplessly. 'Let me help you.'

She was aware of Bob drawing alongside her. 'Come on, Professor. Time to get yer skates on.'

He didn't touch her, but she sensed his hand hovering within reach of her arm, ready to grab it should it prove necessary.

Anna got to her feet, not taking her eyes off Sandra.

'Come on, Professor,' Bob said again, a note of warning now entering his voice.

Slowly, deliberately Anna gathered up her voice recorder and other odds and ends, her eyes remaining fixed on Sandra, who was now preoccupied with inspecting some dirt trapped under her thumbnail. Somehow, she thought that if she could just make eye contact with her, she might stand a chance of making her see reason.

But it was not to be. By the time she'd finished packing up her things, Sandra still hadn't looked up. Aware of Bob hovering by her side, she turned and walked out without looking back, not wanting to give Sandra the satisfaction of seeing her having to be dragged out.

As Anna strode down the corridor, her cheeks burning, one of the doors ahead of her swung open and Ruth Laxton stepped into view.

'Well, well,' she said, 'so you're back with us again, Professor Scavolini? I must say, you're becoming something of a regular fixture here.'

If Anna had felt so inclined, she could have pointed out that Ruth's woefully transparent attempt to make this out to be a chance encounter rather than a deliberate ambush wouldn't have fooled a five-year-old. But right now, she had bigger fish to fry.

'So it would seem,' she grunted, not breaking her stride.

'It's all highly irregular,' the prison governor went on, hurrying to keep pace with her. 'All these ... *meetings*. For the last five years, Sandra hasn't seen any visitors besides her solicitor, and now, all of a sudden, you're here three times in the space of just over a month. It can't be doing her any good – getting so exercised this often.'

'Well, don't worry,' Anna replied. 'After today, I doubt you'll be seeing me again.'

With that, she quickened her pace and strode on towards the exit, leaving the aggrieved Ruth to stare after her in helpless indignation.

26

The journey home did nothing to ease Anna's sense of frustration. She couldn't for the life of her understand why Sandra was so utterly unwilling to help herself – why her only response to a sincere offer to listen to her version of events without fear or favour was to sneer and mock. She understood that Sandra had little reason to trust people, but Anna liked to think that, over the course of their three meetings, she'd done enough to demonstrate that she wasn't the equivalent of some unscrupulous tabloid hack out to profit from the grisly deaths of a man and two infant children or a quack psychiatrist determined to add another feather to his bow by pinning some spurious diagnosis to her. She'd gone out of her way to treat the most hated woman in the country without prejudice, only to have it thrown back in her face.

The one moment when Sandra had seemed to briefly engage with the spirit of the proceedings had been when she'd entreated Anna to look into the eyewitness reports of strangers in and around Hillend prior to the night of the murders. Did she genuinely believe the sightings of a young man with long hair and vaguely Manson-esque appearance constituted a significant lead, or had she been trying to distract Anna from something else? Anna thought back to that part of the conversation, mentally replaying their respective contributions leading up to Sandra's reference to the sightings. She'd just stated that, in the criminology journals, there were umpteen examples of women who'd killed their own children because they became convinced someone was going to take them. And before that, she'd raised the matter of the rumour that Sandra had been impregnated at the age of fourteen by her own father.

Could it really be true?

Anna had always been inclined to view the pregnancy story as the result of McEnaney either getting carried away after listening to unsubstantiated gossip or else concocting his own twisted fantasy to satisfy whatever mental aberration caused people to come up with such disgusting ideas – but was that because the story itself was genuinely improbable or was it because she desperately *wanted* it not to be true? She still sincerely hoped it was the former, though she had to admit that the latter seemed increasingly plausible. Unless, of course, Sandra was playing an elaborate double bluff and had, for reasons unknown, engineered her response specifically to plant the seed in Anna's mind. It seemed unwise to put *anything* past her.

Either way, Anna knew she was unlikely to get an answer now. As far as she could see, with no other credible leads and Sandra actively refusing to cooperate, she'd come to the end of the road. She supposed she'd better get in touch with Pamela and give her advance warning that Sandra was wise to the ruse they'd concocted together and that there was a not insignificant chance she would shortly have one less client on her books.

But not yet. She'd had enough drama for one day.

All this was to say that Anna was hardly in the most positive frame of mind when she got home. Upon entering the house, she promptly tripped over something lying just beyond the threshold and lost her footing. She only saved herself from landing flat on her face by grabbing onto the nearby console table, causing most of its contents to spill onto the floor. She righted herself, cursing under her breath, and turned to see what she'd tripped over. A pair of Gabor ankle boots sat directly in front of the doormat, one knocked over onto its side, the other still standing provocatively upright.

This time, she didn't bother to stifle her curses. 'For fuck's fucking *sake*!' she yelled, violently kicking the boots out of the way. 'Who the fuck left *these* in the hallway?'

She knew, of course, precisely who was responsible. There was only one person in the house who wore shoes of that style, and it was neither her nor Zoe.

On cue, the guilty party emerged from the living room.

'What do you mean by making such a racket?' Leah demanded, striding into the hallway. 'Anyone would think World War Three was starting.'

Anna jabbed a finger at the offending items. 'I just tripped on your fucking boots and nearly broke my neck.'

Leah folded her arms and regarded Anna without sympathy. 'Well, that'll teach you to look where you're going, then, won't it? You probably had your head in the clouds as usual.'

'I wouldn't *have* to look where I was going if you didn't leave your overpriced wellies lying in the middle of a walkway,' Anna retorted, her voice an angry snarl.

'Well, where am I *supposed* to leave them? It's not as if you even have a shoe drop.'

'Oh, perish the thought that I wouldn't have one of *those*—'

'And another thing,' Leah cut her off. 'The language you use around this house is *completely* inappropriate. What hope has that child of yours got of learning how to express himself civilly if his own mother curses like a football player at every opportunity?'

'I'll use whatever language I please in my own fucking house!' Anna shouted, her voice rising to fever pitch.

'Hey, hey, hey!' Zoe had now appeared on the scene as well, a look of dismay on her features. 'What's all the hullaballoo? Folk can hear yese fae here tae Timbuktu. Time out, awright?'

As one, both women turned to face Zoe – their chastened expressions, if Anna only had the self-awareness to realise it, a perfect mirror image of one another.

'There's no need for thus sorta strife, yese hear me?' Zoe went on, addressing them like a pair of recalcitrant children. 'We're all just gonnae take five big, deep breaths – in and out, in and out …'

She looked so patently absurd, puffing her cheeks like a bellows while she conducted with her arms, that Anna found herself having to stifle a laugh. Out of the corner of her eye, she saw that Leah, too, was watching Zoe with wry amusement.

'There now!' Zoe declared, satisfied that the tension had been suitably defused. 'Isn't everything much better when we can all get along?' She regarded mother and daughter in turn, hands on hips, and shook her head disapprovingly. 'Ye've been able tae cut the air in this hoose wi a knife for yonks now. It's no good for the blood pressure. Well, I'm putting a stop to it here and now. The morra, the four of us are going on a day out – a proper family pleasure trip. When was the last time we had one of those?'

'It's a weekday,' Anna protested feebly. 'I've got to work.'

'Ah, c'mon,' said Zoe. 'Y'think I havnae noticed ye burning the midnight oil every night for weeks now? Ye can afford tae start the weekend early just the once. 'Sides, it's non-negotiable. Doctor's orders.'

'But—'

'Ah!' Zoe held up a hand, silencing her.

'I—'

'What did I just say?'

Anna looked at Zoe, then at her mother, who appeared to be privately enjoying this whole spectacle, then felt her shoulders slump in defeat.

'Fine,' she muttered.

Zoe beamed, instantly mollified. 'All righty, then! Leave it tae me. I'll take care of all the particulars.'

She spun on her heel and sauntered off, humming cheerfully. Anna shot a baleful look at Leah, as if to say, *Now see what you've caused?* Her mother merely shrugged innocently and headed back to the living room, the spat over her boots seemingly forgotten. Anna remained in the hallway, still in her coat, the very air around her seeming to crackle with electric tension. For a moment, she didn't move. Then, with a sigh of resignation, she bent down and began to gather up the various objects that had fallen from the table.

27

Friday 19 April

They set off late the following morning, taking the M8 out of Glasgow. Zoe's chosen destination, as she'd informed them after she was safely installed behind the wheel and they were on their way, was Blair Drummond Safari Park in Stirling, roughly an hour's drive away. As they rolled north up the M80, Anna told herself it wouldn't be the end of the world if she took one day off, and that it might even serve as something of a palate cleanser, allowing her to put the Sandra Morton business firmly behind her before she redoubled her efforts on the now seriously behind schedule first draft of her book. Nonetheless, it wasn't until they'd passed through Cumbernauld and the countryside had begun to open up before them that she felt the tension in her shoulders beginning to loosen and the cloud she belatedly realised had been hanging over her for weeks start to lift.

Her mood continued to improve as they meandered through the park, heading from attraction to attraction at a leisurely pace, letting Jack's ever-changing whims dictate their direction of travel. Leah, too, seemed more at ease and, to Anna's surprise, didn't even complain about getting mud all over her good shoes. Jack seemed to have picked up on the more harmonious family dynamic and was in high spirits himself, shrieking with delight at the lions, hippos and other creatures that, until now, he'd only ever seen in books. He was particularly enamoured by the tall, majestic giraffes, who regarded him with cool indifference from their enclosure.

Watching him, Zoe nudged Anna conspiratorially. 'You thinking what I'm thinking?'

Their eyes met, both reading the other's mind perfectly. '"Look at me, Damien!"' they recited in unison. '"It's all for you!"'

As they collapsed in peals of laughter, Jack beamed at them cluelessly, not understanding why they were laughing but happy all the same because Anna was happy, while Leah watched them in bemused incredulity and declared that she didn't get it.

They set off for home a little after 3.30, stopping, at Zoe's enthusiastic suggestion, for ice creams at a parlour in Cumbernauld Village which, based on previous experience, she declared were 'good enough tae give ye a braingasm'. She wasn't far wrong, and as they sat clustered around a tiny circular table with a red-and-white-chequered cloth, digging into their respective dishes, Anna felt a deep and profound sense of warmth spreading throughout her that belied the chill of the massive sundae she'd barely made a dent in.

'Thanks for today,' she said to Zoe, who was making considerably more headway with her own bowl of ice cream and waffles. 'I don't think I was ready to admit how much I needed this. How much we *all* needed it.'

Zoe grinned and aimed a friendly slap at her arm. 'Ach, any time, doll. We all need tae chillax every once in a while – 'specially those of us that're overworking our noggins all the time. Howsabout you, Mrs S?' she asked Leah. 'You looked like ye were having a grand ol' time.'

Leah pondered the question, carefully working her tongue around inside her mouth. 'It was certainly stimulating,' she eventually concluded – which, by Anna's reckoning, was high praise indeed. 'At any rate, Jack seems to have had a whale of a time.'

They all turned to look at Jack, who appeared to be managing to get more ice cream on his face than inside his mouth.

'Aye,' said Zoe, with a contented sigh. ''S all about building memories, in't it? Like, odds are a day like this is gonnae stick with him forever. Who knows? Mibby, in years to come, it'll even be his first memory. What's the earliest thing *you* remember, Mrs S?'

'Gosh!' Leah gave an awkward little laugh. 'I suppose it would probably be Saturday mornings at Garnethill Synagogue with my parents … but really, I'm so long in the tooth it's hard to recall.'

'Aye,' Zoe grinned, 'at your grand auld age ye've prob'ly forgotten mair than us whippersnappers'll ever know.' She turned to Anna. 'What about you, doll? What's your earliest memory?'

Anna became acutely aware the every pair of eyes at the table – even Jack's – was now locked on her. She shifted uncomfortably in her seat, tugging at the neckline of her blouse, which suddenly felt improbably tight.

'I … I don't know,' she eventually muttered. 'Honestly, I've no idea.'

It took several more denials to convince Zoe, but eventually she gave up the ghost and moved onto her own first memory – a journey in the back of her parents' car which she insisted, in the face of all logic to the contrary, was her coming home from the hospital at just a few days old. For Anna, however, the mood had irreversibly shifted, and she remained distant and subdued for the remainder of their time at the parlour and throughout the drive home.

Contrary to what she'd told the others, she could, in fact, recall her first memory with perfect clarity. She'd been about Jack's age at the time – somewhere between three and four. Her father, on a rare afternoon off, had taken her on a stroll down to the Botanic Gardens at the top of Byres Road. She'd left him sitting on a bench and gone wandering off to explore the glasshouses with their collection of rare and endangered plants.

On returning to the bench some fifteen minutes later, she'd found him gone. At first, she'd assumed he was somewhere nearby. Perhaps he'd seen someone he knew and gone over to say hello? Gradually, however, the realisation that he was no longer there had set in, and she'd begun to panic.

At first, she'd managed to hold it together, and had made her way up the path in search of him, heading back the way they'd come. It hadn't taken long, though, for the tears to begin to flow, and while a handful of passersby had expressed concern, she'd remembered her parents' frequent lectures about not talking to strangers and had steadfastly ignored them, even as her legs grew increasingly leaden and the tears made it impossible to see where she was going.

She'd made it almost as far as the west gate when one of the park wardens finally apprehended her. By then, she was verging on exhaustion and in the grip of what, with the benefit of age and experience, she now recognised as her first ever panic attack. The warden had carried her back to the gatehouse, where he and a colleague had asked her all manner of questions. *Where do you live? Do you know where your parents are? What's your mummy's name?* Ordinarily, she'd have been able to ream off the answers to all these questions without a second thought, but at that moment, she'd been too distraught to even tell them her own name. One of the wardens had said something about calling the police, and that had only caused her to panic even more, consumed by the irrational but nonetheless sincerely held belief that they were going to put her in prison.

In the end, things never progressed that far. Both her parents had turned up at the gatehouse, breathless and full of apologies and gratitude. Phrases like 'wandered off' and 'had no idea where she'd gone' were bandied about, and the wardens, seemingly satisfied that the crisis had been resolved, gladly returned her to the bosom of her family, no doubt congratulating themselves on a job well done.

The recriminations had begun as soon as Anna and her parents had left the park. All the predictable lectures about the fright she'd given them both had ensued, and Anna, exhausted and barely able to think straight, had quickly accepted that she'd been in the wrong and had put her parents through merry hell. It wasn't until many years later, revisiting the events of that day for the umpteenth time, that she'd started to question the narrative her parents had imposed on her. She was sure she'd told her father exactly where she was going, so the 'wandered off' line didn't stack up. And then there were the logistical anomalies, like the fact he'd taken her to the Gardens himself but both he and her mother had turned up at the gatehouse. Eventually, she'd deduced that her father – distracted, no doubt, by work matters – had forgotten why he was there and that he'd brought her with him and had gone home, only realising the error of his ways when confronted by his wife as to their daughter's whereabouts.

Even to this day, the entire episode and the way it had been dealt with pained her on a visceral level. It was bad enough that she'd occupied such a low rung on her father's list of priorities that he'd forgotten all about her and abandoned her in a public space. What made it all so much worse was that her mother, despite it being impossible for her not to have realised what had really happened, had taken her husband's side and allowed Anna to believe she was the one at fault.

What sort of parents did that to a child? To a *three*-year-old?

* * *

These thoughts were still preying on Anna's mind when the time came for them to make tracks. Anna and Leah headed outside while Zoe took Jack for a pre-emptive visit to the toilet ahead of the journey home. As they stood under the awning, Leah contemplated her watch. Her expression told Anna that she didn't like what she saw.

'What time do you suppose we'll get home?' she said, turning to Anna.

'Hard to say,' said Anna, half-wondering what the big hurry was. 'We'll probably hit the evening traffic, so I'd imagine anywhere between half an hour and fifty minutes. Why? Have you got somewhere you need to be?'

Leah made a noise at the back of her throat that sounded somewhere between a scoff and a sigh. 'Not till later, but it's just … well, I'm going to need time to get ready.'

'Ready?'

'You know.' Leah's expression was one of incredulity, mixed with a side order of something resembling weary forbearance. '*Passover.*'

'Oh,' said Anna. She'd forgotten it was today – or, to be more precise, it had never occurred to her in the first place. That was the trouble with holidays whose dates changed every year – especially if you didn't observe them yourself. At least you always knew where you were with April Fool's Day.

'Oh,' she said again, rather more feebly; then, 'I don't … I mean, *we* don't … '

Leah gave a rather strained smile. 'I *had* worked that out. The Kupermans have invited me for supper at theirs. I'm due there at seven.' She gestured to her mud-stained shoes. 'I can't very well turn up looking like *this*, can I?'

'Oh,' said Anna, for the third time. 'Well, don't worry. I'm sure we'll have you back in plenty time.'

'Yes. I … ' Leah hesitated for a moment, then began again. 'Sara asked me to tell you that you're very welcome to come along … as is Jack. I mean,' she went on – already, it seemed to Anna, tripping over herself to talk her out of it, 'I imagine you probably wouldn't want him there, but … well, the offer stands nonetheless.'

For a moment, Anna didn't respond. It had been a good twenty years since she'd last participated in a Passover seder, and longer still since she'd regarded it as anything other than a collection of archaic and faintly ridiculous rituals which were of no relevance to her. And yet, she couldn't deny the existence of the faintest stirring inside her of a yearning for … well, for *something*. Not so much the rituals themselves, but perhaps the earlier, more innocent period in her life with which she associated them.

The moment passed, and the spell was broken. 'I can't,' she said, stirring. 'I'm going to have to work this evening – you know, to make up for today? It's just, I'm *really* behind with this draft, and … '

Leah gave a tight smile. 'It's fine. Another time, perhaps.'

Anna returned the smile, grateful to her mother for saving them both from the embarrassment of having to listen to her on-the-hoof excuse-spinning. 'But listen,' she said, 'tomorrow night, we'll all eat together at home – you, me, Jack and Zoe. I'll lay on a feast that'll put Mrs Kuperman's cooking to shame.'

For a moment, Leah simply stared at Anna. Clearly, this wasn't something she'd been anticipating. Nor, for that matter, had Anna, who'd formulated the plan on the spot.

'That would be very nice,' said her mother, in a tone of great magnanimity. 'After all,' she added with a ghost of a smile, 'it's customary for the Diaspora to celebrate with a second meal the following night as well.'

'Hey,' said Anna sharply, 'don't make this into something it's not. It's just a bog-standard family dinner – no religious connotations whatsoever.'

Leah said nothing, but she continued to smile to herself in a knowing sort of way. It was an unreadable smile and, for that reason, all the more irritating to Anna, who, for reasons that she couldn't explain, was left feeling like she'd just conceded some ground she hadn't meant to.

At that moment, the door opened behind them and Zoe emerged from the parlour with Jack in tow.

'Right, then,' she said briskly, 'we gonnae get this show on the road?'

It was after five when they finally pulled onto Clarence Drive. They got out of the car, Zoe carrying a now exhausted Jack, and headed indoors. Leah went straight upstairs to get changed, while Zoe took Jack through to the kitchen to make him some dinner. Anna joined them for long enough to fix herself a quick sandwich, which she took upstairs to eat in her office while she got down to business. Having used her book as an excuse to turn down her mother's invitation, she now felt obligated to actually do some work on it to avoid proving herself a liar.

As she re-read the last couple of paragraphs she'd written, trying to pick up the thread of her argument once more, the sound of brief, meandering little morsels of song reached her ears from the room next door, rising and falling like waves on a gentle sea. Stopping to listen, she recognised the words and melody of 'Chad Gadya', the playful children's song traditionally sung at the end of the Passover feast.

'*Chad gadya, chad gadya, dizabin abah bitrei zuzei…*'

Even now, two decades after she'd last heard them, the tune and words came back to her as readily as if she still sung them every day. They brought with them a comforting sense of familiarity, again with a tantalising sense that something indefinable and yet yearned for lay just beyond her reach.

She shook her head, forcing these thoughts from her mind, and resumed reading.

She remained shut up in her office for the next several hours, hunched over her keyboard as she attempted the literary equivalent of drawing blood from a stone. It was always the same for her with any sort of writing project. You couldn't do these things piecemeal, writing a few sentences here, a paragraph there, expecting to jump back in after a lengthy absence and immediately hit the ground running. You had to properly dedicate yourself to the task. That was, after all, meant to have been the entire point of the sabbatical. While metaphorically bashing her head against the wall over and over, she heard Leah heading out and, just over an hour later, Zoe putting Jack to bed. She listened to Zoe's voice rising and falling at the other end of the corridor, the story she was telling Jack capturing her imagination far more readily than the section on the financial cost of incarceration that she was currently trying to power through.

She left it until around a quarter to eleven before throwing in the towel, having added fewer than two hundred and fifty words to the total, most of which she suspected she was going to end up deleting tomorrow. She got stiffly to her feet and made her way along the corridor to Jack's room. She put her ear to the door, listening for signs of life inside, but heard nothing. Cautiously, she eased the door open a crack and peered in. A sliver of light from the corridor illuminated the mop of dark hair resting on the pillow. The duvet, cocooned around his body, rose and fell in time with his steady breathing.

Anna remained where she was for a few moments longer. Then, shutting the door once more, she sloped downstairs to the living room, where she found Zoe lounging on the sofa, half-watching a late-night chat show on TV while she scrolled through her phone.

'Oh hey,' she said, reaching for the remote and muting the sound. 'How'd it go with the key-bashing? Manage tae conquer Mount Everest?'

'Getting there,' said Anna, concluding that Zoe didn't need to know about her severe case of writer's block. 'Leah say when she'd be back?'

Zoe shook her head. 'She reckoned it'd be a late one. Said we weren't tae wait up for her. I gave her the spare key.'

'How'd she seem to you?'

'Oh, y'know – just her usual indefatigable self. Went sauntering oot the door in her glad rags, looking like she'd just won the EuroMillions. S'pose we all need a quality knees-up every now and then, don't we?'

'Heh, yeah.'

Anna slid into the armchair facing the sofa. She watched as Zoe's eyes returned to the now mute television screen, following the lantern-jawed celebrity with the Brylcreemed hair as he regaled the host with an extended monologue that involved a lot of expansive hand gestures and baring of his frighteningly white teeth.

A quality knees-up. When was the last time Zoe had had anything of the sort? Here she was yet again, relegated to childminding duty on a Friday night while Anna hid in her office, behaving as if Jack was someone else's child. If Guy Morton's actions in isolating Sandra from friends, family and the world at large amounted to abuse, what label ought Anna to put on her own relationship with the woman who was her best friend, lodger and childminder rolled into one?

'Zoe?'

'Aye?'

'Are you … y'know … happy?'

Zoe shifted her eyes from the TV and gave Anna a puzzled look. 'Aye?' Her rising intonation made her sound decidedly uncertain.

'What I mean is …' Anna stopped, already fervently wishing she'd never said anything. She began again. 'Let's say, five years ago, if you could have seen into the future, where would you have pictured yourself?'

Zoe gave a dry laugh. 'Five years ago, I couldnae picture a future for masel in five *days'* time, let alone five years.'

'OK, but say, for talking's sake, you could snap your fingers and have any life you wanted, right now. What would it look like?'

Zoe shifted upright into a sitting position. 'What's brought this on?'

'Just humour me.'

Zoe laughed softly and turned her eyes towards the ceiling as she thought about it. 'I'd have … I dunno, a villa in the Costa del Blanca, servants at my beck and call twenty-four-seven and a hunky gigolo called Esteban tae attend tae my every desire.' She gave Anna a knowing but kindly smile. 'I know what it is ye're really asking. The answer's no.'

'No?' Anna blinked in confusion. 'How d'you know what I'm—'

'Cos I can read you like an open book, Scavolini. I know your mind better than ye know it yersel. I know when it's fretting about something, and I've usually got a pretty good idea about what. And I'm telling ye, I havnae got itchy feet, and I don't wish my life was any different fae what it is now.'

Anna's shoulders sagged. 'I just want you to be happy,' she said helplessly. 'I don't want you to feel obligated to stick with this … arrangement for my sake.'

'Anna,' said Zoe firmly, 'this is my life, and I like it. And if that ever changes, believe me, I'll no be shy tae tell ye.'

They faced one another in silence for what felt like an eternity, Zoe meeting Anna's gaze unwaveringly. Anna studied her face, searching for some sign that she was being untruthful, but she couldn't see any.

'So we're good?'

'We're good,' said Zoe.

Anna exhaled heavily, realising she'd been holding her breath for some time. 'Good. We're both good, then.'

'Aye,' said Zoe, her nodding a little too deliberate to appear entirely natural. 'Good talk.'

'Good talk.'

Zoe stretched her arms behind her head and got to her feet. 'Well, that's me done my share of introspecting for the night. I'm heading tae bed. Coming?'

Anna remained seated. 'Nah, reckon I'm gonna wait up for Mum after all. You know what she's like – she'll probably find she can't get the key in the lock and raise the entire street in the process.'

Zoe chuckled. 'And we both know she *hates* being the centre of attention.'

She headed for the door, giving Anna's shoulder a brief squeeze as she passed her. In the doorway, she stopped and turned to face Anna once more.

'Meant what I said, by the way. Ye're no tae worry about me, awright?'

'All right,' Anna nodded. 'N'night.'

'Night.'

Anna remained in the armchair, listening to the sounds above as Zoe dotted back and forth between her bedroom and the bathroom, getting ready for bed. Even if she still wasn't wholly convinced by Zoe's denials, she saw little choice but to take her at her word and accept the current situation for what it was.

Overhead, she heard Zoe's door closing, then silence. Hoping her mother wouldn't be *too* late getting back, she dimmed the lights, kicked off her shoes and lay down on the sofa, settling in to wait.

She came to some time later at the sound of the front door opening. She hadn't intended to fall asleep – but then, she supposed that was what tended to happen when you were tired and lay down in the dark with your eyes closed. She remained perfectly still, scarcely breathing, as the front door closed and footsteps that she recognised as Leah's advanced along the hardwood floor before stopping just outside the living room door. For around thirty seconds, there was complete silence. Anna pictured her mother standing on the other side of the door, listening as intently as she was herself. Did Leah sense her daughter's presence?

The moment passed. Leah's footsteps resumed, heading up the stairs. A door closed on the floor above, then silence.

Anna let out the breath she'd been holding in and wondered just why she felt so relieved to have avoided an actual face-to-face encounter with her mother. Was it guilt over turning down her invitation to dinner at the Kupermans'? She couldn't think why. She had no reason to feel guilty. She'd had a prior engagement and had received virtually no notice. Anyway, she was an adult, free to make her own decisions. Perhaps, she supposed, it wasn't guilt so much as a sense of residual awkwardness. A sense that all their massive disagreements – about religion, about parenting, about a thousand and one other things – had not been resolved but merely put on hold. Today's trip had unquestionably defused a lot of the tension between them, but Anna was acutely aware that the current state of affairs was merely a ceasefire rather than a full armistice, and she knew it was only a matter of time before some spark or other reignited the kindling.

She heard movement above: Leah's footsteps heading along the landing to the bathroom. Resolving to wait till her mother was safely settled before heading upstairs herself, she tucked a cushion behind her head to make herself more comfortable, confident this time of remaining awake.

Within minutes, however, her eyes had closed and she was once more fast asleep.

28

Saturday 20 April

She awoke with a start. It was light in the living room, the sound of morning birdsong drifting in through an open window, accompanied by the creak of slow, deliberate footsteps on the stairs. Jack's booming voice rang out as he began to say something, only to be swiftly interrupted by a hushed 'Shh!'

Anna lurched upright with a start, only to wince as her neck, which she'd seemingly cricked during the night, gave a sharp jolt of complaint. She checked her watch. 8.15. She groaned and rubbed her crusty eyes with the heels of her hands.

Behind her, the door opened a crack and Zoe poked her head in. Seeing Anna awake and upright, she opened the door fully and stepped in, grinning.

'Morning, lazybones! See ye've decided tae join the rest of us in the land of the living.' She tutted disapprovingly. 'Falling asleep on the couch – honestly! You musta been properly plum tuckered last night.'

'Seems that way,' Anna agreed, tilting her head sideways to try to loosen up her neck.

'That's what ye get for working like a beast fae dawn till dusk. Listen, I'm about tae put the kettle on. I'll make ye a coffee, aye?'

'Please. Strong and black.'

'Coming right up.'

Zoe ducked out of the living room, leaving Anna to continue her head-tilting exercises. A moment later, though, she was back.

'Forgot tae mention last night – buncha mail came for ye while we were out yesterday. Here.'

She handed Anna a bundle of envelopes of varying sizes before exiting again. Stifling a yawn, Anna began to sort through them. They included the usual mix of bills and circulars, the latest issue of *The New European*, a flyer for a new deli on Hyndland Road that looked halfway tempting … and a padded envelope hand-addressed in block capitals to 'PROFESSOR A. SCAVOLINI', containing a small, solid, rectangular object. She gave it a shake. Something rattled inside. Frowning, she slit the envelope open with a thumbnail and tipped it upside down.

An audio cassette in a see-through plastic case landed at her feet. The words 'LISTEN TO ME' were written on the label in the same hand as the envelope. Anna picked it up and stared at it for several seconds, trying to puzzle out the meaning of it, then …

'Zoe!'

Something about the tone of her voice must have given away her anxiety, for Zoe reappeared from the kitchen almost instantly, a frown of apprehension etched on her features.

''Sup?'

Anna wordlessly showed her the cassette.

Zoe's frown intensified. 'Where'd that come fae?'

By way of explanation, Anna handed her the envelope. Zoe took it, turned it front to back to front again.

'It's stamped,' she pointed out. 'Musta came wi the regular mail.'

'Mm,' Anna nodded, not sure what, if anything, this information told her. 'No postmark, though.'

Zoe gestured to the tape. 'Ye gonnae listen tae it?'

'I think I have to.'

Zoe sucked her teeth in consternation. 'Aye, I'm no disagreeing. Just … take it fae someone who's been there, done that – when someone sends ye an anonymous tape through the post, doesnae tend tae make for pleasant viewing … or listening, in this case.'

Anna clutched the tape in both hands, squeezing it tightly as she considered Zoe's words. A part of her desperately wanted to put it back in the envelope, head through to the kitchen for breakfast with Zoe and Jack and forget all about it. But she knew that would only mean delaying the inevitable, and that she wouldn't be able to concentrate on anything else until she learned, for better or worse, what the tape contained.

She got to her feet. 'You go ahead and sort breakfast for you and Jack. I'll get something myself later.'

And then, forestalling any objection from Zoe, she headed for the stairs, clutching the cassette in her clammy hand.

She strode into her office, shut the door and spent a good ten minutes rooting through various cupboards and drawers before finally finding what she was looking for: her old, well-worn Sony Walkman, which she'd hung onto despite not having used in years. After fitting it with fresh batteries and attaching her headphones, she settled in her chair and inserted the tape. She took a deep breath, steeling herself for whatever was to come, then pressed Play.

At first, she heard nothing but the hum of the tracking heads rubbing against blank tape. After about thirty seconds, there was a loud thump, followed by heavy rustling. Then, faintly, voices began to reach her ears, unintelligible beneath both a persistent hiss and what sounded vaguely like a heavily muffled drilling noise. She fiddled with the volume slider, which only succeeded in intensifying the background interference without making the speech any clearer. Even the device's built-in noise reduction control did little to alleviate the problem. But gradually – whether as a result of the interference decreasing, the voices becoming louder or her own brain adjusting to what she was hearing, or indeed a combination of all three – she found that she was able to understand a surprising amount of what was being said. There were two voices – one male, one female. The former, she recognised from his various television appearances as that of Detective Superintendent Frank Dalston. The latter, Anna quickly surmised from her accent and the nature of the questions being asked, belonged to Adjoa Asante.

'—wasting my time and answer the bloody question!' Dalston shouted.

'I … I do … do not … ' Adjoa stammered, seemingly confused and frightened in equal measure.

'You you do do not what?' Dalston repeated Adjoa's words back to her in a singsong voice, clearly intended to mock the cadence of her speech. 'Spit it out.'

'My son, Samuel. Please, we wait for him.'

'But I don't *want* to talk to your son – I want to talk to *you*. He's not the eyewitness here. You are. What the hell's he going to tell us that you can't, hmm?'

'Please. He help me to—'

'Help you to what? To know which lies to tell?'

Silence.

Dalston chuckled humourlessly. 'You know what I think? I think this is all a bit of an act for you. I think you speak far better English than you're letting on. Is that not right, Mrs Asante?'

Again, no response.

'Let's go back to what you told PC McLaverty. On the night of the murders, you were travelling home to Ecclefechan by bus from the house in Browhouses where you're employed as a cleaner. Correct?'

There was another silence. Then, after a lengthy delay, Adjoa said glumly, 'Yes, sir.'

'And at roughly twelve minutes past ten, as you were heading north along Haysend Road, you looked out the window and saw a figure scaling the wall at the foot of the field on your left. Yes?'

'Yes.'

'Excellent,' said Dalston, considerably more cheerful now, though no one could have failed to pick up on the dangerous edge that remained in his voice. 'You know, I really feel like we're making progress here – don't you? Now, this figure was wearing a blue coat and—'

'No,' said Adjoa.

'No?' Dalston's tone was one of confusion.

'I say the figure wearing a coat. Not blue.'

'I'm quite certain you said it was blue.'

'No,' said Adjoa, without a shred of doubt. 'Not blue. Green.'

Dalston muttered something like, 'For Christ's sake.' There was a sound of pages being shuffled, followed by silence for almost thirty seconds as he presumably consulted his notes. When he finally spoke again, it was in the universally recognisable tone of the aggrieved blowhard whose self-assured assertions have just collided with the immovable force of concrete evidence to the contrary.

'Well, it's always possible you were mistaken. After all, green and blue aren't too dissimilar. Though I think, if you concentrate very hard, you'll remember that what you saw was in fact a blue raincoat.'

No response.

'Let's assume, for the sake of expediency, that the coat you saw *could* have been blue.'

'I,' a befuddled Adjoa stammered, 'I do not think…'

'Blue,' Dalston snapped. 'The woman you saw was wearing a blue raincoat, was she not?'

'I…a woman?' Adjoa was more confused than ever now. 'No…no… I see *person*, but I think not…' A note of pleading entered her voice. 'Is dark. Hard to see…'

Dalston sighed heavily. 'You told PC McLaverty the person you saw had long hair. Or are you going to tell me you were mistaken about that too?'

Adjoa was becoming increasingly flustered. 'Long hair, yes. Long hair, but no…I see no face…'

'Do women have long hair?'

'Do…women…' Adjoa repeated falteringly, as if the words were unfamiliar to her.

'Yes or no – DO. WOMEN. HAVE. LONG. HAIR?'

'…yes.'

'And do men?'

Silence.

'I said, do men have long hair?' A pause. 'Do *I* have long hair?'

'No,' said Adjoa.

'Does PC McLaverty?'

'No.'

'Does Detective Sergeant Gunning?'

'No.'

'Of course we don't,' said Dalston. 'Because women have long hair and men have short hair. Yes?'

'Yes,' Adjoa agreed.

'So, the figure you saw climbing over the wall was a woman with long, dark hair, wearing a blue coat.'

Again, no response.

'We already have another eyewitness who's stated on the record that he saw a woman in a blue coat fleeing the scene of the murders. What are you trying to suggest? That he's lying?'

'No,' Adjoa began, 'I—'

'Then what *are* you saying, Mrs Asante? Because the two of you can't both be right. From where I'm sitting, it seems plain that only one of you is telling the truth, and so far, I'm sorry to say, you've given me precious little reason to believe that someone is you.'

Another period of silence followed, during which Adjoa presumably tried to find the logic in this statement.

'Look,' Dalston continued, his tone more conciliatory, 'we know all about your troubles with the immigration people. We're not interested in that. Not unless you give us a reason to be. If you cooperate with us like a good girl and answer our questions, you can be home before Samuel gets back from school. If not …' He left the rest unsaid. 'Come on – you help us, we help you.'

There was another lengthy silence, followed by a heavy sigh, which could have come from Dalston or Adjoa, or some unidentified third party.

'Let's try this one more time,' said Dalston. 'You saw a figure climbing over the wall bordering Haysend Road. Yes?'

'Yes,' Adjoa agreed unhappily.

'And that someone was a woman with long, dark hair and a blue raincoat. Yes?'

'… yes.'

'And if anyone asks you – whether that's me, or Mr Gunning, or a lawyer, or even your next-door neighbour – what are you going to say?' He paused, barely long enough to give Adjoa time to draw breath. 'Come on – chop chop! What did you see?'

'I saw woman with long dark hair and blue raincoat climbing over wall,' said Adjoa, in an unhappy monotone.

'Good. And don't you forget it.'

There was a brief pause. Then, Dalston piped up again, his tone instantly more cheerful.

'See? Don't things go a whole lot more smoothly when you tell the truth?'

No response.

'We'll stop for coffee, I think,' Dalston declared. 'Then, when we're all suitably refreshed, we'll sit down and go through all this properly. Sound good?'

There was a sound of fumbling as someone fiddled with the controls of whatever device was being used to record the interview. Then, with another abrupt thump, it cut out, leaving only the familiar hum of the tracking heads.

Anna stopped the tape. Slowly, she lowered her headphones and sat, unmoving, the heavy silence of the tiny office oppressive after hearing the background interference on the recording for so long. It was difficult to shake the feeling that what she'd just heard changed everything. It had always been clear in her mind that, for Sandra's alibi to have been true, both of the prosecution's star witnesses would have to have been either lying or gravely mistaken about what they had – or hadn't – seen. Well, here was incontrovertible proof that one of those witnesses had been coerced into changing her statement. There could be no doubt about it: Adjoa Asante had been bullied and railroaded into agreeing to a version of events that, in the most charitable reading possible, imposed certainty where, in fact, significant doubt existed. By the end, she'd sounded like a completely broken woman – one ready to agree with whatever narrative Dalston presented her with in order to make it stop. And what was all this about another eyewitness who saw someone matching Sandra's description fleeing the crime scene? If such a person indeed existed, why had no record of it been found in the (admittedly incomplete) case file, and why hadn't they been called as a witness at the trial?

She retrieved the envelope the tape had come in and examined each side in turn for some clue as to its origin. Nothing. The block capital lettering could have been the work of anyone – young, old, male, female, cop, civilian. She turned the envelope upside down and shook it, just in case there was anything else inside it. Nada. In desperation, she grabbed a pair of scissors and sliced it open, in the slim chance that there was something attached to the inner lining. Zilch.

She let the envelope fall to the floor, her mind still churning. Presumably, what she'd just heard had been the first of Adjoa's two interviews with Dalston, all trace of which had previously been thought lost in the fire at the storage facility in Giffnock in 2012. But who could have sent it to her – and why?

At length, she decided that, before she did anything else, she was going to head downstairs for that black coffee Zoe had promised her. Perhaps *it* would help her to see things more clearly. After that, she was going to get straight on the phone to Pamela Macklin to let her know what she'd just heard. Given the significance of this new development, she couldn't justify putting off contacting her for a moment longer.

29

Rousing Pamela proved to be easier said than done. Each of the half-dozen or so calls Anna made to the solicitor's work mobile – the only method of contact she had for her – over the course of the morning went straight to voicemail, the chirpy, pre-recorded invitation to contact her during office hours becoming increasingly irritating with each successive performance. Eventually, she was forced to accept that Pamela was entitled to take the weekend off from answering work calls and left a message entreating her to ring her back as soon as possible. She just hoped it wouldn't take her till Monday.

In the meantime, she forced herself to turn her attention to other matters. She hadn't yet received any contact from Katie Morton, and, if she was being honest with herself, she didn't entirely trust Jeff to keep his word and pass on her contact details, despite his protestations to the contrary. She spent some time on various social media platforms, inputting various permutations of Katie's name – Katherine, Kathryn, Catherine, Caitlin, Katy and so forth – but to no avail. She couldn't say she was overly surprised. Given the level of interest in the case, and the intrigue surrounding 'the one that got away' in particular, Katie would have had more reason than most to stay off social media. Still, she persevered, moving onto marriage records once she'd exhausted her patience with Facebook, in case someone of that name had gotten married in Canada as some point in the last fifteen years. Once again, she drew a blank.

She also listened to the tape twice more, just in case she happened to spot something she'd previously missed. She was able to make out a handful of words here and there that had eluded her the first time round, but they didn't alter her understanding of the conversation in any significant way, other than to further intensify her anger at Dalston's treatment of a confused and clearly frightened woman.

It was mid-afternoon by the time Pamela finally got back to her.

'Anna!' She sounded in high spirits – presumably *she* hadn't cricked her neck sleeping on an uncomfortable sofa the previous night. 'So good to get your message! You know, I was just *thinking* it was time we had a catch-up. What's new?'

'I don't want you to get *too* excited,' said Anna, aware that there was a not insignificant possibility of this happening, 'but there's been something of a development.'

She heard a sharp intake of breath at the other end of the line. 'You mean, to do with' – Pamela dropped her voice to a whisper – '*Sandra? What sort of development?*'

'The sort that casts the circumstances surrounding her conviction in a somewhat different light. It's also the kind of thing you really need to hear in person. Is there any chance we can meet?'

'Let me check. I've got back to back client meetings all day, but I think— Oh, fudge. No, that's not going to work. Listen, though – I ought to be finished by 7.30. If I run like the clappers, I should be able to get the 7.45 out of Waverley and be in Glasgow for—'

'I've got a better idea,' Anna interrupted, not wanting their meeting to be delayed for a second longer than it needed to be. 'I can be in Edinburgh for seven-thirty. Just let me know where to meet you and I'll be there.'

'Are you sure that's OK?' The relief in Pamela's voice was palpable. 'As long as it's not a massive headache for *you*, that would be completely amazing. Tell you what – call it eight and come straight to my flat.' She gave a little squeal of glee. '*Oooh*, this is exciting!'

Anna proceeded to spend the remainder of the afternoon alternating between clock-watching and pacing in circles, wearing out the already threadbare rug on her office floor. She did wonder, if she'd revealed what the 'development' entailed, whether Pamela would have immediately dropped everything and jumped on the first train to Glasgow. But then, that wouldn't have been fair. She had clients depending on her not just to honour her appointments with them but to give them her undivided attention – something Anna wasn't certain she'd be able to do if she knew they were potentially on the verge of blowing the Sandra Morton case wide open. Besides, there was a part of her, however small, that couldn't help thinking turnabout was fair play. This entire saga had, after all, begun with Pamela insisting Anna meet her in person to hear her proposal. So she bided her time as best she could, alternating between pacing and taking care of various non-taxing admin tasks till it was time for her to set off.

She was just heading down to the kitchen to make herself a sandwich to eat on the train when Leah appeared at the foot of the stairs.

'There you are,' she said, as if Anna had been deliberately evading her. 'I was just coming to find you. Leaving things a bit late, aren't you?'

'Sorry?'

'For dinner. You haven't forgotten, have you?' And then, seeing the expression on her daughter's face, she sighed wearily. 'Oh, *Anna.*'

Perhaps the most crushing aspect of all this was that she didn't even seem surprised. It was as if she'd anticipated precisely this turn of events from the beginning and had set her expectations accordingly.

'I hadn't forgotten,' Anna lied, unable to meet her mother's eye. 'It's just ... I've got to go out. It's ... '

'Let me guess. A work thing.'

'Something like that. But listen,' she went on, producing her wallet, 'let me leave you some money. You can get yourselves a carry-out, or go out to a restaurant, or—'

'That's all right,' said Leah, pushing away the bundle of cash Anna had tried to press into her hand. 'Zoe and I will manage to come up with something between us.'

They stood facing one another for an uncomfortable moment, Anna holding the rejected fistful of banknotes, not sure what to do with them, Leah – deliberately or otherwise – blocking her path to the kitchen.

'Are you sure it's all right?' asked Anna. She knew, of course, that it wasn't, but she needed to hear her mother tell her that it was.

Leah gave a strained smile. 'I imagine we'll cope somehow.'

They continued to face each other for a few more seconds, neither seemingly wanting to be the one to blink first. Then Anna, succumbing, cleared her throat and strode forward, giving Leah no option but to step aside. As she turned off into the kitchen, head hanging low, she was left with the unshakeable feeling that something had just slipped through her fingers, like fine grains of sand.

An hour and a half on the 17:58 train to Edinburgh Waverley and a brisk walk later, Anna turned onto West Richmond Street, nestled in the shadow of the Salisbury Crags, and, as directed, followed the row of terraced houses to the one at the end with the green door.

Pamela was in a state of giddy excitement when she answered said door, instantly vindicating Anna's decision not to reveal the nature of this morning's development beforehand. If this was what she was like when she didn't know what lay in store for her, odds were she'd have been barely functional if she'd realised just how explosive the news actually was.

'Come in, come in,' she effused, ushering Anna over the threshold. 'I'm just in the door myself. Haven't even had time to change, but no matter. I'm afraid we're on the top floor. You don't mind the climb, do you?'

Anna assured her that she didn't, and followed her up the stairs.

As they tramped up the thickly carpeted staircase of what had evidently once been a single dwelling but had now been broken up into multiple flats, Anna wondered whether Pamela had had any contact with Sandra since her own disastrous encounter with her, during which Sandra had revealed that she knew Pamela had contracted her to re-examine the case. Presumably not, as otherwise the subject could hardly have failed to come up. She considered warning Pamela that Sandra was onto them – had been onto them from the start – then decided against it. No sense creating any unnecessary drama.

'Have you eaten?' Pamela asked, as she opened the door on the top landing and led Anna into a hallway so narrow there wasn't room for two people to walk abreast. 'I was going to fix myself something quick but I'm so excited I'm not sure I'd be able to keep anything down.' She let out a high-pitched giggle.

'I'm fine,' said Anna, not wanting to be responsible for provoking a fit of vomiting. 'If it's all the same with you, I think we should just get on.'

'Of course, of course.'

Pamela ushered Anna into a living room that seemed more like an oversized cupboard than Anna's own one back in Glasgow. Her host hastily grabbed a pair of rumpled tights from the back of the threadbare sofa that consumed most of the floorspace, stuffed them in her trouser pocket and turned to face Anna with an expectant smile.

'So don't keep me in suspense. What's this big news? I've not been able to sit still all day.'

30

Anna sat at one end of the sofa and watched as Pamela, head dwarfed by her massive headphones, listened to the tape of Dalston and Adjoa's exchange on the Walkman. Though the leakage from the headphones was minimal, the fact that Pamela had one of those hyper-expressive faces that made hiding her emotions impossible meant that Anna could tell, from its ever-changing expression, exactly which part she was listening to at any given moment.

When the recording finally ended, Pamela pressed Stop and slowly lowered her headphones. For a moment, she simply looked at Anna, eyes wide with disbelief.

'Blimey,' she eventually said.

'My thoughts exactly,' said Anna.

'This is really something.' She reached for the envelope, which Anna had brought with her. 'And you've no idea where this came from?'

'Only that it must have been sent to me by someone who both knew I was investigating the Sandra Morton case and was in a position to access that recording.'

Frowning, Pamela turned the envelope this way and that, clearly looking for any identifying features. Anna resisted the urge to tell her she was wasting her time; that she herself had already examined every millimetre of it umpteen times and come up with nothing.

'The quality's pretty ropey,' she said instead. 'so it stands to reason what we're hearing is probably a couple of generations removed from the source tape, at minimum. So presumably we can't necessarily assume whoever sent it had access to the original ... which doesn't exactly help narrow down the list of suspects.'

Pamela set down the envelope, brows furrowed as she considered the matter. 'Who *does* know you're looking into the case?'

'I've already thought long and hard about that,' said Anna, 'and I'm fairly confident I can rule out every single one of them.'

'Humour me.'

Anna suppressed a sigh, reminding herself that Pamela hadn't had the benefit of the better part of a day to consider the various options. 'Well, there's Drew Barriscale, Sandra's original solicitor. It's certainly conceivable he might have access to a recording of a police interview, but he made it abundantly clear to me that he had zero interest in helping me in any way.'

'I know him,' said Pamela. 'By reputation, at any rate. He's a by the book sort of guy. This sort of thing isn't his style. Who else is there?'

'There's Malcolm Gunning – Dalston's old second-in-command. I've left him umpteen messages asking to speak to him about the case, but he's never gotten back to me. Either he wants nothing to do with me – in which case, why send me this? – or—'

'—or he never got your messages.'

'Which makes it even *less* likely the tape came from him.'

Pamela nodded soberly. 'So not him, then. Who else?'

'Well, obviously, there's the surviving members of the Morton family – the grandparents and Guy's brother, Jeff. But I can't concoct a scenario in which any of them has access to a police interview. Besides, they've all made their feelings about Sandra crystal clear – George and Eunice especially. I can't see any of them doing anything that casts doubt on her guilt – and I think we can both agree that that's precisely what this tape does.'

Pamela massaged her jaw, deep in thought. 'What about that skeevy journalist? The one you spoke to who wrote that book about the case? Mc-something-or-other.'

'McEnaney,' said Anna. 'Actually, for a while I thought he was the most likely candidate, but the more I think about it, the less convinced I am. I think, if he was sitting on something this explosive, he wouldn't have been able to resist telling me. And I can't see him sending it to me anonymously – he's far too self-aggrandising not to want to take all the credit. Plus, why sit on it for twenty years and then suddenly decide to turn it over?'

'To be honest,' said Pamela, 'that question applies irrespective of who sent it.'

They ran through the remaining individuals Anna had contacted during her investigation – people like Paul Kempley's mother and Cressida Bagshawe. The odds of any of them being behind the delivery were slim to non-existent – a fact on which Pamela was forced to agree.

'What I want to know,' said Anna, once they'd thoroughly exhausted every possibility, 'is this: regardless of who and where this tape originates from, if we took it to the appropriate authorities, would it be enough to get the case reopened?'

Pamela's expression was dubious. It seemed to Anna that, as they'd run through the list of potential suspects, her initial excitement had slowly given way to solemn pragmatism.

'Thing is,' she said at length, 'I'm not sure how much of a bombshell it really *is*. Obviously, it proves Dalston was a thoroughly nasty piece of work who browbeat a vulnerable witness into agreeing with his version of events. But I've spoken to people who work for the anti-corruption unit, and they tell me their in-trays are full of just this sort of thing and worse besides. Odds are, if we take it to them, they'll just say, "Thanks for bringing this to our attention", then add it to the bottom of the pile and continue slogging through whichever investigation they're currently working on. Like, I can't see them claiming it doesn't need looking into, but in their eyes, there's no reason why it should take precedence over the thousand and one other cases that got there first.'

Anna thought back to her own phone call to the anti-corruption unit and to the nasal-voiced Detective Inspector's almost gleeful dismissal of her request for information. *'We don't simply bump cases to the top of the pile because they happen to be especially juicy.'* And, however much she hated to admit it, he had a point. Ascertaining the legitimacy of Sandra Morton's conviction might be the single most pressing matter to both herself and Pamela, but for every case in the unit's in-tray, there would be someone who felt exactly the same way about *it*. In the pursuit of justice, there was no room for favouritism.

'Plus, at the end of the day,' Pamela went on, 'whether we like it or not, this still doesn't prove Sandra didn't do it. Not conclusively. For all we know, she *could* have been the figure Adjoa saw climbing over the wall, and her coat *could* have been blue, not green. And to get her conviction overturned, we need evidence so compelling the Appeal Court'll have no choice but to sit up and take notice.'

Anna nodded morosely. She saw now that, despite all her concern about the possibility of Pamela becoming too excited, she had in fact allowed *herself* to get completely carried away, almost to the point of believing the tape would be enough to get Sandra's sentence quashed with immediate effect.

'What now, then?' she asked.

Pamela licked her lips pensively. 'Back at the beginning, I asked you to review the case for new evidence, and you've certainly done that … even if you *didn't* technically uncover it yourself,' she added with a wry smile. 'The point is, you've more than upheld your end of the bargain. You're well within your rights if you want to go back to your *actual* job and leave this with me to take forward however I can.'

Anna pondered this for well over a minute. Deep down, she knew this was the sensible option. Over the last few weeks, she'd sunk more time and energy than she could possibly justify into a venture that, at the end of the day, had nothing whatsoever to do with her. Work on her book had suffered – and, if she was being honest with herself, so too had her relationship with her family. Really, there shouldn't even be a decision to be made.

And yet …

'A woman has spent the last eighteen years in prison for a crime she insists she didn't commit,' she said eventually. 'If there's the slightest possibility her conviction is unsound, she deserves the chance to see justice while she still has her health and her wits about her.' She fixed Pamela with a look of determination. 'And I want to be a part of that.'

Pamela's smile of relief was almost enough to convince her she'd made the right choice. For a while, they sat in companionable silence, listening to the sounds of late evening birdsong filtering through the half-open living room window. Anna wondered if Zoe, Leah and Jack were still at dinner; if they *had* ended up preparing a meal in her absence or thrown in the towel and ordered out. At the mental image of the three of them sitting round the kitchen table together, one place conspicuously empty, she felt a fresh pang of shame over her decision to abandon them and go haring off to Edinburgh.

Just then, Pamela stirred. 'I wanna listen to the tape again,' she said. 'I've just had a thought.'

Anna watched, not daring to say anything lest she break whatever spell Pamela appeared to be under, as the solicitor wound the tape back to the start, fitted her headphones over her ears, pressed play and sat, hunched forward, her brows pursed in concentration as she listened. After a couple of minutes, she stopped the tape and lowered her headphones again.

'I'm right,' she declared. 'I'm sure I am.'

'About what?'

'I think we've been on the wrong tack all along. I mean, I don't think it's what we both thought it was.'

'How d'you mean?'

'I mean I don't think it's an interview at all.'

Anna sat up a little straighter. 'You're going to have to explain.'

'All right, so something's been bothering me since the beginning, and it's this: if this *was* a formal interview, recorded at a police station and properly logged and everything, it would have been handed over to the prosecution during the disclosure phase, and there's no *way* they wouldn't have brought this up during the trial. I mean, it might not *prove* Sandra's innocence, but if the senior detective responsible for investigating her was bullying witnesses into changing their accounts in order to shore up his case, then it's more than enough to create an absolute *ton* of reasonable doubt. Which means the only logical conclusion I can come to is that it was never disclosed.'

Anna stared at Pamela intently, waiting for her to continue.

'So I reckon there are two possibilities. One is that it was deliberately suppressed. That's not an impossible proposition, but it would have required a *whole* lot of organisation – like, multiple dodgy officers and admin staff cooperating behind the scenes to make sure it never saw the light of day.'

'And possibility number two?'

'OK, bear with me. We know there was an earlier interview with Adjoa Asante that went AWOL – tapes destroyed, transcripts up in smoke in the fire at the police archive. And then, suddenly, along comes this recording that *sounds* like an interview, so naturally we both immediately assume that's what it is.'

Anna was at a loss for words.

'It's confirmation bias, isn't it?' Pamela went on, unable to suppress a smile of delight at the effect of her words on Anna. 'We heard what we wanted to hear. But what I'm saying is, what if what we're listening to *isn't* the missing first interview at all but something else entirely: an off-the-record chat *before* the interview even took place. For all we know, it might even have been taped on the way to the station. All that background noise? The more I think about it, the more I reckon it sounds just like a moving car. And the bit where Dalston says, "We'll stop for coffee"? Well, maybe that meant swinging by the nearest Starbucks or whatever. Did they have Starbucks back in those days?'

'I'm not sure,' said Anna. Right at this moment in time, that didn't seem like the most pressing issue. 'OK, so if this *was* an informal conversation, that means someone else must have recorded it covertly. Who?'

'Well, let's go back to our original list of suspects. Forget about motive for a minute. Concentrate on means. Out of all of them, who's the one person that could plausibly have been there at the time, sitting quietly with a tape recorder in his pocket? Dalston even mentions his name at one point.'

'*Gunning?*' Anna almost spluttered. 'But why? What possible motivation would he have to record something that casts his boss in such a negative light? That potentially holes the entire case below the waterline? They were thick as thieves. He worshipped the ground Dalston walked on.'

'Did he, though? Or maybe that's just what he *wanted* everyone to believe. Put it this way – those allegations against Dalston must have come from somewhere. Who's to say it wasn't from Gunning? Maybe he wasn't quite as much of a loyal servant as everyone thought?'

For several seconds, Anna didn't speak. Her heart was pounding, her skin prickling all over with excitement.

'Fuck,' she eventually breathed. 'Holy *shit.*'

Pamela giggled. 'My thoughts exactly, only without the sweary words. But we're both agreed it's the explanation that makes the most sense, right?'

'I think so,' said Anna, a part of her still not quite ready to believe it. 'So what now? I mean, knowing who sent the tape – or *thinking* we know who sent it – still doesn't get us past the inconvenient fact that, according to you, the tape on its own isn't going to be enough to get the case reopened.'

Pamela was silent for a moment, gazing off into the middle distance, hands steepled under her chin as she racked her brains.

'OK,' she said eventually, 'let's assume we know for a fact that the tape *did* come from DS Gunning.' She spoke slowly and deliberately, as if she was still working things out in her head. 'I know he wouldn't take your calls, but if he sent you the tape, then he must have reservations about how the case was conducted, or – I don't know, maybe a sense of guilt at having kept what he knew about Dalston's behaviour to himself for so many years. If he had the presence of mind to record that conversation with Adjoa, then that suggests it was part of a pattern of behaviour – that he already had concerns to begin with. If we could just persuade him to talk to us…'

'I see your point,' said Anna, 'but I just don't see how we go about *doing* that. If he was willing to go on the record, he wouldn't have sent that tape anonymously, would he? He'd have taken it to the appropriate authorities years ago.'

Pamela shrugged. 'Maybe he did. Maybe they hushed it up. We know how far the Shadow Men's reach extended back in the day, and we know Dalston was linked to them at some point.'

'OK, but I don't see where that—'

'Bear with me. Off the top of your head, do you think we have anything to lose by confronting Gunning?'

Anna thought about it. 'Probably not. But we've already established he's not taking my calls – in which case, I doubt he'll take yours either.'

'I'm not talking about phone calls.' There was a note in Pamela's voice that bordered on exasperation, as if Anna was being deliberately dense. 'I'm saying let's head down to Lockerbie tomorrow, you and me, and confront him directly – see if we can get him to talk. It has to be worth a shot.'

It wasn't immediate, but as she sat there, digesting this, Anna felt the thrill of adventure slowly rekindling in her belly.

'I think it just might be,' she said.

Pamela grinned, obviously buoyed by the fact Anna hadn't dismissed her plan out of hand. 'And if we *are* going to visit Gunning, there's something else I'd like to do while we're in that neck of the woods.'

'What's that?'

'Go to Hillend. Actually visit it. I've read so much about it, but I've never once set foot in the place. Have you?'

Anna shook her head. 'Not exactly a top holiday destination, is it?'

'No,' Pamela agreed, 'but being there in person, seeing it with our own eyes, might just reveal something that hasn't come to light from looking at maps and reading police reports.' She gazed at Anna intently, flashing her improbably tiny teeth in a determined smile. 'So what do you say? You in?'

PART FOUR

YES! I AM A LONG WAY FROM HOME

31

Sunday 21 April

That night, and much to her surprise, Anna slept soundly. She awoke on Sunday morning, feeling refreshed and ready for whatever the day might hold. The sun was already riding high in an expansive blue sky, seeming to suggest a day full of promise. Pamela had vowed to be at the house by 9 a.m. at the latest to ensure they'd be on the road promptly, and as Anna emerged from the bathroom shortly after 8.30, she heard voices downstairs – the solicitor's high-pitched chirps mingling with her mother's more gravelly intonation.

She arrived in the living room to find the whole lot of them standing or sitting on ceremony: Pamela, dressed in high-waisted slacks and a matching blazer, was on her feet near the door, facing a dressing gown-clad Leah, who stood, arms folded, eyeing her appraisingly. Zoe occupied the sofa, Jack perched on her knee. The whole tableau had such a 'meet the parents' feel to it that Anna almost burst out laughing.

'Anna,' said her mother, turning to face her. 'Your friend's just been telling us about your plans for the day.'

Her disapproval was implicit in every syllable. Whatever steps forward their relationship had taken during their trip to Blair Drummond on Friday appeared to have been undone in their entirety by the double whammy of Anna bailing on dinner last night and announcing, upon her return from Edinburgh, that she would be gone all day on Sunday on a work-related fact-finding mission.

'Is that right?' she said, choosing to direct her response to Pamela instead. 'Hope they haven't been giving you the third degree.' She blew out an exaggerated breath. 'Right, I reckon we'd better get this show on the road, don't you? No sense in dilly-dallying.'

'It was really nice to meet you, Mrs Scavolini,' said Pamela, practically curtseying as Anna ushered her out the door.

Anna sent her on ahead to the car and hung back to make her goodbyes to Jack and to exchange a few words with Zoe, reminding her to put the washing on so Jack would have clean clothes for playgroup tomorrow. After giving Jack one last hug and entreating him to be good while she was away, she hurried down the steps to join Pamela, who was already securely belted into the passenger seat, beaming like an excited child who'd been allowed to ride up front.

'All good?' she asked.

'All good,' Anna confirmed, wondering whether Pamela was so spectacularly unobservant as to have failed to pick up on the tension between mother and daughter or was simply pretending not to have noticed for politeness' sake.

Pamela rubbed her hands together in excitement. 'Yay! Thunderbirds are go!' She grinned sheepishly in response to Anna's look of incredulity. 'Sorry. I've always wanted to say that.'

Not trusting herself to say anything, Anna turned the key in the ignition.

They set off, heading south down the A739 and through the Clyde Tunnel before joining the M74 as it wound its way out of Glasgow and on towards Uddingston. As they roared south down the dual carriageway, Pamela, who'd said little for the first leg of their journey, broke the silence.

'I don't think your mum likes me very much.'

Anna's eyes left the road and glanced across at her sharply. 'Sorry?'

'Oh, nothing. Just something she said.'

'Why? What did she say?'

'Something like, "So you're the reason my daughter skipped out on Passover dinner last night".'

'Mother*fucker*!' Anna swore. She shook her head in disbelief, thinking that this had to be a new low even for Leah. 'I am *so* sorry about that.'

'No, no,' Pamela put in quickly, 'she didn't say it in a *nasty* way or anything. She just … y'know, said it.'

'*Had* to make her point,' Anna muttered, wondering what a non-nasty way of directly accusing someone of scuppering your dinner plans could possibly look like. 'Anyway, last night's dinner had nothing to do with Passover. She's just trying to make it into something it wasn't.'

They drove on in silence for another mile or so, Pamela gazing out of the window, Anna concentrating on the road. At length, Pamela piped up again.

'I never realised you were Jewish.'

To her credit, she said it in an *oh, that's interesting* rather than a *why aren't you walking around with it branded on your forehead?* way.

'I'm not,' Anna said immediately. 'Well, I am. I mean … it's complicated.'

Pamela gave a sympathetic grimace. 'Tell me about it. My wee mum's a Catholic and my dad's the son of a grandee of the Orange Lodge. Makes for some *veeery* colourful family get-togethers.'

'It's a *bit* more complicated than that,' said Anna. 'It's not just a religion. It's a culture, an ethnicity, a whole identity.'

And no matter how hard you try, she thought, *you can never truly leave. You'll always be 'one of us', even if you reject every last tenet of the faith.* She still vividly remembered the moment when, at the age of thirteen, she'd announced to her parents that she didn't believe in God, never had, and would no longer attend synagogue or practise any of the associated rituals. The outrage and horror from her parents had seemed, to her, to have far more of a whiff of 'what will people *think*?' about it than any genuine concern for her immortal soul. For several weeks afterwards, she and her parents had barely spoken, and, to her mind, relations between them never truly recovered. Eventually, it became a subject they simply didn't talk about – the elephant in the room which they all studiously ignored or swiftly changed the subject whenever an acquaintance asked them what the family was doing for Rosh Hashanah or when Anna was finally going to have her Bat Mitzvah. Eventually, they stopped asking.

'Well,' Pamela continued obliviously, 'it must be nice, having that sense of belonging. Hey – d'you know the Bergmans in Inverleith?'

Anna gave a glib smile. 'It's not like we're all in the same WhatsApp group or anything.'

'Of course, of course!' said Pamela immediately, her face a picture of mortification. 'Sorry. Wasn't meaning to be flippant about it.'

Anna sighed heavily. 'No, it's fine. It's all a load of ahistorical bollocks anyway. The Hebrews were never enslaved by the Egyptians, there was no plague of locusts, and the Red Sea never parted.'

'OK.'

Pamela's wary expression told Anna she'd gone too far. Not trusting herself to say anything more, she gritted her teeth and fixed her eyes on the road as they continued their southward journey.

Shortly before 10.45, they crossed from South Lanarkshire into Dumfries and Galloway. Twenty minutes later, they took the turn-off for Lockerbie. Fields and meadows opened up before them, while rolling, tree-capped hills loomed in the distance. Anna had never been to this part of the country before and was ashamed to admit that the only thing she knew about the small town was that it was where the wreckage of Pan Am Flight 103 had landed in 1988 after a bomb ripped through its fuselage. She wondered what sort of effect it must have on the collective psyche of the local populace to inhabit a town whose very name was synonymous throughout the world with catastrophic loss of life. The residents of Hillend must be in a similar situation, she supposed, albeit on a smaller scale.

According to the phone book, Malcolm Gunning lived on Atholl Grove, a cul-de-sac on the south-eastern outskirts of the town. The dozen or so houses which lined it were all detached bungalows with white pebbledash walls and neat, well-tended lawns – all except one, Number 8, whose overgrown, weed-strewn garden was in urgent need of some TLC.

It also happened to be their destination.

They pulled to a halt in front of it and sat, gazing up at it.

'How do you want to play this?' said Anna.

'Perhaps let me take the lead?' Pamela suggested. 'To begin with, at any rate. Only, he hasn't been receptive to your advances before, so ... ' She trailed off, wincing apologetically.

'Fair enough,' said Anna, unconvinced that Pamela had what it took to be an effective interrogator.

They got out of the car and headed up the overgrown path, Anna standing a little way back as Pamela rang the doorbell.

Nothing happened.

'Maybe he's out for his morning constitutional,' Pamela suggested, but without much conviction.

'Maybe,' said Anna, with even less. She glanced across at the nearest window, which, now that she was up close, she noticed was covered with a layer of grime. If she didn't know better, she'd have assumed the place had been abandoned for years.

Pamela rang the bell again. This time, her finger had scarcely left the button when a cantankerous voice rang out from inside the house.

'All right, all right! Hold your horses. I'm coming.'

There was the sound of shuffling footsteps behind the door. A few moments later, it opened a few inches and a beady eye peered out at them from behind a pair of almost comically large glasses.

'Yes?'

'Mr Gunning?' said Pamela brightly. 'May we have a word?'

'What's this about?' Gunning demanded, the gap between the door and the jamb still little more than a crack.

'My name's Pamela Macklin. I'm a solicitor with Riddoch MacLetchie.'

'And? What do you want?'

'If we could come inside, we can explain everything.'

'You can explain from where you are.'

Pamela glanced over her shoulder at Anna, who shrugged as if to say, *This is your gig.*

Pamela turned to face the door again. 'Actually,' she said, in a voice several decibels higher than the one she'd been using until now, 'it's about the tape Professor Scavolini here received in the post the other day. If that's a conversation you want to continue to have on the doorstep, we can go right ahead. But if you'd rather the whole neighbourhood didn't hear about it, I suggest you let us in.'

Anna's eyes widened in surprise. This was a far bolder gamble than she would ever have anticipated from the mousy lawyer.

And it seemed to do the trick. After a moment's pause, there was a rattling noise as Gunning removed the security chain, then opened the door, revealing himself in his entirety. He was in his late sixties and sported a sleeveless woollen pullover and baggy corduroy trousers, the latter looking like they could do with a good wash. At one point, he'd evidently been a tall, imposing presence, but age and a pronounced stoop had diminished his stature considerably. Behind him, Anna could see that the hallway was piled high with old newspapers and other detritus.

'All right, all right,' he growled. 'Hurry up and get in here.'

Anna followed Pamela across the threshold. The hall corridor was overflowing with piles of newspapers to the extent that only a single, narrow walkway remained, like the path carved by a snowplough through a deep drift.

'Well?' Gunning glowered at them expectantly.

'Is there somewhere more comfortable we can go and sit?' asked Pamela, smiling pleasantly at him.

From the look on Gunning's face, Anna thought he was about to treat them to a stream of invective. After a moment, however, he gave a surly grunt and, turning wordlessly, continued down the passageway.

She and Pamela followed him into the living room, which, much like the hallway, was a hoarder's paradise. Every available surface was taken up by newspapers, books and magazines. Anna clocked an issue of *Gardeners' World* dated March 2006 and suppressed a shudder. She had no idea how anyone could possibly live like this. It certainly put the comparatively modest amount of clutter that had accumulated in her own house since Jack and Zoe had arrived on the scene into perspective.

'Sit wherever you can find a space,' said Gunning.

He gestured vaguely to the various items of furniture, of which only a low armchair, its seat hollowed out by years of use, wasn't strewn with piles of aged publications. Concluding that this was Gunning's preferred perch, Anna and Pamela discretely cleared spaces for themselves on the facing sofa and sat down, waiting as their reluctant host eased himself into the armchair. Despite the bright sun shining outside, the living room was dull and gloomy, the air chilly and slightly damp. Coupled with the dated décor, it was as if it had been hermetically sealed off from the rest of the world for decades.

'Before we start,' said Pamela, 'I'm very much hoping we can skip the preliminaries and agree that it's a matter of factual truth that the tape in question came from you and contains a covert recording of a conversation between Detective Superintendent Dalston and Adjoa Asante.'

'I'm not admitting to anything,' said Gunning tersely, 'and I'm not under any obligation to answer your questions.'

Pamela gave him a look of weary disapproval, as if to suggest she'd thought better of him than this. 'Now, now, Mr Gunning, there's no need to make this into a drama. We're not here in any official capacity. We've just come for a quiet chat, off the record. Of course, if anything comes to light during our conversation that proves relevant to an ongoing investigation, then of course the police may ask you to give a formal statement at some point in the future, but we're a long way from that yet. You are, of course, within your rights to refuse to talk to us.' She gave a small smile of understanding. 'But I reckon we're cut from the same cloth, you and me. We both prize justice above all else – and I think that's what you were trying to achieve, in a slightly roundabout way, when you sent that tape to my friend Anna. Am I right?'

Gunning glanced briefly at Anna, then lowered his eyes and gave a small, almost imperceptible nod.

Pamela smiled encouragingly. 'I thought so. So let's just have a nice, relaxed, friendly chat, and we'll see if we can't work things out. Sound good?'

Gunning shrugged, as if it was neither here nor there to him. 'All right. Get on with it, then.'

'OK.' Pamela crossed one leg over the other, hands in her lap. 'So, you made the recording of Detective Superintendent Dalston and Adjoa Asante without their knowledge?'

'Yes.'

'Where?'

'In a squad car, en route to Dumfries and Galloway Divisional Headquarters.'

'And in addition to yourself, DSU Dalston and Mrs Asante, who else was present?'

'No one.'

'No driver?'

'*I* drove. Frank— DSU Dalston wanted some ... ' He sighed heavily. '... some time with the witness before we reached the station.'

'To make sure she had her story straight?'

At this, Gunning seemed to flinch, but he gave a nod of acquiescence. 'Something like that.'

'And is that why you recorded the conversation? Because you knew, or suspected, that he planned to bring pressure to bear on a witness.'

Gunning said nothing. His eyes remained downcast, his shoulders drawn in.

'The two of you went back a ways, didn't you?' said Pamela, trying a different tack. 'You worked together, off and on, for the better part of fifteen years, if my information's accurate.'

Gunning nodded. 'That's right. We first cooperated on a missing person case back in '93. I was an experienced DS and he'd just made DCI. We… well, I suppose he must have thought we were a good match, because he requested me again on his next case, and the next one after that. Far as I could tell, he trusted me to make sure things ran smoothly behind the scenes, so he was free to get on with the big picture stuff. He used to call me his workhorse,' he added, with a trace of a smile.

'He was promoted again a few years later, to Detective Superintendent. You stayed a DS for the rest of your career.'

'That's right,' said Gunning stiffly.

'And there was never any ill-feeling because of that?'

'Why should there be? He was ambitious. A high-flyer. Someone who got results. Whereas I…' He gave a rueful grimace. 'Look, I never had any interest in being thrust into the limelight. Dealing with the press, the pressure of the success or failure of a major investigation resting on my shoulders – that sort of thing. Frank… he had this ability to turn on the charm for the cameras. If you'd seen him work a room full of hungry reporters, answering question after question designed to trip him up without so much as breaking a sweat, you'd understand.'

'And during Operation Bluegrass, would you say he was under more pressure than usual?'

Gunning's eyes narrowed. 'How d'you mean?'

Pamela shrugged. 'It was the highest profile murder investigation in the country in living memory – one of those cases that comes along once in any detective's career, if that. I expect anyone would feel the pinch.'

'I supported him wherever I could.'

'I'm sure you did,' Pamela replied smoothly, 'and I'm sure he appreciated having you there to stand shoulder to shoulder with him. But I know a thing or two about high-pressure cases. I'm not coming at it from quite the same angle as you, but I definitely know what it's like to have people breathing down your neck, demanding you magic a result out of thin air – whether that's your boss or a client or the general public who just want you to announce that you've made an arrest so they can stop worrying about the multiple murderer on the loose.'

Gunning gave something approaching a smile of understanding, but it was half-hearted.

As this exchange unfolded, Anna had watched Pamela with surprise and growing admiration. Until now, she would never have credited her with the ability to be so forthright, so self-controlled, so persuasive. With just the right amount of deftness and firmness, she was conveying to Gunning that, under the circumstances, it would have been perfectly understandable if Dalston's behaviour had been less than impeccable; that it wouldn't be a betrayal of his former boss to acknowledge the shortcomings in his handling of the case. Anna had to concede that she'd underestimated the small, unassuming solicitor considerably.

'The reason I ask,' Pamela went on, 'is that it wouldn't be the first time corners were cut under pressure to get a result. And given the mood at the time, it would be understandable if you had concerns but didn't feel able to raise them – at least, not through any official channels.' She leaned towards him, her expression open and encouraging. 'Was Frank cutting corners because he was getting it in the neck from his superiors? Is that why you recorded his conversation with Adjoa?'

Gunning let out a great, shuddering breath that looked almost physically painful. When he finally spoke, it was in a low, doleful tone, his eyes remaining fixed on the floor.

'Actually, I'd been uneasy for a while. Since before the Sandra Morton investigation, I mean. The top brass loved him for his solve rate, and as long as he kept delivering on that front, they weren't inclined to ask too many questions about the whys and wherefores. And at first, I didn't either. Whatever he was doing, it seemed to be working. And it wasn't as if he was the only copper in town who ever bent the rules in the name of expediency. But the more time I spent with him, the closer we worked together, the more my eyes began to open to some of the things he was doing.

'Now, don't mistake what I'm saying,' he added quickly, as Anna and Pamela exchanged a look. 'Most of the things that've come to light in the last few years – the child abuse and the murders and whatnot – Frank never had anything to do with that. Or, if he did, I never had any knowledge of it. But no,' he muttered softly, 'I'd have known – I'm certain of it.'

It seemed to Anna that this last statement was intended to reassure himself rather than his audience.

'Mostly, though,' he went on, 'it was the sort of thing you'll have heard on that tape. Coaching witnesses, pushing them that little bit harder than he probably should have, telling them another witness had already picked out the suspect when in fact they'd done no such thing – that sort of thing. He was always a big believer in going with your gut. From the word go, he made it plain to me that he liked Sandra Morton for the murders. That much wasn't controversial. So did everyone, from the man on the street right up to the Chief Constable. He said he wanted to limit the scope of the investigation to stop it becoming unwieldy. But in reality, he already had an outcome in mind from the word go, and he gave short shrift to anything – and any*one* – that contradicted it.'

'People,' said Anna, 'like Adjoa Asante.'

Gunning looked pained. 'That was several orders of magnitude more extreme than anything I'd witnessed from him before. He seemed to really take against her. I think he figured she'd be a pushover – you know, being undocumented, not having a good grasp of English. The fact she pushed back against him really got his hackles up. He seemed determined to break her – and not just because so much of the case rested on her saying the right thing.'

'He was teaching her a lesson.' Anna couldn't hide the distaste in her voice.

Gunning twisted the plain gold band on his ring finger distractedly. 'If a witness or a suspect said something which contradicted his theory, it would never occur to him that it might just mean his theory was wrong. His instinct was always to assume they were lying. It wasn't always like that. He used to be much more open-minded. But over time, he became more and more dogmatic in his approach. And the thing is, I can pinpoint the precise moment when it first started.'

'Go on,' said Pamela.

Gunning shifted his gaze from Anna to her. 'What do you know about the Kinnaman Method?'

'I don't think I've heard of it.'

Gunning smiled dryly. 'No reason you should have, really. It's not something that ever took off in this country, but it's big business in the States. Used by all the major law enforcement agencies. An ex-police officer from New York came up with it in the 1950s. Basically, you put as much pressure on a suspect as possible in order to extract a confession from them, using a range of intensive interrogation techniques. In the mid-nineties, Frank spent three months with the NYPD as part of an exchange programme. He came back determined to put the techniques he'd learned there into practice.

'At the time, I think we were all a little bit in awe of what he was telling us. *I* was, at any rate. It had a veneer of being scientifically sound. Plus, anything coming out of America tended to make folk slightly starstruck. Frankly, I think we all *wanted* it to be true – for there to be this catch-all solution that delivered results reliably and efficiently. If you want something badly enough, you'll overlook all the evidence to the contrary and only see the things that reinforce what you already believe.'

'And he used this technique on Sandra too,' said Anna. It was a statement of fact rather than a question.

Gunning gave an inkling of a dry smile. 'That's the thing – it didn't work on her at all. Right from the get-go, she was completely monosyllabic. She had no interest in telling us her version of events. We had to wheedle it out of her, bit by bit. Frank said she was trying to conserve her energy. He had this theory that people who've got nothing to hide will always be desperate to prove their innocence, while with the guilty ones it's the opposite: they're quiet because they're keeping their powder dry, putting all their mental energy into not cracking.' He shrugged slightly. 'Of course, I also heard him say more than once that a suspect who can't keep their mouth shut is hiding something as well. I suppose, if you look at it from the right angle, *anything* can be a sign of guilt.'

Anna said nothing, though she couldn't help but think of the witch trials of days gone by. If you drowned, it proved you'd been innocent all along. If you floated, you were declared guilty and condemned to death anyway. *The lady doth protest too much.*

She realised Gunning was still talking. 'Once you're confident a suspect is lying, you're supposed to imply to them that you have incontrovertible evidence against them, then steer them towards confession as the path of least resistance. You tell them their actions were understandable; that it's in their best interests to own up now and save themselves a whole lot of grief. But Sandra wouldn't bite. She just kept denying it over and over, and when Frank refused to take no for an answer, she'd goad him with jibes to the tune that he was inept. And when she didn't respond the way the manual said she was supposed to, rather than accept that his approach wasn't working, that the methodology was flawed, he just took it as further proof that she must be guilty. Sometimes I wonder whether his determination to put her away had more to do with getting back at her for making him look like a mug than it did locking up a child-killer.'

A silence settled on the room that somehow made it feel even darker and colder than it had previously.

'There's an obvious question to all of this,' Anna said after a moment, 'and that's: if you were so concerned about Dalston's behaviour – so concerned you made covert recordings of him – why's it taken you till now to do anything about it?'

Once again, a pained expression crossed Gunning's features. 'I was going to. I'd made up my mind I was going to take the matter to Complaints and Conduct as soon as the case wrapped up. But then I saw what a hero the press made him out to be – the man who took down the Ice Queen. I saw the TV deals, the glowing op-eds, and I knew no one would thank me for calling the verdict into question – which is exactly how an investigation into Frank's conduct would have been perceived. So I let it be.

'You have to understand, Frank might not have done it by the book, but I never for a moment doubted justice had been served. Besides, we were both just a few years out from retirement. There was a time limit on how much more harm he could do. I thought, why kick up a fuss at this stage? Anyway, sometimes calling attention to this sort of thing does more harm than good. You only have to look at what a low opinion folk have of the police these days to see that.'

'Better for them to remain blissfully ignorant, hmm?' said Anna, unable to help herself.

'Yes, well,' said Pamela, interjecting with forced brightness before Gunning could respond, 'I think we're probably just about done here.' She glanced at Anna. 'Unless you've got any further questions?'

Anna caught the note of warning in both her expression and her tone: *Behave yourself.*

'There's one thing I'm wondering,' she said, addressing Gunning with strained civility. 'We know Dalston bullied Adjoa Asante into changing her testimony. That's a matter of record. But what about the other key eyewitness the prosecution relied on? Did he put pressure on Paul Kempley too?'

'I don't know,' said Gunning. 'I wasn't there when he was interviewed. And I've no idea what may or may not have happened before he made it as far as the interview room. But if what you're asking me is whether I think Frank compelled him to say Sandra Morton wasn't present at the petrol station when she actually *was*, I'd say no. It would have been too great a gamble on his part. Besides, he wasn't in the business of fitting people up. That sort of thing's in no one's interests.'

'What about the CCTV that failed to record? And the missing receipt and painkillers? There's no possibility he could have made them disappear?'

Gunning shook his head emphatically. 'Absolutely not. Tampering with evidence was never his style. Besides, I'm not sure it would even have been possible. The number of people you'd have to persuade to turn a blind eye...'

Anna thought about the activities of the Shadow Men – both the ones she'd uncovered herself and those that had subsequently come to light over the last three years – and felt like saying she suspected it would have been *entirely* possible. But she resisted. They were here to probe Gunning's recollection of events twenty years ago, not persuade him to alter his outlook on those events.

Pamela glanced at Anna, which Anna interpreted as her asking her if she had any further questions. She shook her head almost imperceptibly.

Pamela got to her feet, the movement stiff and unnatural. 'Well, in that case, I think we've got all we need for the time being. Thank you for answering our questions, Mr Gunning. It's very much appreciated.'

'I want to be clear about one thing,' Gunning said as Anna joined Pamela on her feet. 'I had a lot of respect for Frank Dalston. I *still* have a lot of respect for him. There may have been some mistakes made along the way, but whatever's come to light since then can't erase all the good we accomplished together.'

'Well,' said Pamela, her tone remaining impeccably chirpy and good-natured, 'that probably depends on whether you're sitting inside a prison cell or outside one, doesn't it?'

32

They got back into the car and sat for a moment, each privately digesting what they'd heard. Anna became aware that Pamela was flexing her fingers compulsively, her lips quivering as she muttered inaudibly to herself. Both movements were increasingly in speed and intensity, building towards a crescendo.

'Pamela,' Anna began cautiously, 'are you—'

Pamela suddenly lashed out, slamming her fist against the dashboard. 'That ... that *bugger!*' she exploded.

Anna stared at her in surprise. She would never have guessed Gunning's words had had such an adverse effect on her. This sudden, uncharacteristic explosion of anger made the fact she'd managed to keep her cool inside the house all the more impressive.

'I'm guessing you weren't swayed by the pity-me speech, then,' Anna said.

It was, by her own admission, a feeble attempt at levity, and Pamela's response – a stony-faced glare – immediately told her she'd misjudged the mood.

'Yeah,' Pamela shot back glibly, 'he's a real stand-up bloke. All that self-serving rubbish about how he was going to do something about it, honest he was, and not making a fuss, and anyway Frank wasn't *that* bad, not really, it just ...' Her stream-of-consciousness tirade came to an abrupt halt as she inhaled a lungful of air. The act of catching her breath seemed to stall her momentum and she ended with a limp, almost apologetic shrug. 'It just really grinds my gears, that's what.'

'Mine too,' said Anna gently, 'but it's obvious he feels bad about what happened, whatever excuses he might make. You said it yourself – he wouldn't have sent that tape if at least *some* part of him didn't want to make amends.'

Pamela expelled a heavy breath, blowing a loose strand of hair out of her eyes. 'If there's one thing I can't stand, it's people who won't take responsibility for their own actions.'

Her tone was so apologetic, it was almost as if she thought this was something to be ashamed of.

Anna smiled sympathetically. 'Same here. To be honest, I was struggling a bit to keep my emotions in check back there. You did a lot better than me. But it was worthwhile, right? I mean, it'll help our case, won't it, if he can be persuaded to go on the record?'

Pamela considered the question. 'It's not the smoking gun we need,' she said eventually, 'but it's certainly not going to *hurt*.'

She fell silent for a moment, sitting slumped forward in her seat with her head bowed in apparent concentration, as if drawing on her inner reserves. Anna briefly wondered whether she might be praying. Then, abruptly, she straightened up, sucked air in through her nostrils and turned to Anna expectantly.

'Right, then,' she said, her earlier air of melancholy having evaporated completely, 'shall we crack on?'

They set off once again, heading out of Lockerbie and continuing south down the A74. As they passed Ecclefechan, Adjoa Asante's one-time place of residence, a signpost loomed ahead of them: 'EASTRIGGS – 8 MILES'.

'Eunice and George Morton live in Eastriggs, don't they?' said Pamela.

'That's right,' said Anna.

'Huh.'

Anna glanced in Pamela's direction. 'What?'

'Oh, nothing. Just, we're heading that way anyway. Might be worth swinging by, see if they're in. Nothing ventured, nothing gained.'

Anna turned to look at her in surprise. Pamela merely shrugged and gazed back with that familiar butter-wouldn't-melt expression of hers.

'I'm just saying – be a shame to pass up the opportunity while we're practically in the neighbourhood…'

A smile slowly spread across Anna's features. She wondered whether this was a genuine spur-of-the-moment idea inspired by the signpost or if Pamela had planned this all along.

'I suppose it wouldn't do any harm,' Anna mused, trying to sound like she wasn't bothered either way. 'After all, they can only tell us to get lost.'

And probably will, she thought ruefully, mindful of how her phone call to them had ended three weeks earlier. Nonetheless, she reached for the sat-nav and entered their new destination. *Nothing ventured,* indeed.

Fifteen minutes later, they pulled into Eastriggs – home of the now decommissioned Devil's Porridge munitions factory, as the Wikipedia entry on Pamela's phone helpfully informed them. As they cruised along the Annan Road towards the village green, they passed the Black Swan, the pub where Sandra had been photographed in an intimate clinch with one of her many paramours. This was, of course, also the place where Paul Kempley had grown up and Katie Morton had lived for the seven months prior to the murders of her father and brothers. For Anna, who'd read about these locations more times than she cared to remember, the whole thing had a whiff of the surreal about it, as if she'd just stepped onto the set of a familiar television series. Though she'd never been here before in her life, everything looked exactly as she'd expected it to, right down to the last shopfront sign.

They continued along the Annan Road, passing through the northern limits of the village, before turning off onto the East Road and following it until they came to a gravel track leading to the renovated farmhouse where, according to the phone book, Eunice and George Morton lived. By the time they made it to the end of the track, a man of about eighty, no doubt alerted by the sound of the Skoda's engine, had emerged from the sprawling, two-storey building and was making his way towards them, moving with both a briskness and a determination that belied his advanced years. Anna and Pamela got out of the car and stood on either side of it, waiting till he drew to a halt facing them.

'This road doesn't lead anywhere,' he informed them. 'Wherever it is you're headed, you'll need to turn round and go back the way you came.'

'That's all right,' said Pamela cheerfully. 'As it happens, *this* is where we're headed. You'll be George Morton, I take it?'

'I am,' said the man, eyeing them both dubiously. 'And who might *you* be?'

'Pamela Macklin. I'm a solicitor with Riddoch MacLetchie.'

'Are either of those names supposed to mean anything to me?'

'Possibly not, but the name of my client might. I represent Sandra Morton.'

For a moment, George didn't respond. He simply stared at Pamela in open-mouthed disbelief. Then his eyes narrowed and his hands balled into fists. He moved towards Pamela until he was right in her face, forcing her back up against the car.

'You've got some bloody nerve coming here,' he snarled. 'After everything that … that *woman* put us through, you show up, bold as brass, expecting – what? To be welcomed with open arms?'

The moment George had begun to advance on Pamela, Anna had hurried round to the other side of the car. She now drew alongside the beleaguered solicitor, partly to provide strength in numbers, but also so she'd be ready to intervene physically should the need arise.

'Mr Morton,' she said, her tone level but with a warning edge to it, 'I can assure you, neither of us expects anything of the sort. All we're here to do is—'

At the sound of Anna's voice, George swung around to face her, eyes flaring. '*You?* You're that busybody who was haranguing my wife on the phone the other week, aren't you? I might have guessed all that drivel about researching the case was a smokescreen. So, you're working with *them*.'

He gave her a look of such contempt that, for a moment, she thought he was about to spit on the ground in front of her. But instead, he merely shook his head and half-turned away from them, giving them the cold shoulder in the most literal sense.

'I've got nothing to say to either of you. I'm giving you thirty seconds to get off my property before I call the police to report you for trespassing.'

'George?'

A woman's voice, high and quavering, rang out behind him. All three of them turned towards the house to see a small, wizened figure standing in the doorway.

'Who is it, George?' she called, her voice instantly recognisable to Anna as that of the woman she'd spoken to on the phone.

'It's nothing, love,' said George, with a reassuring hand-wave. 'Go back inside.'

But Eunice Morton either failed to understand his instruction or pointedly chose to ignore it. With some effort, she clambered down from the front step and set off across the gravel courtyard towards them, her stride faltering but purposeful. Despite it being well past midday, she was wearing slippers and a housecoat.

With his control over the situation rapidly unspooling, George looked wildly from his wife to Anna and Pamela. 'Now's *really* not a good time,' he told them in a low growl.

'Who are these people, George?' Eunice demanded, drawing alongside him and blinking at the two visitors in confusion.

'Nobody,' said George, drawing a protective arm round her frail shoulders. 'They were just leaving.'

'We'd *really* appreciate a few words with you and your wife, Mr Morton,' said Pamela, in a tone that positively oozed deference. 'Please – we've come all the way from Glasgow.'

'You've come all the way from Glasgow?' Eunice echoed in shock and wonderment, as if Pamela had just told her they'd trekked there on foot.

'That's right,' said Pamela cheerfully. 'We've been on the road since first thing.'

'And you came down specially to speak to *us*?'

'That's about the level of it,' said Anna.

Eunice fixed her husband with an imploring look. 'We can't send them away, George. Not after they've come so far.'

George looked from his wife to Anna and Pamela again, his face contorted in exasperation. Pamela smiled at him hopefully, a picture of innocence.

George sighed. 'Well,' he said uncharitably, 'provided this isn't going to take long. You'd better come in, I suppose.'

As the four of them set off towards the house, George leading Eunice by the arm, Pamela turned to Anna and flashed her a surprisingly devilish wink. Too stunned to respond, Anna simply followed the others in a daze.

33

'So let me get this straight,' said George, with an air of incredulity. 'You're investigating the possibility of the creature who murdered my son and grandsons being innocent … and you want *us* to help you prove it?'

They were in the farmhouse's large, airy kitchen – about as far a cry from Malcolm Gunning's dark, cramped living room as it was possible to get. Anna and Pamela sat on one side of a wide oak table, facing the elderly couple on the other. George sat, straight-backed, glowering at the two visitors, while Eunice picked compulsively at the frayed edge of her housecoat's sleeve.

'That's not quite how I'd put it,' Pamela replied levelly. 'We're gathering information and would be grateful if you'd share your memories with us to help us build up a better picture of what happened. Yes, Sandra Morton is my client, and yes, that makes it my job to secure the best possible outcome for her, but it's not my place to offer a view on her guilt or innocence. The fact of the matter is, a jury of her peers found her guilty in a court of law, and until compelling new evidence to the contrary comes to light, she remains so in the eyes of the law.'

George shook his head adamantly. 'Oh, no. I know where this is headed. I've seen it happen umpteen times in the news – criminals getting off on a technicality because the evidence was stored in the wrong colour of envelope or a particular form wasn't submitted to the right department. I know what you lawyers are like. Always looking for an opportunity to poke holes.'

'I can assure you, nothing like that is going to happen here,' said Pamela.

'Nothing short of overwhelming evidence of innocence is going to get your daughter-in-law's conviction overturned. In fact, if our findings end up proving conclusively that she *did* do it, it'll put any possibility of her appealing the verdict to bed once and for all. And since you're so confident of her guilt, I don't see why you'd have anything to fear.' She gave a slight smile. 'If you like, you can think of this as a chance to make doubly sure she remains behind bars.'

It seemed to Anna that George's expression softened ever so slightly, his posture becoming less flagrantly standoffish. At any rate, he seemed, for the first time, to be giving due consideration to the implications of answering versus not answering their questions.

'All right,' he said, after a moment. 'What do you want to know?'

'Let's start from the beginning,' said Pamela. 'What were you doing on the evening of the sixth of May 2001?'

There was little in the account George now gave that deviated significantly from what Anna already knew, barring the occasional insignificant detail. He did all the talking, barring the occasional interjection from Eunice, most of which added nothing to the proceedings, other than to confirm Anna's earlier suspicion that she was in at least the early stages of dementia. It wasn't even clear how much of the conversation she understood. For the most part, she sat quietly, blank-faced and impassive, though she would periodically latch onto a specific word or phrase, especially a name she happened to recognise.

'He was a *nice* man,' she said of Dalston, in a tone that conveyed how important she felt it was that Anna and Pamela knew this. 'He helped us with what to say.'

'That's enough, Eunice,' said George in a low voice, laying a hand on her arm. 'She means for the appeal,' he explained to Anna and Pamela. 'Neither of us had ever done anything like that before – obviously – but Mr Dalston was extremely patient. He sat with us for hours, helping us with the statement – to make sure it was in our own words but that we didn't say anything wrong, you know? Anything that would prejudice the case, that is.'

'And at what point did you begin to suspect your daughter-in-law was responsible?' asked Pamela.

'It was obvious from the start,' George retorted with a scoff. 'Who else had both the means and the motive?'

'What motive would that be, Mr Morton?'

George huffed noisily, making clear just what he thought of the question. 'Well, there was always something not right about her. The whole marriage was a mistake from the beginning. We both thought so – didn't we, love?'

'She wasn't right,' said Eunice, nodding emphatically.

'She was a cold woman. *Unnaturally* cold. That much was plain from the word go. And she didn't love those children – not one bit. Treated them like they were an inconvenience. I lost track of the number of times I saw her point blank ignoring one of the little mites screaming with a dirty nappy or because he needed a feed. We helped out wherever we could, of course. Eunice barely left that house when the boys were first born. Not that she got a word of thanks for it. Quite the opposite, in fact. *She* made it clear just how much our presence was appreciated.'

'Is that why Katie was sent to live with you?' Anna cut in. 'Because Sandra was failing her as a mother?'

'I don't see what that has to do with anything,' George snapped, turning to Anna as if he'd only just remembered she existed.

'We're just trying to build up as complete a picture as possible,' said Pamela, her tone gently reassuring. 'Any background information you can provide will be incredibly useful. Why *did* Katie end up staying with you?'

'I don't ... I mean, I'm not sure why it was. Do *you* remember?' He turned to Eunice for clarification – an act that he must surely have realised was pointless. Indeed, Anna had a sneaking suspicion it was a deliberate ploy to stymie this line of questioning.

'There wasn't a single reason, as I recall,' he went on, when Eunice failed to respond. 'It just seemed more practical that way. Meant she wouldn't have so far to travel to school and whatnot. Besides, Guy had his hands full with the twins by then. It was just easier all round.' He bristled self-righteously. 'Anyway, I hardly think it matters in the grand scheme of things. As like as not, she'd be dead today if we hadn't got her out of there when we did. I wish to God we'd done the same for the boys.'

Eunice covered her mouth and choked back a sob, which George didn't seem to notice. He glared at Anna and Pamela with a single-minded focus that eclipsed everything else from his consciousness. An uncomfortable hush fell, broken only by the ticking of the wall clock and Eunice sniffling quietly by George's side.

'Mr Morton,' Pamela began, after a respectful period of silence had elapsed, 'would you say your daughter-in-law was—'

'For the love of God, would you stop *calling* her that!' George shouted, slamming his fist on the table. 'As far as I'm concerned, that *thing* ceased to be my daughter-in-law the moment she butchered my son and grandchildren as they slept in their beds.'

Eunice let out a loud sob. This time, George did notice. He turned to his wife, putting his arms around her and laying his chin on top of her head. 'It's all right, love, it's all right,' he murmured. Still holding her, he turned to glare at Pamela and Anna. 'Does my wife *have* to be involved in this? Can't you see this is upsetting her?'

Anna resisted the urge to point out that George himself seemed to be the principal source of Eunice's distress.

'Of course, Mr Morton,' said Pamela. 'I see no reason to subject her to any further discomfort, provided *you're* happy to answer the rest of our questions yourself.'

Describing George as *happy* about any of this was probably something of an overstatement. For the time being at least, however, he seemed willing to go along with this proposal. There followed a murmured conversation between himself and his wife, none of which Anna caught, after which Eunice got to her feet and wordlessly made her way out of the kitchen. As George watched her go, Pamela shot Anna a look, the meaning behind which she quickly grasped. Nonetheless, for the time being, she kept her powder dry.

'Mr Morton,' she began, seizing the opportunity to ask a question of her own during this interruption to the flow of Pamela's interrogation, 'I wondered if you happened to know anything about the whereabouts of Paul Kempley?'

George, still distracted by his wife, frowned. 'Should I know that name?'

'I should think so. He was the petrol station employee who contradicted Sandra's alibi at the trial.'

'Oh.' George sounded slightly surprised – or perhaps perturbed by the fact that he'd forgotten this detail. 'Yes, of course. I remember his evidence. Gave a good account of himself, I thought.'

'He also lived here in Eastriggs at the time.'

'Did he? Now *that* I didn't know. Hmm! Small world.' He sounded almost amused.

'I'd wondered perhaps if you'd had any contact with the family,' Anna explained. 'Maybe heard something about where he went after he moved out ...'

George gave a weak shrug. 'To the best of my knowledge our paths have never crossed. Eunice and I, we've always tended to keep ourselves to ourselves. And we don't have much cause to go into town, so ...' He trailed off with a limp gesture with his hand.

'Oh well,' said Anna. 'It was worth a shot.' She tried to ignore the sinking feeling in her gut as yet another potential avenue of enquiry was shut down.

'Listen,' she went on, sensing that now was the time to make her move, 'sorry to be a pest, but would it be OK to use your bathroom? We've been on the road since early, and ...' She gave a sheepish grimace.

'Hmm?' George looked confused, his train of thought momentarily derailed. 'Yes, yes, of course. Up the stair, then first on your left.'

Anna took her leave, heading up the steep wooden staircase to the first floor. She used the bathroom – she hadn't entirely been feigning the need – then conducted a quick search of the upstairs rooms. Finding no trace of Eunice, she crept back downstairs on tiptoe, pausing at the bottom to listen to the rise and fall of voices from the kitchen. Noticing that the door on the opposite side of the corridor was slightly ajar, she crept across and pushed it open cautiously.

Eunice was seated on a floral-patterned sofa at the far end of the wide, low-ceilinged living room, a large hardcover book open in her lap. She was making her way through it methodically, pausing to inspect each double-page spread before turning to the next. Anna stood watching her for a few moments, then shut the door softly behind her, cleared her throat and made her way over.

'Hello, Eunice. How are you doing?'

Eunice responded with a noncommittal expulsion of breath but didn't look up.

'I'm sorry you were upset back there,' Anna went on, inching closer to her. 'It can't be pleasant to be asked to relive those memories.'

'It was a bad time,' said Eunice.

'Yes,' said Anna, feeling spectacularly useless in her inability to come up with anything more profound. She looked down at the book in Eunice's lap and realised it was a photo album. She gestured to it. 'May I … ?'

Eunice nodded.

Anna sat next to her on the sofa, drawing in close so they could both look at the album at the same time. Eunice continued to turn the pages at her own pace, as if Anna wasn't there. Most of the photos, secured in place with yellowing tape, were of people Anna assumed were family friends or members of the extended Morton clan. She recognised the twins, Guy and Jeff, and Eunice and George themselves. There was no sign of Sandra – which, on reflection, she supposed wasn't remotely surprising. What *was* surprising was that, barring the occasional isolated image, Katie, too, was conspicuous by her absence.

Remembering that she was meant to be on a mission to actually *talk* to Eunice, Anna began asking her about the various pictures and the people in them – 'Who's that?', 'Tell me about this day' and so on. Not all of Eunice's responses were entirely coherent. Sometimes she would hit upon a name, though often Anna had no way of knowing whether it was the correct one or not. Other times, she would *um* and *ah* for an extended period, before saying, 'That's … oh, *you* know.' But she certainly recognised the twins, whose faces she paused to stroke with her pinkie, murmuring endearments towards them.

'You must miss them a lot,' Anna said, recognising that this must count as stating the spectacularly obvious.

Eunice gave a soft 'mm' of agreement.

'And Katie – you miss her too, don't you?'

'She was a good girl. Never any trouble. She went to stay with my other son – you know, over the water.'

'And do you still see her at all?'

'She was a good girl,' Eunice repeated, with an earnestness that suggested she felt Anna hadn't sufficiently understood her the last time she said it.

Anna suppressed a sigh. She knew she was getting nowhere; that anything Eunice *did* say, even if it superficially seemed to make sense, had to be treated with a sizeable grain of salt. And yet she had to try.

'Mrs Morton,' she said, laying a hand on the older woman's shoulder, 'why *did* Katie come to live with you and your husband?'

Eunice turned to Anna with something akin to fear in her cloudy eyes. She opened her mouth and inhaled a wheezing breath, seemingly on the verge of saying something.

Just then, the door swung open behind them. Anna spun around as George came striding in with a look of molten fury on his face. Pamela was hot on his heels, though she hung back in the doorway, as if she feared getting too close to him in his current mood.

'What the devil d'you think you're doing?'

'Oh!' said Anna, concluding that feigning blissful ignorance was the best option at her disposal. 'Your wife was just showing me your family photos.'

Once again moving with surprising speed, George cleared the space between them in a couple of brisk strides and snatched the album out of Eunice's hands. He faced Anna, glowering down at her with barely disguised rage.

'I thought you were going to the bathroom.'

'I was,' said Anna brightly. 'I took a wrong turn on my way back and ended up in here by mistake. I thought Eunice could do with some company.'

George scowled and said nothing. She could tell he knew perfectly well what she'd been up to, but she guessed he wasn't willing to come out and accuse her for fear of upsetting Eunice again.

'Yes, well,' he said stiffly, 'we're done here, so you can be on your way.'

'Actually—' Pamela began.

'No.' George held up a hand, silencing her. 'I've been *more* than patient. I've allowed you into my home and answered all your questions – neither of which I was under any obligation to do. And now, if you don't mind, my wife and I have things to do, so I'd be grateful if you'd leave so we can get on with the rest of our day.'

Neither Anna nor Pamela attempted to talk him round. They followed him obediently to the hallway, where he led them to the front door and stood, arms folded, waiting for them to leave.

As Anna collected her jacket from the coat rack, a phone began to ring somewhere in the house. George glanced in its direction, his features contorted in frustration. Clearly, the timing was, from his perspective, far from ideal.

'It's OK, Mr Morton,' said Pamela. 'We can see ourselves out.'

George remained rooted to the spot for a few seconds longer, the phone continuing to trill from deep within the cavernous building. Evidently, he would have preferred to supervise Anna and Pamela's exit to make sure they left.

'You just make sure you do that,' he said at length, then gave a curt nod, turned and headed down the corridor towards the ringing phone.

As Anna and Pamela stepped out onto the gravel courtyard, they heard shuffling footsteps behind them. They looked back to see Eunice coming after them, moving with the same unsteady but determined gait as before. They stopped and waited for her to catch up.

'I have to talk to you,' she said in an urgent whisper, sounding, to Anna's mind, a good deal more clear-headed than she had at any point until now.

'What is it, Mrs Morton?' asked Pamela.

Eunice regarded the two younger women beseechingly. 'There are things you don't know,' she insisted, her voice fading to a strained hiss.

'What? What don't we know?'

But Eunice wouldn't say any more. She looked apprehensively towards the house, from inside which George's voice could be heard, the words unintelligible but his tone unequivocally one of exasperation as he attempted to extricate himself from the call.

Eunice turned to Anna and Pamela again. 'There are things you need to know,' she repeated plaintively.

'All right,' said Pamela. 'I hear what you're saying. Are you able to get away from the house?'

'Or,' Anna interjected, as Eunice looked uncertain, 'is there a time we can come back, when your husband will be out?'

'He has golf on Thursday afternoon,' said Eunice, with a small smile that indicated – what? Pride at having remembered this? Or simply an eagerness to be helpful?

Anna opened her mouth to say yes, they could come back then, but Pamela got in first.

'No, I'm afraid that's no good,' she said, in a tone that was far more forceful than Anna had heard from her before or felt comfortable hearing her use to address such an elderly and clearly infirm woman. 'It needs to be sooner – later today, or tomorrow at the absolute latest.'

'Tomorrow,' said Eunice slowly, as if testing the word in her mouth to see how it sounded. 'Yes, perhaps I could do that. But not here.' Her eyes widened as a thought struck her. 'I could take the bus into the village. George doesn't get up until late.'

'That would be perfect,' said Pamela, once again pipping Anna to the post. 'Shall we say nine o'clock at the Cornerstone Café?' They'd passed it on the Annan Road on their way through the village. It wasn't far from the farmhouse.

'The Cornerstone Café,' Eunice repeated, nodding slowly as she committed this to memory.

'At nine a.m. You won't forget?'

Eunice's eyes flashed with an uncharacteristic display of anger. 'Of course I won't forget,' she retorted, as if the very idea was insulting.

Just then, they heard George's voice calling out from inside the house.

'Eunice? Where are you, love?'

A look of fear came into Eunice's eyes. 'You need to go,' she hissed.

She gave them a final, pleading look before turning and hurrying back towards the house. Anna and Pamela waited till she disappeared inside before turning and heading back to the car.

34

They drove back down the East Road in silence. By now, it was approaching two o'clock, and Anna's stomach was rumbling something fierce. After stopping to share a doughy, undercooked pizza from a rather down at heel takeaway opposite the village green, they set out once again, making the short drive east along the B721 to Hillend.

It began as a couple of detached cottages by the side of the road, followed, a hundred metres or so later, by a left-hand turn-off leading to the village proper – if you could even call it that. Anna had known already that Hillend would be about as far from the busy cities in which she'd lived her entire life as it was possible to get, but nothing could have prepared her for the sense of melancholy and despair that now rose up to smother her. As the day had progressed, she'd had the feeling of leaving civilisation increasingly behind her, with each successive destination constituting a further stage of removal. Now they really were at the ends of the Earth.

They drove up the hill from which the village took its name, pulling up outside the former home of Sandra and Guy Morton. Framed against the virtually cloudless sky, the bungalow dubbed the Hillend House of Horror by the press appeared completely innocuous, a million miles removed from the horrific crime with which it had become associated. And then, as Anna got out of the car, she experienced a sudden, vivid mental image of a young man with long hair and a Manson-esque appearance gazing up at the house from the very spot where she now stood, and it was all she could do to stop herself from shuddering violently.

She hung back while Pamela headed up the garden path to the front door. As she stood there, gazing out at the view afforded by their elevated position, she felt, for the first time, something approaching a proper understanding of just how isolated Sandra would have been here, holed up in this Godforsaken place day after day, with no friends, no job, no link to the rest of the world. As someone who was used to never being more than a few minutes away from the shops, the cinema or her friends, this tiny hamlet with its double-digit population and single convenience store – where all but the most basic necessities were several miles away and the bus passed through a couple of times a day at best – was the stuff of nightmares. She'd have gone out of her mind if she'd had to live here – she was sure of it.

Is that what happened to you, *Sandra?*

She stirred at the sound of footsteps and saw Pamela making her way back down the path.

'Looks like no one's home,' she said, thumbing over her shoulder towards the house. 'I suppose that puts paid to us asking if we can do a walk-around of the premises.'

'Too bad,' said Anna, privately thinking that it was probably a good thing they didn't have to have *that* conversation with the current owners.

Pamela drew alongside her and stood, arms folded, surveying the same view Anna had just balked at. They stood there in silence for a few minutes, both lost in their own thoughts. At length, Anna stirred.

'So what now?'

She wasn't exactly savouring the prospect of having come all this way only to immediately turn round and head back up the road to Glasgow – especially not with the prospect of driving back down to Eastriggs again first thing tomorrow morning for their appointment with Eunice.

Pamela wrinkled her chin thoughtfully. 'Well, as I see it, we've got two conflicting accounts: Sandra's and the official one. How about if we put them both to the test? The investigation team would have done a full reconstruction at the time, but sometimes it's useful to go through the motions yourself. You know, to get a proper feel for the logistics. What do you think?'

'All right,' said Anna, opting not to voice her opinion that this was probably a colossal waste of time. 'Where shall we start?'

Pamela considered the question. 'It's a beautiful day,' she said eventually, 'and I quite fancy a bracing post-lunch constitutional. I vote we start with Sandra.' She pointed in a northerly direction. 'She said she walked up to the convenience store to buy painkillers, right? 'Cept she found it shut and set off over the fields to the petrol station on the A75. Which took her – what was it? Just under half an hour? Let's see if that really is doable.'

They set off, heading up the village's solitary main road, following the directions provided by Pamela's phone. Every so often, they passed a house on one side of the road or the other, but they were spaced so far apart that Hillend began to seem less like a unified settlement than a series of individual, unconnected dwellings placed at random in the middle of the countryside.

'You didn't like the way I was with Eunice back there, did you?' said Pamela, after they'd been walking in silence for a few minutes.

Anna stirred from her own thoughts. She'd been unaware, until now, that she'd been nurturing any ill-feeling towards Pamela for the way she'd spoken to the older woman, but now she'd been forced to confront it, it was impossible to deny it.

'Not really, no,' she said.

'Well, sorry if you thought I was too hard on her, but I'm not sorry I pushed her. If we'd given her time to change her mind about telling us whatever she's been bottling up for twenty-odd years, chances are she'd have done just that. For all we know, she *still* might. Who knows what she'll decide now she's back under the control of that not at *all* coercive husband of hers? But at least this way she's only got eighteen hours or so to have second thoughts instead of the better part of a week.' Pamela glanced sidelong at Anna, seeing her doubtful expression. 'You don't agree.'

'I'm not saying I don't agree. I just, back there, you suddenly seemed an awful lot like … well, like Dalston, I suppose.'

For a moment, Pamela didn't respond. She just trudged along, eyes downcast, lips pursed in deep thought. 'Look,' she said eventually, 'I know you think I'm just a daft wee lassie…'

'I don't think you're a daft wee lassie.'

'Please.' Pamela gave a strained smile. 'Let me finish. I know you think I'm a daft wee lassie, but like it or not, I've got a job to do, and sometimes that involves giving people who need it a dunt in the right direction.' She fixed Anna with an entreating look. 'She *wants* to talk to us. I can feel it. She just needed a bit of a helping hand.'

Anna remained far from convinced, though she resolved to say no more on the subject.

Less than a mile from their starting position, they came to the 8 Till Late – a cosy-looking little nook with brightly coloured frontage at the end of a row of terraced houses.

Pamela checked her phone. 'Eighteen minutes. That fits with Sandra's account, assuming she was moving just a tad faster than us.'

'Which, if she was desperate for painkillers, she would have been.' Anna turned in a circle, orienting herself. 'From the 8 Till Late, she set off over the fields on the northern edge of the village.' She pointed up the road towards the expanse of undulating farmland that began about two hundred metres away and extended towards the horizon. 'Those ones, I'm guessing.'

Pamela shrugged. 'Shall we, then?'

Together, they headed along to the end of the road and clambered over the low stone wall that separated the village from the farmland. The ground in front of them rose steadily and steeply, and the sun beat down on them from directly overhead, with the result that, by the time they reached the top of the first slope, Anna was struggling to catch her breath and cursing herself for not having left her jacket in the car. Pamela, though on the face of it coping rather better, seemed to be entertaining similar thoughts: she'd already shed her blazer and was in the process of tying it round her waist.

Before them, the ground continued to rise and fall, fields spreading out before them as far as the eye could see. In the distance, the A75 was a thin, ill-defined line bisecting the otherwise uninterrupted sea of green, the twin streams of traffic resembling multi-coloured ants marching steadily in either direction. A little way off to the left and on the far side of the road, the yellow and red canopy of a Shell petrol station served as a vibrant marker of their intended destination.

Pamela stood, arms folded, gazing out at the view before her. 'Pity we can't ask *them* what happened that night,' she observed, nodding to the dozen or so cows spread throughout the field, lazily chewing cud and swishing their tails.

Anna, still somewhat winded from the climb, managed a chuckle. 'Yeah, I bet *they* make for reliable eyewitnesses.'

'Well, I doubt they've got the capacity to lie.' Pamela raised her arms above her head in a full body stretch. 'Right, enough lollygagging. Let's get a shifty on.'

'Hang on.' Anna held up a hand in a plea for clemency. 'I just need a moment.'

Pamela grinned. 'Climb too much for you, auld wumman? All right, all right – we'll wait till you've got your breath back.'

Anna shook her head in disbelief. Say what you liked about this trip being a waste of time, but it seemed to be having a profoundly liberating effect on Pamela, revealing a hitherto unseen playful, irreverent side to her.

'Laugh away,' Anna shot back. 'I'll have you know, before I got pregnant, I used to run 5K every morning before breakfast.'

Pamela tutted. 'Excuses, excuses. Tell you what – given that we're supposed to be recreating the movements of a woman in a mortal hurry, what d'you say I go on and you stay put and keep the coos company?' She gave a cheeky nudge in the ribs. 'Don't worry – I'm sure they won't judge you for taking a breather.'

It felt an awful lot like admitting defeat, but Anna ultimately conceded that Pamela's plan made sense. Using her jacket as an impromptu picnic blanket, she sat down on the grass and watched as the younger woman set off down the slope, weaving this way and that as she picked out the safest route underfoot. Before long, she was out of sight.

Anna inhaled the country air deeply, held it for a moment, then let it out in a long, satisfying exhale. She liked it up here more than back down in the village. The sense of isolation was, if anything, even more pronounced, but it was a different, more liberating sort of isolation, the wide-open space all around her a stark contrast to the cloying, backwater oppressiveness of Hillend. It might not be for her, but she could see why the country life appealed to some people.

She wiped her brow with the back of her hand. On a day like this, even sitting doing nothing was thirsty work, and she wished she'd had the forethought to bring a water bottle with her. Her thoughts turned to the 8 Till Late. She wasn't sure whether, in a place like this, the local convenience store would be open on a Sunday, but she had nothing to lose by going to look. She got up, tucked her jacket under her arm and set off back the way she'd come.

35

The place looked as quiet as the proverbial grave, and when she tried the door, she found it locked. She crossed over to the window and peered through it, searching for signs of life inside. She could make out several aisles of well-stocked shelves and, at the far end of the shop, the cool glow of a refrigerated unit filled with drinks bottles – including, tantalisingly several varieties of sparkling water.

As she admitted defeat and turned to go, she heard a window being thrust open above her, followed by a woman's voice.

'Hello there! Can I help you?'

Anna turned and looked up to the now open window above the shop, out of which a rotund, curly-haired woman in her mid-thirties was leaning.

'Sorry.' Anna gestured to the shop. 'I thought this place might be open.'

'Why? What are you after?'

'Oh, no – it's fine. I just—'

'Nonsense! Be down in a tick.'

Before Anna could say another word, the woman had disappeared, slamming the window shut behind her. Less than a minute later, there was a sound of jangling keys behind the shop door, before it swung open to reveal the woman, beaming at Anna a trifle breathlessly.

'We're closed on a Sunday,' she explained as she stooped to prop the door open with a rubber wedge, 'but I'll usually open up if one of the locals needs something. Perks of living on the floor above. Come on in.'

Grateful for the respite from the heat outside, Anna stepped into the cool of the shop. As she made her way over to the fridge, the shopkeeper piped up again.

'I'm Heather, by the way.'

Anna glanced up from inspecting the row of water bottles. 'Anna.'

'Pleasure to meet you, Anna. You aren't from around here, I take it.'

'Just in town for the day.' Anna shut the fridge door and turned to face her host, holding up the bottle she'd selected. 'How much do I owe you for this?'

'So what brings you to Hillend?' asked Heather as she rang Anna's purchase up at the till. 'Sorry, I don't mean to pry. I just can't help it. Naturally nosy, that's me!'

Anna took a grateful swig of water before responding. 'It's fine. Actually, I'm on something of a fact-finding mission. I'm looking into—' She suddenly stopped, having second thoughts. Something told her the locals were unlikely to take too kindly to having that moment in their collective history dredged up yet again.

'Yes?' Heather smiled at her expectantly. 'Looking into what?'

'A crime that was committed here a number of years ago,' said Anna, unable to meet her eyes.

'You mean the murders at the house on Hill Road.'

Anna gave a small nod.

Heather smiled ruefully. 'Figured as much. I mean, it wasn't likely to be anything else. It's what put Hillend on the map. So are you a reporter, or ... ?'

'No, nothing like that,' Anna reassured her hastily. 'I'm an academic. I'm conducting some research on the case.'

She kept it deliberately vague, but even so, she half-expected Heather to snatch back her water bottle and angrily demand that she get out of both her shop and Hillend post-haste. However, to her relief, Heather simply smiled and gave an exaggerated shudder.

'Well, rather you than me. Personally, I do my best to steer clear of anything to do with that business. Though, around this neck of the woods, it's kind of unavoidable.'

'Did you live here at the time?' Anna asked.

Heather beamed proudly. 'Hillend born and bred. Most folk my age got out as soon as they turned eighteen and never looked back.'

'But not you?'

'Oh, believe me, I tried. Spent a couple of years in Newcastle only to come crawling back with my tail between my legs. Couldn't hack the pace of it.' She laughed ruefully. 'Reckon I've got "small town" in my blood, for better or worse. Good thing there was an opening for an assistant here at the shop, otherwise I don't know *what* I'd have done to earn a crust.'

'Do you remember much about the investigation?'

Heather frowned, thinking back. 'I remember the place crawling with police. I'd never seen so many before in my life. Heck, I don't think the village had ever seen so many people full *stop*. And I remember people doing a lot of crying. Especially the older folk. At the time, I found it dead strange. Like, why are they crying? It's not *their* kids that died. Now, though ... ' She shrugged. 'I suppose, in a way, a lot of them saw it as an attack on us all. Nothing like that had ever happened in Hillend before, you see. People thought it was safe. And then, in the blink of an eye, all that innocence was suddenly taken away.'

Anna nodded soberly. To allow for a respectful silence, she took another sip of water before continuing.

'You didn't know the Mortons yourself, then?'

'Not the victims, no,' said Heather. 'But I knew Katie. Not *well*,' she clarified, 'but we went to the same primary school over in Eastriggs. She was a year younger than me, but we were in composite classes two or three years running, I think.'

'How did she seem?'

'She was ... ' Heather frowned, trying to decide how to answer that question. 'I'm not sure,' she admitted eventually. 'She kept herself to herself mostly. Sort of quiet – except when she wasn't.'

'How d'you mean?'

'She'd get these mood swings. Sometimes, she'd be perfectly well behaved, just getting on with her work, not bothering anyone. But then, other times, she'd act out like nothing on earth. Refuse to do what the teachers told her, give them lip, stuff like that. Some of the other girls used to pick on her. Nothing physical, but they'd laugh at her, call her names behind her back, that sort of thing. She was off sick a lot too – I remember that. We all thought she was on the skive ... ' She frowned again. 'But looking back, I'm not so sure. She was awfully pale and weedy-looking.

Maybe she had an illness the rest of us didn't know about. You don't consider those things at that age.'

An uneasy silence settled on the little shop. Heather brushed some imaginary dust from the countertop while Anna gazed around and sipped from her water bottle to avoid having to come up with something to say.

'You haven't spoken to her, I'm guessing?' said Heather after a moment, a slight note of hopefulness entering her voice.

'No,' replied Anna. 'I've tried to get in touch with her, but I've not had any success. I *have* just come from speaking to her grandparents, though.'

'Oh,' said Heather, brightening slightly after her initial disappointment. 'They're still around, then. How are they doing?'

'All right, I guess,' said Anna. She didn't feel the need to share details of Eunice's declining mental faculties. 'Katie went to live with them for a while before … before it happened. Did you know anything about that?'

Heather shook her head. 'I'd essentially lost touch with her by the time that happened. We were both at different schools by then. She went to Annan Academy while I got sent to St Joseph's. I heard about it on the grapevine – I mean, you *do* hear things in a place like this – but I never knew what lay behind it.'

'And you weren't in touch afterwards.'

For a moment, Heather gazed down at the countertop, not responding. Eventually, she sighed and lifted her head to meet Anna's eye. 'I thought about reaching out to her, offering my condolences … but in the end I never went through with it. I suppose I just didn't know what to say – too caught up in how *I'd* feel to stop and think about what *she* was going through. I mean, I was only fourteen. I know it's no excuse, but still.'

She fell silent for a moment, toying with the hem of her blouse. Anna finished her water and looked around for a recycling bin.

'I did see her once more,' Heather piped up, causing her to turn to face her again. 'Before she left for Canada, I mean. She came to tell me she was going, and to say thank you for being her friend.' She gave a humourless laugh. 'Some friend! I mean, I wasn't nasty to her like some of the other girls … but still, that's just doing the bare minimum, right? It's not as if we hung out or went round to each other's houses or anything like that. To be honest, I barely even knew her.'

'I'm not sure *anyone* really did,' said Anna quietly.

She wasn't so much speaking to Heather as thinking aloud. Other than Sandra herself, Katie was the biggest enigma in the entire affair. So much about her remained unknowable – the particulars of her childhood, why she moved out of her parents' home, what had become of her after she left Scotland.

'You know,' she went on, once more turning to Heather, 'her grand-mother has this album full of family photos. There's pictures of Guy and the twins, but hardly any of Katie. It's very strange.'

'I think I might be able to help with that,' said Heather unexpectedly. 'It's funny – you've just jogged my memory. When she came to see me – to say goodbye and whatnot – she dumped a whole load of stuff on me. A bunch of clothes and books and the like. She wasn't taking anything with her, she said. Didn't want any reminders of her old life. I ended up giving most of it away to charity. But there was a shoebox as well, full of pictures, mostly of her.'

Anna straightened up in sudden interest. 'Have you still got them?'

'Of course. I wouldn't have given *those* away.' Heather sounded almost offended. 'They're at the flat. Come on up and see.'

Anna followed Heather up a narrow wooden staircase to the tiny flat above the shop. It was just two rooms, really – a bedroom with a kitchenette, and a bathroom the size of a small broom cupboard. Anna wasn't convinced they were both going to fit in the bedroom at once, but somehow they managed to squeeze in, and Anna perched on the bed while Heather rooted around inside the wardrobe before finally producing an old, battered shoebox tied with string.

'Here,' she said, joining Anna on the bed.

Anna took the box, undid the string and lifted the lid. Inside were around a hundred photographs of varying sizes and in various states of preservation, from the dog-eared to the pristine. At least half of them featured Katie – a pale-faced, blonde-haired girl with the same cleft in her chin that both Guy and Jeff had sported. Many of them were formal affairs – yearly school portraits; her confirmation photograph; one of her and her brothers, seemingly taken shortly after the twins' birth, in a professional studio setting. In almost every one, her expression was the same: unsmiling, her blonde locks framing a thin, drawn face with pale blue eyes that instantly reminded Anna of someone else.

She continued to flick through the pictures, skimming past the ones of landscapes and animals and concentrating on the ones of Katie. As she drew near the end of the bundle, one in particular caught her eye. It was noticeably different from the others. For one thing, Katie was smiling. For another, there was someone else with her. Someone Anna didn't recognise.

She looked to have been in her early teens at the time. Anna guessed it must have been not long before the murders, for the simple reason that she couldn't imagine anyone being capable of smiling in such an unselfconscious, carefree manner *after* her father and two brothers had been so horrifically butchered. She sat astride a motorcycle that was far too big for her, head thrown back and grinning to reveal a wide gap between her front teeth. A boy in his late teens stood behind her, leaning over to hold the handlebars steady. He was tall, with dark, shoulder-length hair and a strong, chiselled jawline with a mere hint of five o'clock shadow.

'D'you know who that is?' she asked Heather, pointing to him.

Heather frowned. 'I'm not sure. I always assumed he was one of her cousins or something. That or a boyfriend. But he's got to be at *least* five years older than her, which ... ' She suppressed a shudder. 'Yeah, not sure I wanna go there.'

Anna examined the photo again, studying the boy's features intently. She placed him in his late teens, and while there was a sense of intimacy to his and Katie's closeness, she couldn't detect any hint of inappropriateness. On the contrary, the vibe she most got from the boy was one of protectiveness, like that of an older sibling. She supposed it was possible he was one of her cousins from Canada – Christopher, was it? – and that the picture had been snapped during one of their sporadic visits to Scotland.

Her eyes drifted to Katie's face again – to that wide, devil-may-care smile, so unlike the other pictures of her. For the umpteenth time, she wondered just what this thin, pale-faced girl, with her father's chin and her mother's eyes, had experienced in the thirteen years before her life was transformed utterly by the events of that night in May 2001. She hoped Eunice might be able to shed some light on the matter when they met her tomorrow – assuming the meeting actually ended up happening.

Anna was debating whether it would seem obsessive or creepy if she asked for permission to take a copy of the photo when there was a sound of footsteps on the linoleum of the shop floor. A moment later, Pamela's voice called up the stairs, effectively making the decision for her.

'Hello? Anyone there?'

Anna stirred. 'That's my friend. I'd better be going.' She gathered up the pictures and handed the box back to Heather. 'Thanks for showing me these. I really appreciate it. And thanks for the water.'

They headed back down to the shop to find Pamela standing by the checkout counter. Her brow sparkled with sweat and both her shoes and the hems of her previously pristine trousers were caked with mud, but she otherwise didn't look any the worse for wear.

'*There* you are,' she said, as Anna made her way over. 'I was wondering where you'd got to. I was starting to think you'd got bored and gone back to Glasgow, leaving me stranded here.'

'Ignore her,' Anna told Heather, taking Pamela firmly by the arm and marching her towards the exit. 'And thanks again.'

'It's been a pleasure,' Heather called after her. 'Come back any time.'

'I'll be sure to do that,' Anna replied, privately thinking that the odds of her ever coming to this neck of the woods again were small to the point of non-existence.

36

'So?' said Pamela, once they were back in the street. 'What was all that about?'

Briefly, Anna filled Pamela in on her conversation with Heather and the photographs of Katie, before turning the conversation to the solicitor's own manoeuvres.

'So what's the verdict? Does Sandra's account of her movements stack up?'

'It stacks up – just about. I reckon the route's doable in the timeframe Sandra claims, provided you're running full tilt and don't mind risking falling and breaking your neck. I lost my footing a couple of times going at an easy trot in broad daylight. I wouldn't've fancied my chances in the pitch black and lashing rain. If she really did that trek inside of thirty minutes, she must've had the toothache to end all toothaches.'

Anna looked at her watch. It was approaching 4.30 p.m. Once again, her thoughts turned to the journey home.

'Do we want to do the route the prosecution thought Sandra took?' she said, half-hoping Pamela would say no.

'Might as well,' Pamela shrugged, 'seeing as we're here.'

'All right,' said Anna, with a feeling of weary resignation. 'As long as it doesn't involve any running.'

Pamela laughed and patted Anna's arm. 'Not to worry. I promise we'll take it nice and slow just for you.'

* * *

They headed back to the Morton home and went through the gate to the back garden. As they passed the rear door, Anna half-expected it to fly open and the house's current resident to come charging out to confront them for trespassing, but nothing happened.

They made their way down the gentle slope leading to the foot of the garden, where a simple wooden fence separated it from the field below. They climbed over it one at a time, Anna stubbornly waving away Pamela's offer of help, before making their way down to the stone wall Adjoa Asante had seen the figure with long hair and a blue – or was it green? – coat scaling. From there, the Haysend Road continued north for several hundred metres before looping around in a roughly one hundred and forty-five degree arc to avoid an area of marshland, then continued in a south-easterly direction towards Shaw Road, hugging the perimeter of the reservoir.

What was referred to locally as 'The Reservoir' was, in fact, two separate bodies of water, which together formed a loose U-shape, divided vertically by a narrow stone footbridge leading north towards Haysend Farm, beyond which, in a more or less straight line, was the portion of Shaw Road where PCs Coughlin and Bennie had come upon Sandra in their patrol car. Keeping to a leisurely pace, Anna and Pamela continued along Sandra's supposed route, following a well-trodden dirt track leading from the road up to the reservoir, where they found access to the bridge barred by a six-foot-high metal gate.

Anna tried it. It opened easily. She turned to Pamela with a shrug. 'Right of way, I guess?'

They set off across the bridge, flanked on either side by high metal safety bars, presumably to prevent anyone foolhardy enough to consider doing so from taking a dip in the water. The roar from the nearby spillway was loud enough to render conversation impossible, so they walked in silence and single file, Anna leading the way.

They were about halfway across when Anna noticed a figure waiting for them at the other end of the bridge. He was dressed in the overalls of a park warden and was gesticulating animatedly with both arms. Anna glanced back at Pamela, whose responding grimace wordlessly conveyed her views on the man's presumed mental state. They quickened their pace, continuing towards him.

'Did you not hear me shouting?' he demanded, when they reached him a few minutes later. 'The gates close at five on the dot.'

'Do they?' Pamela's tone was light and breezy. 'We didn't see any signs.'

'Well, there aren't any *signs*, obviously,' the warden retorted, some of his earlier bluster fading. He was in his sixties and had the weatherbeaten features of a man who'd spent most of his life outdoors. 'You're not local, then, I take it?'

Pamela shook her head. 'Nope, just visiting.'

'In that case, I'll excuse you for not knowing.'

'Knowing what?'

Rather than respond, the warden swung the gate shut and busied himself securing it with a chain. It wasn't until he'd fixed a padlock into place and given the chain a sharp tug to make sure it was secure that he turned to face the two women once more.

'I've been the warden here for nigh on twenty-five years.' His tone made clear that he felt each and every one of them. 'Anytime some drunken youth falls into the drink, it falls to *me* to fish them out – rain or shine, day or night.' He shook his head mirthlessly. 'Must've done something unspeakable in a previous life. Anyway, after getting called out once too often at two in the morning, I took to locking the gates out of hours. It's the only way I'm guaranteed a decent night's kip,' he added, a touch defensively.

'And how do your employers feel about that?' asked Pamela innocently.

The man smiled dryly. 'Hmm, yes, well. What they don't know can't hurt them, can it? It's not as if I'm preventing anyone from going about their lawful business.'

As he and Pamela continued to converse, their voices blending into the churn of the water, Anna, her mind wandering, experienced one of those all-too-rare epiphanies that occasionally visited themselves upon her. She felt her heart rate ratcheting up; the skin on her palms becoming clammy.

'Excuse me,' she said, cutting the warden off mid-flow. 'When you said you started closing the gates after a couple of years, did you *mean* a couple or were you using the term more loosely?'

She saw, from his look of incomprehension, that she'd singularly failed to express herself with anything approaching clarity.

'What I mean,' she said, trying again, 'is would these measures have been in place in 2001?'

'Of course,' said the warden, bemused by the specificity of the question. 'I first started locking up in the summer of 1996. Improved my quality of sleep no end, I can tell you, and kept more than a few foolhardy teenagers out of mortal danger to boot.'

Anna shot a glance at Pamela and saw that she was staring at the warden intently, her own mind racing as it made the same connections Anna's own had made mere moments before.

'And if the gates were closed,' she went on, 'how long would it take someone to get to the other side?'

'On foot? Well, let's see – they'd have to go east along Haysend Road, then up Shaw Road. Going at a brisk clip, I'd say about forty minutes.'

As he spoke, Anna's eyes remained locked onto Pamela's. There could be no doubting that she too understood the significance of this information.

'You've been very helpful,' said Anna, turning to the warden once more. 'Thanks so much for your time.'

'Any time,' he said, scratching his neck in bemusement. 'You ladies enjoy the rest of your holiday now.'

Neither of them spoke until they emerged from the reservoir park. Anna felt light-headed, the adrenaline coursing through her veins, her mind going nineteen to the dozen. Beside her, Pamela was perfectly still, apart from her hands, which she was clenching and unclenching over and over without any apparent awareness of what she was doing.

Anna took her bag from her shoulder and rummaged inside, silently cursing her clammy hands for their clumsiness. At last, she found what she was looking for: the notebook in which she'd jotted down the known sequence of events on the night of the murders. She rifled through it, mumbling to herself as she did so.

'Let's see … forty minutes to circle round the reservoir plus, say, at least ten before that from the house. That's fifty, minimum …' She found the page she was looking for. 'The 999 call was made at 23:09. Adjoa's sighting of the figure hopping the wall was at 23:12. The patrol car picked Sandra up on Shaw Road at 23:49. From the 999 call to the pick-up, that's forty minutes, practically to the second.'

She lowered the notebook and stared at Pamela.

'She couldn't have done it.'

'Seems that way,' breathed Pamela.

37

'OK,' said Anna, 'let's think this through. There's still an outside chance she could have made it in thirty, provided she ran all the way.'

They were sitting in Anna's car, still parked outside the Morton house. Anna's mind had been racing with possibilities all throughout the walk back, testing the feasibility of every possible permutation of events. Pamela, seemingly sensing that she was working things through, had wisely remained quiet, though she'd watched her like a hawk every step of the way, as if hoping to spot some advance indication as to any revelations that might come her way.

'Though having said that,' she went on, now playing her own devil's advocate, 'we know she did a lot of walking, but she wasn't a trained runner. I'm not convinced she could have kept up that sort of pace the whole way. And if her goal was simply to put as much distance between herself and the crime scene as possible, why take such a circuitous path? Why not head west towards Eastriggs instead – or north over the fields like she claims she did?' She gave a groan of frustration. 'Urgh! So many questions!' She turned to look at Pamela, who was still watching her intently. 'It's enough to count as reasonable doubt, though, right?'

'Possibly,' said Pamela, after considering the question for a moment. 'At any rate, if the defence had led with this during the trial, I'd struggle to picture the jury reaching the same verdict.'

'Why the hell did this not come to light during the investigation? You said yourself – the police did a full blown reconstruction of the route they thought Sandra took.'

Pamela shrugged. 'Perhaps it was just one more thing Dalston ignored because it didn't fit his theory? But even then, locking the gates wasn't official policy. They'd have had no reason to even consider the possibility.'

Anna shook her head and said nothing. She knew she ought not to be surprised at this point, but she still couldn't believe how many corners had been cut simply because the lead detective had made up his mind he didn't like the woman at the centre of it all.

'We should go straight to the Appeal Court with this, right?' she said, after a moment. 'Surely they'll *have* to reopen the case now.'

Pamela's brow furrowed. 'Maybe. But remember we've still got our chat with Eunice tomorrow morning. I vote we wait and see what she says before we rush into anything. No sense going in all guns blazing before we know the whole story.'

'I guess,' said Anna, reluctant to admit she'd forgotten about their meeting with Eunice in all the excitement. She glanced at her watch. 'Look at that – it's gone six. We really ought to be heading for home.'

'Actually,' said Pamela, 'I was wondering if it'd make more sense to find somewhere local to spend the night. Saves us both having to be up at the crack of dawn tomorrow to come back down for a nine o'clock appointment.'

Anna didn't respond immediately. In truth, she hated these sorts of last-minute changes to a previously agreed itinerary. They invariably left her feeling unmoored and at the whim of forces outwith her control. And she hadn't brought pyjamas, toiletries, a change of clothes. Nor, for that matter, did she like the thought of being away from Jack for more than twenty-four hours. Lately, she'd been paying him precious little attention as it was, without abandoning him overnight into the bargain. Mind you, given that Zoe was invariably the one who put him to bed and got him up in the morning, she did wonder how much of an impact her absence would actually have on him ...

Her thoughts turned to Pamela, who also had a lengthy train ride back to Edinburgh to look forward to once they got back to Glasgow. She could, she supposed, offer to put her up at the house, but they were already desperately short on beds with Leah there. Plus, she could see, from Pamela's point of view, why it made little sense to spend an hour and a half in the car and then not even get a night in her own bed out of it when she could just get a hotel room somewhere nearby.

It's just one night, she told herself. Besides, the way things were working out, it looked like all this would soon be over – at which point she'd make it up to Jack in spades. Leah already thought she was a negligent mother anyway, so it wasn't as if this was going to change her views in any way.

'Why not?' she said. 'It makes total sense from a practicality standpoint.'

Pamela gave a little squeal of excitement. 'Yay! This'll be so exciting! It's been ages since I had a night away.'

'Just one condition,' said Anna.

'What?'

'I don't know about you, but I've had my fill of quaint little villages with more livestock than people. If it's a hotel we're looking for, I vote we hop across the border and head into Carlisle – treat ourselves to a slap-up meal in a place with hot *and* cold running water.'

'Sounds like an adventure!' grinned Pamela. 'You're on.'

'By the way,' said Anna, as they set off, following the A75 towards the English border, 'I take it there's no prospect of you claiming back the costs of this little excursion as a business expense?'

Pamela chuckled. 'I think we'd probably be pushing our luck.'

They arrived in Carlisle half an hour later and proceeded into the city centre, where they managed to secure a twin room at the Station Hotel, a four-storey Victorian-era affair within shouting distance of the city's main railway terminus.

'You've timed it just right,' the receptionist informed them cheerfully as she handed over their key cards. 'It's a good thing we had a cancellation an hour ago, or you'd have been fresh out of luck.'

They headed upstairs to dump their things and freshen up. While Pamela was busy in the bathroom, Anna phoned Zoe and let her know what was happening.

'Oh right,' said Zoe, to Anna's ears making an effort to sound unfazed. 'Aye, no, makes total sense when ye put it that way. Prob'ly save ye a packet on the petrol as well.'

'Are you sure it's OK?' said Anna, increasingly convinced that Zoe was taking a dim view of her for neglecting her responsibilities at home. 'I don't mind—'

'Ach, don't be talking shite, doll. You have a grand time. Mind and no drink the minibar dry, but.'

'Everything OK back home? Leah hasn't set fire to the kitchen curtains or started a fight with the neighbours or anything, has she?'

Zoe chortled. 'Naw, naw, nothing like that. Just keeping calm and carrying on – aren't we, kiddo?'

A few feet away, Jack gabbled something incomprehensible.

'Is he there?' said Anna. 'Can you put him on?'

Zoe hesitated. 'Ach, he's kinda got his hands full at the mo – daein' something *super* intensive wi different colours of slime. Beats me what he's making, but I'm sure it'll be dead impressive when it's done.' She paused again. 'I can see if I can prise him away fae his labours if you want, but?'

As Anna considered her response, Pamela emerged from the bathroom, face freshly scrubbed and the worst of the muck cleaned off her trouser-legs.

'Righty-ho, I reckon I've managed to make myself look *just* about presentable. We all set?'

'It's fine,' Anna told Zoe. 'I've gotta go anyway. Just … tell him Mummy says she loves him.'

She hung up and gave Pamela a thumbs up. 'All set.'

The in-house restaurant was mobbed – so much so that Anna suspected the receptionist hadn't merely been making conversation when she'd said they'd been lucky to get a room. Despite her late and extremely stodgy lunch, she found herself to be ravenous, and for a time after their food arrived, the only sounds coming from their table were those of chewing and the clatter of cutlery as they both attacked their plates with gusto.

Only after they'd done justice to their meal did they trouble themselves with such trivial matters as making conversation. Unsurprisingly, they spent a good amount of time picking over the day's events and the revelations that had come to light. The very air around them seemed to crackle with excitement at the knowledge that they were on the cusp of potentially overturning one of the highest profile cases in legal history.

Afterwards, they retreated to the considerably quieter bar and carried on their conversation over drinks. As the alcohol flowed, Anna found herself opening up to Pamela about her research into women's experiences of prison, her visits to Cornton Vale, Broadwood and Dungavel, and her despair about the state of the penal system in general.

'I just…' – she threw up her hands in exasperation – '…hate this obsession with the notion that people can be sorted into goodies and baddies, the deserving and the undeserving, and to hell with you if you end up on the wrong side of that divide. All any politician has to do to get elected is to promise to be "tough on crime". Because, if you break the law, you've forfeited your right to be treated as anything but a political tool – right? And the solution to every crime, whatever the story behind it, from petty theft to serial murder, is "lock them up".'

She sighed and drained her glass. 'Honestly, there's a part of me that doesn't know why I bother. The part which knows, deep down, that nothing's ever going to change, no matter how hard I bang my drum. There are easier paths through life than as the patron saint of hopeless causes.' She fixed Pamela with a hard look. 'You've felt the same way – I know you have. There's no way you can do the work you do and not feel like you're bashing your head against the proverbial brick wall.'

Pamela slid their empty glasses towards the bartender and nodded in response to his silent query before turning her eyes to Anna once more.

'I get it,' she said. 'It's a terrible curse, caring. And yeah, absolutely, I have my days when I wonder what it's all for. We're understaffed, underfunded, under-resourced and *seriously* underpaid. And like you, I see the effects of the system on a daily basis. I see how counterproductive it all is. I see how it makes monsters out of women and men who were victims of circumstance or just made one bad choice. I see how the whole thing's irretrievably broken and in desperate need of rebuilding from the ground up.'

'So what keeps you going?'

Pamela gave a watery smile. 'The good days. The ones where I'm able to persuade the sheriff to take extenuating factors into account and get my client who's a single mum who only stole to feed her kids off on a suspended sentence. Or where my client, who's sworn blind that she's innocent from the very start, walks from court a free woman because of all the all-nighters I put in making sure her case was as strong as it could possibly be. Those are the days when I feel like what I'm doing really matters.'

The bartender arrived with their drinks. Pamela nodded her thanks and slid a £20 note across the counter, before nudging Anna's glass towards her.

'I know it sounds dead cheesy, but I do what I do because I want to make a difference. Because I believe in the principle of justice for all, regardless of who they are or what they may have done in a previous life. And because, without me, what hope would my clients have? I'm not saying I'm anything special or that I give them something they wouldn't get from a thousand other solicitors, but it's what gets me out of bed in the morning. It's why I continue to do what I do.'

Anna was silent for several moments, digesting Pamela's words. At length, she nodded soberly and raised her glass. 'To making a difference, then.'

Pamela did likewise. 'To making a difference.'

They clinked glasses and downed a mouthful each.

'You didn't go to your own dad's *funeral*?'

Pamela stared at Anna in disbelief. Anna sipped from her glass and wondered how on earth they'd come to be talking about this. She wouldn't normally have shared this information with anyone; even Zoe didn't know the full story of the origins of the rift between her and her mother. But the genie was out of the bottle now and she couldn't put it back in, even if she wanted to – which she wasn't sure she did.

'I hope you don't mind me saying so,' Pamela went on, 'but that seems a bit … nuts.'

Anna shrugged but didn't dispute this assessment.

'You didn't want to be there?'

Anna gave no reply. That wasn't a question that could be summed up with a straightforward 'yes' or 'no.'

'And what about your mum? Surely *she'd* have wanted you there by her side.'

Anna chuckled dryly. 'I wouldn't be so sure about that.'

Pamela's eyes widened incredulously.

Anna sighed heavily. She knew she was going to have to provide an explanation for that cryptic statement. She swallowed another mouthful from her glass before continuing.

'I was studying in Rome at the time. I hadn't been home for a while. My mother rang me up one night out of the blue. "Your father's been having some tests," she said. "He's a little under the weather." I found out later that "tests" actually meant a biopsy, that "under the weather" meant oesophageal cancer, that they'd known since the previous year, and that it was inoperable. I found out about the inoperable part last of all, just a few weeks before the end – but even then, she didn't tell me just how far things had progressed. She just said, "It might be a good idea if you came home at some point in the not-too-distant future."

'Of course, I was knee-deep in my PhD at the time. I had deadlines and teaching commitments. I couldn't just drop everything. I mean,' she corrected herself hastily, 'I *would* have, if I'd had so much as an inkling of how bad things were, but I didn't. So I put off going home for another week, then another, then another.'

She drew in a heavy breath to steady herself, warding off the conflicting emotions that rose up inside her, threatening to derail her account. 'Next thing I know, I get a call from a friend of the family, Mrs Kuperman, telling me that Dad died in the night.' She let out a disgusted scoff. 'Couldn't even bring herself to pick up the phone to tell me in person. Instead, she outsourced it to one of her lackeys – who, I might add, took no small amount of pleasure in telling me he'd died without seeing his daughter's face one last time because I was too wrapped up in my studies.'

'I'm sorry,' said Pamela quietly. The shock on her face was palpable.

'By the way, I haven't told you the best part. They scheduled the funeral for the next day.'

Pamela gave her a quizzical look.

Anna sighed. 'In Judaism, it's tradition to bury the body within twenty-four hours. I mean, it's not mandatory, and nowadays they'll often delay the service so family members living further afield have time to get home. But my mother's nothing if not a traditionalist in these matters. Besides, she couldn't resist one last twist of the knife.'

Pamela stared at her incredulously. 'You're saying she did it deliberately? That she arranged the funeral for the following day to stop you getting home?'

Anna shrugged. 'Whether it was exclusively contrived for my benefit or not, she must have known what the result would be. There was an airline strike on at the time. It was all over the news. There's no way I could have got a flight to Glasgow. It was as if she was rubbing it in my face – saying, "Well, if you'd come sooner, you wouldn't have this problem".' She shook her head contemptuously. 'So like her.'

'Blimey,' said Pamela softly.

'If I'd known, I'd have gone. I'd have dropped everything.' She'd said as much already, but for some reason, she *needed* Pamela to know this. To believe her. 'But my mother had other ideas. She kept how ill he was from me, then made out it was my fault I hadn't known.' Her expression hardened. 'So as far as I'm concerned, I'm not really interested in what *she* would have wanted.'

She fell silent, her account having reached its conclusion. Pamela said nothing for a long moment, before eventually stirring.

'I guess,' she said carefully. 'Only … '

'Only what?'

'Well, I mean, have you ever *talked* to your mum about any of this?'

'What is there to talk about?' Anna snapped. 'She made her feelings perfectly clear thirteen years ago.' She reached for her glass and downed the remaining contents in a single gulp.

'What about your dad?' said Pamela, after a moment. 'What was your relationship with *him* like?'

'We were … ' Anna began, then stopped. Suddenly, she found herself back in the living room at the house on Cleveden Road, defiantly facing him down as he tried every trick in the book to dissuade her from her chosen subject of study, from laying down the law to predictions of penury to bare-faced bribery. This really was her abiding memory of him, she thought – the singular moment that had come to define their relationship for all time.

'Honestly,' she said wearily, 'my enduring feeling is that I was this perennial disappointment to him. He hated the choices I made, and nothing I did ever seemed to be good enough. I'm not even sure we really *had* a relationship to speak of. He was hardly ever home, and when he was, he was distant or short-tempered or holed up inside his office hiding from the rest of us.' She shrugged philosophically. 'I'm sure he'd say I didn't understand the pressure he was under, and maybe I didn't. But all the other girls at school, their fathers would hug and kiss them and ask them how their day had gone and tell them they loved them. Dad never did any of those things with me. It was like he wished I wasn't there.'

And that apple sure as hell didn't fall far from the tree, did it, Anna?

For almost a full minute, Pamela sat in silence, digesting this. 'I really think,' she said eventually, 'you should talk to your mum.' She shrugged encouragingly. 'She might have a perspective on all this that's different from yours. Sounds like you've been carrying these feelings round with you for most of your life. And bottling things up for that long? That's *never* healthy. Little things get blown up out of all proportion and you lose sight of the bigger picture. I bet things between you and your folks weren't half as bad as you think they were.'

Anna sighed. 'What's the point? She'll never admit it.'

'Won't know unless you try.'

'I *do* know, though,' Anna snapped, 'because I know *her*. It's not worth the hassle. It never is.'

Pamela folded her arms and regarded Anna appraisingly for several long, uncomfortable moments. Eventually, she gave a knowing smile.

'I think I've worked out what your problem is.'

'Oh, really?' said Anna, without much interest. 'What's that, then?'

'You're incapable of compromising. You want all things and all people to be perfect, or else they're not worth bothering with. Well, here's what *I* think. If your minimum standard's perfection, nothing's ever going to measure up. Not your friends, not your family, not the institutions we spend our lives criticising even as we try to navigate them the best we can. But the fact they're not perfect doesn't mean they're not worth fighting for. It means it's doubly important that we *do* fight for them; that we find ways of changing them for the better. Take your crusade against the prison system or the job *I* do. People like us, we don't do these things because they're easy but because, deep down, we know they're worth it.'

She paused to sip from her glass. 'We've all got things we don't like about the world we live in. But if ideological purity's what you're chasing after, you might as well give up on society altogether and go and live in a hut in the woods – provided you're sure the way it was built was completely ethically uncompromised, that is.'

This time, she *almost* got a laugh out of Anna.

'No system's ever going to be perfect,' she concluded. 'Doesn't mean we can't fight like heck to change them for the better, though. And that' – she dipped her glass in Anna's direction to accentuate her point – 'begins at home.'

Anna exhaled a heavy sigh and said nothing. Privately, she still felt that what Pamela was proposing was a colossal waste of time and, given the old wounds it would reopen, stood a strong chance of doing more harm than good. But she decided she wasn't going to argue anymore. It'd been too long a day and she'd had too much to drink for any hope of making herself sound coherent.

Pamela blew out an exaggerated breath and shook her head. 'Well, I reckon that's enough soul-searching to last us the rest of the night. Tell me something light and frivolous.'

Anna looked around in search of inspiration. Her eyes became drawn to a pair of youngish-looking men in business suits perched on stools at the opposite end of the bar. Catching sight of her, the one nearest nudged his friend, then smiled at her and raised his glass in toast.

Anna turned back to Pamela and leaned in close to her. 'Well, don't turn round too quickly,' she said in a low voice, 'but I think those two are checking us out.'

Pamela glanced in the direction of the two men, then turned to Anna with a look that was somewhere between scandalised and thrilled. 'They *totally* are. Hey, do you think we should go over to them?'

Anna considered this for a moment, then smiled and shook her head. 'I'll pass. I reckon it's time I turned in. After all, us golden oldies need our beauty sleep.'

The look Pamela gave her was one of pure, undiluted glee. 'More for me, then. I'll try not to wake you when I get in.'

For a moment, Anna simply stared at Pamela, wondering what had become of the guileless, unassuming and – dare she say it? – virginal young woman she'd first encountered a few weeks ago. She decided not to trouble her already overworked brain attempting to make sense of it all. Instead, she drained her glass and got to her feet. As she reached the exit, she turned to look back. Pamela had already drawn up a stool next to the two men and had engaged them in earnest conversation. From the looks on their faces, it was clear neither of them could believe their luck.

Anna shook her head ruefully, laughed softly to herself and headed for the stairs.

38

Monday 22 April

Anna came to the following morning to the sound of the door to the en suite opening. She eased herself upright, blinking heavily, as Pamela emerged in a cloud of steam, one towel wrapped around her head, another around her body.

'Morning,' she said cheerfully.

'Morning. What time is it?'

'It's just gone half-seven.' Pamela crossed over to her side of the room and, perching on the end of her bed, proceeded to rub her hair dry. 'I figured we'd want to be on the road by eight, in case the roads are busy.'

Anna gingerly wiped crusts of sleep from her eyes with her index fingers. 'What time did you get in last night?'

'Just after three. You were out like a light.'

'So you and those two blokes ... I mean, you didn't *actually* ... did you?'

Pamela shrugged. 'We stayed at the bar chatting till they chucked us out. They were both completely charming.' She wrinkled her nose in amusement. 'Why, what did you think? That we all went back to their room and had a massive sex orgy?' She nodded towards the en suite. 'Bathroom's all yours, by the way.'

Feeling decidedly sheepish, Anna threw back the covers and headed into the bathroom, where she showered hastily, before putting back on the clothes she'd worn yesterday, pants inside out. *I really* am *reliving my student days,* she thought ruefully. Not that she'd ever worn the same pants two days in a row, even as a student. She was far too organised, not to mention too hygiene-conscious, for that. For good measure, she borrowed Pamela's Dove Go Fresh, applied it liberally and, after hastily grabbing a bite to eat downstairs, they were on the road again.

They arrived in Eastriggs twenty minutes ahead of their scheduled appointment and made straight for the Cornerstone Café – an intimate, homely affair with half a dozen tables, all empty. They ordered coffee at the counter, then commandeered a table with a clear view of the entrance to wait for Eunice.

'D'you reckon she'll show?' Anna asked, once they'd made themselves comfortable.

Pamela shrugged. 'Difficult to say. We're banking on her getting out of the house without her husband noticing, then managing to find her way here. That's assuming she even remembers she's meant to be meeting us. Those are all pretty big asks.'

Anna nodded glumly. The whole situation was far from ideal. Even assuming Eunice *did* make it here successfully, there was always the question of just how reliable anything she told them would actually be.

Time continued to tick by. 9 a.m. came and went with no sign of Eunice. Neither Anna nor Pamela passed any comment on this, but Anna knew perfectly well they were both thinking the same thing: one way or another, they'd been stood up, and each fresh minute they spent here was a minute they wouldn't get back.

She was on the verge of suggesting to Pamela that they head towards the farmhouse in case Eunice had got lost along the way when the bell above the entrance tinkled. Anna looked up, then froze. Making his way towards them was not Eunice but *George* Morton. She gave Pamela a warning nudge. Pamela looked up, stiffened, and shot Anna a worried look. Anna found herself having to fight the urge to get up and flee.

'Mr Morton!' Pamela exclaimed, with rather too much enthusiasm, as George came to a halt facing their table. 'This is unexpected. To what do we owe the pleasure?'

'Cut the crap,' snapped George, so sharply Anna dropped the spoon she'd been footering with. 'You know perfectly well why I'm here – and if you don't, I'm sure you can guess.' He shook his head in derision. 'Did you think I wouldn't find out about the little scheme the two of you had cooked up? Eunice told me everything.'

'Mr Morton,' Pamela began, 'before you judge your wife too harshly, please understand that she simply offered us her help—'

'I'm not judging *her*!' George almost roared. 'I'm judging *you*!'

The effort of this outburst caused his balance to momentarily falter. Anna was already halfway out of her seat to help him before he grabbed the side of the table and managed to stop himself from stumbling.

'She gets *confused*,' he said, once he'd righted himself – his tone less aggressive now, but no less insistent. 'She doesn't know what she's saying half the time. You had no right taking advantage of that – no right at all.'

Even though the rational part of her knew it had been Pamela who'd come up with the plan and harried Eunice into agreeing to it, Anna nonetheless felt a pang of guilt for not paying more heed to her own reservations and putting a stop to it. She lowered her gaze, unable to look George in the eye. Pamela, however, held firm, staring up at him unblinkingly.

'Mr Morton,' she said levelly, 'you can order us to leave if you like. But if you do, I'll be back. Not tomorrow, probably not next week, maybe not even this year. But rest assured, I'll find a way to get this investigation officially reopened. And if I have reason to believe you've deliberately withheld information and obstructed our work, when I come back it'll be with the police and a warrant for your arrest.'

Anna listened with a sense of mounting apprehension. She knew enough about the law to be reasonably sure Pamela didn't have a leg to stand on when it came to compelling the Mortons, or indeed any other witness, to talk to her – but bluff or not, her words constituted an indisputable raising of the stakes.

'We can do this the easy way or the hard way,' said Pamela. 'What's it to be?'

For a moment, it looked like George was very much minded to do it the hard way. Then Anna saw an almost imperceptible slackening of his shoulders.

'All right,' he said quietly. 'What I'm going to tell you, I'm telling you in the hope of persuading you to put to bed this foolhardy notion of trying to get that *woman* exonerated.'

Gingerly, he eased himself into the seat opposite Anna and Pamela and folded his hands on the tabletop.

'You must understand, my wife and I are of a generation that was brought up not to air its dirty laundry in public. For years, we kept quiet about it, doing our best to deal with it behind closed doors, without involving a whole bunch of interfering busybodies. Hard as it may be for folk of your generation to fathom, we believe that what happens in the family should stay in the family.'

'If you don't mind my asking,' said Pamela, 'what exactly is "it"?'

George fixed Pamela with a long, hard stare. Only when he appeared satisfied that there would be no further interruptions did he continue.

'It started when Katie was just a toddler. From around the time she started going to nursery, she was a sickly child – stomach upset after stomach upset, all without any obvious explanation and invariably clearing up after a few days. We didn't realise the extent of it at first, Eunice and I. This was when they were still living in Linlithgow, and I'm ashamed to say we didn't visit anything like as often as we should have. Mostly, we just picked up on things Guy would mention in passing over the phone. "Oh, Katie's not well again, poor mite" – things like that. It wasn't till she was six or seven that I began to realise something was seriously wrong.

'I still remember the moment when it became impossible to ignore for a moment longer. It was Christmas Day, 1995. The three of them were meant to be driving down to us for Christmas lunch. Then, mid-morning, I got a call from Guy, saying they were going to have to call it off on account of Katie. She'd been up half the night, he said, with sickness and diarrhoea. I could hear her in the next room, vomiting and retching uncontrollably. It was awful, just awful to listen to. Then I remembered that, in the weeks leading up to Christmas, Guy had been havering about coming down. Sandra wasn't keen, he'd said. And then it hit me, and I thought to myself, "She's done it deliberately. She's poisoned her own daughter to get out of coming."'

Anna swallowed heavily, the mouthful of saliva going down like a rock. She remembered what Heather had told her the previous day about Katie's frequent absences from school.

We all thought she was on the skive … but looking back, I'm not so sure.

'Of course,' said George, 'I couldn't be *certain* she was responsible, even if there was no other credible explanation. But I knew there was no point sharing my suspicions with Guy. He'd never hear a bad word said against her. Always bent over backwards to make excuses for her behaviour. But I pressed him to have Katie examined by a doctor – we both did, Eunice and I. At first, he told us we were making something out of nothing. "Kids pick up bugs all the time," he said. "She's just got a sensitive stomach. She'll grow out of it in due course." He was so deep in denial he might as well have been in Egypt.

'But I like to think, by refusing to let the matter lie, that we managed to plant a seed of doubt that grew till it finally became too great to ignore. Over the next two years, he became increasingly suspicious, to the point that he finally began to make noises about taking Katie to see a specialist. Naturally, her mother poured cold water on that idea – and whenever it was floated, Katie always seemed to perk up remarkably quickly, and then there would be a spell of a few weeks or even a few months when she was right as rain … though as soon as the hue and cry died down, she'd inevitably suffer a relapse – more proof, to my mind, that her mother was doing something to her.

'Then, one night, it all came to a head. We got a call from Guy to say that Katie had been rushed to hospital after a prolonged spell of vomiting and, latterly, difficulty breathing and swallowing. The doctors found bleach in her digestive system. She had burns to her stomach lining, her oesophagus and throat. Sandra claimed it had been an accident – that she'd left a bottle of bleach on the work surface and Katie must have thought it was juice. When it was put to her, Katie more or less agreed that that was what had happened.' George shook his head vehemently. 'But I didn't believe it for a second. She wasn't like that. She *wouldn't*.'

He took off his glasses and pinched the bridge of his nose, eyes clenched shut. He was trembling slightly, as if exerting all his energy into keeping his emotions in check. At length, he opened his eyes and began to speak again.

'That was the last time anything like that ever happened. From that moment on, Katie was never seriously ill a day in her life. I don't think Sandra ever meant for it to go that far; that coming that close to being found out gave her a genuine fright. And of course, Katie was growing up. It was becoming more difficult for her mother to get her to do her bidding.

There's a world of difference between persuading a toddler to drink a glass of juice laced with washing up liquid and getting a nine-year-old to do the same. And, after the hospital incident, Guy was a lot more vigilant. He never admitted as much, but it was a major factor in why he moved the family to Hillend – so we'd be closer at hand.'

'And is that why Katie ended up moving in with you and Eunice?' asked Anna. 'To protect her from her mother?'

George blinked sharply, seemingly surprised by the question. 'This may surprise you, but that had very little to do with it – at least, not directly. By then, it had been years since Katie had had anything worse than a runny nose. No – by far the bigger issue was the total breakdown in relations between her and her mother. They were barely on speaking terms by the end, and if you'd seen the way that girl used to look at her...' He shook his head, evidently still troubled by the memory. 'You can chalk it up to traditional teenage angst if you like, but I'm convinced it all stemmed from what that woman did to her when she was little. Would *you* be able to forgive someone who made you drink bleach when you were a child?'

Anna said nothing. She sensed that George wasn't really looking for an answer.

'Neither one missed the other, I can tell you that much. If Katie told anyone about her mother and the things she did to her – well, neither myself nor Eunice was any the wiser. She certainly never talked to *us* about it. Not that we pried, you understand. Nothing to be gained by digging up old bones. And after...' He hesitated. 'After everything that had happened, and with the press sniffing around hoping for a scoop, it made complete sense for her to go and live with our other son in Canada. Eunice and I were broken-hearted, of course, but the last thing we would have wanted was for her to have remained behind on our account. After what she'd been through, it was only right and proper that she got a chance to start over.'

George fell silent, his account having seemingly reached its end. Anna glanced at Pamela, silently asking her if she had any other questions she wanted to put to him, but Pamela gave no response. She sat very still, her eyes vacant, almost as if she'd gone into a trance.

'Mr Morton,' said Anna carefully, 'we're not for a moment doubting what you've told us. But you yourself said it: none of this *proves* Sandra was responsible for making Katie sick. Certainly not enough to stand up in a court of law. And even if it *is* true, there's a big difference between deliberately making a child sick and committing murder in cold blood.'

George's features contorted into an ugly scowl. 'Don't give me that. I've read up on the criminal mind. I know a thing or two about how they operate. They *escalate*. Start small, then work their way up. Katie was just a trial run for what was to come.' He sighed heavily and shuddered violently, clutching himself as if to stop the grief from leaking out. 'I should have listened to what my gut was telling me – done whatever I could to get these children as far away from that woman as possible. But I didn't want to rock the boat. And now my son and those two little boys are dead – and there's not a single thing you or anyone else can say or do that will make that all right.'

He exhaled heavily, his arms dropping limply to his sides. 'I'm aware there's nothing I can do to stop this investigation of yours.' He glanced at Pamela. 'You're duty-bound to do whatever you can to get the best outcome for your client. But just know who it is you're trying to help.'

He lifted his head and gazed at them both imploringly, a degree of vulnerability in his expression that Anna hadn't seen from him before – an acknowledgement, perhaps, that the matter was out of his hands.

'Please – don't allow her conviction to be overturned on some technicality so she can do the same thing again to a fresh set of innocents.'

Pamela again said nothing. If she'd heard a word George had said, she gave no sign.

Anna saw no option but to take charge of the situation herself. She stood up, taking Pamela's arm and lifting her to her feet too. Pamela put up no resistance.

'Thank you for your time, Mr Morton,' she said, with practised formality. 'We'll be in touch in due course.'

39

They returned to the car and sat side by side, each preoccupied by their own thoughts. It wasn't until several minutes had passed that Anna finally broke the heavy silence hanging over the car.

'None of this changes anything. We've no idea how much of George's recollection of events is even accurate. He could have been talking things up for effect, or even adding in details that didn't happen.'

'Right,' said Pamela, her voice devoid of either enthusiasm or sincerity.

'And even if everything he said is completely true, there's still no *proof*, only supposition.'

Pamela said nothing.

'Think of everything we've uncovered that pokes holes in the conviction. There's Dalston's failure to consider alternative theories, his coaching of witnesses – behaviour that worried his own DS enough that he was on the verge of shopping him to the authorities...'

Still nothing from Pamela.

Anna pressed on, her voice rising to compensate for the stony silence coming from Pamela's side of the car. 'And then, quite apart from anything else, there's the business with the reservoir gates. I know it's impossible for us to be one hundred percent sure, but surely, if this had come to light during the trial, it would have been enough to create reasonable doubt—'

'For the love of God, STOP!' Pamela exploded, so suddenly and violently that Anna all but jumped out of her seat. She turned to gape at the solicitor, who glowered back at her, eyes brimming with unshed tears.

'After everything we've just heard, you really want to keep going with this? To keep poking holes in the case till she gets off on a technicality? Doesn't it, even for a moment, make you second-guess what we're doing?'

'I—'

'Bleach.' Pamela spat the word out like it was poison. 'She made that wee girl drink bloody BLEACH.'

Anna was lost for words. All she could do was stare back at Pamela in disbelief, her mouth hanging open like a landed fish.

'Say she didn't do it,' Pamela continued. 'Say she really didn't kill Guy and the twins. Is there not even a *part* of you that wonders whether we wouldn't still be doing the whole world a massive favour if we left her behind bars for the rest of her natural existence, so no other child ever has to go through what Katie did?'

'We don't *know*—'

'Don't we? You think a child just keeps magically getting sick again and again, only for it to mysteriously clear up any time someone suggests taking her to the doctor's? Then, one time it gets so bad she nearly dies, and then, wonder of wonders, it never happens again? You're seriously telling me you think there's any other realistic explanation?'

'No,' Anna admitted helplessly, 'but what about everything you said yesterday? About having a duty to secure the best outcome for your client without fear or favour? About believing in justice as an ideal in and of itself, regardless of whatever they've done in a previous life? Whatever Sandra might or might not have done to Katie shouldn't change that.'

'It shouldn't,' said Pamela, 'but it does.'

'You don't mean that.'

'Don't I?' Pamela's eyes flared angrily, so much so that Anna found herself instinctively drawing back from her, her back pressing up against the driver's door. 'You might have all the hifalutin academic knowledge in the world, but you know bugger all about people if you think for a minute that this doesn't change things completely.'

Anna sat, chastened into silence, as Pamela inhaled a deep breath and let it out in a heavy sigh.

'You're right,' she said, with an air of both finality and of having made peace with herself. 'I have a responsibility to pursue the best outcome for my client. And I'm sure, somewhere out there, there's an idealistic young solicitor who's just chomping at the bit to take Sandra's fight to the very top. But it won't be me. I'm done.'

Neither of them said a word throughout the entire ninety-minute journey back to Glasgow. Pamela sat, arms folded, gazing out the window with her head turned away from Anna. A couple of times, Anna was on the verge of saying something, but each time, she stopped herself at the last moment. What was there to say?

They reached the city centre at the back of eleven. Anna brought the car to a stop outside the entrance to Queen Street Station. Pamela got out and hurried into the terminus without a backward glance.

For a while, Anna continued to idle at the kerb, gazing after her. She wanted to believe that, before long, Pamela would come around – that she'd been speaking in the heat of a moment and didn't really mean the things she'd said. And yet, there was a part of Anna that couldn't help but agree wholeheartedly with every word. While there were no certainties about anything they'd uncovered over the last twenty-four hours, she could hardly deny that there was a certain moral justice in the act of leaving a Sandra who was innocent of the murders of Guy and the twins but guilty of a years-long campaign of abuse against her surviving child to languish in her cell at HMP Broadwood for the rest of time.

With a leaden feeling in her stomach, she headed for home. As she wearily climbed the steps to her house, the prospect of a change of clothes and the chance to digest, in peace, the various revelations from her trip – both good and bad – caused her step to perk up marginally.

She was just fishing out her key when the door swung open of its own accord to reveal Zoe, a stricken expression on her face.

'Ye're back,' she said.

'Obviously,' said Anna. She was in little mood for statements of the blindingly obvious. She made to cross the threshold, but Zoe blocked her path.

'Just a sec.' She stepped out onto the front step to join Anna, shutting the door behind her. 'Look,' she said in a low voice, 'before ye go in, there's something ye need tae know.'

A wave of trepidation washed over Anna. 'What is it?'

'Eh, it's like this.' Zoe curled one foot round her other leg, struggling to make eye contact. 'I didnae wanna say over the phone, but see yesterday afternoon? Yer mum decided she wanted tae take Jack tae the swing park. She asked me if it was OK and I said aye, fine – y'know, thinking it'd be good for him tae spend some time alone wi his granny.'

'Did something happen?' demanded Anna, her mind immediately conjuring up all manner of upsetting images, from Jack lying at the foot of the swings with a bleeding head to him being hit by a speeding lorry as they crossed the road.

Zoe held up both arms in a placatory gesture. 'Jack's fine. He's absolutely jim-dandy. Only … well, like I say, I didnae wanna bother ye with it last night on the phone so I never said, but … well, she never made sure he'd gone for a wee-wee first, and he ended up having a bit of an accident while they were out.'

Anna's shoulders sagged in instantaneous relief. She almost wanted to laugh. 'Is that *all*? Christ, Zo, he's three years old. It's not the end of the world.'

'Naw, there's a bit more.'

Zoe's eyes flicked up to meet Anna's. Once again, Anna saw the look of apprehension in them – the knowledge that whatever she was about to say would not be well-received.

'See, when she got him home, she took it on hersel tae change him and … ' Her eyes lowered again. 'She noticed … something.'

Her brain addled from the long drive home and the million other concerns vying for her attention, Anna couldn't make head or tail of any of this.

'Noticed *what*?'

But even as she said the words, something clicked into place and, with a suddenly burst of clarity, she understood precisely what Zoe was trying to tell her. Her eyes narrowed. Heat flushed through her body like a wave of angry fire.

She nodded towards the house. 'Is she in there?'

'She's up the stair,' Zoe began, 'but listen—'

'And Jack? Where's he?'

'He's at playgroup. Ye know he has playgroup on a Monday morning.'

'Right,' Anna muttered. Then, brushing past Zoe, she wrenched open the door and stormed inside.

'MOTHER!' she roared at the top of her lungs. 'WHERE ARE YOU?'

Not waiting for a response, she went charging up the stairs, taking them three at a time. By the time she reached the first landing, Leah had emerged from her bedroom and was waiting for her, arms folded, her mouth a line of tight-laced disapproval. Anna came to a halt facing her, her breathing laboured from a combination of the climb and the fury broiling inside her.

'Where the *fuck* do you get off?' she snarled.

'I might ask the same of you,' said Leah starchily, 'only without the gratuitous profanity.'

Anna jerked her head back, mock-affronted. 'Oh, *I'm* sorry. Does my profanity upset you? Well, too *fucking* bad. See, I'm just a *tad* ticked off myself, on account of having just discovered that apparently you've been casting aspersions about the state of my son's genitalia in my absence.'

'Well, what sort of response did you expect?' Leah retorted, immediately retreating into self-righteous indignation. 'I don't for a moment imagine it never occurred to you that I would have something to say when I found out.' She snorted indignantly. 'Honestly! You could at least have prepared me for the fact that he has … that he still has … ' She trailed off into a series of incomprehensible splutters.

'A *foreskin*, Mother.' Anna spoke the apparently unutterable word with undisguised relish. 'He has a foreskin, just like every other male child who hasn't been mutilated in the name of a mythology dreamed up by Bronze Age goat-herders.'

'Oh, good grief.' Leah sighed and threw up her hands. 'I swear you do these things deliberately to get a reaction out of me.'

Anna barked a harsh, humourless laugh. 'Get over yourself, Mother. Hard as it may be to believe, this is not all about you.'

'It's so utterly typical,' Leah went on, as if Anna hadn't spoken. 'You always feel the need to make some sort of a *statement*, don't you? To stick two fingers up at your heritage. You can't just be normal.'

'*Normal?*' Anna spluttered, eyes agog. 'Does that word mean something different to you than it does to the rest of us? You're the one that thinks I should have subjected my child – *my newborn, premature child* – to unnecessary surgery in order to … to *brand* him so that you can … what? Lay claim to him in the name of the ancient tribes of the Israelites?'

Leah scoffed and shook her head. 'All this talk of mutilation – honestly! You're being completely melodramatic. Millions of boys the world over—'

'*I'm* being melodramatic? *Me?*' Anna pressed her hands to her temples, pacing away from Leah. 'This is not happening. I am not having this conversation. This sort of thing is *exactly* why I never wanted you in his life.'

'Do you know, I'm actually glad your father isn't alive to witness this?'

Anna swung around to face her mother. '*What?*'

Leah sniffed, unrepentant. 'He always showed remarkable restraint when it came to your endless acts of contrarianism; your contempt for our beliefs and traditions. But I suspect this is one stunt he wouldn't have been able to thole.'

For a moment, Anna simply stared at her, unable to believe that, of all the cards she could have played, she'd chosen this one. Then her resolve hardened.

'Get out.'

Leah blinked in surprise. 'What?'

'Get the fuck out of my house.'

For several seconds, Leah simply stared at her in astonishment. 'You can't throw me out,' she eventually said. 'I'm your mother.'

Anna laughed grimly. 'Like that means anything.'

Seizing Leah by the upper arm, Anna began to frogmarch her down the stairs. Taken aback both by Anna's reaction and the ignominy of being manhandled in such a way, Leah could only splutter in indignant disbelief as she struggled to keep pace.

'But… but where am I supposed to go?' she demanded, her voice wavering with a hint of uncertainty.

'Not my problem. Go and stay with the Kupermans. Or why don't you go back to whatsisname – see if *he'll* take you back? Maybe his dick's reconfigured more to your taste, or maybe you're just less picky when it comes to him.'

They reached the ground floor. Zoe, doing her best to make herself appear unobtrusive, watched from the living room doorway but didn't try to intervene. Anna let go of Leah's arm for long enough to snatch her coat from the peg in the hallway. Then, shoving it into her hands, she grabbed hold of her again and marched her the remaining few steps to the door.

'Thanks for dropping by, Mother,' she said, briskly and insincerely, as she thrust it open. 'It's been a real pleasure as always, having you here, sticking your oar in. Feel free not to come back for at least another decade.'

With that, she shoved her mother out onto the front step, slammed the door behind her, locked it and, for good measure, slid the security bolt into place. As she turned away, she half-expected Leah to ring the bell in defiance, but no sound came from outside. Reaching the stairs, she stopped and, looking back, saw, through the frosted glass, the shape of her mother turning and heading down the steps.

'*Don't,*' she said, as Zoe moved towards her, opening her mouth to speak.

Then, without another word, she stormed up the stairs.

40

Though she knew full well she should sit down and take some deep, calming breaths, Anna found herself unable to do any such thing. On at least some level, she recognised that the fury coursing through her needed an outlet, lest she lash out at the wrong person – most likely Zoe, given that there was no one else left in the building. She was also determined to eradicate all trace of her mother from the house with immediate effect.

Before she'd even taken off her jacket, therefore, she headed to her bedroom, where she proceeded to gather up Leah's belongings and stuff them into the two suitcases she'd brought with her and, like everything apart from the clothes on her back, been forced to leave behind when she was forcibly ejected. With that business taken care of, she headed to the kitchen and emptied the fridge of every item of food Leah had added to it, reserving particular venom for those of a kosher variety. Having shoved the lot into a black plastic bag and dumped it in the wheelie bin outside, she plonked herself on a chair at the kitchen table and finally remembered to breathe.

As the adrenaline slowly ebbed from her system, she heard approaching footsteps. Until now, Zoe had wisely stayed out of her way, letting her burn herself out rather than risk becoming a victim of friendly fire. Now, though, she edged her way towards Anna with the sort of trepidation one might associate with a lion tamer entering the ring.

Anna sucked in a breath and managed a tired grimace. 'It's safe to approach. I'm not going to bite your head off.'

Zoe drew up a chair and sat down a couple of feet from Anna – close, but still keeping a respectful, or perhaps self-preserving, distance.

'Well,' she said cheerily, 'that went about as smoothly as a slow-mo pile-up on the dual carriageway at rush hour.'

Anna gave a thin, humourless smile and said nothing.

'S'pose it was aye gonnae be a big ask that the two of ye'd sit doon and have a civilised convo about it.'

'From where I'm standing, there's precious little that's civilised about the topic in question.'

Zoe lowered her eyes. 'Aye, well.'

Anna sighed and ran a weary hand over her face. 'At least tell me she didn't cause a scene in front of him.'

'Naw, actually she was dead discreet about it. She only came tae me after and said how come he wasnae … y'know.'

Anna let out a sigh of relief. Throughout the whole confrontation, her worst fear had been that Leah had said or done something in Jack's presence to make him think there was something wrong with him.

'Well, thank heavens for small mercies. How did you respond?'

'Just said it wasnae my place tae comment. That it was a conversation she was gonnae have tae have wi *you*. But I did say I was surprised *she* was surprised. I mean, she knows ye're no religious.'

'Yeah, well, evidently there are some aspects of the doctrine that are too sacred even for heathens like me to disregard.' Anna barked out a shrill, almost manic laugh. 'I mean, maybe I'm just missing what's obvious to everyone else. Help me out here. Explain to me how me keeping my child's genitals intact somehow makes *me* the unreasonable one in this debate.'

Zoe looked at her with an expression of strained forbearance. 'I'm no trying tae tell ye ye're wrong tae see it that way … but mibby ye should-nae've gone in all guns blazing and chucked her ontae the street before ye'd both had time tae count tae ten.' She reached out and laid a hand on Anna's forearm. 'She got a surprise is all. Just cos she's got funny ideas about willies doesnae mean she's a bad person.'

Anna sighed. 'Why do you *always* give her the benefit of the doubt?'

Zoe gazed at Anna helplessly. 'Because she's yer mum.'

There was nothing Anna could say in response to that simple but loaded statement of fact. Zoe, she reflected, had always had something of a tendency to put parental figures on a pedestal. Perhaps it was because she'd lost her own at a young age, but she seemed incapable of comprehending the notion that a person could be so ideologically at odds with theirs as to want them to have no role in their life.

'I'm not apologising to her,' she said.

Zoe sighed. 'I'm no saying ye have tae apologise. I'm just saying don't leave it like this.'

At lunchtime, Anna headed down to Hayburn Park to collect Jack from playgroup. Zoe had offered to go, but Anna insisted on doing it herself. On some level, she recognised that she was doing this out of a misplaced desire to make amends for the previous day. If she hadn't gone to Hillend with Pamela, the whole incident would never have happened and they'd still be carrying on their strained but semi-convincing impression of happy families. Not that Jack, mercifully, was any the wiser about any of this, and as Anna sat on the step at the back door, watching him stalking an oblivious pigeon on the lawn, she thanked her lucky stars once more that he was utterly oblivious to the battle that had played out between her and his grandmother over his bodily integrity.

The sound of her phone ringing snapped her out of her thoughts. She fumbled for it and looked at the screen. The call was coming from the PJ Kempley Facebook profile.

Feeling a sudden rush of nervous anticipation, she accepted the call and put the phone to her ear.

'Anna Scavolini.'

'Ah, good. You are who I am wanting.'

The voice was that of a woman, heavily accented. German, she thought.

'Can I help you?'

'Yes. It is … I am sorry, my English … '

'*Das ist OK,*' said Anna, switching into German. '*Ich spreche Deutsch.*'

As a rule, she avoided speaking German if at all possible. Her grasp of the language couldn't be faulted – having maternal grandparents who'd emigrated from Frankfurt in the thirties helped significantly – but she was acutely aware that she spoke it with a pronounced Kelvinsider's twang, which native speakers had varyingly described as 'adorable' and 'hilarious' – at times to her face.

The woman on the line wasn't laughing, however. On the contrary, her relief once she realised Anna was fluent in her mother tongue was palpable, and she showered her with effusive thanks in what, to Anna's reasonably attuned ear, sounded like a Düsseldorf accent.

'How can I help you?' Anna asked, once she managed to get a word in edgeways.

'Yes, sorry. I should introduce myself. My name is Heike Schulze, and I must apologise for how long it's taken me to get in touch. This probably won't surprise you, but I don't often check the account – Paul's, I mean. His Facebook page. I'm his girlfriend,' she added, as if belatedly realising that this context might prove important. 'Or I should say, I *was*.'

'Was?' Anna repeated, unable to shake the feeling that her brain was playing catch-up and that she should be more on the ball than this. 'You mean you split up, or … '

'No, I mean that Paul died in 2009. A lorry hit his bike on the Autobahn.'

Silence. Anna found herself lost for words. Instinctively, she got to her feet and moved back inside the house, out of earshot of Jack, while still keeping him in her sights.

'I'm sorry,' said Heike, as if Anna was the one who'd lost a loved one. 'I know you wanted to speak to him for your research, but … ' She trailed off. 'Well, anyway, I thought I should do you the courtesy of calling you rather than telling you via DM.'

'Thank you,' said Anna, finding her voice at last. 'It was very good of you. And' – she belatedly remembered her manners – 'I'm sorry for your loss.'

Heike drew in an audibly strained breath. 'We had four good years together. I wish it could have been longer, but … we had some good times.' She gave a dry little laugh. 'Him and that damned bike.'

They exchanged a few more words – mostly banal pleasantries which Anna, for her part, offered up without really thinking about what she was saying – then made their goodbyes. Less than thirty seconds after she'd rung off, her phone pinged a notification. She checked the screen.

Heike had sent her a message with an image attachment. She tapped it open.

It was a picture of the order of service from Paul's funeral. The photo on the front of the cheaply printed pamphlet showed him in his mid-twenties, with a leather jacket and his hair swept back, perched on a motorbike – probably the same one he'd ridden to his death. Unlike the pictures the press photographers had snapped of him arriving at court, he was clean-shaven, which changed the shape of his face significantly. Despite being a good five years older in this picture, he looked younger, not to mention considerably more carefree.

For a sudden, brief moment, Anna experienced a profound sense of déjà vu – a certainty that she'd seen his face somewhere before. She told herself her response was irrational – that she was merely recognising him from the paparazzi snaps. But no, that wasn't it. It was almost as if she'd seen him again more recently, in an entirely different context, looking more like he did on the order of service.

The feeling passed. She'd looked at so many different faces, in press cuttings and social media profiles and whatnot, that they must all have started to blend together. Besides, it hardly mattered now. Pamela had made it crystal clear she had no intention of playing any further part in seeking Sandra's acquittal, and while Anna knew there must be steps she herself could take to ensure that the evidence they'd uncovered reached the appropriate authorities, any enthusiasm for doing any such thing had long since evaporated. The woman in question was as undeserving as they came – and besides, what proof of her innocence did she have, really? Certainly nothing a semi-competent prosecution lawyer couldn't pick to pieces with one hand tied behind their back.

And somehow, that forlorn photograph on a sheet of folded printer paper – *Paul Jackson Kempley, 14.3.1982–10.11.2009* – felt like the perfect marker for the end of a journey that had begun on a March afternoon almost two months ago with a visit to the women's super-prison in Cumbernauld.

This really was the end.

41

That afternoon, Anna went for a long, solitary walk. She tramped halfway across Glasgow and back, in the hope that it would clear her head and allow her to somehow make her peace with the day's events. It accomplished neither. Late afternoon was giving way to early evening by the time she finally coaxed her aching legs up the steps to the house.

'Yer mum rang while ye were gone,' Zoe told her as she shut the front door behind her. 'She's staying over at the Kupermans', then flying back to Saint-Tropez the morra.'

In fact, Anna had half-expected to find Leah waiting for her when she got home. She wasn't sure how she'd have reacted if she had; whether she'd have turfed her out for a second time or somehow found it within herself to tolerate her presence – temporarily, at any rate. She was glad she didn't have to find out.

'Um.' Zoe chewed on her bottom lip, eyes shifting awkwardly. 'Jacko asked when his nana's gonnae be back.'

Anna's heart sank. There was, she recognised, a certain bitter irony in the fact she'd thrown her mother out on Jack's account but that, out of all of them, he would be the most cut up about her departure.

'Ye figured out what ye're gonnae say tae him?'

'I'm working on it.' *One problem at a time.*

Zoe gave her a look that wasn't quite disapproving but wasn't quite *not* either. 'Her flight's in the afternoon,' she said, after a moment. 'I said we'd drop off her stuff sometime before then.' A moment's hesitation. 'I can take her bags over in the morning if you're no up for it.'

'No, it's fine,' said Anna heavily. 'I'll do it tonight after dinner.'

'Ye sure? I don't mind—'

'I'm sure.' She gave a strained smile. 'Might as well get this over and done with.'

The Kupermans lived in Broomhill, barely a fifteen-minute walk away, but she took the car to save herself having to lug two heavy suitcases behind her. She pulled up outside the large two-storey sandstone building on Marlborough Avenue a little after seven and sat behind the wheel for a few minutes, steeling herself.

You don't have to see her. Just hand the bags over at the door and be on your way.

She inhaled a deep breath, then got out and made her way up the driveway, cases in tow.

The door was opened by a slight, high-cheekboned woman in her mid-sixties with dark hair in a bun and a pearl necklace fastened around her neck. She regarded Anna coolly, her lips a thin, puckered line.

'Hello, Mrs Kuperman,' said Anna weakly.

'Anna,' said Sara Kuperman, with forced civility. 'What an unexpected surprise. Last time I saw you, you were still in school uniform.'

'Yes, it's been quite a while,' Anna agreed, resisting the urge to point out that a surprise was, by its nature, unexpected.

Mrs Kuperman looked at the two suitcases at Anna's feet, then at Anna again. 'Well, no need to ask why you're here.'

'No,' said Anna, wondering just how much Leah had revealed to her old friend about the circumstances behind her rapid departure.

They faced each other in silence for several awkward moments, both seemingly having exhausted their respective stock of banal pleasantries. Anna blinked first.

'Well,' she said, picking up the cases and depositing them on the other side of the threshold without crossing it herself, 'if you could just let her have these ...'

Mrs Kuperman continued to gaze at her, unmoving, an expectant look in her face as if to say, *Well, off you go, then.* Anna made to do just that, but even as she turned, she found herself hesitating. Perhaps it was Zoe's plea to her earlier not to leave things as they were. Or perhaps it was the sheer number of damaged or irretrievably broken families she'd encountered during her investigation into the Sandra Morton case. But whatever the reason, when it came down to it, she found she couldn't just leave – not without either attempting to repair the rift between her and her mother or else putting to bed, once and for all, any prospect of reconciliation.

'Actually,' she said, turning to face Mrs Kuperman again, 'I'd like to see her if that's OK.'

Somehow, Mrs Kuperman's lips became even more pinched. 'I'm not sure that's going to be possible. Your mother is very upset.'

Anna counted to three in her head. 'Mrs Kuperman,' she said, with as much civility as she could muster, 'I would very much appreciate it if you would allow me to speak to my mother.'

Mrs Kuperman regarded her for a long, tortuous moment, during which Anna felt her eyes drilling into her like hot pokers.

'Wait here,' she finally said. Then, before Anna could respond, she shut the door.

Anna remained on the doorstep for the next couple of minutes, feeling both ridiculous and more than a little humiliated. *I suppose it's no more than I deserve,* she reasoned. Not that she regretted what she'd done. On the contrary, if she could wind back the clock, she'd do it all over again. Or so she told herself.

She heard movement behind the door. Quickly, she rearranged her face into a neutral expression. It opened once more to reveal Mrs Kuperman.

'You can come in,' she said curtly. Evidently this wasn't the outcome she'd been hoping for.

Anna followed her down the long hallway corridor, past framed photos on the walls of Sara and Richard Kuperman and their two grown-up sons, both of whom had been ages with her and had, at least as children, been fairly obnoxious specimens – a classic case of two sets of parents assuming their respective offspring would get along simply because *they* happened to be friends.

At the door to the living room, Mrs Kuperman stopped and, standing to one side, gestured to Anna to go on in.

Leah was sitting on the sofa with her back to the doorway. Anna took a deep breath, steeling herself, then stepped into the room, shut the door behind her and circled round to face her. Leah sat straight-backed with her hands folded in her lap, eyes half-closed and gazing past Anna to some indeterminate spot on the wall.

'Hello, Mother,' said Anna.

'Hello,' said Leah, her voice devoid of all emotion, still not looking at her.

'Can I sit down?' said Anna, already convinced this had been a massive mistake.

'If you like.'

Anna resisted the urge to roll her eyes. If she'd ever thought there was any prospect of her mother making this conversation easy for either of them, she'd now been comprehensively disavowed of that notion. She moved over to the chair facing the sofa and sat down, automatically folding her hands in her lap, before realising she was mirroring Leah's own pose and swiftly unfolding them again.

'I hear you're going back to Saint-Tropez tomorrow,' she said, when it became clear Leah wasn't going to break the ice first.

'That's right.'

'What time?'

'Three o'clock.'

'Is that with a change of flights?'

'Yes. Layover in Schiphol.'

'Ah.'

Truth be told, this exchange wasn't progressing any worse than she'd anticipated. At least Leah was talking to her, even if their conversation resembled that of two strangers who'd found themselves alone together in a dentist's waiting room.

Leah opened her mouth to say something, then changed her mind and shut again.

'What?' said Anna.

'Nothing.'

'No, go on. You were going to say something.'

'I was merely going to ask how Jack was.'

'He's fine,' said Anna, instantly on guard.

'What are you going to tell him?'

No need to ask about what.

'I'll figure something out.'

Silence descended again. A car drove by outside, both women listening as the overpowering roar of its exhaust receded into the distance.

Anna took a breath. 'I—' she began, then stopped.

Leah's ears pricked up. 'Pardon?'

Anna lowered her eyes, shook her head. 'Nothing.'

Another prolonged silence, even more uncomfortable than the last, now that they both knew she had something she wanted to say.

Just say it. Get it over and done with.

'I'm sorry I had such a meltdown earlier.'

It came out in a rush, as if getting through the words as quickly as possible would take the sting off saying them.

Leah's expression was difficult to read. She frowned, as if not quite sure what to make of this.

'I'm *not* sorry for what I said,' Anna added quickly, determined that there should be no uncertainty in the matter, 'or *why* I said it. You have no right to an opinion on my decision to leave my son the way nature intended – none whatsoever. And what you said about Dad ... ' She stopped herself – unwilling, for the time being at least, to follow that train of thought to where it led. 'But I admit my response could have been more measured. The way I behaved, it was ... unbecoming.'

She fell silent, her eyes lowered to her lap, unwilling – or unable – to risk meeting her mother's gaze. Her cheeks were burning, her back and underarms slick with perspiration – though that might just have been the ridiculously high setting at which Sara Kuperman insisted on keeping the thermostat.

'Well,' said Leah after a moment, a barely perceptible note of surprise cutting through her otherwise crisp, controlled diction, 'that's ... fairly magnanimous of you to say. I suppose, for my part, I could have been slightly more diplomatic in how I expressed my views.'

And just like that, Anna's hackles were up once more. 'The issue isn't the way you expressed yourself. It's the views themselves I find abhorrent.'

Leah made a sound that was somewhere between a disgruntled harrumph and a sigh of genuine regret. 'I hadn't realised you held such a strong opinion on the subject. But then, I suppose it's not something we've ever had cause to talk about.'

Anna gave a rueful grimace. 'We never *have*. Talked, I mean.'

'What on earth does *that* mean? Of course we talk. Perhaps not as often as a mother and daughter should, but it's not as if we never exchange words. We're doing it right now.'

Anna couldn't tell whether her mother was deliberately missing the point or genuinely didn't understand. 'That's not what I'm saying. All right, yes, we exchange words, but we don't *talk* talk. Not about the big things.'

Leah merely frowned, the distinction evidently lost on her.

Anna sighed. 'When I was a teenager – when I was figuring out who I was, *what* I was – I *wanted* to talk to you about these things. You *and* Dad. I wanted us to find some way for us all to reconcile the differing ways in which we saw the world. But every time I tried, you'd shut down, or change the subject, or pretend you hadn't heard. It was as if I was this inconvenient problem and you hoped, by ignoring it, that it would just go away. But problems don't go away when you ignore them. They *fester*.' She gave a small, ironic smile. 'Thing is, I actually thought you'd be pleased I was figuring things out for myself. I always thought Judaism was meant to be about the search for the truth. And isn't truth supposed to be personal?'

'That's not how I remember it,' said Leah, with unexpected vehemence. 'I remember you rubbing our faces in it; telling us our beliefs were nonsense and that we were wasting our lives on pointless mumbo-jumbo. You'd try to argue theology with your father all the time. You saw everything as an ideological battle to be won. Some of my most vivid memories of that time are of you stomping around after him, trying to goad him into fighting with you. It's a measure of his forbearance that he rarely ever rose to the bait.'

Anna stared at her mother, stunned. This didn't accord at all with her own memories. And yet, the uncomfortable feeling of guilt in the pit of her stomach not only told her that Leah wasn't just making this up but that, deep down, she'd known it all along.

She realised Leah was still speaking. 'We could just about cope with the whole "atheism" business. You'd hardly have been the first Jew to turn your back on God. It was your wholesale rejection of everything else – your roots, your culture, your very sense of identity. Are you really so ashamed of who you are?'

'I'm not,' said Anna fiercely. 'That's positively the last thing I've ever been. And it's got nothing to do with a need to assimilate or an aversion to being different or anything like that. Fitting in has never been at the top of my agenda – you know that.' She gave an exaggerated, helpless shrug. 'But I don't care about the things you care about. I don't want the things you want. Growing up, I felt suffocated by the lifestyle you imposed on me – the insistence on clinging to tradition, this circular logic that says we've got to continue doing things the same way because that's the way they've always been done.'

'The reason we uphold these traditions,' said Leah, her voice rising, less in anger than in a desperate need to make her daughter *see*, 'is because so much of our history is rooted in a fight for our very survival. When your own forebears are forced under pain of death to hide who they are, continuing to observe those rites – including the ones you deem pointless or irrational – is an act of defiance in its own right.'

'That doesn't mean I've got an obligation to play any part in it,' Anna retorted, her own voice instinctively rising to match her mother's. 'Freedom to practise your traditions without threat of persecution goes hand in hand with an equally immutable freedom to reject them.'

Leah gave an exasperated sigh, threw up her hands and sat back, arms folded. Again, Anna caught herself mirroring her mother's obstinate, arms-akimbo posture and swiftly dropped them to her sides. They sat in silence for several moments, the impasse between them seemingly insurmountable, before Leah spoke again.

'I know you thought we were incredibly strict,' she said, her tone now closer to one of regret; 'that we boxed you into this restrictive lifestyle. But the truth is, we allowed you an exceptional amount of leeway. We sent you to a secular school – a private school, yes, and I'm well aware of your views on *that* subject, but just be glad we didn't pack you off to a Jewish-only institution.

'Of course,' she went on, before Anna could say what she thought of *that* proposal, 'we knew you were getting up to all manner of things that would have appalled even the least devout practitioner of the faith. But we didn't try to stop you. We knew there would have been no point – that you'd just have carried on anyway and resented us even more than you already did.'

Another heavy sigh racked her shoulders. 'I just wish … I wish you and your father could have buried the hatchet before he passed. He went to his grave convinced you hated him.' She looked at Anna imploringly, her voice cracking with emotion. 'For pity's sake, why didn't you come home for the funeral?'

'You know why,' said Anna stiffly.

'I don't!' Leah exclaimed, exasperated. 'I want you to explain it to me. I want to understand how things can possibly go so badly wrong that a daughter refuses to attend her own father's *levaya*. Is that so much to ask?'

'Refuse?' Anna stared at her mother in disbelief. 'Are you...' A thin, almost hysterical laugh escaped from her. 'Don't you *dare* try to rewrite history to make me out to be the villain. Just don't. It's beneath even you. You know perfectly well you did everything you could to make it impossible for me to be there.'

Now it was Leah's turn to gawp. '*What?*' she spluttered. 'I did no such thing! Do you seriously imagine that I didn't want you there by my side? That I didn't *need* you?'

Anna opened her mouth, ready to fire back, but something stopped her in her tracks. The vehemence of her mother's denials had thrown her off balance. There hadn't been so much as a hint in them to suggest that she was trying to cover her own back.

'You kept how ill he was from me for months,' she said, her tone sounding both brittle and petulant in her own ears.

'Because that was what he *wanted*!'

Anna stared at her mother uncomprehendingly. 'What he...'

'He always felt guilty for the way he handled your decision to study criminology. For the rest of his life, he wished he could take back what he said that night. He wished he'd given you more support. He wanted you to be the best you could possibly be – at *whatever* you chose to do. And the last thing he wanted was for you to abandon your studies only to spend the next six months by his bedside, watching him waste away.'

Anna opened her mouth, then shut it again. She was all set to deny it all; to accuse her mother of spouting a bunch of self-serving lies to cover for her own dereliction of duty. But something stopped her. A tiny niggle of doubt had started to worm its way into her head. Could it be that she'd put two and two together and spent all those years convinced she'd made four when in fact she'd been completely off the mark?

'We thought we'd have longer,' Leah went on, more subdued now. 'As soon as we knew we couldn't delay any longer, we told you. But neither of us expected him to go downhill so quickly. And even then, we still thought, once you knew …'

She left it unsaid, but Anna immediately understood what she meant. Tendrils of guilt began to coil themselves around her. In desperation, she thrust them off, flailing for an excuse – *any* excuse – to justify her actions.

'But … but the funeral. You waited hours to tell me he'd died. If I'd known sooner, maybe I could have …'

'I was in *pieces*!' Leah shouted, and to her astonishment, Anna saw tears glistening in her eyes. 'There were umpteen arrangements to be made. I only had room in my head for so much. I tried to call you the morning after it happened, but you didn't answer the phone and I didn't have a number for you at the university. I asked Sara to keep trying to reach you while I …'

She broke off, too overwhelmed by emotion to continue with that train of thought. After briefly covering her mouth in expectation of a sob that never materialised, her eyes flared accusingly once more.

'You could have made it. If you'd put your mind to it, you could have made it. Don't even *try* to deny it.'

Anna said nothing. She'd run out of excuses.

'And then, for days and weeks afterwards, I heard nothing from you. *Nothing.* You didn't come for the shiva. You didn't call me. You didn't even send a miserly "sorry for your loss" card. In the name of God, *why?*'

'I … I needed more time,' Anna muttered helplessly. She was talking to herself now, desperately trying to convince herself of what she was saying. 'If I'd just had more time …'

'For *what?*'

'I …'

'Why didn't you come?' Leah's voice was a whisper.

'Because I was afraid, OK?'

It came blurting out before she even had time to realise what she was saying. She shut her mouth immediately, as if that might somehow allow her to take it back. But it was too late. Leah was staring at her, her face a mask of incomprehension, but with something else mixed in – something close to anguish.

'I was afraid of being vulnerable,' Anna muttered, her eyes lowered to her lap. 'Of the emotions it'd make me feel. Of not knowing what to say. What to do. How to be. It was easier to bury myself in work and pretend it hadn't happened. That it had nothing to do with me. That it was someone else's dad.'

'I wish you'd told me,' said Leah quietly.

Anna shook her head. 'I couldn't. We've never had that kind of relationship. And … and I don't know whether it's me who's to blame for that, or you, or both of us equally. I just know I've never been any good at expressing feelings like love or grief or joy.' She gave a grim smile. 'We Scavolinis, we've never been big with wearing our hearts on our sleeves. Dad was just the same. Maybe that's where I get it from.'

She slumped low in her seat, head bowed, arms resting on her knees. 'And I hate it. I hate that I'm this way. I hate feeling like my brain is wired differently to everyone else's. I hate not being able to let people in because I'm afraid of how it might make me feel. But most of all I hate that I wasn't there when you needed me.' She lifted her head to look at Leah, eyes glassy and empty. 'And that Dad thought I hated him.'

Leah lowered her own head in contrition. 'I shouldn't have said that. He didn't think you hated him. You had your differences all right, but he knew that, deep down, you loved him throughout it all. He knew that because he felt exactly the same way about you, even though he found it every bit as hard to express as you did.'

Anna shook her head, still not convinced. 'I always felt like he resented me. It was as if he saw me pursuing my passions and, instead of being pleased for me, he got mad and tried to sabotage my chances.'

'He wanted what was best for you. We both did.' Leah fixed her daughter with a sad, tired smile. 'Your father was far from a perfect man. He made mistakes, and I know there are things he wished he'd done differently. But he understood all about pursuing one's passions. He understood more than you can ever know.'

Anna frowned at her. 'What do you mean?'

Leah's smile was almost wistful. 'He was a different man when I first met him. Believe it or not, back then his life's ambition was to rent a tiny garret in the centre of Paris and spend his days making fine art paintings. That, or become a rock musician. But he put those dreams on hold for a career that allowed him to provide his family with a very comfortable life but which brought him no end of stress and little, if any, sense of fulfilment. I think a part of him always wished he'd done things differently, and for that reason it was incredibly hard for him to watch you leading the life he'd denied to himself.'

Anna lifted her head and met her mother's gaze. 'He was depressed, wasn't he?' It came out as barely a whisper.

Leah nodded softly. 'Yes. I mean, I think so. It's not as if he ever saw anyone about it or had any sort of formal diagnosis. Back then, people weren't so determined to stick a label on everyone, ascribing this condition or that to them. I'm not saying it was better,' she went on quickly, evidently anticipating a rebuke from Anna. 'It was just … different. But yes, I think it's likely he was.'

'Oh God,' Anna whispered. 'And I made his life hell.'

This time, she could do nothing to hold the tears at bay. She could count on one hand the number of times she'd cried properly since reaching adulthood. *Bottle up all your feelings – it's the Scavolini way.* Even her father's death hadn't prompted a response on this level.

As the sobs racked her chest and she buried her head in her hands, she still had sufficient presence of mind to consider the possibility that this was, in part, a reaction to his death, thirteen years overdue. But that wasn't all it was about. She was crying because of how unfairly she'd judged him. And because he *had* loved her after all.

As she continued to weep, she sensed a presence beside her, followed, a moment later, by arms enveloping her. Amidst her untrammelled outpouring of grief, she registered the shock of what was happening. Her mother was sitting beside her, hugging her like a small child – something she hadn't done since she was a toddler.

'There now,' Leah murmured, resting her chin on Anna's forehead. 'It's all right.'

'I never knew,' Anna choked helplessly. 'I didn't realise.'

'That was how he wanted it,' said her mother. 'The last thing he wanted was for his problems to become yours.'

They continued to sit together, squeezed into the same armchair, Leah holding Anna as her sobs gradually subsided. At length, Anna straightened up and turned to gaze at her mother, eyes and cheeks glistening. Using her thumb, Leah wiped the tears from under Anna's eyes, one after the other. Then, as Anna sniffed and hastily composed herself, her mother got up and retrieved her handbag from next to the sofa. She rummaged inside it and, a moment later, returned with her purse. Sitting down next to Anna once more, she opened it and took out a dog-eared Polaroid photograph.

'Here. This is how he'd want you to remember him.'

Anna took the picture and gazed down at it. It had that pastel-hued, slightly otherworldly quality so common to old photographs. She recognised the location as the large back garden of the house on Cleveden Road. She was in the foreground, a dark-haired toddler sitting astride a tricycle, pedalling for all she was worth as she tore along the crazy paving path among the rose bushes, her head thrown back in ecstasy. Loping behind her, bent over almost double in an effort to hold the handlebars steady, was her father – a tall, spidery figure, his grin as wide as his daughter's as he shared in her unbridled joy.

Anna stared at the picture, lost for words. 'I . . . I remember this,' she managed to say.

Leah smiled softly. 'That was one of his good days.'

Anna continued to gaze at the picture, drinking in every last detail. It occurred to her that, in addition to demonstrating her father's love for her, it also said something that, despite all the rancour that had existed between them for so long, her mother had nonetheless continued to carry it in her purse for so many years.

Something else occurred to her. She couldn't have been more than three years old at the time, if that, and yet the memory of it now came flooding back with near-perfect clarity. She remembered the smell of the rose bushes in the warm summer air. The bump and rattle of the paving stones under her wheels. The giddy sense of total freedom that enveloped her as she careened down the path at full tilt.

The picture predated the incident in the Botanic Gardens. Which meant that *this*, not it, must be her first memory.

'He would have been proud of you, you know.' Leah's voice reached Anna through the fog of her reverie. 'If he'd lived to see what you've become . . . what you've achieved, all on your own.'

Anna lifted her head in surprise. She understood that Leah, in her own particular buttoned-up way, was conveying that she too was proud of her, even if she was too reserved to come out and say it. More than that, though, there was a sense of validation implicit in this statement – of the life she'd chosen, of the effort it had taken her to achieve it. It was this validation, she now realised, that, deep down, she'd craved from her parents all her life.

'Mum…' she began, her voice cracking.

'Shh.' Leah gently touched her fingers to Anna's lips. 'You don't have to. I know.'

So Anna said nothing. Instead, she slowly slipped an arm around her mother and rested her head on her shoulder. It was an awkward gesture for both of them, but after a moment's hesitation, she felt Leah's shoulders untensing as she embraced this rare moment of mother/daughter bonding.

The moment ended – all too quickly, perhaps, but both women's ingrained discomfort at such overt physical expressions of affection soon kicked in and they drew apart, both clearing their throats awkwardly and smoothing down their clothes.

'Right, then,' said Anna, all business, 'you've a flight to catch tomorrow. Will you be needing a lift to the airport?'

'No need,' said her mother promptly. 'I can manage.'

'And what about whatsisname? Will you be going back to him?'

Leah considered the question. 'I think not,' she said eventually. 'Or at least, not right away. He can grovel for a bit first. Then we'll see.'

Anna laughed. 'We'll make a feminist out of you yet, Mother.'

She got up to leave. Leah stood too – a faintly ridiculous touch of formality that almost made Anna order her to sit down again.

'And will you be back?' she asked instead.

'I'm not sure. It rather depends.'

'On what?'

'Well, on whether you want me to, for a start.'

Anna hesitated. The ball had been well and truly lobbed into her court. She licked her lips. Swallowed a mouthful of saliva.

'I'd like that,' she said.

'Are you sure?'

'Yes,' she said, with quiet conviction. 'Just because we do things differently – just because we don't see eye to eye on … well, *anything* –

doesn't mean I don't want you in my life ... and in Jack's. He ... ' The next part required some effort for her to say. 'Well, I think he needs his granny.'

Leah scoffed softly. 'Oh, stuff and nonsense. He doesn't need me – not really. He's got all he needs right here.' Her expression grew serious. 'But if you want me to be a part of his life, I'll be there, in whatever capacity.' Her lips curled in the inklings of a smile. 'Though I suspect, for both our sanities, we should probably avoid making these family reunions *too* frequent an endeavour.'

Anna choked back a laugh. 'Yeah, I reckon that'd be enough to put us *both* into therapy.'

Anna emerged from the Kupermans' house, feeling light-headed, almost euphoric. The sun had gone down, and the cool evening air hit her like an ice-cold blast after the warmth of the living room. She settled behind the wheel of her car and blew out a long breath, still not quite able to believe the turn the evening had taken. However she'd imagined things panning out, they certainly hadn't involved mending a decades-long feud with her mother and facing up to her own long-repressed guilt.

As she sat there, listening to the rustling of the leaves of the thick oak tree in the Kupermans' garden, the back of her scalp began to prickle as something fought to force itself to the surface. It had been on the edge of her consciousness for a while now, she realised – ever since Leah had shown her the photograph of herself on the tricycle.

What was it about that picture that her unconscious mind had latched onto? Something about the location? No, that wasn't it. The scenario it depicted? Possibly, yes, but it was more specific than that. No, it was the familiarity of the way the two figures were posed: one, younger, on a bike; another, older, behind them, leaning over to steady the handlebars. Where had she seen that before?

It hit her so hard and suddenly that her breath caught in her throat.

'Oh, *fuck.*'

Hands trembling, she got out her phone and navigated to the last text she'd received. Then she switched to Google Images, keyed in a name and hit Search. She scrolled through the results until her eyes alighted on the image she was looking for. She stared at it in stunned silence, her blood pounding in her ears.

She knew now why the photo on the front of Paul Kempley's order of service had seemed so familiar. She *had* seen his face before, but not in a paparazzo's snap of him arriving at court during Sandra Morton's trial.

No – she'd seen it a whole lot more recently than that. Barely more than twenty-four hours ago, in fact.

42

The drive to Hillend might have taken her less than ninety minutes, but it felt infinitely longer. She called Zoe en route to let her know what was happening, then rang off before Zoe had a chance to interrogate her. Her phone, lying on the passenger seat, continued to ping as a volley of texts and missed calls came in, until she got tired of hearing it and switched it off.

Her first port of call was the 8 Till Late on the town's northernmost edge. Heather wasn't over the moon about being roused by Anna's incessant banging on the door, and was clearly taken aback to see her again so soon. However, once she'd rubbed the sleep from her eyes and Anna had explained at least three times what she wanted, she reluctantly obliged.

From there, Anna drove on to Eastriggs. It was just gone 10.45 p.m. when she pulled into the grounds of Eunice and George Morton's farmhouse. The house was in darkness, but she strode across the gravel courtyard and pounded on the front door anyway. Less than a minute passed before a light went on in the hallway, visible through the glass pane above the door. A few seconds later, it opened to reveal George, clutching a dressing gown about himself, his blue-and-white striped pyjama trousers visible beneath it. Upon recognising Anna, his eyes widened in angry disbelief.

'*You?*' he exclaimed. 'What the devil are you doing here? Get off this property right now before I call the police.'

'Go right ahead,' said Anna. 'There's a very good chance their services will be needed before the night's over.'

Not waiting for an invitation which she knew wouldn't be forthcoming, she strode on into the house. George, so disconcerted by her brazenness that he seemed not to know whether he was coming or going, could only splutter impotently as he hurriedly shut the door and shuffled after her into the hallway.

'This is *beyond* insolent,' he declared, his voice an angry whisper. 'My wife is asleep just overhead. If you wake her—'

'I'll tell you what else is insolent,' Anna shot back, swinging round to face him with folded arms. 'Yesterday, you told me what's known in the trade as a bald-faced lie – or at least you were seriously economical with the truth.'

'I don't know what you're talking about. And you're trespassing.'

'When I asked you, you claimed you didn't know Paul Kempley. You said, and I quote, "our paths have never crossed". And for all I know, that's true, but what you neglected to mention is that someone else in the family *did* know him.'

A momentary flicker of anxiety crossed George's face. He recovered quickly, but not quickly enough.

'I'm sure I've no idea—' he began.

'I thought you might deny it. That's why I took a pit stop before coming here.' Anna produced her phone and held it up, the screen already showing the most recent image on the camera roll. 'Recognise this?'

It was evident from the ashen look on his face that George *did* recognise it. Nonetheless, he insisted on taking the phone from Anna and fishing his glasses out of his dressing gown pocket to inspect it properly. On the glossy screen, the grinning likeness of Katie, age thirteen, gazed back at him from behind the motorcycle handlebars, the older boy standing behind her bearing an undeniable resemblance to the picture of Paul Kempley from his order of service.

'The woman who showed me this picture yesterday thought he might be her cousin,' said Anna, as George handed the phone back wordlessly, a slight tremor in his hand. 'But both Katie's cousins are roughly the same age as her, according to their father – something that slipped my mind at the time, given everything else that was going on. Judging by the way they're posed, I'd say theirs was more than a passing acquaintance, wouldn't you?'

George said nothing. He merely glowered at Anna, his jaw set.

'The fact that the only surviving daughter of the woman on trial for murder – who, according to you, spent years deliberately poisoning her – was friends with the witness whose testimony blew apart her alibi seems like information that really ought to have come to light, don't you? I can only conclude that it was withheld for a reason.'

George swallowed heavily. In the space of under a minute, he appeared to have aged at least a decade.

'So here's what I think happened,' Anna continued. 'I think Katie told Paul Kempley about the things her mother used to do to her. And when the opportunity arose, they hatched a plot together to make sure she got the punishment she deserved. Paul got rid of the CCTV footage and claimed he hadn't seen Sandra on the night of the murders and hey presto – the central plank of her defence was fatally undermined long before she ever saw the inside of a courtroom.'

Having delivered her entire speech without stopping to draw a single breath, she now paused for long enough to fill her lungs with air, before fixing George with an enquiring look.

'The only part I'm still trying to work out is whether *you* knew anything about it.'

George, who'd listened to everything without attempting to interject, continued to say nothing, but he appeared utterly deflated, his shoulders slumped and his head hanging low in resignation. As he licked his dry lips, seemingly on the verge of speaking, a tremulous voice called out overhead:

'George? Who are you talking to?'

Both Anna and George turned towards the stairs. At the top stood Eunice. She too was wearing her dressing gown and had the bleary, disoriented look of someone who'd just woken up. She gazed down at them with a mixture of confusion and apprehension.

George raised and lowered his hand in a placatory gesture. 'It's all right, love. I'm dealing with it.'

Eunice, however, was unassuaged. Clutching the handrail tightly, she began to make her way down the stairs towards them, one step at a time. Abandoning any hope of trying to stop her, George gave a sigh of defeat and turned to Anna, shaking his head sadly.

'You're so close to being right, but so wrong. Katie had nothing to do with it. She's an innocent in all of this.'

As Anna stared back at him uncomprehendingly, Eunice completed her descent of the stairs. She drew alongside her husband, laying a hand on his arm.

'George,' she said softly, 'it's time.'

The image on the television screen was fuzzy, black and white and riddled with tracking errors, but what it showed was clear enough to be discernible: a high-angle view of the interior of a petrol station, encompassing the checkout counter and the rows of shelves facing it, plus the sliding doors leading out to the pumps. The date burned into the corner read 06/05/2001, the time 23:05 and counting. The shop was empty but for a solitary figure standing behind the counter, leaning against the back wall while he mashed the controls of a handheld games console.

Paul Kempley's periodic changes in position had a jerky, staccato quality as Anna, on her knees in front of the TV unit in George and Eunice's living room, held the dial on the VCR in the fast-forward position, scrubbing through the footage to get to the part she was looking for.

'He used to do odd jobs for us,' George explained, 'helping out here and there on weekends for some extra pocket money. He was a good lad – always happy to go the extra mile.'

He stood behind Anna, one hand on Eunice's shoulder as she sat on the sofa, gazing at the jittery footage on the screen as if mesmerised.

'That's how he and Katie came to know each other,' George continued. 'She'd not long come to live with us and still hadn't made any real friends her own age here in Eastriggs. They had a lot in common – quiet, kept to themselves, didn't open up to other people easily. The age difference didn't seem to be an issue for either of them. In fact, in Katie's case I fancy it was a bonus. It helped her, I think, having someone a bit more worldly-wise take her under his wing.'

Anna let go of the dial and, leaving the tape playing at its normal speed, turned to give George her full attention.

'He brought the tape to you, didn't he?'

To some extent, she was still playing catch-up, but she reckoned she had a reasonable idea of how things had played out, even if the specifics continued to elude her.

George nodded. 'One evening, just over halfway through the trial, he showed up at the house with it and half a dozen others in his rucksack. He said his conscience had got the better of him; that he'd been going to turn them over but had decided to do us the courtesy of coming to us first to find out what *we* wanted him to do.'

'He stole them the day after the murders.' It wasn't a question.

'The news that morning was wall-to-wall "Hillend House of Horror". Sandra's face was on every front page, and several of them were already hinting that she was responsible. He went in and swapped the tapes for blanks before the police got round to seizing them.'

'Because of what she did to Katie.'

George nodded. 'You were right about that part. She'd told him all about the bleach and the rest of it. I was flabbergasted. She'd never talked to us about it – her own *grandparents* – but she'd happily shared it with some boy she'd only known for a few months.'

Sometimes it's easier to discuss difficult things with complete strangers, Anna thought. It was why therapy was such a lucrative business.

Aloud, she said, 'So the three of you hatched this plan to frame Sandra for the murders.'

'No!' George sounded affronted by the suggestion. 'It had nothing to do with framing her. It was about making sure justice was served. That woman is as guilty as sin. I believed that then and I believe it now. But we knew the defence would use the fact she'd been seen at the petrol station to muddy the waters and get her off. You know what lawyers are like. They'd have found a way.'

'It's not about finding a way,' Anna protested, her frustration at his apparent inability to understand this point tipping over into outright exasperation. 'If Sandra was at the petrol station when she claims she was, it's physically impossible for her to have committed the murders.'

As she spoke, she wondered if it was remotely plausible that George genuinely didn't know this. During both the trial and the ensuing two decades, he'd have had ample time to consider the logistics involved; to plot the timings down to the last minute. Or was it simply the case that his determination for Sandra to be guilty was so overwhelming that, consciously or otherwise, he'd glossed over the ramifications of her being at a location two and a half miles from the house within minutes of the murders having taken place?

It seemed to her that he faltered momentarily, a look of uncertainty briefly flickering in his eyes before he found his resolve once more.

'She did it,' he muttered. 'I *know* she did.'

'She was an evil woman,' Eunice declared – her sole contribution since she'd sat down. George responded by squeezing her shoulder, and she once more sank into her earlier state of blank inertia.

'And Katie,' Anna prompted. 'You're telling me she knew nothing about any of this?'

'I told you,' George's response was immediate and emphatic, 'she had nothing to do with it. Paul swore he hadn't discussed it with her, and *we* certainly never told her anything. We all agreed it was for the best that she wasn't involved.'

Anna briefly considered the possibility that he could be lying – denying his granddaughter's involvement to avoid incriminating her. She sensed, though, that there was little point in pressing the matter. Besides, she had bigger fish to fry than pursuing someone who, at the time, had been a thirteen-year-old girl grieving the loss of her father and brothers.

'I suppose it's all going to come out now.' George's voice cut into her thoughts. 'You'll take this to the police, and Eunice and I will be prosecuted for withholding evidence and whatever other charges they dream up. Well, so be it. I'd do it all again in a heartbeat.'

Anna didn't respond. Out of the corner of her eye, she'd caught sight of something on the screen. She now gave it her undivided attention, watching the scene playing out before her in silent, low-resolution black and white. Striding in through the sliding doors was Sandra, her thin tank top rendered semi-transparent by the downpour outside.

As Anna watched, she strolled along the aisle nearest the door, pausing midway to grab a packet of pills from one of the shelves. She continued towards the checkout, where she slammed them down on the counter, along with a banknote produced from the pocket of her shorts. Paul, who'd sprung to attention as soon as the doors slid open, proceeded to ring them up, while Sandra stood, hands on hips, her body language radiating impatience.

Anna briefly glanced at George and Eunice. Both pairs of eyes were fixed on the screen, though Eunice's were so glazed it was debatable whether she was processing what she was seeing, far less understanding its significance.

Anna turned back to the screen. Paul had finished ringing up Sandra's purchase and was counting out her change. Sandra's lips moved as she said something. Paul glanced at her, shrugging. Sandra spoke again, her lips moving more aggressively now, accompanied by her jabbing her finger at Paul's chest. Again, Paul shrugged. Sandra snapped her fingers under his nose, then pointed them at her eyes. *My eyes are up here, not down there.*

Paul raised his arms in aggrieved protest, but Sandra wasn't interested. Grabbing the box of pills, the receipt and the change he'd slid across the counter, she turned on her heel and strode towards the exit. As she went, she paused to grab a bottle of juice from the fridge next to the magazine stand. Paul, still watching from behind the counter, shouted something at her. Sandra responded by flipping the bird in his direction, then strode out of the building, taking her unpaid-for orangeade bottle with her. Paul threw up his hands in exasperation but made no move to follow her. A moment later, he shrugged, retrieved his games machine from under the counter and settled back into button-mashing mode.

Anna hit Pause on the VCR. The timecode in the bottom corner read 23:17 – eight minutes after Guy Morton, with his last ounce of strength, had called 999, and five minutes after Adjoa Asante had sighted the figure the prosecution had claimed was Sandra scaling the wall at the foot of the field adjoining the Mortons' back garden.

PART FIVE

THE MOTHER WE SHARE

43

Friday 31 May

Sandra Morton was released from prison at 10.30 a.m. on Saturday 27 April, a mere six days and nine hours after Anna handed the CCTV tapes over to Pamela Macklin. Whether because her sense of duty to the ideal of due process ran deeper than she'd previously realised or simply because, having seen the evidence with her own eyes, she could hardly suppress its existence, Pamela immediately petitioned the Justice Secretary to instigate a judicial review, the fact that she'd previously resigned as Sandra's solicitor instantly forgotten. Having gone through a similar process herself mere hours earlier and still experiencing both a profound sense of whiplash and a degree of ambivalence as to whether she'd done the right thing, Anna had little difficulty in empathising with her likely conflicted state of mind.

Two days later, following a hastily convened session of the Appeal Court, Sandra's conviction was overturned and her release ordered with immediate effect. Anna was given to understand that the speed with which this all unfolded was virtually unheard of in the annals of judicial reviews, proving that the wheels of justice can be incited to turn surprisingly swiftly in times of great need – or great embarrassment.

In the ensuing days, much speculation followed as to what charges would be levied against George and Eunice Morton for their role in suppressing the crucial evidence that proved their daughter-in-law's innocence. Several months later, the Procurator Fiscal would announce that no further action was to be taken in the matter. It was widely held that this decision was informed less by the likelihood of a prosecution against them succeeding than their advanced age, coupled with Eunice's declining cognitive faculties. A few of the more malicious pundits speculated that Sandra Morton might feel compelled to take out a private prosecution against them, but theirs appeared to be a minority view. It may be that the same publications that played such a prominent role in the creation of the mythos of the Butcher of Hillend felt it prudent not to give her any ideas about pursuing similar action against *them*.

Four weeks after Sandra's release, on the afternoon of the last day of May, Anna caught a train to Edinburgh. After disembarking at Waverley Station, she walked up Hanover Street until she came to a small café overlooking the George IV statue at the intersection with George Street.

The bell above the door jangled merrily as she entered. She halted just inside, taking in the faces of the dozen or so customers seated at the various tables. At first, she could see no sign of the person she'd arranged to meet, and she wondered briefly if she'd come to the wrong café, or else been stood up. Then she noticed that one of the two women seated at the table nearest the back of the room – the one facing her – was looking directly at her, albeit from behind a pair of dark glasses. She was in her early fifties, with an unseasonal fur-lined coat and a severe-looking peroxide blonde bob. A moment later, she lowered her glasses and Anna saw the familiar ice-blue eyes gazing back at her, almost transfixing her. Anna gave a small wave and made her way over.

The second woman rose to her feet and turned as Anna approached, revealing herself to be Pamela Macklin.

'Anna. You made it.'

Anna got the distinct sense that she was relieved to no longer be alone with her client. She accepted the solicitor's characteristically clammy handshake, took the empty seat between the two women and gestured to Sandra.

'This is a new look. I didn't recognise you for a moment.'

'Evidently,' said Sandra, her tone one of mild derision. 'Wouldn't have been much point in it otherwise.'

'It's to stop her being mobbed by the press,' Pamela explained, evidently angling for first prize for stating the obvious. 'We don't think they've figured out she's staying in Edinburgh yet, but it's probably only a matter of time.'

'Say that a bit louder, why don't you?' Sandra snorted, and Pamela immediately hung her head in mortification. She raised an eyebrow at Anna. 'Who needs the paps when we can rely on our own side to shoot their mouths off, eh?'

'How are you adjusting?' Anna asked, determined not to allow Sandra any further room to humiliate the woman who'd assumed the thankless task of representing her when there was no reason to believe it was anything other than a lost cause. 'To …' She trailed off, unsure how to phrase it diplomatically.

'To my return to the real world? Well, I confess it's been something of an eye-opener. I've spent a good chunk of the last four weeks people-watching. You don't really appreciate how quickly fashions change till you're hermetically sealed in a twelve-by-eight cell for nigh on two decades. When I was put away, plucked eyebrows were all the rage. Now, every woman I see has bloody great caterpillars.'

Pamela let out a shrill and painfully eager laugh. 'Yes, it's so hard to keep up with the trends, isn't it?'

Sandra gave her a withering look, and she promptly shut down again. Anna suspected she was probably feeling a bit like a spare part. After all, in the end, Pamela had played no part in securing her client's release, beyond the formal submission of the request for a judicial review – which had, in effect, amounted to a rubber-stamping exercise.

'And then there are the phones,' Sandra went on. 'In 2001, a mobile phone was this tacky little plastic thing with buttons and a two-inch screen. Nowadays, people use them to play games and make videos of their lunch. I must admit to having a touch of the green-eyed monster …' She shot a sidelong glance at Pamela. 'But my minder here won't allow me to have one.'

'I've suggested she doesn't – for now, anyway,' Pamela explained. 'The press would get hold of the number before you could say "Jack Robinson". For the time being, it's best if all communications go through me.'

'Yes, I've found myself with quite the efficient little PA,' said Sandra, again with the veneer of a sneer. 'Phone's been ringing off the hook, so I'm told. All manner of ambulance chasers have come out of the woodwork to offer me the opportunity to tell my side of the story. Several have made *very* lucrative offers.'

'D'you think you'll take any of them up on it?' asked Anna.

'Depends.'

'On what?'

Sandra gave her an enigmatic look and shrugged. 'Dunno – just depends. I waited eighteen years because of them. Now *they* can wait.'

At that moment, a barista came over, clutching a pen and a notepad. 'Can I get you anything?' she asked Anna.

Anna opened her mouth to speak, but Sandra beat her to it. 'We won't be staying long. Just the bill. You're paying, aren't you?' She addressed the question to Pamela.

Pamela nodded rather glumly, and Anna made a mental note to slip her something towards the cost if she got the chance to do so discreetly.

As the barista departed, Sandra leaned back in her chair with a contented sigh. 'One thing's for sure – I'll certainly not want for money. Quite apart from the offers for juicy tell-alls, there's the small matter of the various publications and their associated hacks who've spent the last two decades dragging my name through the mud – to say nothing of my ongoing application to the Justice Directorate for compensation for my wrongful conviction and lost years. Suffice it to say we intend to take the lot of them to the cleaners – isn't that right, Pammy?'

Pamela, who looked less than enthused by the prospect, gave a small nod.

'Perhaps they'll get round to making that film about me after all now,' Sandra went on, stroking her jaw thoughtfully. 'There was talk of one, years ago, but it ended up being mothballed for reasons unknown. Of course, it'll end on a far more positive note now – and audiences do love a happy ending.'

Anna gritted her teeth and said nothing. The unapologetic delight Sandra was taking in her newfound freedom was beginning to seriously stick in her craw. It took all her willpower not to point out that the fact that she'd been absolved of responsibility didn't change the reality that her husband and two infant children were dead. What was more, it hadn't escaped her notice that Sandra had failed to show even the tiniest hint of gratitude towards her for what she'd done. If not for Anna, she'd still be languishing behind the concrete walls of Broadwood with no hope of release. Not that she'd expected Sandra to throw her arms around her or prostrate herself at her knees, but she'd anticipated – even, she was forced to admit, *hoped* for – some sort of acknowledgement.

She reminded herself that, however unattractive Sandra might be as a person, the evidence was indisputable: she couldn't have committed the murders, and there was therefore no justification for her having remained in prison for a second longer. *I did the right thing,* she told herself.

But the knot in her stomach, which had been there ever since the news had reached her of Sandra's release, and which had grown steadily in intensity over the last four weeks, continued to tighten.

May gave way to June. Summer entered its early bloom, bringing with it the longer days and warmer weather that normally lifted Anna's spirits but which, this year, stubbornly refused to have any effect on the inexplicable feeling of foreboding that continued to gnaw away at her insides.

Meanwhile, as one chapter of the Hillend Murders ended, so another began. The investigation into the events of Sunday 6 May 2001 was re-opened, with Gillian Langley, Assistant Chief Constable (West of Scotland), declaring that establishing what really happened that night and bringing the true perpetrator to justice was her number one priority. Appeals had already been issued for information regarding the various sightings of an unidentified man with long hair that had never been followed up at the time, and a new team was drafted in to re-examine the entire case with fresh eyes.

Mind you, these days Anna had more than enough to occupy her without also finding time to follow the new investigation in exhaustive detail. Since the end of April, she'd been scrambling to make up for lost time with the first draft of her book on women's experiences of the prison system. The race was well and truly on now, and she anticipated having to put in more than a few all-nighters to get it over the finish line, but she was making steady headway and found, now she was back into it, that she'd rediscovered much of her earlier passion for the project.

Somewhat to her surprise, Pamela Macklin had even come good on her long-undelivered promise of access to her clients, and she'd made several genuinely productive visits to Broadwood, returning home with ample material to incorporate. On the couple of occasions when their paths had crossed, Ruth Laxton had been civil but undeniably chilly towards her. Evidently, she'd surmised that whatever discussions Anna was having with her ladies were unlikely to result in her prison being painted in a positive light. Or perhaps Ruth simply resented the fact that Anna had robbed her of the kudos associated with having the most infamous convict in the country under her care. The promised dossier on prison conditions that Pamela was supposedly collating had not materialised as yet, though she continued to insist it would be ready 'really, really soon'. Perhaps, Anna thought, if the book ever got a second edition, she'd be able to incorporate its findings into it.

Late on the morning of the first Friday of June, Anna was upstairs in her office, scrambling to make the finishing touches to the chapter she'd been working on for the last fortnight. She had the house to herself – she'd belatedly arranged with Simone Cole for Jack to go on a playdate with Oscar at their house near Victoria Park, and Zoe, possibly sensing that Anna wanted peace and quiet to work, had absented herself too, with some talk of catching a movie followed by a round of what she referred to as 'therapy shopping'. Anna was planning to swing by the university in the afternoon to pick up some mail the secretary had rung to say was waiting for her, and her mind was just turning to doing that when the doorbell rang.

The woman standing on the front step looked to be in her early thirties, with shoulder-length blonde hair, a septum piercing and a cleft in her chin that seemed vaguely familiar.

'Hi,' said Anna, wondering if she knew this person in a different context and had merely forgotten who they were. It wouldn't be the first time.

'Are you Anna Scavolini?'

She spoke with a North American accent of some variety and exuded a sense of pushy self-confidence that immediately put Anna on the back foot.

'I am,' she confirmed warily.

'Then I think you'd better let me in. I have things to say that you need to hear.'

Then, without waiting for an invitation, the woman strode across the threshold, forcing Anna to reverse into the hallway.

'Now just a minute,' Anna spluttered, fighting to retain some semblance of control of the situation. 'I don't know who you think you are, but you can't just barge in like this.'

'Can't I?' said the woman sardonically. 'From where I'm standing, it seems only fair, given the way you drove a coach and horses through *my* life without a care in the world.'

Anna stared at her uncomprehendingly, wondering if it was possible that one or both of them had lost the plot.

'Who *are* you?'

The woman looked at her for a long, deeply uncomfortable moment, during which the back of Anna's scalp began to prickle as she took in the sight of her pale blue eyes and suddenly realised why both they and that cleft chin seemed so achingly familiar.

'Haven't you guessed?' the woman's voice dripped derision. 'These days I go by Kat Alcott, but in a previous life I was Kathryn Morton … or Katie, if you prefer.'

44

'My uncle passed on your contact details. He told me why you wanted to speak to me.'

Katie had laid claim to the living room sofa and sat, one leg crossed over the other, arms spread across the backrest, looking for all the world like she owned the place. Anna remained standing, feet planted apart, arms folded – a futile attempt to wrest back some of the control she'd comprehensively lost the moment this woman, in whose features she now recognised the pale-faced young girl from Heather's photo collection, had barged into the house.

'I didn't even give it a moment's thought,' Katie went on. 'I knew nothing good could come of it.' She gave a humourless smirk. 'Got that part right, didn't I?'

Anna took a deep breath, counting to five in her head before speaking. 'Your granddad told me how your mother treated you as a child. I know all about the poisoning and whatnot.' She shrugged helplessly. 'But be that as it may, the fact of the matter is that your mother couldn't have committed the crimes she was convicted of. We found incontrovertible proof of that. It took all of five seconds for the appeal judges to be convinced.'

'I don't know how you've got the nerve to stand there and talk about what you "know",' Katie shot back. 'Just cos you get off on sticking your nose into other people's affairs doesn't mean you understand the first goddamn thing about them.' She scoffed softly and shook her head. 'Even before I met you, I knew you'd be a sanctimonious twat.' She pronounced it the North American way – *twot*.

Anna said nothing. She perched on the arm of the chair facing Katie, arms still folded defensively, and waited for her to continue. However out of line this woman might have been in charging in and insulting her in her own house, she nonetheless had some measure of understanding as to why she felt so aggrieved. The least she owed her was an opportunity to get this off her chest.

'She used to give me these glasses of juice to drink,' said Katie. 'I remember it from as far back as when I was three or four, though I'm sure it started way before then. Ribena, orange juice, SunnyD – it didn't matter what it was, it always came with a little something extra added in.' She gave a crooked smile. 'Bleach was an enduring favourite, or toilet cleaner. If she couldn't lay her hands on those, or she wanted to mix things up a bit, she'd pour in half a shaker's worth of salt. I used to watch her making up her little concoctions. "Time for your special medicine, Katie," she'd say. And then she'd stand over me and make sure I drank it all down, all the while with this twisted little smirk on her face, like she couldn't believe she was actually getting away with it.

'It took me ages to work out it was the "special medicine" that was making me sick all the time. I mean, I was just a dumb little kid. It's not like I knew any better. And yet, in spite of that, I somehow knew not to let on to Dad or Granny and Grandpa. I knew, even without her telling me, that it was our little secret.'

Anna forced down a mouthful of saliva. The sound was almost comically loud in the stillness of the room.

'Oh *yeah*.' Katie was clearly deriving no small amount of twisted enjoyment from Anna's unease. 'She's a real peach, my mother. See, she wanted me to get sick, but she always made sure I didn't get *too* sick. That would have been too dangerous. So she was careful. Made sure she got the dosage just right. She used to measure it out using one of those jugs with the numbers on the side. Until that one time she put in too much and I ended up in hospital. She got a fright then.'

She gave a sudden, twisted little smile, revealing the gap-teeth she'd shown off, in an altogether more wholesome fashion, in the picture of her and Paul Kempley.

Anna licked dry lips. 'Do you …' She tried again. 'What I mean to say is, did you ever get any sense as to *why* she did it?'

'You mean like did she have Munchausen's by proxy or whatever? I did consider that at one time. And I know the shrinks have all tried to pin this, that and the other on her – you know, making excuses for what she did to Dad and the boys.' Katie gave a contemptuous snort. 'It's all bullcrap. Sandra isn't sick. Everything she did, she did for one reason and one reason only. She did it cos she enjoys watching people suffer. She's evil, pure and simple.'

Anna couldn't help but feel like she'd had this conversation before – with George and Jeff and just about everyone else who'd ever encountered and formed an opinion on Sandra. And yet, if anyone was entitled to regard her as the devil incarnate, it was surely Katie.

She decided to try to seek a middle ground. 'I hear everything you're saying,' she said – aware, even as she spoke, that she was using the same mealy-mouthed language that always got her back up when she heard it from cod-psychologists on the telly. 'And you must understand that I'm not for one moment trying to downplay or trivialise what you experienced. But there's a world of difference between poisoning a child to watch them suffer and committing cold-blooded murder. The offender typologies are completely different.'

Katie gave a sardonic smile. 'Thought you might say that. That's why I've saved the best for last. Here's a story for you – one you won't have read in any of your books or heard from any of the so-called experts. That's cos I've never told it to anyone before. See, Sandra's got form when it comes to what happened that night.'

Anna felt herself leaning forward. For the first time since Katie had begun to speak, it felt like they were on the cusp of a genuine revelation.

'It happened about a year before I finally got outta that place and moved in with Granny and Granddad. It was the middle of the night. I was in my bed, fast asleep. And then, suddenly, for whatever reason, I woke up. You ever suffer from sleep paralysis?'

Anna shook her head.

'I get it from time to time, and lemme tell you, it's not fun. Your mind's awake but your body might as well not be your own. You can't move, you can't speak, you can't *do* anything. You wanna scream, but you can't even do that. You're completely alone, at the mercy of your own brain's faulty wiring. Anyway, at first it was just like the other times – me coming to, only not, staring up at the ceiling, feeling like someone was pressing on my chest, holding me down.

'But then I realised there was something different this time. There was this other person in the room with me. I felt it at first rather than seeing anything. This ... *presence*. And then my eyes adjusted to the dark and I saw her: my beloved mother, standing over me. And she didn't do anything. She just stood there, looking down at me, her eyes staring into mine. I couldn't move. I couldn't speak. All I could do was stare back at her. Then I managed to move my eyes just a tiny bit, and I saw it, there, in her hand.'

'What?' Anna's voice was barely a whisper.

'A knife. A carving knife from the block in the kitchen, just like the one she used a year later on Dad and the boys. She was just holding it and staring down at me and not moving. We stayed like that for what felt like ages, me and her, just looking at each other, and it was like we both understood. She knew I knew what she wanted to do, and I knew she knew I knew.

'Then ... I dunno, she must've thought I was starting to come out of it or something, cos the next thing I knew, she was gone.'

Anna licked her lips again, choosing her next words carefully. 'I'm sorry if this is asking the obvious, but is it possible you were—'

'Hallucinating?' Katie smirked dryly. 'Yup, I thought so too at the time. Just another bad dream. I had a lot of those back then. But it was too vivid, too specific. And then, when Dad and my wee brothers were knifed to death ... '

There was, Anna thought, something almost heartbreakingly sweet about the fact that, despite her accent not having a trace of Scottishness left in it, she still used the word 'wee' to describe her dead siblings. She opened her mouth to speak, but Katie beat her to it.

'And if you're going to ask,' she said, her voice tight with bitterness, 'yes, I've often thought about how things might've turned out if I'd said something back then. But I didn't, and because of that, they're dead, and I wish to God I'd been there that night and gone the same way as them. Then I wouldn't've been left to carry on without them, knowing I could have saved them, if only I'd spoken up. I carry that guilt with me every day.'

'That wasn't what I was going to ask,' said Anna gently. 'What I was going to say was, even if what you saw wasn't a hallucination, it still doesn't change the fact that your mother *can't* have committed the murders. The CCTV footage—'

'You don't get it,' said Katie, but with weariness this time rather than rancour. 'Even if she wasn't there in person, even if she didn't physically strike the blows herself, she made it happen. Don't ask me how I know, and don't ask me how she did it, but she did.' A thin, humourless smile crossed her lips. 'You think you're so clever, with all your book smarts and your letters after your name and whatnot – but you don't know shit. She's played you like a fiddle.'

Anna said nothing. What else was there *to* say? Regardless of her own scepticism, Katie clearly believed what she was saying with every fibre of her being, and nothing was going to change her mind on the matter.

And now Katie was getting to her feet. 'So there you have it. And if you're going to say, "You should have just emailed me", then yeah, I probably could've – but I wanted to be able to look you in the eyes when I told you what you've set in motion.'

Anna, too, got up. 'And just what is it you think I've set in motion?'

Katie gazed back at her, her eyes like pale blue ice crystals. 'I'm not sure, but I've always thought I only escaped that night by the grace of God, and that, in *her* eyes, I was unfinished business. I took a big risk coming back here now that she's out. I mean,' she added, with a roll of her eyes, 'I was here anyway to see Uncle Jeff and the grandparents. Don't flatter yourself into thinking I flew all this way just for you. You were my last stop, and now I've said my piece, I'm not sticking round to wait for her to find me.'

Feeling a sense of obligation, Anna saw her to the door.

'There's just one thing I've been wondering,' said Katie, turning on the doorstep.

'What's that?'

'How did you know? What was the big breakthrough that let you crack the case?'

'Paul Kempley. A photo of you and him together on a motorbike.'

'Huh,' said Katie. 'That old thing. Well, I suppose that would do it. Have you spoken to him?'

'No,' said Anna. Then, feeling the need to provide further explanation, she added, 'He's dead, I'm afraid. Sorry.'

'Oh.'

To Anna's eyes, Katie didn't look grief-stricken so much as numb. She supposed, when your life was already so filled with heartbreak, there came a point when you became if not used to it then at least inured, to the point that it lost any sense of novelty – if indeed it was ever appropriate to speak of death in such terms. It occurred to Anna that she knew nothing about the life Katie had made for herself. Did she have friends? A lover? Children? A job that brought her a sense of fulfilment? Or did she merely lead an empty, colourless existence, with nothing to look forward to except the day when, as she saw it, she got to re-join her father and brothers in the next life?

'He was abused too, you know,' Katie said after a moment. 'It was different for him than it was for me…but still sort of the same, I guess. His dad. He used to come into his room at night and make him touch his willy. He told his mum and she took her husband's side 'stead of his.' The expression on her face told Anna she didn't see this as remotely surprising. 'I was the only other person he ever told – at least, back then. That's sort of how we ended up bonding. I hope…' A slight flicker of emotion caused her voice to catch momentarily. 'I hope he at least got to live a life that made him happy, even if it was only for a short while.'

'I think he did,' said Anna quietly.

'That's good,' said Katie. 'Better to burn brightly but briefly than to linger on in nothingness for eternity.'

Then, without another word, she turned and made her way down the steps. She set off along the road without looking back and was soon lost from view.

Anna headed indoors, her heart leaden, the foreboding sensation that had weighed down on her for the last several weeks now more overpowering than ever. She told herself Katie didn't *know* anything – not for certain. She had, with good reason, spent thirty-odd years nurturing her resentment towards her mother and had deemed that to be sufficient proof of her guilt, despite the absence of any concrete evidence.

And yet, Anna could hardly pretend this was the first time she'd had second thoughts about her role in securing Sandra's release. A kernel of doubt had been growing in her mind – had been present, in fact, since long before the breakthrough that had led to the conviction being overturned. She'd ignored it at the time, but now, thanks to Katie's intervention, it was staring her in the face once more.

Hadn't she herself considered, at least briefly, the possibility that there had been an accomplice? What if Sandra *had* somehow orchestrated the murders without carrying them out in person?

Her mobile, which she'd left in the office when she came down to answer the door, began to ring. Cursing, she scrambled up the stairs and snatched it up before it rang out.

'Hello?'

'Anna? Oh, thank God. I've been trying to get hold of you. It's Simone – Oscar's mum.'

She sounded even more breathless than Anna. Panicked, too, a note of pronounced urgency in her voice.

'Simone, slow down. What's happened?'

'Oh Anna, it's bad – it's really bad. I realise it's no excuse, but I swear, I only turned my back for a second—'

'Simone,' snapped Anna, both exasperated by the other woman's dithering and, at the same time, feeling a sensation of cold dread creeping over her, 'will you just tell me what happened?'

'I'm so sorry. It's Jack. He's gone.'

45

The Skoda roared to a stop at Simone's front gate. Anna scrambled out, leaving the door swinging. A police car was already parked in the driveway, but Anna barrelled past it and slammed straight through the front door without knocking. Simone was standing in the hallway, wringing her hands as she faced two police officers. As Anna barged in, one of them moved to head her off.

'I'm his fucking mother,' she snapped, and he backed off immediately, cowed by her unfiltered rage.

'Anna...' Simone's face was streaked with tears.

'Where is he?' Anna demanded, coming to a halt in front of her and resisting the urge to grab hold of her with both hands and shake her like a rag-doll. 'Where is my son?'

The tale came out in fits and starts as Simone fought back fresh tears. Jack and Oscar had spent most of the morning indoors, playing upstairs with Oscar's Tonka trucks. When their novelty had worn off, Simone had let them out into the back garden to continue their games in the fresh air. She'd kept an eye on them for a while, but they seemed to be getting on like gangbusters, and when the front doorbell rang with her weekly shopping delivery, she saw no harm in leaving them briefly unattended.

'I swear to you,' she sobbed, 'they were out of my sight for less than two minutes – but it was long enough. When I got back, Oscar was there, but there was no sign of Jack.'

She paused to wipe her eyes on her sleeve. 'I thought at first he might be hiding. But I checked everywhere, and Oscar said they hadn't been playing hide and seek. When I asked him where Jack was then, he just said he was gone.' She gazed at Anna tearfully. 'You have to believe me, I am so, *so* sorry. I never imagined anything like this could happen.'

Anna ignored her words point blank. An apology was of no use to her now, and she was afraid that, if she allowed herself to dwell on Simone's culpability, she wouldn't be held responsible for her actions. There'd be ample time for recriminations later.

'Have you searched the other nearby gardens?' she asked the two policemen. 'The neighbouring streets?'

'It's in hand,' said the one who'd moved to intercept her when she first arrived. 'We've got officers going door to door.'

'And Oscar? Where's he?'

'In the living room.' Simone gestured to the door at the end of the hall corridor. 'My next-door neighbour came over to sit with him.'

'Have you questioned him?' Anna asked the PC.

'Not yet. We're waiting for an officer trained in interviewing child witnesses to get here.'

'It doesn't take a fucking expert,' said Anna.

Then, before anyone could stop her, she strode past Simone and barged into the living room.

A fair-haired boy about the same age as Jack was sitting on the sofa next to a woman in her seventies. Still wearing an apron which bore traces of flour, she'd evidently dropped what she was doing to answer Simone's summons. She rose as Anna approached, clearly reading hostile intent in her, but Anna ignored her, making a beeline for Oscar instead.

'What happened?' she demanded, coming to a halt in front of him. 'I want to know everything.'

Oscar merely stared up at her in wide-eyed silence.

Behind her, Simone burst into the room, followed by the two officers. None of them attempted to intervene, however. All three seemed to sense that Anna was in no mood to be trifled with.

Anna dropped to her haunches, bringing her face level with Oscar's. 'Now you listen to me,' she said, keeping her voice low and gazing straight into his eyes, determined to let him know she meant business. 'You're going to tell me what happened out there in the garden, and you're going to tell me now. Where's Jack?'

Oscar stuck out his bottom lip, his brows knitting together into a frown that, under any other circumstances, would have looked comical.

'Not s'posed to tell.'

Anna stared at him. 'What do you mean?'

Oscar said nothing.

'Please. He's my little boy.'

Still no response.

'WHERE IS HE?'

She grabbed him by the arm and squeezed it tight, causing him to yelp.

'Don't hurt him!' Simone wailed. Anna didn't turn, but she sensed movement behind her and knew she had seconds before either she or one of the officers reached her.

'The man!' Oscar wailed.

A tendril of dread snaked its way up Anna's spine. She let go of Oscar's arm.

'What?' she managed to whisper.

'The man,' Oscar repeated. 'He came and taked Jack away.'

Anna gulped down the bile that had risen in her throat. '*What* man?'

'The man with lady hair.'

A sudden image leapt into Anna's head of a figure gazing up at the detached bungalow atop a small hill, his long, Charles Manson-esque hair fluttering slightly in the breeze. She heard, too, the words Katie Morton had spoken to her not half an hour earlier.

'Even if she wasn't there in person, even if she didn't physically strike the blows herself, she made it happen. Don't ask me how I know, and don't ask me how she did it, but she did.'

'Oh God…'

She let go of Oscar's arm and sank to her knees, no longer possessing the strength to keep herself upright. As she knelt there on the floor, her entire world crumbling to dust around her, she heard one of the officers speaking into his radio.

'You'd better send backup – right away.'

As soon as she'd recovered sufficiently to form coherent words, Anna laid out, to the two infuriatingly slow on the uptake officers, her theory that Sandra Morton and the long-haired stranger had committed the Hillend

Murders in tandem and, for reasons she dared not guess, had now abducted Jack. They nodded and took copious notes but, to her mind, seemed to have little conception of the gravity of the situation. A part of her recognised that what she was telling them sounded like nonsense – in fact, quite possibly *was* nonsense. But her patience for anything less than full and immediate cooperation was non-existent, and her efforts to compel them to take her seriously grew increasingly frantic and expletive-filled, even as the rational part of her mind knew she was skirting dangerously close to being arrested herself.

She was busy explaining that any existing photos of Sandra on file would be useless, as her appearance had changed considerably, when Zoe arrived on the scene. Anna had tried calling her several times en route to the house, eventually giving up and leaving her a voicemail which she'd just had to hope made sense. Zoe, it seemed, had well and truly got the message. She made it as far as the living room doorway before bursting into tears, throwing her arms round Anna and clinging to her for dear life.

Before long, Simone's house was milling with police – mostly uniformed, but there were a couple of plain-clothes CID officers present too. Even if they weren't buying what she was telling them, the abduction of a toddler by an unknown man, long-haired *or* short, had evidently spurred an all-hands-on-deck approach. One of the plain-clothes officers, a glamorous, heavily tanned woman in her late thirties, with a well-cut trouser suit and hair pulled back into a tight ponytail, introduced herself to Anna as DCI Vanessa Tope and informed her that she would be taking charge of the case.

'We're conducting a top-to-bottom search of the house,' she explained, 'and, with your permission, I'd like to send a team to do the same to yours. You're within your rights to refuse, but it's best practice in cases of suspected child abduction.'

'Do whatever you have to,' said Anna. Her voice sounded strange in her own ears, as if someone else was doing the talking.

'Thank you. It would also be extremely helpful if you could provide us with a recent photo of Jack, and … ' She hesitated, her eyes dropping to the floor momentarily. 'Forgive me, but I'd also like your permission to take an item belonging to him so we can get a DNA sample. A comb or a toothbrush would be ideal.'

Her tan had to be fake, Anna thought. There was no way anyone living in Glasgow achieved that sort of complexion without liberal use of spray or time in a sun-bed. She wondered if the police code of conduct had anything to say about excessive tanning, then wondered why she was fixating on such irrelevant details at a time like this.

You know exactly why, Anna. Because it keeps your mind off you-know-what.

'Sure,' she said. 'Whatever you need. Take everything.'

She was aware of handing over her house keys, but once again it seemed to be someone else doing it, not her.

'Chris.' DCI Tope beckoned to the other CID officer – a young man with pockmarked cheeks and a prominent Adam's apple. 'I want you to find out Sandra Morton's current address and dispatch a squad car there to detain her. I don't care whose legs you have to break.'

Chris gave a nod and hurried off.

Tope turned to Anna and Zoe, who were sitting side by side on the couch, Zoe dabbing at her eyes with a sodden tissue. 'I'm going to have a chat with Oscar and his mum now; see if I can get anything more out of him. For now, I'd like the two of you to stick around, OK?'

Anna nodded. She had no intention of going anywhere. Simone had made herself scarce, taking Oscar up to the playroom to keep out of the way. Anna thought it was probably for the best. The mood she was in, she'd probably have decked the idiotic woman if she'd had to breathe the same air as her for a second longer.

Beside her, Zoe sniffed loudly and muttered a tearful profanity to herself. Anna slipped an arm round her and squeezed her shoulder.

'It's OK,' she said. 'It's all going to be OK.'

Why the hell was *she* the one comforting *Zoe*? It was all arse-backwards. She wished she could cry. Wished she could do all the things that were expected of a parent who found themselves in her situation. It was every mother's worst nightmare – or so the cliché went. Anna had no desire to dispute that, but she was acutely aware that her emotional response was, so far, woefully lacking. There was anger, yes, and awful, bone-chilling fear – but more than anything, she yearned for the release provided by a full-bodied breakdown, with tears and snot and eardrum-shattering keening.

What must they all think of her?

Next to her, Zoe gave another sniff.

Anna turned to her. 'What film did you see?'

Zoe blinked at her in teary surprise. 'Wh-what?'

'Film. You were at the cinema.'

'Oh, right,' said Zoe, as if this was a perfectly reasonable conversation to be having right now. 'Cannae remember. It was shite anyway.'

Hearing footsteps, they both looked up to see Vanessa Tope approaching, armed with an iPad.

'I want you to have a look at this,' she said, passing the tablet to Anna. 'One of the residents further along the street has CCTV at their front door.'

She tapped an icon on the screen, and Anna watched as the footage began to play. It showed a high-angle view of a front porch, the street visible behind it. For several seconds, there was nothing to see – just the large, blocky compression artefacts changing every now and then as the image refreshed. Then she saw them: two figures, walking hand in hand along the pavement beyond the low garden wall. One was a tall, lanky man wearing a bomber jacket, his long hair trailing down his back to below his shoulder-blades. The other was a small, dark-haired boy. To the unenlightened observer, they could easily have been father and son. Anna, though, stared at the image in silent dread. Beside her, Zoe let out a soft moan.

'Is that your son?' asked Tope.

'Yes,' Anna managed to whisper.

'And do you recognise the man he's with?'

'No,' said Anna, though that wasn't strictly true. Though she'd never laid eyes on him before in her life, it was as if he'd strode fully formed out of her subconscious. Somehow, he looked exactly like the figure she'd so often imagined stalking the lanes of Hillend in the days prior to the murders.

And now he had her son.

Retrieving the iPad from Anna, Tope summoned a couple of uniforms and spoke to them in a low, urgent tone. She'd just sent them on their way when Chris, the CID detective she'd dispatched earlier, appeared in the doorway, his expression grave. He beckoned to Tope, who excused herself and headed over to join him. The pair of them held a furtive exchange in the hallway outside. Anna tried to read their lips but soon gave up.

'What are they saying?' said Zoe, addressing no one in particular. She was staring, glassy-eyed, at the two detectives.

A moment later, the pair appeared to come to a decision and approached the sofa together, their expressions grave.

'Anna,' said Tope, after an agonising pause, 'Sandra Morton is dead.'

46

They'd found her lying on the kitchen floor of the temporary flat in Edinburgh where she'd been staying for the last six weeks. She'd been stabbed multiple times with a sharp, pointed blade – possibly a carving knife, though a more definitive pronouncement would have to wait until the post-mortem. Defensive wounds on her hands indicated that she'd put up a fight, but the degree of blood loss meant that death would have been quick and inevitable – likely in the space of a couple of minutes. There was no sign of a break-in, suggesting that she'd let her attacker in voluntarily. An initial estimate placed the time of death at roughly twenty-four hours prior to discovery.

Whatever sense of urgency the hunt for Jack and his abductor had previously possessed was now magnified tenfold. The working hypothesis was that his abductor and Sandra Morton's killer were one in the same, and that, given the historic eyewitness accounts of a man matching his description and the strikingly similar nature of the killings, he had also been the true perpetrator of the murders of Guy, Iain and Gabriel Morton. Additional forces were drafted in, the search area was widened, and an all-points bulletin was issued to every on-duty police officer in the Central Belt. DCI Tope vetoed the suggestion of a televised appeal on the grounds that it was likely to do more harm than good. The suspect was believed to have killed multiple times already, including within the past twenty-four hours. The last thing they wanted to do was spook him into doing something rash.

At Anna's insistence, Tope also phoned Pamela Macklin personally to inform her about what had happened. Anna couldn't face making the call herself. She had enough on her plate as it was without having to coddle the flaky solicitor.

As evening fell, Anna and Zoe returned home to wait for news. The police had finished searching the house and, realistically, there was nothing to keep Anna at Simone's. Tope offered to have a family liaison officer sit with them, but Anna refused. The last thing she wanted right now was a stranger floating around the place, serving up trite platitudes and cups of tea. She didn't even really want Zoe there, so desperate was she to be alone with her thoughts, but she knew she could hardly turf her out – especially not with her hurting every bit as much as Anna herself, if not more. So she tolerated her presence and her near-constant sniffling, which every now and then gave way to fresh floods of tears.

Anna sat on the sofa, hunched forward, gnawing on a thumbnail. She'd moved on from blaming Simone. If she wanted to apportion responsibility, then it lay squarely at her own door. No one had forced her to send Jack to play with Oscar. Indeed, had she not had serious misgivings about these sorts of forced socialisation experiments all along? She should have stuck to her guns and kept him home. But no – it had been easier to give in to the pressure to do the sociable thing; to attempt to enforce normality on her strange son. And, if she was being honest with herself, a part of her had been only too glad to have him out from under her feet so she could get on with writing that bloody book of hers undisturbed.

She sighed. Who was she kidding? It had nothing to do with any of that. The real reason, the root cause of all her current problems, lay in her decision to accept Sandra Morton's offer to stand in for Martina Macdonald that Tuesday afternoon back at the beginning of March, and her subsequent decision to embark on an obsessive quest to exonerate her.

She'd caused this. It was her fault, no one else's. All of it.

Time passed. 8 p.m. came and went. Neither of them had eaten anything, but food was the last thing on their minds. Eventually, Zoe, worn out after all her crying, fell into an unsettled form of sleep at one end of the sofa while Anna, wide awake and on high alert, kept vigil at the other.

The shadows continued to lengthen outside. There were still a couple of hours to go until the sun was due to set, but it had already disappeared behind dark, heavy clouds and the world had assumed a grey, colourless veneer, like a living death. Rain couldn't be far off. Inside the living room, the atmosphere had become positively funereal, but Anna didn't get up to put on the lights. There didn't seem any point.

Her phone, lying on the coffee table, began to vibrate. Immediately, she snatched it up and checked the screen. *Number withheld.*

'Hello?'

'That Anna?'

'Yes.'

'Know who *I* am?'

The voice belonged to a man – deep, gruff and, judging by the flattened vowels and glottal stops, unmistakably working class.

'No,' she began. Then, as realisation dawned, and the image of a long-haired man in a bomber jacket formed in her mind, she drew in a shallow breath.

'Yes,' she said quietly. 'Yes, I know who you are.'

'You at home?'

'Yes.'

'Anyone with you?'

She glanced at Zoe, whose eyelids flickered slightly, then became still once more.

'Just my friend.'

'Burd with the red hair?'

Is he close by? Has he been watching us all this time?

'Yes.' She paused; then, to convey that they could speak openly, added, 'She's sleeping.'

'No polis, then?'

'No.' She'd managed to restrain herself until now, answering his questions without asking any of her own. Now, however, she blurted out the one thing she'd wanted to know since she'd realised who she was talking to. 'My son – is he—'

'He's just hunky-dory. And if you're wanting him to stay that way, you're gonnae do exactly as I say. Understood?'

'Understood.' She swallowed heavily.

'Good. I want you to come to the old hospital off Dumbarton Road. Know the one I mean?'

'The Western Infirmary.' She was already on her feet, making ready to leave.

'Aye, that one. Head up the road left of the gatehouse and go straight. Bring the car. That's important. And leave your mobile behind. Got it?'

'Got it.'

'Oh, and one other thing. If I see a bunch of polis arriving instead of you, or I get so much as a sniff of you having brought backup … I'll cut his fucking throat. You know I'll do it, don't you?'

Virtually decapitated.

'I'll be alone,' she managed to say.

'Good. You've got ten minutes.'

The line went dead.

Anna didn't think. Thinking could get Jack killed. She sprang straight into action, grabbing her car keys and shoving them into her pocket. Her phone, she switched to silent and jammed behind one of the cushions on the sofa. She was shrugging on her jacket when she heard a voice behind her.

'What's happening?'

She turned to see Zoe sitting up and blinking in confusion.

'It's nothing. Go back to sleep.'

'Where are ye goin'?'

'Nowhere. Just out. Don't worry about it.'

'Out?' Zoe repeated in disbelief. 'Now? Why?'

'I …' She racked her brain for a plausible explanation and came up blank. 'Look, I need to be alone for a bit, OK? Don't ask. Just let me be.'

'At a time like *this*?'

Anna's patience failed her. 'Yes, at a time like this,' she snapped. 'Just go back to sleep, all right?'

Zoe said nothing. She simply stared at Anna, wounded and baffled in equal measure. Anna turned on her heel and walked out without another word. She hated herself for it, but she couldn't risk dropping so much as a cryptic hint to Zoe as to what she was doing. Jack's life depended on it.

She left the house. As she hurried round the corner to where the Skoda was parked, it began to rain.

* * *

The Western Infirmary had closed its doors for good a few years back and was currently scheduled for demolition, though the actual date kept being pushed back. What remained of the once busy hospital was a sprawling cluster of buildings, constructed at different points over the previous two centuries, now augmented by a seemingly random assortment of temporary fencing that, as far as Anna could see, was intended more for show than to actually keep anyone out. She'd heard about urban explorers venturing into the bowels of the old hospital, seeking whatever thrill it was that compelled them to do such things, but the appeal of such feats of recklessness was utterly lost on her. She hoped Jack and his abductor weren't *inside* one of the buildings. If they were, she'd have the threat of falling masonry and Christ knows what else to contend with on top of the fact that her son was in the hands of a deranged child-killer.

She turned off Dumbarton Road and followed the road past the gatehouse towards the multi-storey 'Phase 1' block – an austere granite affair from the sixties, rendered even more unattractive by its array of broken or boarded up windows. She followed the road till she came to the old underground car park, now fenced off, and brought the Skoda to a standstill. She had no idea where she was meant to go now. Was she supposed to continue following the road uphill to the main campus, or was this as far as Jack's abductor expected her to come? Her eyes darted this way and that, taking in all the nooks and crannies where someone might be able to hide. Nothing.

She'd just resolved to drive on when, out of the corner of her eye, she spotted movement beyond the fence: two figures, one tall, one short, holding hands as they emerged from the shadows of the car park. The tall one wore a bomber jacket and a baseball cap, the brim pulled down low to obscure his face. The smaller figure, looking none the worse for his ordeal, was Jack.

Anna lurched out of the car. Even as she did so, Jack spotted her, his face lighting up with surprise and delight.

'Mummy!'

She hurried towards them, only to be brought to a crashing halt by the fence separating them. She cast around desperately, searching for some way round it, before finally noticing a small gap between two sections. By the time she'd squeezed through, Jack had scrambled free of the man's grasp and was barrelling towards her in his characteristic bow-legged gait. Dropping to her knees, she threw her arms around him and held him close.

'Are you all right?' she choked, continuing to press him to her. 'You're not hurt, are you?'

'No,' said Jack, a note of irritation in his voice at what he clearly regarded as a total overreaction.

Anna lifted her head as the man in the baseball cap strode over to them, the trace of a leering grin on his gaunt, greyish features. She guessed he was probably about the same age as her, but he looked so much older, especially around the eyes.

'We've been having a grand old time, me and Jackie-boy,' he said, with what sounded like wry amusement. 'Been hanging out all day, so we have, exploring old buildings and playing peekaboo with the boys in blue. Said I was an old pal of his mammy's ~ that she'd asked me to keep an eye on him for the day. That no right?' He gave her an expectant look.

Anna, still clutching Jack, glared up at him with undisguised hatred. 'That's right.'

'And I told him his mammy promised she was gonnae help me out with a wee problem I've been having. Right?'

'Right,' said Anna again, wondering just what the hell she was agreeing to.

'Good. Knew you wouldnae let me down.' He grinned again, flashing a row of uneven, yellowed teeth. 'Right, that's more than enough time for catch-up. Best be making tracks. We've a schedule to stick to.'

Seizing Anna by the collar of her jacket, he pulled her to her feet – not particularly roughly, but firmly enough to make it clear he meant business. As if she'd ever been in any doubt.

'Let's go.'

Slipping one arm through hers, he seized Jack's hand with the other and flashed him a grin and a wink. Jack, returning the grin, happily fell into step with them. Anna briefly wondered whether, if she snatched Jack and made a break for it, she could get to the street and raise the alarm before the man had time to respond, before swiftly disavowing herself of the notion. Jack was still alive because, so far, she'd played the game that had been set for her. She'd succeeded in earning a degree of trust from his kidnapper. It was in both their interests for that to continue for as long as possible.

They squeezed through the gap in the fence, the man keeping a tight hold on both Anna and Jack the entire time, and made their way to the car. As he walked, his eyes skittered nervously left and right, but the handful of pedestrians in the street were too busy hurrying to get out of the rain to pay them any attention.

They came to a halt in front of the Skoda.

'Nice ride,' said the man. 'Got a full tank of petrol in her?'

'Close enough.'

'Good. Got a bit of a trek ahead of us.'

'Look.' Anna turned to face him. 'If it's the car you want, take it. It's yours. Here.'

She tried to hand him the keys, but he batted her hand away.

'Nice of you to offer, but it's gonnae have to be a no.'

She gazed at him imploringly, drinking in the flaky skin; the sunken, hollow eyes. He looked like he hadn't slept in days.

'Please. I've done what you asked. Just let us go.'

He looked almost regretful. 'No that easy, though, is it? Where we're headed, your part's kind of essential.' He gave her a light shove. 'C'mon – clock's ticking.'

She was forced to admit defeat. 'Come on, Trouble,' she said, trying to sound upbeat. 'You can ride up front with me.'

She extended her hand, beckoning to Jack, but his abductor held him tight, halting him in his tracks.

'Nice try, but nae chance. He'll be happy enough in the back with his Uncle Sean – won't ya, kiddo?'

Jack looked from his mother to the man with whom he'd spent the last several hours, evidently torn. Anna, dreading what would happen if she continued to resist, gave way.

'Do as he says, Jack,' she told him, her heart in her boots.

They bundled into the car – Anna in the front, Jack and the man calling himself Sean in the back.

'Seatbelt,' Sean ordered Jack.

Jack obediently buckled up. The grown-ups did likewise. Anna looked to the rearview mirror, her eyes meeting Sean's.

'Where are we going?'

'Down to the street and start heading east.'

'And then?'

'You'll find out soon enough. Now drive.'

She turned the key in the ignition.

47

They drove on through Finnieston and Anderston, then south across the Kingston Bridge, following the M8 past the suburbs south of the Clyde and on towards the open country. Jack, apparently worn out by his big adventure, soon fell asleep, his head resting on the window. Once they were free of the city, Sean removed his cap and shook out his long hair – an act which, judging by his sigh of satisfaction, he found profoundly liberating. Anna had an inkling as to where they might be headed – an inkling which grew into near certainty as they passed Newton Mearns and continued south down the M77 into Ayrshire – but it wasn't until they were approaching Kilmarnock, some thirty minutes after they'd set out, that she finally decided to risk a direct question.

'We're going to Cairnryan, aren't we?'

Sean said nothing.

'You're trying to catch the ferry to Belfast. I'm right, aren't I?'

Again, no response, but his eyes in the rearview mirror smouldered dangerously, and she knew she was right. It was so obvious as to practically be a cliché: across the water to Northern Ireland, then over the frictionless border to the Republic – and then, presumably, on to mainland Europe to disappear without a trace.

'Look, I'm not trying to trick you. Believe me, I want you to be on your way and out of our hair just as soon as humanly possible. That's why you need to know you can't just turn up at the terminal and buy a ticket over the counter.'

Sean's brows furrowed uncertainly. 'You ... you can't?'

'You need to book in advance. Do you even know if there's a crossing scheduled for tonight?'

Sean hesitated. 'No,' he finally admitted, sounding slightly sheepish.

'If you want my advice,' said Anna, her confidence rising slightly now that, for the first time, she felt she had some measure of leverage over the situation, 'you'll call them now and make sure there's a ferry leaving Cairnryan tonight and that they have room for you on board, then book yourself a place on it.' She looked at him expectantly in the mirror. 'Well, *I* can't do it. You made me leave my phone at home, remember?'

Sean continued to frown, and for a moment she feared she'd pushed things too hard and that he was going to snap. A moment later, though, he reached into his pocket and took out an old Nokia phone with a cracked screen. He held it out towards her.

'You make the call.'

'Why me?'

He shrugged irritably. 'You talk better.'

He continued to hold the phone out to her. Their eyes met in the mirror once more.

'Fine,' she said. 'Let me find a spot to pull over.'

Parked on the hard shoulder, Anna took the phone from Sean and began to tap at the screen. Eventually, she found what she was looking for: a contact number for P&O Ferries. She keyed the number in and put the phone to her ear. As the ringing tone began to sound, Sean tapped her on the shoulder.

'Put it on speakerphone. Book a car ticket for yourself and one for the kid.'

She nodded stiffly, any faint hope she'd been clinging to that she and Jack would be able to simply wave him off at the gate evaporating. She'd long since given up trying to predict all the different – and mostly unbearably grim – ways this might end.

'You're in luck,' the bubbly operator cheerfully informed her. 'We still have a few spaces available on the 23:00 to Belfast. Will you be paying by card?'

Anna looked at Sean. He merely shrugged.

Feeling unaccountably irked by the fact that, not content with having abducted her son and now her, he apparently expected her to fork out from her own pocket to fund his flight from justice, Anna recited her credit card details, thanked the operator and hung up while she was in the process of telling her to *have a nice—*

'Top marks,' said Sean, taking the phone back from her.

'Thanks,' she said, without feeling.

They set off again, continuing down the A77 towards Cairnyran, the tiny village on Scotland's southwestern coast just north of Stranraer, whose two ferry ports served as the country's primary link to the island of Ireland. Glancing at him in the rearview mirror, Anna noticed that Sean was no longer watching her as intently as before. Indeed, he seemed to have relaxed somewhat and had taken to gazing out of the window, watching the countryside passing in the fading light. She decided to risk another question.

'Out of interest, how did you get my phone number?'

Sean stirred from whatever thoughts had been occupying him. For a moment, he looked confused, as if he hadn't understood the question.

'Got it off your wee boy,' he said, as if it was obvious. 'I asked him if he knew his mammy's number and he reeled it off, just like that. S'one smart cookie you got there.'

'I know,' said Anna quietly. It was just like the business with the train timetables. *Mind like a steel trap.*

Another five minutes elapsed. A sign went sailing past them: *Maybole – 7, Girvan – 19, Stranraer – 49.* They'd be there in less than an hour.

'Why us?' Anna broke the silence again.

'Huh?'

'You could have picked anyone, but you chose me and my son. Why?'

For a moment, Sean didn't respond. Then, as she glanced at his reflection in the mirror, she saw the papery skin at the corners of his eyes crinkle into something approaching amusement.

'You know who I am, don't you?'

'I think so,' said Anna, trying to make sense of this non-sequitur. 'You're the person who killed Guy Morton and his two infant sons.' *And his wife Sandra,* she thought – but, for some reason, thought it better not to add.

The expression on Sean's face somehow managed to fall equally between irritation and amusement. 'Aye, but do you know who I *am*?'

It took Anna a moment to understand what he was actually asking her.

'I think,' she said carefully, 'you and Sandra Morton entered into some kind of pact. You'd kill her family for her, giving her the perfect alibi. Only things didn't go to plan and she ended up going to prison while you slipped off the radar.'

'Until you got her out.'

'Until I got her out,' Anna agreed. The reminder of her role in all of this was like lemon juice rubbed into a fresh wound.

'I seen you with her,' Sean went on, 'in that café in Edinburgh. You and her and that lawyer burd. I had no idea who you were, so I followed you. Scoped out your house, watched you with your boy and that ginger lassie who stays with you. A nice wee happy family.'

Anna suppressed a shudder. How long had he been watching them? How long had he been waiting to put his plan into action?

'She always said …' Sean's voice, wavering with emotion, interrupted her thoughts. 'She always said, if anything went wrong, if one of us was ever caught, we'd say nothing about the other, so they'd have nothing to pin on us. So I kept quiet. I kept quiet for twenty years, waiting for her. And then, when I heard the news she was out, I was over the moon. I thought we were gonnae be together. I waited, and I waited, and … nothing. She never came for me. She knew where to find me, but she never came. So I went looking for *her*.'

Anna said nothing. As eager as she was to hear this story, she sensed that this act of unloading was more for his benefit than for hers.

'It wasnae that hard tracking her down – not really. I set up camp outside her lawyer's office and followed her whenever I seen her coming out. After a couple of days, she led me right to her door. She was forever running back and forth to her, like she was her personal messenger. I still held back, but. I figured she must've a good reason for keeping her distance – like, mibby she thought the polis were still tailing her, hoping she'd lead 'em to me or something. But after a while I realised there was no one following her but me while she flounced around, living the life of Riley. Come yesterday, I'd had my fill, so I marched right up to her flat and chapped on her door.

'Right from the get-go, I knew she wasnae too thrilled to see me. First, she pretended she didnae know who I was – like I believed that for a *second.* Then, when she could see that wasnae gonna wash, she hauled me inside and went on this rant about how anyone could've seen me and how dare I show my face after all this time. She just kept going on and on, telling me how I was useless. How I'd let her rot in the jail for eighteen years. I asked her what I was supposed to have done. Well, she didnae like me asking her that, cos she didnae have an answer.

'She mentioned *you,*' he suddenly said, and Anna's eyes snapped up from the road to the rearview mirror.

'What?'

'Aye – I asked her who was that wumman with the dark hair I seen her being so pally with in the café. And she looked dead at me and gave this sneering kinda laugh and said, "Her? She was more help to me than you ever were. She put her nose to the grindstone and got me out while you were off playing with your dick." And so ... ' He trailed off.

'And so you saw red,' said Anna quietly.

Sean nodded, eyes downcast. 'I never thought. I just acted. We were standing in the kitchen and there was this knife on the counter. She'd been chopping carrots when I showed up. And next thing I know, it's in my hand and I'm pointing it at her and she gives me this look – like, to say, "We both know you havnae got the balls to *use* that." And she starts *laughing* – like, standing there, hands on hips, throwing back her head and cackling, like I'm the most pathetic thing she ever seen.'

He sucked in a strained breath. 'And then ... and then it all gets dead hazy. I 'member running down the steps. I 'member washing the blood off my hands in the fountain. I 'member the moment it hit me what I done, and dropping to my knees right in the middle of the street. My legs just gave way under me, like they couldnae hold me up a second longer. And I 'member just kneeling there, greeting like a wean while folk just walked on by, like they'd seen it all before.' He shook his head vehemently, fresh tears glistening in his eyes. 'It never had to end that way. She never had to make me do it.'

Anna tightened her grip on the wheel in an attempt to quell the tremor in her hands. She really hadn't needed such a vivid reminder of what the man sitting behind her, next to her son, was capable of, and the knowledge that his attack on Sandra had been largely outwith his control did nothing to quell her fears as to what he might be capable of doing to her or Jack.

She suspected she'd have felt more reassured if he'd claimed it had been a completely rational, premeditated act.

She became aware that Sean had begun speaking again. 'I needed to disappear before someone found the body. All it'd take would be someone to say they seen me going into the building, and I'd be fucked. Then I thought of you and the kid. And I got this idea. I knew it was a long shot, but I was desperate. So I bided my time. I staked out your house, just like I done before, and this morning I saw you leaving with your boy and dropping him off at his pal's. And then, when the pair of them came out into the garden, I thought, *Now's my chance*.

'I just walked right in and said to Jack I was a friend of his mammy's; that she couldnae come and get him herself so she sent me instead. He was only too happy to come away with me. He said, "Good. It's boring here and Oscar's a pure fanny."' Sean's eyes crinkled in amusement as Anna's darted to the mirror once more. 'He said that. Those were his exact words. Damn near creased myself laughing. I told Oscar not to breathe a word to his mammy, then I took Jack by the hand and just walked out with him. Easy as that.'

Anna swallowed heavily. Under different circumstances, she too would have seen the humour in Jack's obvious Zoe-ism. Right now, though, laughter was the furthest thing from her mind. *Easy as that.* If the two of them got out of this – no, she told herself, *when* they got out of this – they were going to have a serious conversation about going off with strange men.

'What I don't understand,' she said after a moment, 'is how Sandra convinced you to kill her husband and the twins for her. How on earth did she have *that* much leverage over you?'

It didn't matter, of course – not in any practical sense. But she was searching for something – *anything* – to distract herself from dwelling on hers and Jack's plight, and filling in the blanks seemed as good a way as any to keep her mind occupied.

'Cos they were in our way,' said Sean, as if it was obvious.

'In your way?'

'Aye. She couldn't leave 'em. She'd've had nothing. It was all in his name – the bank accounts, the deeds to the house, all of it. He made sure of that. And it's not as if *I* had twa pennies to rub together. But if they died, she'd've inherited the lot. More than enough for us to start over someplace fresh. She said I just needed to help her get rid of them and we could be together.' He shrugged. 'So that's what I done.'

'Just like that?'

His eyes flared angrily. 'Aye, just like that. You don't know what it's like to grow up with nothing. Born with a silver spoon in your mouth, handed everything on a plate … Well, it wasn't like that for me. Passed from pillar to post – foster home after foster home, then kicked to the kerb at eighteen with nothing but a "good luck, sonny, you're gonnae need it".'

'Plenty of people grow up with nothing,' Anna retorted. 'They don't all end up murdering defenceless toddlers in their beds just because the woman they're shagging told them to do it.'

Shut up. Shut UP.

'Shagging?' Sean stared at her in open-mouth amazement. 'You think we were *shagging*?'

'Well, you were lovers, weren't you? I don't exactly imagine you were saving yourselves till after the ground was clear.'

A look of dry amusement crossed his face. 'No,' he said softly, his lips curling in a sardonic smile. 'We weren't lovers.'

'What, then?'

'You really haven't worked it out?'

She opened her mouth to say no, but the word caught in her throat. Like a key finally slotting into place after a long and fruitless effort to make it fit, she suddenly saw everything with crystal clarity. His age; his experience of the care system; the hold Sandra had apparently had over him; his resentment towards her family, especially the children …

'Oh Christ,' she breathed, 'she was your mother.'

Sean smiled. 'Bingo.'

'She never had the abortion. She had you and then gave you up.'

'Lucky me, huh?'

'And then, when you were older, you tracked her down and she—'

'She promised me a future together, if I'd just help her get rid of her *new* family first.' He gave another ugly, humourless smile. 'Funny how things never work out how you planned 'em, in't it?'

'So you murdered three innocent people for her,' said Anna, 'then waited for her for eighteen years, only for her to throw it all back in your face. Sounds like it was totally worth it.'

'Aye, well,' Sean muttered, 'if I hadnae lost it, mibby she'd've come round.'

'Right.'

She knew she was treading on seriously thin ice, but she couldn't help herself. Try as she might, nothing could erase from her mind the image of Iain and Gabriel lying butchered in their beds.

Virtually decapitated.

'It's fucking true,' Sean snarled, his nostrils flaring. 'She *loved* me.'

Not trusting herself to respond, Anna simply gritted her teeth and kept her eyes on the road so she wouldn't have to look at him in the rearview mirror for a moment longer.

48

They entered Cairnryan a little before 10.30 p.m., and arrived at the ferry port a few short minutes later. Off to the west, barely visible in the darkness that now engulfed their surroundings, Anna saw row after row of lorries and HGVs parked beyond a wire fence. Behind them, the waters of Loch Ryan were a black, impenetrable mass, the Rhins of Galloway barely visible on the distant horizon.

As she turned into the port grounds, following the signs for cars and other small vehicles, she became aware of furtive movement behind her. Glancing up to the mirror, she saw that Sean had lowered his seat into the down position and was in the process of scrambling into the boot. She turned round to face him.

'Not a word,' he hissed.

He held her gaze for a moment, before disappearing behind the seat, pulling it upright behind him.

Swallowing the nausea that was building up inside her, Anna faced forward again and continued to follow the signs. The road ahead was eerily empty. She frowned. Surely they couldn't be the only ones travelling tonight?

As they neared the small kiosk outside the terminal, it suddenly occurred to her that it was entirely possible that Jack's abduction would have triggered an all-ports alert. As far as she knew, it wasn't standard practice in cases of kidnapping unless there was a specific reason to believe the abductor planned to take the child out of the country – a foreign father who'd recently lost a custody battle, for example. However, given the threat to life, she didn't feel confident in ruling *anything* out – in which case, the name 'Scavolini' was bound to set red flags waving. Why couldn't she have had a nice, boring name like Smith?

Willing her pounding heart to settle, she pulled up next to the kiosk, winding down the window as directed by the ruddy-faced clerk inside.

'Evenin', luvvy,' he said jovially. 'Where would you be off to, now?'

'One adult and one infant travelling on the eleven o'clock to Larne,' Anna replied, conscious of how stiff and artificial her voice sounded. 'Tickets are in the name of Scavolini,' she added in a lower voice, as if that would help her slip under the radar.

'Ah, well,' said the clerk, regret etched across his features, 'that might be a bit tricky. See, you've just missed the cut-off.'

Anna glanced at the clock on the dashboard. 22:32.

'But the ferry doesn't leave till eleven!'

The clerk shrugged apologetically. 'Check-in for vehicles closes at ten-thirty on the dot. If I let you through, it's more than my job's worth.'

Anna wasn't sure how much, if any, of this conversation Sean could hear from the boot, but she was in no doubt that, either way, he'd be starting to wonder what was causing the hold-up.

'There's really no way you can make an exception?'

'Rules is rules, I'm afraid.'

She racked her brains, frantically searching for a way out of this.

'My dad's dying,' she blurted out.

'Sorry?'

She wasn't sure where it had come from, but she decided to run with it. 'I just got word this afternoon,' she continued, more than a little breathlessly. 'They don't expect him to last the night. I've not seen him in years. I knew he was sick, but … I kept telling myself I'd have more time, and now …' She gazed up at the clerk imploringly. 'If I don't make it … I mean, what sort of a daughter wouldn't be there for her dad in his final hours?'

The clerk's features crumpled in sympathy. He appeared genuinely torn. Capitalising on the ground she'd gained so far, Anna went in for the kill.

'Please. He's never even met his grandson.' She nodded behind her to the back seat, where Jack continued to slumber, before turning to the clerk with puppy dog eyes.

The clerk hesitated, the expression on his face resembling one of physical pain. Then he groaned heavily.

'Aaargh! There'll be hell to pay, but all right.'

Anna watched, hardly daring to breathe, as he tapped away at the keyboard of his computer terminal.

'Scavolini, you said?'

She nodded tightly. This was it: make or break time.

He tapped a few more keys. A moment later, the printer next to him made a grinding noise and vomited out a ticket.

'Hang that from your rearview mirror,' he instructed her, passing it through the window. 'First on your left, through the gate. Follow the signs, and if anyone gives you any hassle, tell them ... ' He sighed. 'Tell them Barry OK'd it, all right?'

Anna held his gaze, giving him a grateful nod. 'Thanks, Barry. You've no idea what a lifesaver you are.'

'Ah, go on,' he said gruffly, waving her through.

She hurriedly wound up her window and drove on, following the directions through the security gate, where two hi-vis-jacketed men nodded her past with nary a second glance, then on across the lengthy stretch of tarmac. At the other end, she could make out the taillights at the back of the queue of passenger vehicles as it inched its way towards the ferry, a great white behemoth looming against the night sky.

As she drove on, forcing herself to stick to the speed limit and ignore her natural inclination to step on the gas, she heard movement behind her. Glancing up at the mirror, she saw Sean re-emerging from behind the seat.

'Nicely done,' he said, with a smile of grim satisfaction. 'Nearly home and dry.'

They joined the queue and progressed up the ramp towards the back of the ship. A succession of men in hi-vis jackets and helmets waved them down to the lower deck. They came to a halt, sandwiched on every side by other vehicles. Around them, people began to emerge from their cars and head towards the stairs. Automatically, Anna reached for the door handle, ready to follow them.

'*Oh* no.' Sean's hand on her shoulder stopped her in her tracks. 'Just you sit tight. We're fine where we are.'

Anna removed her hand from the door handle. She sat rigid in her seat, staring straight ahead. Around them, their fellow passengers continued to exit their vehicles.

A rap on the window caused Anna to jump. She turned to see one of the ferry workers peering down at her. She wound down the window.

'Can I help you?'

'Ye cannae stay in there, pet,' said the man. 'No passengers in vehicles when the ferry's moving. That's the rules.'

'But—'

'That's – the – rules,' he repeated, enunciating each word carefully.

'Fucksake, just do as he says,' Sean muttered in her ear.

Heart hammering, Anna unbuckled her belt. She got out of the car, watched all the while by the deckhand, who evidently didn't trust her not to get straight back in the moment his back was turned. Sean got out too, pulling on his baseball cap and tugging the brim down low. As he tucked his long hair into the collar of his bomber jacket, Anna squeezed past him and, leaning into the back, shook Jack gently.

'Wakey wakey. Come on, Trouble – you need to get up.'

Jack stirred momentarily, then gave a disgruntled moan and, twisting his body away from her, carried on sleeping.

In the end, she had to physically lift him out of the car. He remained fast asleep – or close enough for it to make no difference – as, carrying him in her arms, she set off towards the nearest set of stairs. Sean was just behind her, his hand on her shoulder, once more putting paid to any thought of escape. They made their way up the narrow staircase behind a sizeable queue of their fellow travellers, none of whom seemed intent on going anywhere in a hurry.

They finally emerged onto the passenger deck, a brightly lit interior space with shops, a food court and other attractions geared towards relieving passengers of their cash, in much the same vein as the duty-free section of an airport. Pressed close to her side, she felt the jerky, impulsive nature of Sean's movements.

''Mon,' he muttered. 'Let's find somewhere quieter.'

They set off along the corridor, threading their way through the throng. Sean kept a tight grip on Anna's arm, his hip brushing against hers with each step. Any casual observer, she thought, would see them simply as a mismatched but undeniably close couple, taking their sleepy child, up long past his bedtime, on a weekend jaunt across the water. Even so, it seemed somehow absurd that no one noticed anything off about them – but then, if the last few months had taught her anything, it was that people could be staggeringly unobservant about those around them. Or perhaps it was more accurate to say they made a conscious effort not to notice the signs, even when they were staring them in the face. Anything for a quiet life.

They'd almost reached the end of the corridor when a voice suddenly rang out behind them.

'Anna? Anna Scavolini?'

Anna and Sean both stopped dead in their tracks. Sean remained stock still, as if he was frozen to the spot, but Anna turned and looked back along the corridor. Her heart sank. Striding in their direction was a familiar figure, her presence as incongruous as it was horrifying.

'It *is* you,' said Pamela Macklin, grinning from ear to ear as she made her way towards them. 'Well I never! What are *you* doing here?'

Fuck, fuck, FUCK, Anna thought as hot panic spread throughout her entire body.

Sean let go of Anna's arm and moved off, tugging the brim of his cap down even lower. He remained within reach of her and Jack, turned slightly away from them so he could pretend to be engrossed in the sign for fire evacuation procedure while keeping his hostages in his sights out of the corner of his eye.

'Pamela!' Anna managed to say as the younger woman drew level with her. '*This* is a surprise. Fancy running into you here.'

'Yeah, just fancy it,' said Pamela, her rictus grin stretching from ear to ear. 'You never told *me* you were planning a late-night cruise to the Emerald Isle.' Her gaze strayed to Jack, continuing to snooze with his head resting on Anna's shoulder. 'And I see you've got Jack with you. That's just grand, so it is.'

'Well,' said Anna, with an over-the-top shrug, 'you know what they say: small world.'

'No kidding!'

They continued to smile at each other, like rivals in a contest to produce the most artificial facial expression. Sean continued to watch them surreptitiously, scratching compulsively at the side of his face.

'So,' Pamela gave an exaggerated shrug of her own, 'I was thinking I'd head up thataway and get myself some scran.' She pointed towards the food court, where a trio of staff members were clustered together in earnest conversation. 'You and Jack fancy tagging along?'

'That might not be possible.'

Pamela's eyes flickered in Sean's direction almost imperceptibly. 'OK, no worries. In that case, I'll just hang out here with you.'

'It might be better if you just walked away,' said Anna, aware than Sean had turned towards them once more.

'Honestly, it's no bother,' said Pamela airily, continuing her charade of clueless amicability. 'I mean,' she gave an exaggerated shrug, 'be a bit weird of me to run into my best pal out of the blue and then not stick around to shoot the breeze.'

'Pamela,' said Anna, forcing the words through clenched teeth, 'I really think you should walk away.'

At that moment, the tense stalemate gave way to a sudden explosion of violent action. Sean lunged at her, snatching Jack from her arms and retreating with him to the far wall, clutching him to his chest like a human shield.

'Get away from me! I'll kill him! I'll fucking kill him!'

Jack, roused instantly from sleep, let out a squeal of panic. Anna saw the glint of a knife in Sean's hand, close to Jack's throat, and stifled a cry of her own.

'I'll do it,' Sean insisted, his grip on Jack tightening. 'I'll fucking do it.'

Every pair of eyes in the immediate vicinity was now on them. More people, alerted by the disturbance, were arriving by the second, including the three crew members from the food court, but none dared approach. Mercifully, they all seemed to understand just what a monumentally catastrophic thing that would be to do, though their presence did nothing to calm Anna's nerves – or, for that matter, Sean's.

'Please,' she managed to say. She took a few steps towards him, hands outstretched to show that she wasn't going to try anything.

'Don't you fucking come a step closer,' Sean snarled, his head buried in Jack's shoulder. Jack continued to wail.

'All right, all right.' Anna halted, hands still spread outward, palms open. 'I'm not moving. See?'

Sean looked around wildly, his eyes darting from one face to another before settling on Anna's once more. 'Why did you have to do it?' There were tears in his eyes as he spoke. 'Why did you have to fuck it all up? We were almost home and dry.'

'Please,' Anna repeated, still not lowering her hands. 'This doesn't have to end badly. Just give him to me.' Her voice dropped to a choking whisper. 'Give me back my little boy.'

'Oh no.' Sean shook his head vigorously. There was a wild light in his eyes which, mingled with the glistening tears, was profoundly unnerving. 'See, I got a better idea. When this boat docks on the other side, I'm gonnae leave, and I'm gonnae take him with me. That's how I'll know you won't so much as *think* of coming after me. Cos you know what I'll do tae him if you do.'

'No,' Anna whispered.

Her own eyes had filled with tears, turning her vision blurry. She cast around wildly, looking for someone to do something, *anything*. But no one moved. Everyone was as rooted to the spot as her. One or two, she dimly registered, were even recording the stand-off on their phones. There was no sign of Pamela. She seemed to have simply disappeared. Jack, terrified beyond all measure, howled at the top of his lungs.

'It'll not be so bad,' Sean went on. It wasn't clear if he was still addressing Anna or if he'd forgotten all about her and was talking to himself, so caught up in the impossible fantasy he was concocting on the hoof. 'Cos see if you leave me alone, I'll take good care of him – swear on my life. I'll show him all the love and affection no one ever showed me, and he'll no want for anything.'

His eyes suddenly fixed on Anna once again, narrowing into accusatory slits. 'You never wanted him. I know you never. *She* told me.'

The words hit Anna right between the shoulder-blades, knocking the breath from her lungs. Even as she felt her knees go weak, though, she sensed movement next to Sean. Unbeknownst to him – and, it seemed, everyone else – Pamela had been inching towards him through the crowd, taking full advantage of the distraction provided by Anna. With a desperate cry, she now flung herself onto him, grappling with him for control of the knife.

Several things happened at once. Jack fell from Sean's arms. Springing into action, Anna dived towards him, throwing herself across the floor like a rugby player going for the ball. She was too late to catch him, but he landed on his feet and immediately ran towards her, arms outstretched. She hauled herself upright and enveloped him in her arms, holding him close.

Pamela and Sean continued to grapple – a mass of flailing limbs, so tangled up that it was difficult to determine where one ended and the other began. Then, a flash of metal. A gasp. Pamela let go of Sean and staggered backwards, a look of confusion on her face. Her hand strayed as far as the hilt of the blade protruding from her lower ribs before she dropped to the ground and lay still.

For a moment, Sean remained standing where he was, unopposed, his expression one of surprise. Then he turned towards Anna, who crouched on the floor, continuing to cling to Jack, gazing up at him with pleading eyes.

Even as he took a step towards them, though, a massive shape flew at him. One of the other passengers – a hulky, musclebound man in a Scotland top and a kilt, who looked like he might well have *been* a rugby player – had tackled him to the floor and was now lying on top of him, using the full force of his weight to prevent him from moving. This proved to be the breaking of the dam, and several more onlookers now rushed forward to assist – some to help hold Sean down, others to attend to Pamela, who lay lifeless on the floor just a couple of feet away.

Gradually, Sean's struggles subsided, the combined weight of the four people attempting to subdue him proving too much for him to fight. Nearby, one of the ship's crew had rolled Pamela onto her back and was performing chest compressions, the blade handle still protruding from just below her left breast, while another stood ready with a portable defibrillator. Where once there had been horrified silence, a hubbub now broke out as those who weren't playing an active role now talked animatedly among themselves, their conversations all, no doubt, variations on the same refrain: *Can you BELIEVE what just happened?*

But to Anna, none of it was important. The only thing that mattered to her, the only thing she cared about, was Jack. She continued to cling to him, her sobs mingling with his, her entire world shrinking to encompass just the two of them.

49

Saturday 8 June

Anna stood on the observation side of the two-way mirror, watching as Sean, having now traded his baseball cap and outdoor clothes for a set of police station issue scrubs, sat alone at a table in the small, noise-proofed interview room. The unnaturally cold overhead lighting gave his pallid skin a bluish tinge and threw into unforgivingly sharp relief the various pockmarks and sores on his face. He was dipping a teabag into a polystyrene cup in exactly the same way she'd seen Sandra perform the manoeuvre – with the string tied around his pinkie.

DCI Vanessa Tope drew alongside Anna, arms folded. 'The story he gave you checks out. His name's Sean Hanlon…though "Sean Morton" might be equally valid. Born in '81, spent his childhood in the care system, then in and out of prison throughout adulthood for various misdemeanours, from petty theft to drug-dealing to assault to injury.' She shook her head. 'Not a happy story.'

'No,' Anna agreed.

She knew she was only here because Vanessa had bent the rules for her – 'from one mother to another,' as the DCI had put it. 'You can look,' she'd said, 'but you stay on this side of the glass.'

A wise precaution, Anna now thought as she watched Sean continuing to dip his teabag in the cup. As harmless as he now looked – a pale, gaunt-looking figure in a securely locked room, no longer a threat to her or anyone else – she knew she wouldn't soon forget the sight of him holding a knife to Jack's throat, or of Pamela lying lifeless on the deck, the blade protruding from between her ribs.

Upon disembarking from the ferry the previous night, she and Jack had been transported to the nearest hospital, where Jack was examined from head to toe. To Anna's undying relief, there was no sign that Sean had interfered with him in any way. In fact, as he informed the physician with a mixture of outrage and pride, he'd even had to wipe his own rectum after he did a shit. He seemed to have recovered from his entire ordeal remarkably quickly, showing a degree of resilience which Anna doubted she would've been capable of at his age.

She realised Vanessa was speaking once more.

'From what I've been able to make out, the situation is this. Sandra Morton *did* become pregnant at fourteen, and she *was* sent away to stay with her aunt in Kyle of Lochalsh – but not to have an abortion. She was already too far gone by the time her condition became known. As soon as she'd given birth, they took the baby from her and turned him over to the state. Her aunt's partner, an obstetrician, pulled all sorts of strings to hush it up. Sean spent the next eighteen years being bounced from pillar to post. Then, when he reached adulthood, he set out to track down his birth mother. It took him close to two years, but in the end he found her. He showed up on her doorstep one day while she was home alone and told her who he was.

'By the sounds of it, she wasn't too thrilled to see him at first. Kept trying to tell him he'd got the wrong person. So he said he'd just wait on the step till her husband got home and see if *he* believed him when he said who he was. After that, she quickly changed her tune.'

'She was already thinking about how she might be able to use him,' said Anna. She could think of no reason why, under any other circumstances, Sandra would have been at all concerned about Guy discovering she'd had another child before her marriage to him.

'Probably,' Vanessa agreed. 'They met in secret for a while. He'd come over to the house while the rest of the family was out, or she'd travel into Gretna or Annan to hook up with him. She told him about how she'd been forced to give him up; how she was stuck in a loveless marriage with kids she couldn't stand. She made it clear to him that, if it wasn't for them, she and him could have a life together.'

'So they hatched a plan. Well, *she* hatched it, probably. I can't picture him coming up with anything so underhanded. She worked it all out, down to the last detail. He'd come in and deal with the family while she was out creating the perfect alibi for herself.' She gave a grim smile. 'If only the 8 Till Late hadn't closed early.'

Anna nodded. 'And if only the attendant on duty at the petrol station hadn't been Paul Kempley.'

'What I don't understand,' said Vanessa, 'is why, given everything we know about the sort of person she was, she would willingly spend eighteen years and potentially the rest of her life in prison to protect a man whom it's pretty clear she was simply using for her own ends.'

'I think I know why,' said Anna quietly. 'Pragmatism. Pure, clinical pragmatism.'

Vanessa turned to her, a single stencilled eyebrow raised questioningly.

'She knew she couldn't finger him for the murders without revealing her own role in planning them – or without *him* revealing it. And that would mean they'd both be held equally culpable. The art and part principle. It wouldn't have improved her situation one iota. In fact, it would have made it worse, because, having as good as admitted responsibility, she'd have no hope of ever appealing her conviction. But as long as the police remained blissfully unaware of his existence, there was still a slim chance that, one day, she might get off – and to her cold, calculating mind, a slim chance was infinitely better than no chance at all.'

What she didn't add, but was only too aware, was that Sandra had played *her* every bit as expertly as she'd played Sean. Katie Morton had been right. She saw that now with agonising clarity. From their very first meeting, every word out of Sandra's mouth had been designed to convince Anna to take up the challenge of proving her innocence. She'd known when to give her encouragement and when to deploy a liberal dose of scepticism, correctly surmising that it would only compel her to work doubly hard to prove her wrong. She'd even, Anna now realised, steered her towards the truth, pressing her to focus her enquiries on the long-haired stranger who even now sat on the other side of the two-way mirror. But, of course, she hadn't been able to see the wood for the trees. The notion of Sandra as a kept woman, as a victim of male abuse, had fitted with her own preconceived notions and prevented her from seeing Sandra for what she was, and indeed what everyone else had *said* she was: pure, unrepentant evil.

And now Sean was left to answer for both of them.

She nodded in his direction. 'What'll happen to him?'

Vanessa exhaled heavily. 'He's coughed to everything. The case is open and shut. Suffice it to say, he'll go to prison for a very long time. It's a good outcome,' she added, as Anna continued to say nothing. 'No lengthy trial. No attempt to plead mitigating circumstances. Just a final, definitive end to this whole sorry tale.'

To Anna's ears, she sounded tired and far less satisfied with the situation than her words suggested. Anna could sympathise. As victories went, this was an undeniably pyrrhic one. Four people were dead, and many more lives had been ruined. And at the centre of it all was the broken man on the other side of the glass. She both hated him for what he'd done and pitied him for what had been done *to* him – by Sandra, by the system, by everyone and everything he'd ever trusted, at every stage of his existence. What hope had there ever been for him, really, with a start in life like that?

At the end of the corridor, the door to the rear courtyard opened, heralding the arrival of Chris, Vanessa's second-in-command. The smell of nicotine wafted in behind him.

Vanessa greeted him with another eyebrow-raise. 'All set?'

'Aye – I'll be good for another couple of hours.'

'Right, then. Time for round two.'

She and Chris headed back into the interview room. Anna watched as they retook their seats facing Sean, who didn't so much as look up.

'All right, Sean,' said Vanessa, her voice booming unnaturally loud from the speakers in the viewing booth, 'let's continue our little chat, shall we?'

Sean shrugged, as if it was neither here nor there for him, and continued to dip his teabag.

Anna stood there for the next minute or so, listening to Vanessa's calm, patient questions and Sean's disinterested, monosyllabic responses. There was nothing here for her, she realised. Nothing Sean had to say was going to make any difference to what had happened or how she felt. Whether what ultimately came out of his mouth was unwavering remorselessness, or self-pitying justification for his actions, or pleas for understanding and mercy, she had no interest in hearing it. She turned and walked out without a backward glance.

50

She followed the nurse in navy-blue scrubs along the corridor, past a succession of different recovery rooms. As she walked, she caught periodic glimpses of the patients inside them – some up and about and looking like they had no real reason to be there, others appearing to be barely clinging onto life.

The door they halted at was only open a crack, obscuring the occupant from view. The nurse turned to face Anna.

'Just a few minutes,' she warned. 'She's still quite poorly.'

Anna suppressed the urge to point out that 'poorly' was a term generally reserved for people who had the sniffles or a tummy-bug, not those who, less than twenty-four hours earlier, had been at death's door.

'Understood,' she said instead, and headed on in.

Pamela lay in a semi-upright position on a large hydraulic bed, one arm tucked behind her head. A line of tubing snaked out from under the bedcovers on the side where she'd been stabbed, running down to a drainage bag hanging from the bed-frame. She had her head turned towards the window, but, hearing Anna's approach, she looked round and faced her with a feeble smile.

'Hey,' she croaked.

'Hey,' Anna smiled in return. She made her way over to the bed and squeezed Pamela's fingers, taking care to avoid the cannula protruding from the back of her hand. 'How are you feeling?'

'Oh, you know. Probably not ready to run a marathon just yet, but all things considered …' She gave an ambivalent shrug.

'Nurses treating you well?'

'Can't complain. Sister Mary Margaret's a bit of a dragon, but her heart's in the right place.'

'I think I just met her,' said Anna.

She drew up a chair and sat facing the bed. Pamela might have been putting on a brave face, but she really *did* look poorly – though it was hardly surprising. In all likelihood, the only reason she was still alive was because the ferry had still been in port at the time of her stabbing. As it was, they'd been able to rush her to shore in record time, where an ambulance was waiting to blue-light her to the nearest hospital. Anna knew, from what Vanessa Tope had relayed to her, that if the knife had gone in a couple of centimetres higher up, it would have punctured Pamela's heart, and then it wouldn't have mattered whether they were still docked or halfway across the Irish Sea. As it was, she was now minus a spleen and had several weeks of recovery to look forward to, but, considering the alternative, Anna doubted she'd regard that as too raw a deal.

'Have you got everything you need?' she asked, keen to fill the void of silence. 'Pyjamas and toiletries and such? I can run to your flat or to the shops or whatever. It's no bother.'

Pamela shook her head. 'I'm fine. 'Sides, my folks should be here in the next couple of hours. They're booked on the first flight down from Stornoway. I plan on making full use of them while they're here.' She gave a wry smile, which clearly took some effort. 'Mark my words, they'll be at my beck and call day and night.'

'That's good. About them coming down, I mean. What use are parents if you can't rely on them to wait on you hand and foot during a crisis?'

Pamela winced. 'Don't. This morphine's great and all, but it still hurts to laugh.'

'Sorry. Listen – I wanted to ask you something.'

'Fire away.'

'How did you come to be on the ferry last night?'

'Easy. I followed you.'

'You *what*?'

Pamela smiled at Anna's look of incomprehension. 'Soon as the police told me what had happened – with your wee boy, I mean – I got straight in the car and drove across to your place. I felt awful about ... well, you know. Sat outside your house for ages, trying to think what I was going to say. Then I saw you coming out and getting in your car, and straight away, I thought, *Something doesn't smell right here.* So I followed you up to the old hospital. I saw you and Jack and that bloke with the long hair coming out and ... ' She trailed off with a limp shrug, either worn out by the effort of doing so much talking or concluding that the rest required no elaboration.

'The man at the kiosk almost didn't let me on,' said Anna. 'How did *you* manage to get past him?'

Pamela waved a limp hand dismissively. 'Ah, he was a total soft touch. I told him I was supposed to be meeting my friend Anna, and straight away he was like, "Oh, you're another member of the Scavolini party" and waved me through.' She gave Anna an incredulous look. 'Apparently you spun him some sob story about your dad being at death's door?'

'I might have said something along those lines. In any event, it goes without saying that I'm beyond glad he let you through. If it hadn't been for you ... ' She stopped, the words catching in her throat.

Pamela gave another tired smile. 'Least I could do.'

Anna shook her head. 'It's more than that. You had no skin in the game, but you risked your life for us anyway. I'll be forever grateful for that.'

'No, what I mean is ... well, I sort of felt I owed it to you, seeing as it's basically my fault he was taken in the first place.'

'It's not your fault,' said Anna immediately.

Pamela winced apologetically. 'It kind of is. If it hadn't been for me, you'd never have got involved in any of this. And Sandra wouldn't have been released, and—'

'I want you to stop that right now,' said Anna firmly. '"If there's one thing I can't stand, it's people who won't take responsibility for their own actions." Your words, not mine.'

'But—'

'But nothing. You didn't force me to do anything I didn't want to. I walked into this with both eyes open.'

'But—' Pamela began again.

'Shh.' Anna held up a hand, silencing her. 'Zip it. I don't want to hear another word on the subject.'

Pamela meekly mimed zipping her mouth shut.

They sat in silence together for a couple of minutes, listening to the sounds of the ward: purposeful footsteps on the linoleum floor, the raised voice of the ward sister instructing one of her underlings to 'do obs on Mrs MacInnes in Four', the beep of a dozen monitors.

Eventually, Anna stirred again.

'On the ferry, you said something.'

Pamela shook her head ruefully. 'I suspect I said a lot of things. Don't rightly remember what, though.'

'Well, I do. You called me your best friend. Is that what I am to you?'

'Of course,' said Pamela, as if it was an absurd question to even ask. 'I mean, I know it hasn't all been a bundle of laughs, to put it mildly, and … and I know I'm an aggravating little so-and-so, but I really enjoyed the time we spent together. Our trip to Hillend and all the stuff we talked about that night in Carlisle and whatnot … it meant a lot to me.' She gave a sheepish smile. 'Just between us, most folk wouldn't've been half as patient with me as you've been.' She hesitated, a look of sudden uncertainty entering her eyes. 'We *are* friends, aren't we?'

As Anna met Pamela's eyes, it occurred to her that the solicitor probably had even fewer friends than she did, and that, under the circumstances, it would be cruel in the extreme to disavow her of the notion. Not that she wanted to anyway. She now realised that, for all that Pamela could be incredibly hard work at times, she too valued the bond she'd forged with this skittish but determined young woman. Even discounting the fact that she would forever consider herself in Pamela's debt for what she'd done for her and Jack, she was determined not to allow their relationship to wither on the vine like she had so many others.

'Of course we are,' she said, squeezing Pamela's hand. 'I'm glad our paths crossed.'

Pamela gave a far more fulsome smile than she'd managed until now. 'Me too,' she said quietly.

Anna cleared her throat. 'Listen, you'd better hurry up and get better soon so you can get back to doing what you do best. The legal profession needs more people like you.'

'D'you honestly think so?' Pamela blinked in surprise. 'I was just thinking earlier that I've gotta be a pretty crummy solicitor, really. The way I behaved after our chat with George Morton?'

'Pff.' Anna dismissed this with a wave. 'Anyone would have felt the same.'

'But I let my personal feelings override my responsibilities to my client. That's … well, I mean, it's not on. That sort of thing's a gross misconduct hearing waiting to happen.'

'Well, I won't tell if you don't. Besides, you came round when it mattered, didn't you?'

'I guess.' Pamela sounded far from certain.

'Do you …' Anna stopped, then began again. 'Do you think we were right to do what we did? Getting the conviction overturned, I mean.'

'Of course,' said Pamela immediately, with no uncertainty in her voice this time.

'Are you sure? In spite of everything that happened afterwards?'

'We acted on what we knew at the time. There was no other choice.'

'No, I suppose not,' murmured Anna.

She still wasn't fully convinced herself, but she felt somewhat reassured by the fact that Pamela was and was therefore unlikely to beat herself up over what the pair of them had inadvertently set in motion.

They continued to sit together for a few more minutes, saying nothing. Then the ward sister came bustling into the room, ostensibly to take Pamela's blood pressure – though, from the pointed looks she kept flashing in Anna's direction, it was abundantly clear that it was time for her to leave. Anna got to her feet and stood for a moment, gazing down at Pamela. Then, leaning in, she pressed her right cheek against Pamela's left – the closest she could get to a hug without interfering with the various wires and tubes that were connected to her.

She straightened up. 'I'll see you around.'

Pamela smiled. 'Looking forward to it.'

Anna returned the smile, then turned and headed out of the room, leaving Sister Mary Margaret to her ministrations.

Epilogue

The Jewish section of the Western Necropolis was located on the southern edge of the cemetery, not far from the entrance off Tresta Road. Anna picked her way through the fields of irregularly shaped stones, glancing from one to the next as she read the inscriptions until, finally, she came to the one she was looking for. Leah's directions had been typically vague – 'Oh, it's the one in marble near the end of one of the rows. You'll know it when you see it.'

She'd never considered coming here before – partly because she'd never seen the point. After all, it wasn't as if she believed his immortal soul resided beneath the earth or anything like that. But she was forced to acknowledge that it was also partly – and in spite of her avowed lack of sentimentality about the ceremonial trappings of death – because, having failed to attend the funeral, it had always struck her as somehow insensitive or in poor taste to turn up to the grave. But that was then, and this was now. And, as she gazed down at the words engraved on the stone in both English and Hebrew, she felt a sense of being where she was meant to be. Of having, finally, come home.

FRANCESCO SCAVOLINI
BELOVED HUSBAND AND FATHER
DIED 14 FEBRUARY 2006
FOREVER IN OUR HEARTS

She didn't speak, or mentally commune with her deceased parent. That would have been ridiculous. Nor did she remain there long. After a couple of minutes, she stirred and made ready to leave. Even as she began to turn, however, a sudden thought struck her. Halting in her tracks, she slipped a hand into her pocket and drew out something small, round and black: the pebble she'd picked up on Troon Beach and pocketed so absentmindedly all those months ago. For a moment, she stood there, weighing it in her hand, her fingers tracing its smooth surface. Then, bending down, she laid it on top of the gravestone. It was, she supposed, a concession to her father's faith; a faith she didn't share and never would but with which she'd managed to reconcile herself – some aspects of it, at any rate.

She'd always quite liked the business with the stones. It struck her as a nice gesture – or, at least, in the grand scheme of things, a harmless one. It was a small thing, but it was, nonetheless, a start.

Zoe gazed out at Dowanhill Park from her vantage point on the bench overlooking the children's play area. Below, Jack and a gaggle of other children of similar age were racing in a loop around the swings, their delighted shrieks carrying in the still summer air.

She smiled to herself. Jack seemed to be coming out of his shell more of late – more willing to join in with the games of kids his own age instead of hanging back like a wee lost soul. And he didn't seem to be showing any signs of long-term damage from his ordeal back at the beginning of June – at least, as far as she could tell. But then, she supposed, time would tell.

She continued to watch. One of the children, younger and smaller than the rest, had stopped pursuing the others and was gesticulating wildly at them, jabbering away in a tone that conveyed deep outrage despite none of it being remotely intelligible. Evidently, some unwritten rule of the playground had been breached and he was determined to lay down the law. Zoe leaned forward, grinning to herself, utterly engrossed in this insight into the rules of toddler etiquette.

'They're like little drunks, aren't they?'

Zoe almost leapt off the bench in surprise as a voice piped up next to her. She swung round to find the young woman with the neon-pink hair standing directly beside her, hands jammed into the pockets of her cargo pants.

'Sorry?'

'Toddlers.' The woman nodded towards the play area. 'They go charging around, bumping into everything, barely managing to stay upright, spouting off with whatever gibberish comes into their heads, and they don't give a flying fig what you say back to them.' She grinned, showing two rows of small white teeth. 'Don't you find that?'

'Aye, I guess,' said Zoe, still struggling to recover from her surprise. She gazed up at the woman, wide-eyed, acutely aware that she was staring but unable to look away. To suddenly find herself so close to this woman, whom she'd only previously seen from a distance, that she could practically count the pores in her skin was profoundly disorientating.

The woman gestured to the bench. 'This seat taken?'

Zoe shook her head.

'Amazeballs.'

She plonked herself down next to Zoe and leant back, head tilted up towards the sun, her chest swelling as she inhaled a lungful of air. In the process, her T-shirt rode up, exposing the white skin of her lower stomach. Zoe could only stare, agog, until the woman stirred and turned to her once more.

'I'm Sal.' She held out her hand.

'Zoe,' said Zoe, shaking it absentmindedly.

Sal tilted her head, eyeing Zoe quizzically. 'I've seen you about,' she declared, in a tone that suggested she'd just made up her mind about this fact then and there.

'Aye,' agreed Zoe. 'I mean, I seen you too.'

'Yeah, totally. You and your wee boy come here all the time.'

'Oh, he's … he's no mine. He's my pal's. I just look after him.'

'Cool beans.' Sal nodded approvingly. 'I'm the same. Come here with my sister's two. That's them, there.' She pointed towards the gaggle of toddlers, who, having seemingly resolved their earlier dispute, were once again haring round the swings like a pack of mad dogs. 'She works long hours and I … ' She shrugged airily. 'Eh, it works out nicely for us.'

Zoe nodded like she understood perfectly, even as she tried to work out why her mouth was so dry and a sense of hopeless giddiness was overwhelming her.

Say something. She'll think you're completely doolally if you just keep on gawping at her.

'So listen,' Sal went on, 'real reason I came over was to see if maybe you wanna do something sometime. Like, y'know, just hang out, catch a movie, go eat some waffles or something?' She shrugged expectantly.

'Y-yeah,' said Zoe, nodding again, but with purpose this time. 'Yeah, I'd like that.'

'OK, sweet.' Sal got to her feet. 'Well, I'll have a look at my schedule, you have a look at yours, we'll cross-tabulate and ... ' She shrugged again. 'We'll see what works out. Sound good?'

Zoe nodded, not trusting herself to manage to avoid tripping over her tongue.

'Groovy. Well, I know where to find ya. Catch ya 'round.'

She flashed a wink, then turned and sauntered off, to Zoe's mind waggling her hips just a *tad* more than was strictly necessary.

Zoe remained on the bench, not daring to stand up in case she discovered her legs were suddenly made of jelly. She was light-headed and giddy and tingly all over in all the best possible ways. She hadn't felt this way in forever. Hadn't thought she still *could* feel this way.

'Heh, ye've still got it, Callahan,' she told herself.

Things, she decided, were most definitely looking up.

Anna turned onto Cleveden Road, moving at a leisurely stroll. She'd walked back from the Necropolis, taking the scenic route down through Kelvinside to savour the evening air. Before long, it would be autumn. The new semester was just around the corner, and she was looking forward to getting back to teaching. She'd been away from her natural habitat for too long.

She still had work to do on the book, of course. Her editor's feedback on the first draft was due any day, and, if her previous experience of the world of publishing was anything to go by, she'd have a significant chunk of rewriting ahead of her. But the heavy lifting was over and, as much as it had been a mad dash to get it done, she felt justifiably proud of what she'd turned in.

And there were, it seemed, some rumblings of positive news regarding the plight of the inmates at Broadwood. At a recent cabinet reshuffle, a new Justice Secretary had been appointed – one who, judging by comments she'd made to the media, was considerably less in hock to the idea of tough justice than her predecessor. She'd promised to look again at what was being termed 'the Broadwood question'. From speaking to Pamela, Anna had been able to glean that the consensus within the Government was that the new prison had been a mistake and that, as soon as an opportune moment arose, moves would be made to quietly shutter or at least significantly downsize it and move ahead with the original recommendation of multiple smaller, more community-based initiatives and an emphasis on rehabilitation rather than retribution.

Though the case didn't feature anywhere in her book, she'd been thinking a lot about Sandra Morton recently. From time to time, she wondered whether she'd let herself believe in the possibility of Sandra's innocence because, on some level, that was what she'd *wanted* her to be. She'd allowed herself, if not to empathise with her, then certainly to see the parallels between them – their shared status as assertive, intelligent, independently-minded women who refused to conform to the role society imposed on them. In doing so, she'd succeeded in proving a guilty woman innocent, and in the process had put her own child in mortal danger. It all left her feeling profoundly uneasy, shaken by a sense that many of her deeply held assumptions about the world had been rocked to their core. She couldn't help but think that, in a small way, it gave her an insight into how her parents must have felt when she'd so brazenly rejected *their* beliefs.

Of course, there was still so much about Sandra and what had been going on behind those brilliant blue eyes that Anna didn't know – and would *never* know. What, for instance, had really been her motive in persuading Sean to kill Guy and the twins? Was it purely for the thrill – or even the intellectual challenge – of seeing whether she could manipulate another human being into committing murder? Was her refusal to give him up purely a matter of cold pragmatism – a way of keeping her options open? Or had Sean been right? *Had* she, in fact, had feelings for him after all? Only one thing could be said with any certainty: in death, Sandra remained as much of an enigma as she was in life.

She continued down Hyndland Road, past Caffe Parma and the

Episcopal church with its square, sandstone spire. The evening was drawing in, and while it wasn't exactly cold, there was a more pronounced nip in the air now than there had been earlier and she found herself looking forward to reaching the house, where dinner would be in the oven and Zoe and Jack would be waiting for her.

As she turned onto Clarence Drive, her step momentarily faltered as she experienced a brief, inexplicable pang of something that felt almost akin to mourning. Perhaps it was a delayed reaction to visiting her father's grave earlier. Or perhaps it was a response to the knowledge that everything in this existence was transitory; that the current arrangement she and Zoe and Jack had wouldn't and couldn't go on forever.

But for however long it did last, she was determined to enjoy it to the full – this odd, idiosyncratic DIY family she'd created for herself, with all its warmth and kindness and love. In that regard at least, she knew she was nothing like Sandra Morton – nothing at all.

She quickened her pace and continued towards home.

Acknowledgements

Many authors speak of having written and thrown away an entire additional novel's worth of content by the time they deliver their finished manuscript. In the case of *Women Who Kill*, I'm sure I deep-sixed enough material to fill *two* extra books – and in all likelihood more.

The novel in its current incarnation, and the character of Pamela Macklin, wouldn't exist without the advice of my friend and colleague Neil Snowdon. A shocking amount of *Women Who Kill*'s final form emerged during an impromptu four-hour brainstorming session in the restaurant of a hotel in London last September, which was infinitely more productive than the intended purpose of our trip.

My amazing editor, Suze Clarke-Morris, also deserves copious thanks for helping me tame this unwieldy manuscript and for steering me away from some of the pitfalls into which I'd inadvertently stumbled. Most of the moments where we actually see Anna being a mother to Jack were added at her suggestion, and the book is all the better – and all the more human – for their inclusion.

Thanks to Aaron Caruthers for answering my questions about the Cairnryan–Belfast ferry, and to Stuart Kincavel and Christine Lyden for their guidance on various aspects of police procedure and the restrictions on reporting on children involved in criminal proceedings. As always, any errors are mine, not theirs. Thanks, too, to Louisa Graham for the comparison between toddlers and drunks, which I stole from her almost verbatim.

Much gratitude to Tim Barber for once again designing an incredible cover which perfectly captured the spirit of my pitch to him and nailed the mood I was hoping to evoke.

As always, thanks to my beta readers for lending their eagle eyes to the final draft. In alphabetical order: Luiz Asp, Bev Dodds, Sarah Kelley, Catherine Mackenzie, Una Melville, Alan Nicholson, Daniel Sardella, Anne Simpson and Caroline Whitson.

Finally, a massive, king-sized 'thank you' to everyone who continues to buy and read my books. I wouldn't be doing this if it wasn't for you. See you in the next one!

HMP Broadwood is an entirely fictional prison. In reality, plans for a women's super-prison in Scotland were scuppered in 2015 by the then Justice Secretary, Michael Matheson MSP, following pressure from campaigners. In recent years, the Scottish Government has won plaudits for its trauma-informed, gender-specific approach to women's incarceration.

Nonetheless, the plight of female prisoners remains an ongoing concern, both in Scotland and throughout the wider world.

Printed in Great Britain
by Amazon